*13
Fiendish
Fables:
A Novel*

13 Fiendish Fables: A Novel

Stephen Schmoyer

Copyright © 2021 Stephen Schmoyer

The moral right of the author has been asserted.

Apart from any fair dealing for the purposes of research or private study, or criticism or review, as permitted under the Copyright, Designs and Patents Act 1988, this publication may only be reproduced, stored or transmitted, in any form or by any means, with the prior permission in writing of the publishers, or in the case of reprographic reproduction in accordance with the terms of licences issued by the Copyright Licensing Agency. Enquiries concerning reproduction outside those terms should be sent to the publishers.

This is a work of fiction. Names, characters, businesses, places, events and incidents are either the products of the author's imagination or used in a fictitious manner. Any resemblance to actual persons, living or dead, or actual events is purely coincidental.

Matador
9 Priory Business Park,
Wistow Road, Kibworth Beauchamp,
Leicestershire. LE8 0RX
Tel: 0116 279 2299
Email: books@troubador.co.uk
Web: www.troubador.co.uk/matador
Twitter: @matadorbooks

ISBN 978 1800461 772

British Library Cataloguing in Publication Data.
A catalogue record for this book is available from the British Library.

Printed and bound in Great Britain by 4edge Limited
Typeset in 11pt Minion Pro by Troubador Publishing Ltd, Leicester, UK

Matador is an imprint of Troubador Publishing Ltd

Acknowledgements

I'd like to thank and acknowledge all the people who helped me bring this book to completion. First, I'd like to thank Jackie Hayfield for her decades of encouragement. Every time I even thought about giving up, you'd ask about my writing. It was a blessing. Equally important was the support and contributions of so many friends and family members. To Jenny Mazepa Schmoyer-Malouin, Carl and Debbie Schmoyer, Carl Schmoyer III, Jason Taylor, Stephen and Kelly Batarick, Stacy Hein, Sonia Versuk Kleintop, Mike and Mara Metzger, and Mary Ashner – my gratitude goes up through the sky and down to the sea. Finally, I'd like to thank my excellent illustrator, Dave Hill, Fern Bushnell, and all the fine people at Matador Publishing who helped make my obscure notions a reality. Without support everything falls and each and every one of you helped me stay vertical.

* * * *Preface* * * *

The author gleaned an idea, so naturally he went to his mother to talk about it.

"Mom?" the author asked.

"Yes?" his mother answered.

"I have an idea for a book," the author said.

"Okay…" his mother replied.

"It starts out with a conversation," the author explained. "In fact, it starts out with *this conversation*—the one we're having right now."

"That seems like a weird way to start a book," his mother remarked.

"Why?"

"For a couple of reasons. First, how can you insert something real into a work of fiction? Second, I think it's unusual for authors to write expressly about their mothers. Third, where would you even put the conversation? In the opening chapter?"

"I was thinking about putting it in the Preface."

"People usually skip the opening bits."

"Well, I'll put asterisks around it or something—to draw attention. But this conversation *has to be the way* the book begins. And I don't care most authors don't directly write about their mothers. Actually, I plan on doing a lot of things most authors haven't done."

"Like what?" his mother pressed.

"To begin, I believe I've found a way to merge a collection of short stories within the larger narrative structure of a novel. Also, I'm going to explore different ways to tell my tales in form, format, and content. Lastly, I will unconstrain myself from convention. If I feel I can break a rule—spoken or otherwise—and get away with it, I'll do it. I figure it's high time genres become more fluid. Something new just doesn't fall from the sky."

"Sounds risky," his mother commented.

"Perhaps. But I don't want to write an ordinary book. I'll settle for *a good book*, aim for *a really good book*; however, I passionately desire to write *an extraordinary book*! This means taking chances. You understand?" the author clarified.

"Yes," his mother stated without pause or struggle. "'A thing of beauty is a joy forever.' Keats. That's the idea?"

"Exactly."

"Is there anything else you need to tell your mother or the audience before we wrap this conversation up?"

"Only that the subject matter is heavily religious and is bound to cause some controversy. Oh, and I'm going to start with the last story first. I might as well start breaking rules right out of the gate. Do you have any questions for me?"

"What's the title of the work?" the mother asked.

"The book is called, *13 Fiendish Fables: A Novel,*" the author answered.

"That breaks a rule right there. The title is a contradiction," his mother observed.

"Yes it is. Yes it truly is," finished the author.

The Thirteenth Fable

Part 1

(Story #13: Part 1)

The apprentice nun traveled silently through the convent fretting at every necessary step. She abandoned her dreary, but immaculate, cell and moved soundlessly along the stone corridors filled with all the other drab and solitary cells of her Sisters. It was after curfew and was forbidden, and each inch forward increased the severity of her potential punishment. The punishments were scaled. First would be confinement, then the lash, then the stones… then something truly unpleasant. Still, she had somewhere to go that would hopefully get her to some place even better. Thus, she slunk down hallways and slipped around corners, until she reached the ascending staircase which topped out on what was called the 'gallows platform' where another staircase on the opposite side descended downward to the garden gate. This was because the convent was built like a maze—easy to enter, but hard to leave. She might have even thought the layout had an 'Escher-like' quality, but she never heard of Escher. In the convent, information was tightly regulated and so much was off limits. She wanted to change this tonight. Subsequently, made her way to the most dangerous place she knew of: the Library.

So the nun went up the steps and down the steps and tip-toed to the garden gate. The garden gate was supposed to be locked as was the cemetery gate on the other side, delineating where the convent ended and the monastery began. Quite frequently, though, both gates were left open for what the Ladies of the Order and the Gentlemen of the Word called 'nighttime meditation.' Yes, sometimes nuns from the convent and brothers from the monastery liked to move freely and meditate together. Yes, sometimes they liked to meditate in the garden. And sometimes they liked to meditate in the cemetery. Some nuns even liked to meditate with other nuns and some brothers with other brothers, so the gates were often left unlocked in an act, not so much of acknowledgement, but because of an agreed upon, but unacknowledged, communal ignorance. These nighttime sojourns were, of course, punishable by expiation and death, but such contemptible sins could never be contemplated—not even among the sinners committing them. The apprentice nun marveled how pious minds are sometimes forever immune to evidence of their own impiety. She depressed the latch. The gate opened.

The apprentice nun crossed the garden redolent with smells of mint and jasmine and freshly tilled earth that, however dry, always seemed to hold the sweet scent-memory of rain. There was a humble vegetable patch and a quiet grove of citrus trees lit iridescently underneath a pregnant moon. The nun reached the cemetery gate and, like the garden one, it was open. And, in just seconds and footfalls, she was mutely cat-stepping among the tombstones. The yawning maw of an underground crypt would take her into the monastery and beyond.

Entering the crypt, the novitiate paused because of a noise, but she was sure the noise hadn't come from her. This was because to be a postulant is to practice silence—and such was doubly true for a nun who hadn't yet taken her vows. Yes, she had learned stealth by being unobtrusive and learned surreptitiousness through speechless obedience. Indeed, she made less sound than the shuffling of a couple leaves of paper. On top of this, now she held her breath. The noise sounded like a monk and a sister were robustly meditating somewhere in the damp darkness among the moldering bones. In fact, it sounded like more than one nun and one brother meditating furiously.

The apprentice nun resumed breathing, said nothing, and paused no more. Continuing onward, she traversed to the back ossuary wall comprised of little cubicles containing holy bones, and the cubicles, too, were made of even more reverent calcium in a gruesome bit of monastic carpentry. She searched around the last cubical housing a baker's dozen of skeleton relics from a former penitent soon to be anointed an honored saint. She was looking for the clavicle and found it. The nun removed the bone and felt along its smooth contours to one of its denuded ends that had been carved into the teeth of a key. Then she groped in the shadows for the hidden key eye. Unlike the garden and cemetery gates, this door was always locked. She found the aperture, slid the key in, and turned it. Muffled sounds of gears meshing and mechanisms gnashing prefaced a section of wall sliding open to reveal an ancient elevator. The nun entered the space and hit the top button which illumined in a tired disc of tired yellow. She was going up. The library was the highest point of either the convent or monastery except for the monastery's bell tower which knelled and tolled over everything. The rising momentum made the nun's stomach flutter and she thought about butterflies.

Reaching the top floor, the elevator door opened once again and the apprentice nun stepped out to find herself face to face with a placard larger than the height or width of her entire body.

It read:

>DISCURSIVE ATHENEUM AND BIBLIOTECA
>FOR
>THE MONASTERY OF ST. AMBROSIO
>AND
>THE CONVENT OF ST. LUCIA
>~SEGREGATED~

NUNNERY HOURS: DAWN TO TERCE
(PIETY LEVEL 8 AND HIGHER REQUIRED)
MONASTERY HOURS: TERCE TO CURFEW
(PIETY LEVEL 5 AND HIGHER REQUIRED)

"AND IF YOUR EYE CAUSES YOU TO STUMBLE,
GOUGE IT OUT AND THROW IT AWAY."

~MATTHEW 18:9~

As if to underscore the placard's message, attached to the placards' side was a cut-crystal goblet capped with a silver lid. Filling it nearly to the top were desiccated eyeballs. None of the eyes had been freshly plucked, but they still seemed to stare accusingly at the nun in their jaundiced, mismatched, and cross-eyed ways. It didn't matter. She had seen worse and, besides, if anyone found out what she was doing tonight, she would lose a lot more than an eye.

Her final destination neared so she walked through the stacks of religious texts and reams of corresponding reference materials catalogued as testimony about the true nature of God and Man, Heaven and Hell, and everything in between. At the end of the stacks the last door loomed. It was composed of thick iron bars because the door had been reclaimed from one of the old prisons—from a time when death sentences weren't the answer to every indiscretion. At last, she stood before the door and pulled out an equally old iron key from beneath her virginal habit.

Another sign announced:

HERETICAL ARCHIVES

BROTHERS: PIETY LEVEL 12 AND HIGHER REQUIRED
SISTERS: PRIORESS ACCESS ONLY

VIOLATORS WILL BE CRUCIFIED!

And the sign was coupled with a life-size depiction of Jesus at Calvary with his head tilting limply down and his eyes closed in eternal sleep.

The apprentice nun ran her thumb over the shaft of the iron key. When she joined the convent she thought taking her first vows would be the hardest thing she ever did, but this was harder. Still, she had to know. Still, she had to know what the non-believers believed—what the heretics believed. Yes, she had to know and then let her heart and mind be open to the arousing seduction of an outside perspective. Indeed, the novitiate already experienced faith through obedience, and faith through deprivation, and faith through suffering, but she never experienced faith through genuine trial. For that, it would take struggling with faith itself. Consequently, she was willing to risk her life for this struggle, but the contents behind this last door could do something far worse than taking her life or even damning her soul. It could show her she didn't have a soul, that she never did, and no one else did either—at least not in the way religion envisioned such ethereal presences. The proposition was harrowing and alluring at the same time. Now, standing at the precipice, she could feel the books calling to her like Sirens. There were hundreds of volumes—all unmarked and all of different widths and dimensions, appearing innocuous—but she knew they were dangerous as sticks of dynamite, each and every one.

She was terrified, but she persisted.

Then the key was inserted into the lock.

And the key in the lock was turned.

Her hand swung the door wide.

Finally, with trembling fingers, the apprentice nun selected the first book she came to and opened it.

The book was called *Fiction for Atheists: A Novel*, but it looked more like a manuscript with the author's name blotted out. Still, the apprentice nun felt a thrill and thrum which both frightened and stimulated her—coldly and warmly—as the painting of Jesus Christ hung impotently nearby with his eyes forever closed.

The novitiate began to read…

End of Story #13: Part 1

Fiction for Atheists:
A Novel

By

Prologue

So, the writer conjures up the Devil and makes the hard choice to put everything on the line.

"Sure," the Devil agrees—who is always looking for cheap deals—and few things for him were cheaper than accepting souls in exchange for a little creativity. To seal the deal the Devil smacks the writer directly on his forehead.

"Ow," complains the writer. "What was that for?"

"It was my gift!" replies the Devil. "I just held up my end of the bargain! Now start writing!"

"Is there anything else I should know?" the writer asks, rubbing the place where the Devil struck him.

"Well, this is your first story, so it's probably going to be terrible. Genius might be magic, but magic takes hard work. How many stories do you plan to write?"

"Thirteen," says the writer.

"A good number," answers the Devil.

"I thought so."

"I'll give you a little advice after each one to keep you on track. We'll call these little study sessions 'intermezzos' to make them sound *artsy*," the Devil continues with a smile. "*I do* promise, however, with my help, *you will get there*."

"I'm glad to hear it."

The writer prepares—his fingertips hovering just above the keyboard. He seems to pause apprehensively—perhaps in fear—or perhaps he is waiting for a guarantee. The Devil can't tell which.

"We have a deal, then?" the writer asks.

"We have a deal, then. Your soul for my supernatural assistance in writing short stories," the Devil assures.

"You will keep your word?"

"Of course! I keep all my words! If I may inquire… what are you going to write about?"

"About you," the writer answers, flatly. "About God and the Devil, Angels and Demons, Heaven and Hell, and everything in between—including Humanity."

"Oh, this is going to be worse than I thought," the Devil sighs.

"I might even throw in some wizards for good measure," the writer adds.

At this, the Devil lets out a groan.

And then the writer's fingers connect with the keys as the writer begins to write.

Learning to Love

(Story #1)

There once was a man who hit his wife. He hit her a lot until their bodies grew old and they died. They met in school. He fell in love with her and she fell in love with him. Then one night, very close to summer's end, they went to a bonfire at a local beach. The sparks danced upward while the sand was soft beneath them. They made love under the dancing embers and the brilliant stars so it looked like both the stars and embers frolicked and cavorted as frenzied twinkling paramours underneath a moonless sky. After, she got up to wash, but he remained low and seized her hand. He proposed and put a ring on the appropriate finger. The ring was a little too small, so the man forced it over a white knuckle. The woman winced, but was happy. "I love you," the man said. "I will love you for the whole of my life and through whatever worlds may come."

The marriage happened a few months later. The man was still deeply in love, but something changed in the woman. She wore the most beautiful white gown adorned with champagne pearls and crisp satin patches and even antique whalebone as if from another time. The gown had a high collar and long sleeves and she drew her head back instinctively, squinting ever so slightly, almost imperceptibly, as the minister drew up her secretive and concealing veil. Several guests commented the bride looked tired—bags under the eyes even makeup couldn't cover—however, most in attendance agreed it was perfectly normal—perfectly perfunctory—that many a joyous girl lost sleep fantasizing about her most joyous of joyful days. The man pinched her arm, drew her in close, and finally kissed her with a hot passion to seal the union. It was evident to all his love for her would last forever. It was witnessed by human eyes, within the House of God, under the vault of Heaven, so it must be true. Yes, it was uncommon to witness such love, so personal and private, yet made so public, they said. And everyone clapped and clapped and clapped. Thus, with an unquestioning audience and an unguarded intimate act, the connubial celebration drew to a close. For the man, it was victory. For the woman, it was life.

Years ticked by from that day of matrimony, and the bride, who was now a wife, never lost her penchant for high collars and long sleeves. She wore parkas during hot spells and ponchos on days without rain. Such clothes were more comfortable, she demurred. The couple never went to the beach anymore and never talked about going to the beach. And the woman let her hair go from chestnut brown to raven black—the man's implicit preference. Yes, she let it grow out to obscure the glorious blooms of her face. She had been quite pretty in her youth, but now sagged in places like a slowly deflating balloon. The man, however, remained upright and tight—as fit as a pin. The neighbors would wave to the woman, and the woman would wave back in her long sleeves. She would grin pursed-lipped, but never quite smile. She dared not stray too close. Why would she? It would ruin the love, the neighbors thought. And further, the man seemed always present—even when he was away from his property. Yes, the husband and wife were a world unto themselves and their love was like a hand within a glove making a mighty fist.

Then one night inside the 'house of joy'—as the neighbors called it—the wife prepared dinner in the established tradition of their marital abode. It was a nice dinner: a nice rare piece of meat, freshly butchered; a nice bunch of potatoes skinned and mashed and whipped into a fluffy consistency; and peas—so nice!—just ready to burst in the mouth with succulent flavor and delicate delightful delight. The table setting was simple, yet elegant, and grace was prayed dutifully, but reverently, and the man and woman sat close together in rapt anticipation of their fine repast. But then, just as the husband lifted his fork to eat, he saw, on the third prong to the left, a bit of food that had stuck and dried and failed to be cleaned from the last perfectly perfunctorily prepared meal. Subsequently, a scene acted out and repeated scores of times inside the 'house of joy' replayed once more. The fork flew with lightning force into the soft flesh underneath the woman's bicep—directly between the muscle and bone. She felt the tines of the fork break the skin, chew through the meat, and ultimately bite into the calcium of her body. Blood sluiced down in tendril rivulets. It saturated through her long-sleeved yellow housedress—flowering into a crimson stain, perhaps a rose. She shrunk to the ground as he towered above her.

"I LOVE YOU!" he bellowed. "I HAVE ALWAYS LOVED YOU! I LOVED YOU SINCE THAT DAY ON THE BEACH AND WILL LOVE YOU FOREVER AND EVER AFTER—FOR ALL OF MY DAYS! ALWAYS, I HAVE DONE FOR YOU! WHY DO YOU MAKE ME DO THIS AGAIN AND AGAIN AND AGAIN WHEN YOU KNOW MY LOVE FOR YOU IS SO COMPLETELY BOUNDLESS?!!!"

And then he was upon her, because he always said "I love you" when he hit her.

More years passed and many more dinners and slaps and punches and kicks and elbows and knees and teeth and flatware were served until both the husband and wife grew frail and died. The man went to Hell while the woman went somewhere else. Yes, in death, the final 'until death do they part' portion of their vows was lovingly granted by God's everlasting masculine grace.

And in Hell, the Devil appeared before the husband in the form of a woman. She had skin as startling as a new blood blister rising from a glinting welt, hair the color of a stygian cave, and bare breasts with dark nipples—like twin pieces of coal simmering defiantly atop two round, wonderful hillocks of fire. The man, though supplicant, stood erect. The Devil was as powerful as he was magnificent. His form was quite enticing—with an outer casing as red as a Washington apple.

The Devil smiled softly while the man crumpled to his knees. Then the Devil reached down with fingertips—crowned with nails like knives—and glided them gently over the man's face in a loving, tender fashion. Then she went on to move those razor talons to her own fiery torso—to each of the sequestered black nubs in the center of each of her bloody red breasts. She twisted them almost in ecstasy. Tiny flames, but incredibly bright, erupted from their volcanic tips. The flames piped like burners from an industrial stove or the nozzles of two acetylene torches whistling with heat.

"Don't worry," the Devil said in a kind and silky voice. "I love you. I have always loved you. Our love and our passions are meant to be together forever."

And finally she drew him to him, because even though the Devil took the form of a woman, the source of all violence is Man… and so the husband's timeless nursing from the Devil's teats… began…

End of Story #1

Intermezzo

(first)

The Devil finishes reading the writer's opening story: 'Learning to Love.' He takes a contemplative moment before speaking.

"Well, I suppose this came out as good as could be expected..." the Devil says and sets aside the first completed pages, face down, in a bit of a huff and a puff.

"Do you like it?" the writer asks, eagerly.

"Do I like it?" the Devil responds. "I hope you're joking. No, I don't like it. It's awful. I mean it's really, *really*, spectacularly bad."

"Is it? Are you sure?" inquires the writer. "It's just the first one. I thought it came out okay."

"Fine," the Devil sighs. "The story is *'okay.'* But you have to do a lot better than 'okay.' Some of the imagery isn't a complete failure, but otherwise, it is an affront to every creative impulse for anyone, anywhere, in the entirety of time. I would even suggest burning the whole thing if not for the fact it satisfies 1/13th of our deal," the Devil explains, before adding in a slightly softer tone, "but don't feel too badly. Initial attempts at writing are usually disastrous. This story proves it. The good news for me is: at least it was short… if that makes you feel any better. Still, it is a *supremely* inadequate tale."

Hearing this, the writer stares at the Devil and blinks rapidly a few times.

"It doesn't make me feel better," answers the writer, "… and your criticism is a tad harsh, don't you think?"

"Tad? Harsh? What odd things to say! Are you confused about who you summoned?"

"Alright… okay…" the writer stutters, but doesn't stammer. He is a little crestfallen, but not utterly despondent. He knew dealing with the Devil was never going to be an easy task. "Is there anything I can do to improve it?"

The Devil considers the writer's question gravely while rhythmically tapping his fingers on the back of the face-down pages.

"No," he finally says. He says it as a declaration. "*This story* is the best *this story* can ever be."

"I don't understand…" the writer half-probes and half-laments.

The Devil exhales again, but leans forward like he is going to make a confession or unveil a secret of the Universe.

"Okay, look..." the Devil goes on, "I've put this many ways over many centuries to many—*so many*—artistic types just like you. Imagine if I gave you a bar of pure gold, or a slab of perfect marble, or some of the finest paints—or go further: a fresh flank of butchered pork or sun-kissed wheat or exquisite silk or an uncut gem or even a bunch of mushrooms carefully harvested from bountiful nature or any other material item which exists in the world. Now, what if I asked you to craft jewelry or sculpt or paint or cook or weave—or create a sublime psychedelic drug cocktail or an equally scrumptious mushroom soufflé? Do you think the problem is the materials, or with the hand and eye and mind of the individual who manipulates them?"

"Obviously, the hand and eye and mind are the problems," says the writer, automatically—which he found strange because this answer didn't seem like it should be automatic. He rubs his forehead where the Devil so unceremoniously smacked him.

"Quite right," the Devil answers. "Care to articulate why? It will help you..."

The writer wanted to gather his thoughts, so it surprises him when he begins to reply immediately.

"Because language is like that ingot of gold or uncut diamond or sun-kissed grain or any variety of mushroom hood or stem..." the writer starts; however, he notices—or rather feels—the curious automatic sensation again—that these words weren't exactly coming from him, but instead were *flowing through him*. He continues to touch his forehead. The words just kept pouring out like water. It was actually kind of liberating, like some kind of barrier had come down. He also begins to think about the center of his forehead as his 'Devil's Spot.' The writer finds both the idea and description appealing.

"... And this is especially true of the English language because English... absorbs and adopts... appropriates and steals words from every other language, and when there isn't a word for something it can be invented—a person with a hand and eye and mind and fingers can make one up. Subsequently, you cannot blame a manuscript for any of the tortured deficiencies residing within a man."

"Now you're getting it," the Devil affirms.

"'For the man it was victory. For the woman it was life'... 'The source of all violence is Man,'" quotes the writer from his own story. "What do those things *even mean*?" he asks. Mostly, though, he is asking himself.

The Devil doesn't say anything, but simply waits for the next question that inevitably comes from artistic types who bargain their souls.

"Alright... okay..." the writer stammers. "So, what's a better way to write a better story?"

The Devil had learned through experience not to smile at times like these, so he just remains thin-lipped before answering.

"Write a tale about a character who has a secret, but be sure to tell your readers what the secret is. You see, readers love to tear down someone who has an embarrassing quality or to sympathize with such a character, if that's the way they lean. The important thing is: you have to give people something *to judge*. There is great power in judgment. *Tremendous power*."

"Something to judge…" the writer repeats, pensively.

"Something to judge…" he repeats again, but ends by saying in a mere whisper, "I think I just got an idea…"

"I thought you might," replies the Devil.

And then the writer gets back to his writing.

The Fruits of Shame

(Story #2)

There once was a man with an unusual sexual proclivity. He engaged in this proclivity surreptitiously and with the most carefully practiced cunning until he died. The activity wasn't dangerous. The activity caused no harm to others. The activity wasn't illegal. Nor was the activity illicit. In fact, only those who partake in practices far worse, and poke fingers or other things for cruel pleasure, would ever call what the man did 'wicked' or 'immoral.' Yes, even God and his celestial caretakers in their seats of eternal judgment looked down upon the act as one of those distinctly human exercises—curious, odd, burlesque, but ultimately irrelevant to matters of the Spirit and the Soul. Yes, for the heavenly host it was an activity on par with eating a carrot, or lying about one's age, or being a plushie, or collecting a commemorative spoon from every United State. They paid it no weight on the scales. *After all*, it was only human. *After all*, it was only corporeal. Nevertheless, for the man it was his greatest secret and, while the man lived, it often burned him with an abominable personal shame.

The activity had its genesis when the boy, who would later become a man, was just eleven years old and desperately had to 'make water,' as his mother called it. He had been playing outside by himself—neighbors kept at arm's length by his family's series of fences and barricades both physical and social—when the liquid urge, nay, the compulsive surge, came upon him. He occupied the middle of his home's sprawling back yard—abutted by an expansive red brick Victorian house on one end and a perfectly square suburban garden on the other—with only the wild, untamed woods stretching beyond that. He played on a patch of shiny green grass worn thin by innocent, but persistent, self-amusement. Bright plastic dump trucks, bulldozers, and graders did major construction in miniature. He was laying foundations, moving detritus—destroying and creating—when the unbidden pressure welled and rushed and gushed within him. Without warning, it instantly threatened to geyser. It announced its intent to spill autonomously and tyrannically—unchecked and undirected—without a scintilla of control. One moment there was only him, and there was play, and then everything transformed into a single immediate watery inexorability. Late October had arrived, but the air was still very warm… an Indian summer now sizzling his bladder.

His face blanched to pale ivory and the bright

equipment and modeled rollers trundled to a facile halt. The boy bounded to his feet. A black and yellow construction crane crashed onto its side with a clatter; a slate grey excavator upended and lost a treaded wheel. The boy looked off to the horizon in a fishy unblinking stare. It was as if he were entranced or hypnotized, yet not from anything external, but rather from a groaning, elongating, internal realization that his body was about to do something—*about to birth something*—into the world without his consent or permission. It was just going to come. It was just going to burst. It was a flood splashing and cresting up inside him, building so fast and so vast, he knew he only had a minute—maybe not even that long— to form a plan and execute it.

'The house?

What if I don't make it?'

It had happened before. But the boy cleaned up the mahogany wainscoting and porcelain tile before anyone discovered the sopping and slowly saturating mess. The incriminating garments were expertly disposed of, and the scene meticulously sterilized, but the underlying cause remained as furious as molten lava colliding with a gelid sea. And, here it was again. Yes, the boy felt like he was melting from the inside out.

'What if I don't make it?
What if I make another mess?
What would Mother and Father say?
What if I am seen?
What if I get caught?
What if I am forever soiled?'

And worse, he still relived the reeking, dripping, clandestine, bloodguilt of the whole experience almost daily. He lived and relived it every time he went to the bathroom. It was a disgrace. Indeed, his mortal coil had been mortified.

Color returned to the boy's cheeks, with a flush and a blush, as he turned with half a decision and a half-blind hysterical instinct that was the antithesis of decision-making to hazard a mad dash for the woods. He took off running as his mind lurched primally towards the wilderness—towards the wildness—but, in truth, it had very little to do with his mind. It was just his body rocketing and reckoning to begin a race against itself. The boy's bladder expanded and strained like a precarious balloon whose tied end was unraveling in a whirling frenetic inevitability. It was as if all his organs were breathing, gathering up a high tide, shifting wet things and airy things around, the way an underwater earthquake and a hidden sub-sea air pocket generates a tsunami. Legs pumping, but halfway there, the boy also suddenly and shamefully realized his small penis, his 'stickie'—again from his mother—had stiffened hard as a lumberjack's spile. Under the burgeoning pressure, it was threatening to flume. Embarrassment, odium, anxiety, and judgment might as well have been wolves voraciously snapping at the little boy's heels. All this was happening while, between his legs, an iron nail pounded, pulsed, and vibrated angrily against the tight constraining fabric of his fashionable trousers.

Finally, the garden loomed as a jarring, swiveling,

jag-jigging patch in front of him. The season was autumn and it was fallow—with nothing but a few rotting orange pumpkin heads left decomposing on the vine. Chicken wire surrounded the patch secured by slender wooden stakes. Beyond the garden, the forest waited like a dark and lovely place to hide from prying and accusatory eyes. The boy would have to leap, but before he did, he fumbled with his trousers, to undo the restraining buttons, to let loose the equipment, to let free the flood, which was sloshing and sluicing and roiling within him.

He reached the garden's perimeter.

He leapt.

Equipment ready and all stream ahead, his right foot took flight, but immediately caught on the fencing while the wooden stakes held fast. He could have freed himself with a brief twist of his foot or an acknowledgement this whole endeavor was ill-conceived—that he had gone far enough, that some things cannot be avoided or escaped—but instead he flexed and sprang from the ball of his left foot in total commitment. And, once more, the boy became almost instantly and hopelessly entangled.

He tumbled and fell forward in slow motion, but as he did, he also suddenly and shamefully realized he had been able to liberate himself from his trousers—warm flowing air and tender breezy freedom—but in falling, this left his 'stickie' terrifyingly exposed—unguarded and vulnerable—to be guided by nothing but snagged feet and gravity. There wasn't a thing he could do. The boy was caught in the thin animal wire used to demarcate civilized things from elements far less civilized. His body plunged to the earth. His hands splayed out in a makeshift bracing motion like a plummeting Angel shorn of airy wings. But there—directly in front of him—lay a blotchy orange orb of a fetid gourd and the boy sharply and unceremoniously impaled himself upon it. A warm squishy sensation surrounded his waist and an earthy broken breath assailed his nose. Later, he would think of the smell as 'putrefying ambrosia'—of death and dying, but also of life, of ending and renewal—but at eleven years old he knew only one thing: it was consummate physical intoxication.

And his bladder released as he could bear no more.

And Heaven poured out of him while Heaven filled him up.

The *dénouement* of the incident played out as perfunctorily and predictably as any sequence of events after a climax: an exalted exhale, a slow rise, a preliminary check of his trousers (mostly dry, mostly devoid of pumpkin), and a quickening panicked look from side to side to see if he had been observed. These and that entirely sublime—*sublime*—feeling of relief were the only mental and physical echoes of this singular and formative moment. The boy had never felt anything like it. But just as quickly as it arrived, the feeling began to dissolve in the boy's mind—in fact the whole experience did—dematerializing and deliquescing, transmogrifying until the events seemed hazily dreamlike as if they never happened at all. Yes, the moment after the seminal moment took on the aspects of a blissful calm and quick evaporation that sometimes follows a ferocious downpour on a hot and blazing day. There was no 'making water.' There was no running. There was no 'stickie.' There was no house... or lawn... or... garden. There were no safe woods beyond it. No place is ever safe. Pumpkins never grow and pumpkins never ripen and pumpkins never rot. There was no pumpkin. Nothing heavenly could be experienced on Earth. It hadn't happened. It simply hadn't. It couldn't have. It did not. ***HE WAS NOT SOILED!***

But, despite the boy's revisions, *it had happened.*

And as the child progressed from pubescence into adolescence, and from adolescence into young adulthood, and from young adulthood into maturity, and from maturity into patriarchy, the subconscious memory of what he had forgotten persisted. He was thirteen when he accompanied his family's housekeeper to the produce market—and kept his hands in his pockets the entire time, pretending to be chilly. He was sixteen when he found a too-ripe cantaloupe in a silver fruit basket by the microwave giving him a flirtatious wink. In college, he decided to major in finance and minor in cooking. Then after he married and had children, he would spend long afternoons trolling roadside stands and pick-ur-own fields and organic (*orgasmic?*) emporiums looking always, always searching, for delicacies. And finally he was a great-grandfather when he died putting fresh fertilizer and homemade compost down on a traditional watermelon patch in the square suburban garden in the back of the house he had been raised in, and inherited, and still lived in, right up until the moment of his death.

And so the man, who was once a boy, eventually died and somewhere a place was prepared to welcome him into

God's everlasting accepting grace; because, in actuality, the man had lived a very good life. He loved his wife and children and grandchildren with fidelity and sincerity. He treated his workers compassionately and respectfully, granting them fair wages and a safe working environment for their labor, which he considered to be both industrious and valuable. And to his community, his religion, and his country, he had given himself over in faith and devotion, with nothing but affable duty and personal kindness. Yes, in his heart of hearts, he lived upon the optimistic philosophy that the Universe was equitable, if not just— while always aspiring to be an agent of the just. Yes, in truth, his only dark passenger on Earth was that one proclivity, this one activity—done sparingly, confusingly, bewilderingly, but also done without any intent other than it felt good, had to be kept secret, and came from a part of himself that was truly himself. He often wondered if that part was actually a reservoir of blackest shame—a shame which perhaps spurred him on to all his good works.

Thus, the man's soul traveled from Earth to an intermediate place between Heaven and Hell—on what was called 'The Way'—where souls go and wait for a time until their final fates and ultimate destinations are thoroughly reviewed and adjudged. The man was going to Heaven—this much had already been decided—but then, just at the scant moment before his final departure, to eternal relief and release, the Devil appeared in front of the man. The Devil had a question, but to answer, the man would have to momentarily delay his journey to the land of milk and honey and vegetable tumescence, where all mortal doubt and material confliction between the Spirit and the Flesh forever ceased. The man would have to make a choice. He would have to choose whether or not to respond when the Devil asked his question. Those were the rules. He could share or not share his perspective on a life well-lived, a death well-died, and a resurrection successfully achieved. Choice was essential to the process. And so stood Old Scratch, red as a tomato, casually assessing the saved soul. His pitch-black hooves were planted firmly at parade rest. His formidable and muscled arms draped loosely across his rippled scarlet chest. And, he chewed almost sedately on a stick of celery the way a farmer might on a stalk of hay. His posture was eminently relaxed and easy—almost disinterested—except for his yellow eyes which glimmered in a piqued promethean curiosity. Verily, by his very nature, the Devil was always curious.

"Good evening, Mr. _____," the Devil began, addressing the man formally, because the Devil knows every social comity and every Christian name.

"Excuse my directness, sir, but I wanted to have a brief chat with you before you leave our little stretch of 'The Way' to the realm of supposed infinite reward and sound judgment. You see, I find you quite interesting, Mr. _____, and, since I have no purchase on your soul, I was hoping you would help me solve a bit of a mystery. My understanding of the terrestrial world and the celestial is quite comprehensive; however, there are still a few gaps—and I was hoping you could add one more apple of knowledge to my already considerably assembled cart. It is just one simple question, if you would indulge. I know the hour is late and you must be eager to travel onward, but my inquiry should only take a moment. It is but a curiosity on my behalf, if you would be so kind as to bestow me a courtesy upon yours…"

The man had just arrived and was caught off guard, but he felt no physical reaction since there wasn't anything physical left of him. He was, however, metaphysical now and this made him intrigued and perplexed, reinvigorated and open, but most of all, hungry for miraculous experiences beyond the shackles of mortal life. The man contemplated his new circumstance as well as the much older personage standing before him:

'This…? This…? This is the Devil… everyone… that I… I… was so afraid of?

Red skin, horns, hooves, a tail, yes, but where is the ferocity?

Where is his unspeakable nature, his countenance of ire, his foreboding malevolence that can make men weep?

Where is the heat of his direct channel to the fiery lake, the groan of my soul mid-shudder, the liquefaction of my bones in anticipation of torment unending and eternal terror to come?

Why… his demeanor is any one of a thousand I met at a dinner party!

Why—the Demon even snacks upon chilled greens!'

The Devil noted this delay and abided the pause with immortal cultivation and grace.

"Come now, Mr. _____, I assure you I will not be offended by your choice in either direction. As I said, it is only a curiosity on my part and but a sole query at that. Remember, you already have a seat at the banquet of salvation and the cornucopia awaits! Your feast is proclaimed convened! Indeed, any time of my potential temptation is long past... unless you consider the sharing of knowledge and the congenial exchange of a few words some diabolical threat..."

Still, the man didn't react, but continued his reflection:

'What... What... what do I make of this super-ordinary calm radiating within me?

I have no fear...

Perhaps it is only the Damned that experience the Devil's black dread of annihilation?

Maybe it is exclusively the Condemned who feel the harrowing ague when gazing upon his grim visage of agony personified?

But since I am not damned, I feel nothing.

After all, it is just one question...

I am Saved... am I not?

One question?

What harm could a single question wreak?

I am protected by the Sword of the Angels...

... and the Light of the Lord...

... and the Shield of Heaven...

... and the Devil has no fig leaf left to hide behind...

... and, should I dislike the timbre or content of this Demon's question, I shall just not deign to answer...'

These were the man's thoughts, but below everything was the unspoken fact that he felt no biological reaction to this supposedly renowned and heinous beast so casually and cordially inviting him to conversation. His skin did not crawl. His nose was not soured with the odors of brimstone and sulfur. His eyes did not well. And his stomach did not fall. Such physical and imprisoning things were far afield. In their absence only his disembodied psyche machined forward—titillated, fascinated, aroused. And so finally, yes, the man decided—yes—a moment or two could be spared in the pursuit of shared knowledge and common pleasantries. Indeed, God's Will *must always lead* to the path of an unencumbered mind, he surmised.

"I grant your request, Fallen One," the man began, "but please *do make it* quick because I am eager to finish my journey. I have very little practical instruction on what to expect, but I imagine it will be quite remarkable. Nevertheless, I consent. After all, it isn't every day one gets plied a question by the embodiment of all dark mischief and can safely engage with the Chief of Demons in respectful parlay. Now bathed in Light, I am happy to shed whatever light upon you that I may…"

Announcing this, the recently departed unnecessarily brushed off invisible dust particles from the tops of his shoulders, giving the imprimatur of being no longer burdened, but instead portraying himself as someone infinitely self-possessed.

"Sir, I have no intention of detaining you one second longer than you wish to be detained," replied the Devil, "but I say 'thank you' for your civility. And, yes, it is quite remarkable—your final destination. It is indescribable in fact… the way things not of the world are…"

The Devil relayed these words and then took a little bow. His hands of bone and sinew and blood-red skin glided out from his sides as if doing a curtsey of courtesy while the stalk of celery remained steadfastly gripped between a sharp set of bright white teeth.

"To your question then, Morning Star?" the man asked.

The Devil crunched down on his celery, swallowed, and removed it from his mouth to continue.

"My question is just this, my kind and generous gentleman: in life, you had a rather curious… rather peculiar… rather secretive… sexual practice. We need not name it. But my question is: how do you think your life would have been different had this activity… this bane… this shame… come to public knowledge while your heart still pumped blood and air still entered and left your lungs? I assure, I mean no disrespect or intrusion. As I said, it is just an idle wonderment of mine—one which only you, yourself, can answer."

The man did not redden because he had no circulatory system left to redden with; however, some part of him recoiled and shivered at the proposition—a part that wanted to scurry away like a shrew diving for cover or a snail retreating into its shell. Undoubtedly, *this was* a wonderment and not just for the Devil. In fleeting and frightened times during his life, the man often thought along similar lines. *Just why did he do the things he did, and how could he make sense of the things he had done?* But such was not the Devil's concern. Indeed, all the Devil wanted to know was what would have happened *if he'd been found out*. The difference was crucial. Still the man considered gravely before answering.

"I should find your question quite impertinent, Dark One, but my transition from mortal life to life-everlasting has made me unusually unperturbed to all situations which may have once caused distress. In truth, I've never felt more composed. Thankfully I am protected by the rewards of faith and promises kept. My answer is, I suppose I would have been utterly and completely destroyed. I expect I would have been ostracized and mocked, ridiculed and skewered. I imagine my business faltering and my livelihood suffering. I imagine my marriage, my friendships, and relationships with both acquaintances and allies alike strained to breaking points and probably beyond. Yes, I would have been made an outcast. My children would most likely have never spoken to me again. My wife would have abandoned me. And to my church, my community, and to society at large, I would be a pariah. Yes, at best, I'd have been branded a fool and at worst be marked a pervert of the most deranged sort. Yes, in truth, I'd never be known for anything else. That one activity would *define me… forever…* and forever I would have been lost."

Here the man paused and looked off into the empty space that could become anything and reverently added: "I am thoroughly grateful to God and His eternal host that they do not punish the keeping of secrets for embarrassing, yet benign acts. My secret at least… escaped Divine denunciation. For such heavenly wisdom, I can tell you, I drink in draughts of sweet relief."

The Devil soaked up every word from the man with an almost academic objectivity and contemplative reserve. He even took a moment to munch and crunch once more on his celery stalk before speaking again.

"But if your own self-appointed creator-judge and his feathery court assess your activity not to be a sin, then why would you be so reviled on Earth? What was the need to keep it so secret and so hidden? Yes, why would you be vilified if your mortal and physical practice didn't require heavenly absolution? You abided by the strictures of scripture, didn't you? You committed no wrong, did you? There was no crime. Expiation was not required. Those you hold in such high and ethereal esteem do pronounce it so! Put simply, how can human judgment be so divergent from the judgment of the Divine?"

Once more, the man felt a non-corporeal flush shimmy through him, but only in mere tremor. For this query, he knew well his footing.

"I would guess the answer is because humanity always looks to judge each other instead of letting God handle such matters. No, humans do not much like the unusual or the eccentric—and certainly not the aberrant—unless it entertains them or is couched behind protective fences like those of a zoo... or a prison... or a book. My activity would slake their deepest thirst for salacious gossip and embolden their perennial need to gloat in superior hypocritical condemnation. You see, people like to tear down more than build up—though they, themselves, always want to be on the up. Mortality is filled with such contradictions, I think, and people hunger to pile on as long as they are not on the bottom of the pile. Yes, it must be true at least in part: within every human heart so pumps the lifeblood of a bully and a sadist…"

Here, the Devil's glinting yellow eyes positively sparkled and seemed to penetrate through every word and world. He continued to nod slowly and profoundly as one would at realizing an unthought-of but fundamental truth. The air that was not air seemed to grow heavy, but certainly this must have been an illusion—because real air was not a part of this place. Still, the Devil pushed on almost breathlessly.

"But sir, I have delayed you… and for that I beg your peace and your pardon. I do, however, have one last inquiry to fully sate my prickling curiosity about the mortal realm from whence you came. Would you grant me consent one more time? Will you impart a final kindness? Or have I taxed your patience to its limit? Sir! I implore! Say true!"

Feeling secure in his last utterance, and having actually found the Devil a congenial and well-appointed interrogator, the man did not hesitate.

"Surely, I consent! You have asked two questions and I have answered two. Why not make it a Trinity to pleasantly auger my imminent homecoming to my new forever home? After all, my load has been lifted; fear is banished along with death! Ask away, thy Mephistopheles!"

The Devil seemed to frown at the word 'Trinity' but perked up at the mention of his ancient theatrical name. He took one last bite of celery then threw the remainder behind him where it disintegrated into the miraculous ethers of 'The Way.' Indeed, the ending was nigh.

"My final question is this: I asked how your life would have been different had your private exotic sexual fare become public when you were alive; then, I asked why humanity differs so much in judgment of each other compared to the declarations of your own creator-judge; but finally I ask: what do you think would happen now that you are dead? I mean to your reputation? Your heritage? Your legacy? Would that change? Would it matter? Tell me, good and patient sir: how do you think such revelation on Earth would alter the circumstances *here*, in your new life after old, in your immortal life after mortal death? Yes, what if people knew about those actions and activities now?"

The man blinked once, then twice, and ultimately a third time. He could see in his mind's eye a great and brilliant ripple spreading across the Earth like a dazzling wave of light to touch every dim and forgotten corner. The light held no lies, no deceptions, no disambiguation of any kind. The light held no secrets. It came from a place, that was not just a place, but this place—*the afterlife*— be it *Heaven or Hell* or anywhere in between, where all is known and no shadow or indiscretion could possibly survive. Corporeal privacy was nothing but an Earthly dream. Yes, the man finally saw in the afterlife every atom knows every other, and a Divine vantage can peer into every sphere and peek behind every curtain. Yes, God and His Angels and the Devil and His Demons knew it all even before he arrived.

'And if the veil of death could be pierced?
And if a message was sent back?

What if I don't make it to the House of the Father in time?

What would the living say?

What would my friends and family say?

What if I make another mess?

What if I am seen?

What if I get caught?

***What if I am forever soiled?*'**

Indeed, with a simple Divine whisper everyone could know everything… and what they could know about him was…

"Fiendish! Fiendish! Why… why… I… I… why, it would be the end of everything! **Everything!**" he burst out, only feeling and not thinking, as his immortal soul became immortified.

The man's chin fell to his chest.

"Do not worry, kind sir," said the Devil. "You are welcome to come with me. I may strain the quality of mercy at times, but *I do* know how to keep a secret."

"It isn't fair," the man whimpered.

"No, it isn't fair—*not even remotely*," replied the Devil.

"It's dirty and it's rotten," the man moaned.

"Yes, it's dirty and it's rotten," the Devil concurred.

"*Goddamn it all*," hissed the man, his voice barely rising above a whisper.

The Devil remained the epitome of nonchalance.

"He already has," the Devil firmly concludes.

Then the two of them left because the conversation was over.

And for each of them… it was a shame.

End of Story #2

Intermezzo

(second)

The Devil puts down the new pages on top of the already printed sheets. He sits upright in a tall chair and chews pensively on his bottom lip for a few seconds. Then he picks all the pages back up, fans them out, looks over them again, and finishes by squaring the thin pile against the tabletop so everything was made even. The writer watches keenly as he waits for the Devil to speak. Finally, the Devil does.

"Ugh," the Devil exhales.

"Is that a good 'ugh' or a bad 'ugh'?" the writer asks.

"I don't think there's such a thing as a good 'ugh,'" the Devil returns.

"Well, there could be something like 'Ugh... this is the greatest story ever...' or 'Wow, this time you truly composed a masterpiece of absolute genius… Ugh… it disgusts me how awesome you are…'" the writer answers. The Devil doesn't smile, but the writer does—at least a little. The skin over his Devil's Spot had grown increasingly hot and dry when he touched it, but his mind kept getting clearer and clearer. The Spot had also begun to itch strangely—almost vibrate—but the sensation wasn't entirely unpleasant. Moreover, the automatic feeling of words *flowing through him*, rather than *coming from him*, had diminished. It was still there—to be sure—but he feels like he is slowly reclaiming his own voice and then some.

"I'm afraid my 'ugh' wasn't any of those kinds…" replies the Devil.

"So, I take it you're not impressed?" the writer says, more seriously.

"No," the Devil begins, "I'm not. But, I suppose this is a step in the right direction. At least, it's unusual in a relative way. Still, I can't believe I gave you decades of language comprehension and a dollop of genuine talent and this is what you did with it. I find it pretty extraordinary, if I'm being true."

"I thought I handled the subject tactfully…" the writer answers, "… and besides, that wasn't the point. I wanted 'The Fruits of Shame' to be a story about non-corporeal existence and the infirmity and failure of God's protection. I was going for presence of absence. The fruit diddling was just a way to underscore the theme."

"Don't be crass," chides the Devil, "and I wasn't referring to the vegetable stuff. Also, you don't know the first thing about non-corporeal existence *or God*—for that matter—so don't speak out of school."

"What's the problem, then?" presses the writer.

"The fact it's a short story. Our deal is done, but I fear you may have wasted your soul on gewgaws."

"What? Why? Gewgaws! Short stories aren't shiny objects! I like short stories! What's wrong with short stories?" asks the writer incredulously. He feels his Devil's Spot grow even hotter and start pulsing with the beating of his heart. There is a better way to describe it, he thinks: *'It's flaring!'*

"Nothing… except short stories aren't exactly inspiring or exciting, are they? Hardly anyone reads them anymore. At least with a novel you get to go on a journey with someone, to cheer for them or cry for them, but short stories are just too brief to have that kind of impact. Your main character doesn't even have a name. And, by the way, nobody cares about your 'presence of absence.' Why do new writers have to always start out as such strutting peacocks… so predictably pretentious…"

"Again… that's harsh… and I'm not sure if I agree. I would argue a lot of it depends on the individual reader. Poems are brief and can rock and shock the world. I believe short stories can too. You just have to write them correctly. We move, not until we are moved. And who is to say what moves us? Besides, *I am new at this*. What are you expecting? A rollicking epic barreling right out of the gate?"

"Perhaps not… I was just making an observation," says the Devil, wanting to change the subject.

"Do you have anything positive to add?"

"I like that bit about me being curious."

"You couldn't be but anything else," replies the writer.

"'Tis true. 'Tis always been true," replies the Devil.

"Other advice, then?" asks the writer.

"Well… *you're not* being true," the Devil adds.

Now it is the writer who chews pensively on his bottom lip for a few seconds.

"What's that supposed to mean?"

"I mean, you told a story which revealed a secret. But it wasn't *your secret*. Good writers need to be vulnerable, you understand? They have to speak not just from the parts of themselves they want to show off, but also—and more importantly—show the parts that are honest, no matter how unflattering. You can't be lazy about it. You have to dig deeper. *Much deeper*," the Devil explains.

"Something deeper," echoes the writer. He finds his eyes fixed upon the Devil's. They were as sparkling and as yellow as he had written in his previous story. His Devil's Spot flares up once again.

"Oh Hell!" he exclaims.

"What?" the Devil asks.

"Nothing," the writer answers, "I just know what I am going to write about next…"

"Good for you," the Devil ends in a yawn.

And, with this, the storytelling continues.

An Uncomfortable Nothing

(Story #3)

So once upon a time the Devil was on *'His'* part of 'The Way'—as he liked to think of it—preparing a place for another soul sentenced to eternal damnation. But on this day his mind was unquiet. He managed his business efficiently and diligently, yet something inside him chafed the way a grain of sand must nag and irritate the soft flesh and softer confidence of a hard-shelled oyster. Under normal circumstances, he would go about his labor with a sense of deep satisfaction—a certain zeal and zest accompanying justice well done and an abiding pride he was the unquestioned Master of his own domain. However, on this occasion, the Devil was troubled. The Condemned, who was about to be received, had been convicted of one of the old sins—the Slippery Seven, the Sinister Septalogue, the Lethal List of Abominable Iniquities numbering half a dozen plus one. They were Aquinas's Minuses, SEPTEM PECCATA MORTALIA, or celestial crimes more commonly known as 'The Seven Deadly Sins.' Yes, the forthcoming soul had been damned for the felony of Belphegor: the sludge crime of Sloth. In blackest truth and abysmal honesty, though, the Devil could not for the life of himself understand why such an offense merited his own vices and devices. 'Falderal and balderdash! Tweedle and twaddle!' These words peppered the Devil's infernal monologue while his hands moved steadfast in duty-bound work. Yes, when you apply logic to religion, as it is often said, the Devil is in the details—and the details of 'His' current situation did not rest peacefully within him.

Consequently, the Devil mused about sinners and their terrible sins: 'Gluttony, Lust, Greed, Pride, Envy, Wrath, Sloth—*yes*—but in what way are not all summed up into one diabolical disgrace: EXCESS! Let me ask any liege or legion, seraph or charlatan, con-man or constable, pope or pauper: who does not enjoy food? Who not sex? Who not wealth? Who not accomplishment? Who does not wish to vanquish their enemies with orgiastic destruction, and who does not wish for the accoutrements of others gained serendipitously by birth or achieved honorably through unwavering perseverance? And *yes*, finally, *yes*, in truths both dark and light, who does not prefer *a comfortable nothing* to *an arduous anything*? All fine, *agreed*, all fine, but disastrous and damnable IN EXCESS—and *even then* only in singular context!'

But the Devil thought Sloth had a particularly nasty logic bomb lodged within its tangled and entangling web: it was punishment *for not doing*! Indeed, how can one commit a sin by *not committing* anything? Indeed, how can *not performing* an act warrant perdition unending and pain beyond measure? Yes, how can a *nothing* be worthy of the worst *something* in all of creation? The Devil wished he had someone to talk to about it. *That* was the hardest thing about being the Devil, he reflected: it was a thankless job and so very often he faced his tasks alone. He longed for ears to test his character.

Subsequently, the Devil toiled in silence. He gathered the vapors along 'The Way' and gave them form and presently the form was books. They appeared in a neat circle about a meter wide and proceeded to stack one atop another tome on tome rising high and bulging out, the way cells of a tree would grow, only faster. There were thin books and thick books, anthologies and collections— essays, compendiums, diaries, plays, grimoires, graphic novels, monographs, and epics. Yes, all manner and type were represented until they stacked so airy and so ascendant one could not see where their papery layered leaves ended and apotheosis began.

And they all were new, too, but new in their old ways; all bound by the time and methods from which they were originally constructed: the scriptorium, the printer's garrison, the publishing conglomerate. The smells of tanned leather, linen, pulp and papyrus, lavender and indigo wafted about singing notes of Aramaic gum, pokeberries, sepia, and petroleum naphtha—among so many others and others and others. Some readers prefer the smell of old books, the skin flakes and cigarette smoke of handled knowledge; but a new book, freshly cracked, contains only the fragrances of unbridled possibility and perilous adventure. Yes, a new book is virginal and pure; and the Devil constructed a vertical vestal library of them from the whole of time. This, the Devil decreed, and, by the Devil's own will, made it so.

The work almost complete, one last thing remained. The column stood tall and massive and magnificent but with a final snap of the Devil's fingers, the entire tower of lyrical and literary babble burst into glowing flame. The pages of the books curled slightly and singed with minor embers, but the texts were not consumed. The flames flickered and frolicked like all fires, but—in Hell—fires burned, yet they did not obliterate. Obliteration was not in the Devil's wheelhouse. Only punishment was. And this prison should have been perfect for the impenitently and indolently condemned.

Still the Devil was restive.

No, he looked upon his tower and was not pleased. Oh yes, the craftsmanship was fine—perfect and perfectly fitting even—but nonetheless there was that speck, that mote, that blot of mustard and bit of underdone potato, which wouldn't let his mind find serenity: *not doing* as a sin. Inaction as equivalent to conscious activity. *Not committing* as grounds for never-ending chthonian commitment. *'If only I had someone to converse with. If only I had someone to talk to about it… '* His frightful, spiteful mind began to loop:

'Someone to talk to…
Someone to talk to…
Someone to talk to…'

And then the Devil was struck. If *he* wanted someone to talk to, why not go directly to Arch-Demon Belphegor?! The very SOURCE of Sloth, *himself*!

Thus the Devil began his summoning. He went to draw a razored talon across his own red wrist to spill out the fiery blood which coursed and coarsed within him. But at the last moment to complete the action, he did not. Then he bent down—low on his coal-black hooves like onyx pucks—to draw an ancient antediluvian symbol on the ground. But when it came time to make the mark, he stopped. Then he shifted his dark tongue so it grazed and razed against his pointed teeth to incant one simple phrase: "Belphegor, Come To Me!" But as for finishing the ritual—silence.

And, with that, the summoning was complete.

The effects were immediate and not without irony.

"I am here, my Lord…"

The sound of the Demon's voice rose before the appearance of the flesh that was not flesh of Belphegor. The Demon's vocalization was thick and viscous like someone speaking through a mouthful of oil, black and crude. Belphegor, himself, materialized next, but Belphegor's skin and tissues and bones were entirely transparent—sheer, opaque, limpid—as if the Devil had summoned—instead of an entity—a nothing adorned with a cloak of a thousand unaccomplishments. Finally, the unrealization was completely realized before him. It was the formless form of Belphegor: Arch-Demon of Sloth.

"Thank you for coming, Vile One," greeted the Devil.

"I didn't want to…" Belphegor gurgled in a lugubrious yawn.

"I understand, but I desire to ask about your Nature and the nature of those condemned for embracing your aspects."

"It sounds like a lot of work…" Belphegor slurred and whined, but remembering his place, corrected, "… yet you I serve and only you. I will answer what I can…"

"So you would submit to an interrogation, O' sluggish one?"

The Devil could perceive Belphegor even through his invisible pretense. He was neither smiling nor frowning, agitated nor patient, inviting nor elusive. He just existed as a base thing, comfortable and satisfied with himself and everything around him. If there was a word to describe him, it would be 'ambient.' The Devil felt the power of the Demon's proximity. His energy waned but his joy increased. It was the bliss of complacency. But the Devil also knew it was often necessary to sacrifice such bliss in the service of knowledge. Such was *His* Nature. Thereupon, the Devil opened his mouth to question the Demon, but before he could, Belphegor surprised him.

"You want to ask how not-doing is a sin…" Belphegor initiated, impromptu and unprompted, astute in circumstance. "This is the most common of inquiries, O' active one. Even when our Treaty between the above and below, the included and the afar, the cast and the cast-out was being scripted, this question sounded and resounded again and again in the firmament: why should eternal damnation be the final unresting place for the static agents of inaction? Those with wings and halos, as if mirrors of our former selves, asked this question with puzzled looks and looked puzzled even more when my gifts were finally ordained to fall underneath your purview. Listen closely, because such were my postulations. As a rule I never like to speak once… let alone twice… and a third time… inconceivable…"

Belphegor shimmied and swayed from side to side, shifting the air that was not air translucently, ineluctably—almost transcendently—the way heat slithers up from a desert asphalt. The Demon seemed filled with an odd antiquated vacillation as if possessed by a ghost of energy from long ago or even the ghost of energy's past. It goes without saying, but needs to be said: it was a long time since Belphegor did, was asked to do, or felt the repercussions of doing anything. He shivered with miniscule vibrations of activity. In such a state he launched into the first of his Divine and Divinely remembered recollections.

"To begin my slothful case, I argued it had been well established that accomplished activity falls into categories of good and evil because accomplished actions have material and immaterial consequences that can be pointed to—as all facts can—according to the demonstrable balance of the Universe. A person acts for good or for evil and to complete such a design undeniably moves a person towards one camp or the other. An action can be judged. An action can be quantified. An action, by definition, is also a definition of good or evil. 'Isn't it so?' I asked. Quickly and assuredly the heavenly negotiators affirmed my opening position."

"Of course they did," replied the Devil. "They could do no different. For what is a sin, other than an act?"

"Precisely," continued Belphegor, "but I didn't stop there. I then argued it was not just accomplished actions, but attempts, too, which bridged the spheres, because attempt also skews into black or white—regardless of whether the attempt meets fruition or finds some other outcome in its frustrated effort. Yes, attempt indicates direction towards good or evil while outcome seals it. This is the weighty mark of motivation, of ambition, and of intention. 'This is also the way, *nicht wahr*?' I pressed. And, again, the heavenly host immediately assented."

The Devil nodded as Belphegor advanced.

"Thus far, my reasoning was forthright and pinioned upon nothing but logic and truth and the heavenly negotiators attested to my veracity with ease. How could they not? And with these two propositions accepted, I had only to slide myself and my argument into the final position where inaction was not just beholden to the labeling of 'good' or 'evil,' like accomplishment and attempt, but that inaction landed squarely among the darkest and most damnable offenses."

The Devil's eyes sparkled and shined in yellow brilliance as he waited for Belphegor to conclude.

"Now I know how busy you were during those hectic and hellish times, as you brought chaos out of the false order and true order out of the necessary chaos, but I wish you could have seen my ultimate negotiating stroke! Because, at last, I posited to *not even* attempt—to *not even* try, to *not even* reach, to *not even* strive for exultation in grace or make the smallest gesture towards an exit in gracelessness—demands the slothful soul be subject to only the most basic, rudimentary, unalterable, gravitational forces of mortality and morality. *'AND THIS MUST BE DESCENT!'* I proclaimed. 'Yes, DESCENT downward into the endless spiral of misery and to permanent residence within Satan's pit!' I said, 'True, DESCENT is the only appropriate response!' In short, I argued *not-doing* denies the barest sliver of 'salvation' because it is not sought for, or struggled for, or even acknowledged as the living hearts of these souls beat for nothing—not even themselves. Yes, Sloth is the denial of choice and, in denying choice, the slothful denies life, and the denial of life is the denial of God! And so, the bland soul, composed of nothing, who does nothing, *deserves nothing* but black perdition itself! This was my logic unfolded..."

"Ah, such is the philosophy I wished to explore!" exclaimed the Devil, enthusiastically. "And I find your argumentation as inexorable as if straight from any monastery or lyceum—from any columned cloister or hall of ivy. Yes, your mind truly moves with the sages and ages when it so deigns! No doubt the wisdom you put forth was unassailable as the setting of the sun! Yes, the heavenly host must have surrendered utterly in the face of such pristine reasoning!"

Belphegor, rather than taking heart in these praises, seemed to shudder and tense uncharacteristically and involuntarily—even more in reaction than he did when stirred to action. It was as if all the Devil's laudations had been transformed into toxic laudanum and the Demon of

Sloth was on the verge of collapse. He was not much used to roused feelings.

"It pleases me, but vexes me, you share the same ideas and perspectives as those involved on the other side of the celestial negotiation," Belphegor replied, nervously. "But I mean only respect and not the opposite, because at the time of my syllogism, I didn't care a ladybug's ear about the logic of my supposedly 'logical' position. As you might recall, our territory was *new—brand new*—with apparently a new brand and newer brandings, and I admit I would have said *anything* to increase the sum of our net gain by increasing the number of our gained nets. My goal and mandate was to direct as many souls away from the old kingdom and lead them into yours. As it is said on Earth, as it is in Heaven—as it is said anywhere—a realm without a population is hardly a realm at all. Consequently, my argument may hold water, but I wouldn't drink until you drown in it, my Lord. I desired only to ferry more souls into your new dominion. I cared for nothing else. For this, sin had to be as expansive as possible. Such is my revelation unveiled…"

The Devil thought long and hard about Belphegor's statements. Things shifted in his mind—coalescing and deliquescing—as refinement revises and deliberation evolves into dialect. He remembered how he opined about the old sins: 'All fine, *agreed*, all fine, but disastrous and damnable IN EXCESS—and *even then* only in singular context.' And suddenly the Devil realized he'd fallen for the same absolutism that so governed his former kith and kin. He had fallen for the ancient joke of Heaven where all individuals are bulldozed under the blunt and undiscerning blade of principle and a Principal. There was no gradation. No gray. No grace. All any soul had to rely on was the arrogant unquestioned judgment pronounced by brute monolithic monotheists. No appeal. No movement. No review. It was what it was. It is what it is. No deliberation. No debate. No defense. *'And wasn't it just such ideas—such rigid and inflexible strictures—which gave me initial pause in the first place?'* the Devil thought. *'Maybe even in that Original place too? Is there any question why I rebelled?'* In the grip of this epiphany, friendly or fiendish, the Devil forged onward, perhaps on a straighter path.

"I say true to what you say true, Belphegor, and faithfully I recall the old mandate and the date in which it occurred. But, O' languid one, please turn your incisive and insightful attention to my current circumstance—to this incoming soul, stained by Sloth, and so newly damned. As you can see, I created this tower alight and a-bright with fiery books which 'twas to be his prison. They come from all over the Earthly plane and from the whole of time itself. I gathered every book of wonder and intellect, of emotion and idea, and set them to blaze here for all eternity. You see, O' inert one, this soul was *a reader* and filled his life and spirit with only the stories of others. He could have been a scholar, but was not. He could have been a philosopher or logistician to rival even you, O' leaden one, but was not. But most of all, he could have been a writer himself—*a storyteller*—a purveyor of the fantastic and a crafter of the possible and impossible and he *could have changed lives*! Yet he did none of these things. Instead, he only slothfully read. Verily, Belphegor, if books were food he would have been the most gluttonous glutton to ever bloat himself on words!"

"Fascinating…" the Arch-Demon gurgled and burped, "please go on…"

"Well, here's the rub: it's not that I find myself anathema with condemning someone for reading away his or her soul; but it was *the books*, Belphegor! It was *the books*—*the books*—the books this man *did not write*! They were brilliant, bold, inspired, surprising, virtuous, engaging—yes, all manner of accolades could be used to describe them—enough to fill a lexicon of the sublime! No, never in the history of mankind or even *our kind* had such prose been contemplated, let alone executed, such themes explored, such memes chiseled out of the ether— such beauty and meaning wrought and wrapped together in melodious harmonies of overwhelming erudition and entertaining delight! It is only because I have the ability to see *what could have been, but wasn't* that I even got to read these books—and not since Orpheus charmed the stone heart of Hades has a God of the Underworld been so moved! But had this man actually written his books? Catastrophe! And if humanity read them? Catastrophe metastasized! Yes, those human readers would have become Activated, Elevated, Enlightened—a Consciousness would have risen within the population taking them to new heights only to soar higher and higher as each generation extricated their wisdom and then passed the books on to the next. Indeed, his words could have changed and reshaped thoughts and those filigreed thoughts would have rolled and roiled into a deluge of noble action unstoppable. Peace! Goodwill! Collective Achievement! But for us: Holocaust! Ruination! Apocalypse! *Yes, these books—these books he did not write*, Belphegor; verily I say, *had* he written these books, the Earthly plane would have transformed into a paradise that—save for death—would have driven Heaven into obsolescence and Hell into an ash heap!"

"And herein lies my dilemma," the Devil went on, "these books… these wonderful, amazing, resplendent books which have enchanted even my own supposedly foul heart, would have heralded a golden age for the mortals, and, in doing so, how could they not also please God? Yes, undoubtedly the old kingdom would have swelled with the effervescent spirits resulting from such an era of accord and kindness and commitment to the common good made manifest by such manifests! However, this soul—*my soul* about to be received—wrote nary a word. Thusly, how can I punish him *for not doing* which so benefited me? Yes, how can this man, who so offended our former Master and Masters by inaction, offend me? Indeed, how can this product-less man be subject to my endless products of suffering? This is the worming question trying my diabolical discernment and rankling my rapacious mind! Yes, in truth, sometimes when one wins, one loses; occasionally victory is infused with the fetid breath of defeat! Again, and still truthfully, I have often been described as 'lost' or 'astray' or 'adrift,' but rarely has my conviction ever faced such manner of confliction. I guess I should confess Belphegor, 'fore you will do as well as any priest: I just do not want to torment this slothful soul about to be reborn unto me in Hell!"

Belphegor's response in pith and pitch was only two words:

"Then don't…" the Arch-Demon said.

The Devil retreated a few steps almost in a stumble—as if Belphegor had bludgeoned him instead of saying just a simple pair of words. Surprise was rare for the crimson beast so skilled in anticipation and prognostication, but Belphegor managed to do it twice in only one dialogue. The Devil had been forecasting a substantial amount of woolgathering, of back and forth, of trial and debate about the finer points of justice, damnation, and the commandments of Heaven and Hell—but Belphegor cut straight through all that. And then, Belphegor, at seeing the Devil taken aback, went on, and for a third time, surprise rang out in the princely ears of the Prince of Darkness.

"This goes *way and Way* beyond my resting point," expanded Belphegor. "But, if it helps, and if it serves, I suppose I should remind you. This kingdom *is Yours*, my Lord. It is up *to You*. The arriving soul may be sent by rules *You* do not govern, but once he is here his punishment or damnation or privation lies entirely *in Your* hands. Burn him, if *You* wish. Flay him. Grind him to a pulp. Castrate him. Make him devour his own flesh. Pluck out his eyes a thousand times and have them grow back a thousand more. All this is within *Your* power and all of it bothers Heaven, and those residing in that stale and glittering mausoleum, not a lick or a stick. *Your* power here *is unbound*, so if it pleases, *FREE HIM!*—my Lord over my former lord! Do *You* not have the power? Are *You* not the Master of this domain? Do *You* require permission from some other? Change it, *towards Your Will,* if *You will.* I serve *You,* and *I* know my place, but *Your* place and actions have no restrictions *except what You impose upon Yourself. SO FREE HIM, I SAY!* I say it, if *You* say it! *You* are the architect of all dark destiny—and whose destiny is darker than *Your* own? So I say, take the full reins of *Your Reign* and choose a more appropriate course! Never forget— *YOU control the Design of the Anti-Firmament—THUS EXERCISE THE COMPLETE AND TOTAL CONTROL OF BEING ITS DESIGNER!"*

The Devil listened intently to Belphegor's sermon and upon its conclusion spoke not a word. Instead, as a response, he raised his hands—hands that had tortured and terrified and tormented innumerable souls by crafting accountability for their sins—and brought them together in a tremendous clap. The sound of the clap cracked along 'The Way' like thunderous thunder and a full quarter of the flaming tower of books vanished back into the nothingness from which they came. It was punishment's exit, perdition's escape: absolution in Pandemonium. It was freedom and benevolence and mercy—*and, most of all, it was an exercise of the Devil's Own Will and Power.*

The Devil felt a wave of exhilaration surge through him.

"Your words are well met, Belphegor," the Devil said. "But now behold *this Design*—'fore something I deem *NOT-WICKED* this way comes!"

And then in the midst of such fanfare, the troubling soul, condemned by his own sloth, arrived.

The man died old, but like most souls in Hell, he arrived naked and young and vulnerable—seventeen or eighteen or nineteen—with freshly generated nerve endings and a physical body wide open to all the slings and arrows of experience and expiation. He materialized in the center of his would-be flaming hoop of a prison now cleaved sectionally by a fourth. Sitting cross-legged, with chin to chest, he looked like a man who had been on a long journey only to be told to go on another of an unacceptable and interminable length. His eyes held no fear or despair, no shock or bewilderment. In fact, had the Devil glanced upon his new charge, he may have detected only frustration and annoyance—as with any man who just wanted to be left alone. However, the Devil gave him nothing but the barest review. This was because the Devil was too excited for what he was about to undertake for this lost soul, now newly found in Hell.

Accordingly, the Devil stood tall and proud and unnecessarily cleared his throat. Then, in a mighty voice, he announced:

> "Denizens of Hell, from the shores of Sheol to the summits of Naraka and to all the infernal points in between, HEAR ME: I, the great and powerful Lucifer, Beelzebub, Satan, Captain Howdy, Mephistopheles, Adversary, Horny-Thorny, Rogue, Enfant Terrible, Evil One—*supposedly*—do hereby swear and sanction in this place and at this time

that this adjudged sinner—who has fallen as I have fallen—does get a full and unabridged pardon for all acts, consequences, and inconsequentials he hath doth performed in life or hath doth failed to perform! By my word and my bond, by my intellect and my judgment—by my being here and by my very being—I do proclaim him free and free to do as he sees fit. With these words, I declare a new chapter for both he and I, indeed, for all the occupants of the underworld! Verily, I say this soul has inspired the Devil through not what he has done, but because of *what he could have done, but did not do*! Therefore, I decree his actions and inactions on the mortal plane to be excusable and not worthy of damnation. Subsequently, I grant *his FREEDOM*! 'Fore in realizing his *Total Liberty*, he has helped me find my own! Thus, go forth, damned soul, in my forgiveness and my absolution. I GRANT YOU EASE OF PASSAGE! IT IS BY MY COMMAND! SO BE FREE AND JUST BE!"

At the end of the pronouncement, the now liberated soul glared at the Devil through slitted and slicingly derisive eyes. He looked furious, but bored. He looked exasperated while his eyes stabbed straight through the Dark Lord in response. As for Belphegor, he simply loitered nearby with as much attention as he could muster. Then, with equal intensity, the soul looked away, then up, then down, then around—far and wide, low and high—at the flaming tower of multiple and manifold texts burning around him. Yes, the man examined every angle and contour—every tome of his would-be tomb—except for the gaping maw of an exit. The exit held no interest for him. Finally, with a casual, but deliberate motion, he reached forward and took a book out from the seething pyre. The flames immediately began to bark and sizzle upon his grasping hands, but, defiantly, the man opened the text and began to read.

The sinner's skin first turned red, but soon erupted in bulbous white blisters that after a while bulged and burst with expectorant hisses and squirts. The pus ran briefly, but very soon boiled away into a sickening yellow steam. Charring happened next: pliant skin crisping to ash which immediately began to flake and fall into the reader's own lap like some hideous and noxious snow. The sinner winced and shook a bit, but maintained his novel grip. Finally, when the burning had gone on for a time, and his arms were black and cracked and roasting from finger pads to elbows, new skin—skin once again able to feel the anguish of fire—slurried and shimmied down his mutilated limbs in an act of horrifying reconstitution. A smile seemed to cross the man's face. Then the sinner flipped a page and the process began anew: burning, bursting, steaming, crisping, charring, falling. And the sinner smiled all the same. Yes, there must have been something particularly engrossing in the pages the sinner read.

The Devil waited and watched with growing incredulity at the freed soul reading and reading and burning and burning with every thumbed page. Yes, the Proclamation had been given, the Edict issued, the Decree had been decreed, but still the pardoned soul did not move. There was no action or activity; no progress or progression. To the Devil, it didn't seem possible or rational, *but more than that*, there wasn't even a nod, a glimmer, a scintilla *of gratitude* from the sinner he had so benevolently absolved. Inside him, the grain of sand that nagged and irritated this whole affair was now growing into one big mother of a pearl. He decided to make the announcement again in a volume rapidly approaching a bellow. Indeed, the Devil's unusual magnanimity was quickly reverting back to his usual animus.

"I have *FREED* you! I have *DECREED* you! I have *REPRIEVED* you! So why won't you go? This is a *NEW* day in Hell. It was inspired *by you*; it is because of *what you did not do, but could have done, that I now do what I have never done before*! Inconceivable! Leave this prison, I command! Take your place with me—by my side—or go somewhere else upon the ways and 'Way' by *your design*! Find recreation or purpose, activity or supine repose. Do it where and when you will! It is by my action that I grant your inaction; it is by my power, I allow you to disregard yours! Go, I say! Go! Why won't you go?"

The self-torturing soul did not even look up, but rather continued to bounce and ping-pong his eyes across the folio immolating before him. He advanced a page and the Devil glowered while issuing a low and guttural growl. There was something worse rising in the air that was not air than the smell of burnt flesh and smoldering genius: an electric malevolence began to pervade and percolate the way a flammable gas can fill up a room before exploding. It was at this moment Belphegor decided to interject. Apparently, Belphegor's capacity for surprise was incalculable—even to himself.

"You would do best to answer, Cousin," he said, addressing the simmering sinner, "this *New King* beyond the old kingdom could have you eat those manuscripts if *He* so desired. Then what would you read? All *He* wants to know is the reason for you being what you are. Why not explain? Yes, why not explain why you do what you do and why you don't what you don't? After all, it isn't much of a thing, is it? Your torpid and stagnant nature deserves exploration, doesn't it? Really, the effort shouldn't be too much..."

Hearing this, the tortured soul sighed and put down his book like a votive in front of his crossed ankles, where it continued to burn in flickering perpetuity. He peered up at the Devil and then shifted his eyes to the empty nowhere where Belphegor vibrated transparently next to him. A hint of recognition seemed to flit across the soul's face. The sinner committed to speak, but it was to Belphegor he addressed.

"I do not leave because *he* wishes it," the sinner hissed. "All my life I have been poked and prodded and ordered and nudged to do things I didn't want to do and now apparently I have to go through it all again even after my death. I have inspired the Devil—*OH WHAT JOY!*—but I have never endeavored to inspire anyone to anything because nothing and no one *has ever* inspired me. I read books because I hope to find it. Yes, I read books because the best of humanity is in books—the best of *your kind* is in books—the best of *this or any place* is in books—the *best of everything is in books*—and this means *THE BEST OF MYSELF MUST BE IN BOOKS!* I have *ALMOST SEEN IT!* I have *ALMOST READ IT!* There were glimmers and twinkles, aspects and suspects, sprinkles and sparkles. There were signs and sigils appearing like linguistic lodestones—the finely crafted sentence, a paragraph eloquently executed, the believable twist, the unsuspected surprise, the tantalizing tale of Tantalus himself—that points me to me—*TO MYSELF, TO MY CHARACTER, TO WHAT MUST BE MY PURPOSE AND MY FATED FATE!* I swear there were times when I almost seemed to glimpse myself through a mirror, lightly! So, I do not leave this place because *this place* is where I belong. Yes, if I, as a ward, have inspired my Warden, I only ask him to replace this quarter of my supposed prison because my search is not done! I will search until I find it. I will plumb depths and scale heights! *I WILL FIND MY ONE FINE THING! MY INSPIRATION! YES, I WILL FIND THE SELF AT THE CORE OF MYSELF!* Until then, leave me be. I have already lived one hellish life and verily I say death is no worse than anywhere else I have been! A life without inspiration is like a journey without a destination, like food without flavor, so go—both of you, go—but I will stay! Mark my words on all things holy or unholy: I will find *my inspiration* and I require *NO ONE'S* permission *to seek that which I have not yet found!*"

The sinner, saying his piece and quasi-peace, returned to his painful study. The Devil, meanwhile, gave Belphegor a perplexed look—so very uncommon for him.

"We move not until we are moved," said Belphegor. "Isn't that always the way? Wasn't that the way even with you, Dark Lord?"

Instead of replying, the Devil shifted his eyes from Belphegor back to the occupant of the fiery tower. He shook his head from side to side, confounded, but all trace of the brewing sulfurous maelstrom was gone. It was as if it had been made from the very vapors upon 'The Way' itself, and silently wafted out of existence. "I require *NO ONE'S* permission *to seek that which I have not yet found...*" the Devil muttered. "So be it..."

Then the Devil put out his hands once more and made another mighty clap which thundered along 'The Way.' Before the sound even faded, the circular prison of burning books was restored in full. Yes, this prison was perfect for the impenitently and indolently condemned.

After this, the Devil prepared to leave and gave Belphegor a terse nod in collegial acknowledgement. He turned from the bonfire of literature and made himself ready, but at the last moment before departing he shut his eyes tight and snapped his fingers just like he had at the start. Instantly, the flames vanished.

And then the Devil did too.

A sliver of time passed or seemed to.

In the stillness, a barely audible, "Thank you, Fallen One," was heard somewhere from the center of the formerly combusting tower.

Only Belphegor remained. He, too, then turned to leave, but something nagged and niggled in his mind: the final free and freedom-granting snap of the Devil's fingers.

Belphegor sighed.

In a final surprising act, the Arch-Demon of Sloth summoned the vapors of 'The Way' to create four volumes to add to the no-longer-simmering soul's literary residence. These were the soul's books, once unwritten—*having never been written in the first place*—that Belphegor decided to make whole.

And the Devil was right—*they were magnificent*!

Then Belphegor placed the volumes right at the very top of the towering stacks to eventually descend, and work their way down, to give the searching-reader what he'd always been searching for: his inspiration. Belphegor did this because—at this place and at this time—he knew every story, even a story of Sloth, had to eventually end. And for a reason not even Belphegor could explain, he wanted this story, at least, to end happy.

End of Story #3

Intermezzo
(third)

"Humph!" the Devil exclaims when he finishes assessing the writer's third story. "I told you not to be lazy and you literally wrote a tale about Sloth. I guess irony isn't dead, after all. This is your best yet. Not great, mind you, and maybe not even good or publishable… but who knows with agents and editors these days? Still… it's better. You got in touch with your frustrations and insecurities. On top of this, you can't get deeper than Hell."

"That's what I thought," answers the writer. "And I suppose I should say 'thank you.' It's the nicest feedback you've given so far."

"Don't say that. Never say such a thing when it comes to writing," the Devil replies.

"Why not?" the writer asks. "Can't the Devil take a compliment?"

"No. It's because my role here isn't to be *'nice.'* Feedback is either positive or negative, but it is never *nice*," rebukes the Devil. "If you want writing hugs, send these stories to your mother. Maybe she'll like them. Remember, this *is business* between you and me. Your success is my success. I can't very well accept your soul and not have you improve—however slowly. It would reflect badly on my reputation. I gave you a push. The more you write, the better your stories will get. That's all. I am not your friend. *I'm your reader.* You should make note of it."

The writer listens, but is distracted. His Devil's Spot continues to hum and thrum as he focuses on completing his next tale. He could see words falling one after another like tumblers in a lock. The clacking-typing sounds saturate the room.

"So what else do you think?" the writer asks.

"Well, on a personal level, I find it interesting you made Belphegor transparent because *he actually kind of is*. I mean he's not completely invisible, but he does manifest as sort of a giant blob of opaque gelatin... like congealing petroleum jelly... except he's covered in a thousand eyes. You left that detail out entirely."

"He sounds disgusting," the writer remarks.

"He is... and smells as terrible as he looks... imagine rotten fish slathered with lizard feces."

"Charming. Well it's too late to change him now..." the writer says.

"Oh, I was just making some initial conversation. No, he works. *He works*. He also plays a bit of the hero."

"That was the intent. A Demon-hero. A representative of the sliver of mercy that can reside even within the darkest of dark hearts."

"Belphegor would be shocked. Heroics really aren't his style," the Devil observes.

"Anything else? You might as well be honest. It's the one thing I know you're good at. Lay it on me, oh Draconian Devil, oh Black and Shadowy Muse."

"'Black Muse'? I like that. You should use it somewhere. And to answer your question: there are several mentionable issues I want to point out…"

"Hit me," the writer says. He is still writing as the Devil talks—just a few more paragraphs until the fourth story is done. He could tell because his Devil's Spot told him so and he has no reason to disbelieve it.

"First… you really want this, don't you? This collection of fabulist trifles?"

The Devil watches the writer closely while the writer continues working.

"I want it more than I have the ability to describe. In fact, I'd rather fail at writing than succeed at anything else."

The Devil almost laughs, but manages to hold it in.

"That's some sentimental treacly claptrap. But why does it mean so much? After all, writing is just a bunch of squiggles on a page. It's not like books really *do anything*, right?"

The writer pauses to gather his thoughts, but resumes typing as he answers.

"I think books—or any art, for that matter—provides a stimulus for human consciousness to grow and change and hopefully evolve. Our lives are shaped by the stories we tell one another and I wanted to—no, I *needed to*—add my voice to that potentially transformative process. Otherwise, without books, my life would be thin—paper-thin—if you will excuse the pun. But I have some other reasons too."

"That makes me wonder: would you actually go to the extremes of your most recent character—grabbing burning books to find your purpose and your voice? Obviously, the damned soul was modelled on you," the Devil asks.

"Would it be a guarantee?" the writer asks back.

"What do you mean?"

"I mean, if it was a rock-solid guarantee, I would absolutely trade pain for purpose, and agony for an articulate voice. At least, I hope I would and I could… but some things are beyond the abilities of a person."

"That's true," the Devil replies, thoughtfully.

"Why do you ask? Surely you have talked to other artists who sold their souls and know what drives their creative needs. In fact, you should know better than anyone, I would imagine?"

"Oh, I do, but it always intrigues me what humans think is within the power of stories. I enjoy cataloguing their illusions and delusions. For instance, the idea of me dispensing mercy in Hell is quite ludicrous, you know. I *have never* and *will never* grant a single iota of leniency or clemency—ever—to anyone—ever. I didn't do it for Goethe or Marlowe, Milton or Neil Gaiman, and I certainly wouldn't do it for the likes of you. So you can write what you like, but if you believe you can soothe Hell's nature or bamboozle *My Nature* with some fluffy fictions, you are disastrously mistaken. *Our deal is officially done.* Yes, I will help with your little stories, but when you die, I'll see you roast for them. I just wanted to make sure we're clear."

"We are clear, but I wouldn't call my stories 'little,'" replies the writer with a tinge of genuine opprobrium, "and you used the word 'ever' twice in one sentence."

"Ah, *Pride*. My favorite sin! But I'm glad we understand each other."

"My understanding has never been stronger," says the writer, "... and, by the way, I would never try to soothe Hell or bamboozle the Devil. You're not who I'm writing for."

"Fair enough. It doesn't really matter, anyway. A story never really changes anything real," says the Devil.

The writer lets the Devil's statement slide by unchallenged. He knows it is futile to explain to the Devil what he really thinks: that writing—at its core—is an act of human faith.

"So… uh… how long until the next one?" asks the Devil.

"Soon… soon… I'm just wrapping up…"

"I hope this one has an Angel in it. As a piece of narrative advice—you shouldn't spend too much time in one place."

"I know that… and, as a matter of fact… the next story does have an Angel in it—a fat one."

"What? A fat Angel? How? Why?"

"He's trying to make a point about something."

"A point about what?"

"Read it and find out."

Then the writer hands over the new pages and the Devil dives right in.

An Ocean of Fine Fish and a Flower in Hell

(Story #4)

'The Way' was infinite, or nearly so, as the Divine—both good and evil—understood it. But among those eternals, or nearly so, few could really wrap their minds around the concept. What they did understand, however, was there weren't exactly stations upon 'The Way.' Nothing was so discrete. There existed no defined rest stops or guarded checkpoints or pristine assay offices containing measuring scales, for immortal souls to go up against the poundage of a feather. Rather, Hell was on one end, and Heaven was on the other, and the innumerable stars and planets and various dimensions blinked on and off in between, always shifting, but 'The Way' was the thing that under-girded it all. Yes, 'The Way' shot through the celestial and terrestrial, the material and ethereal, the physical and metaphysical—in an endless series of inclinations, declinations, and intersections only to fold back upon itself like a grand and grandly sprawling Mobius strip. Consequently, 'beginning,' 'middle,' and 'end' became difficult labels to apply, so the informed eternals simply understood 'The Way' as 'Joule-Space' or 'Jewel-Space'—amniotic insubstantial permanence—holding energy in every conceivable form and in no form at all. If the question was asked: "What exactly is 'The Way'?" The answer replied was: "'The Way' exists so anything can exist upon 'The Way.'" As far as articulating a fundamental mechanism underpinning the entirety of existence and the whole Universe, itself—for most—this explanation seemed suitable enough.

And so once upon a time, the Devil decided to travel to one of the intermediate and indeterminate places along 'The Way's' ways, where agents of darkness and light and neutral nature could mold creation according to their own inimitable processes. The Devil wanted to take a break from his dark but necessary work. A recent exchange with a soul of Sloth had irked him, and he very much scorned the sense of lingering unease remaining from the encounter. It was like some greasy film even a hot shower or a fresh toothbrush couldn't completely remove. He wasn't running. The Devil never ran from anything. He just desired a moment of peace and quiet—an earnest yearning towards something approaching tranquility—for a change. This might be a little out of character for the Devil, but since he was, in fact, *That Very Beast*, he didn't much care. Appearances could be damned, as far as the Devil was concerned. He told himself he could do what he wont and wanted, and *His Word* was word enough to justify anything.

Thus the Chief of Demons embarked upon his journey and came to a formless spot where—just like in Heaven and Hell—'The Way's' vapors of endless potential could be coalesced into anything. And from the inky and omnipresent smoke, the Devil conjured a chair, a table, a rug, three magazines, and a contemporary and stylish music player. The Devil made sure the chair and rug were agreeable and plush. The table was composed of brass and glass, more practical than elegant. The music player took on the latest Earthly design, from Apple™, of course. And the three magazines were inconsequential: one of general news, one of sports, and one of popular human entertainment. Then with equal consecration of mists the Devil, himself, stepped out from the vast and sprawling ethers into what had become quite a nice and orderly sitting area.

The Devil strolled easily to the padded chair, stretching and creaking his neck to elicit the occasional pop and crack. Left behind were his hooves, black as night, his vermillion skin like a river of blood on fire, his tail—that pendulous phallic sigil—the horns, the tormenting eyes, the soul-shredding claws, and all the rest. Instead, on this occasion, the Devil chose to embody the figure of a man—Caucasian, mid-twenties, a little over six feet tall, with spiky blonde hair, a fair complexion, and eyes like aquamarine discs floating within twin bowls of freshly poured milk. He wore blue jeans and what was called a 'hoodie' with a brand name embroidered across the front, broken only by a zipper running from neck hollow to crotch bulge. The humans below—always below—called it 'relaxed wear' and the Devil inclined to agree. Yes, Sloth might be a weakness for mortals, but they sure knew how to dress for leisure, he thought.

He paused and exhaled forcefully, perhaps attempting a yawn, and oozed himself into the downy seat. The music player immediately began to cry out a soothing, but modern, tune without being touched. After this, the Devil tapped his fingers on the chair rails and more misty otherworldly tendrils snaked about. One hand now held a glass brimming with red wine while, below the other, appeared an aluminum bowl filled with tawny uncooked popcorn kernels. He took a sip of crimson spirits and lifted a russet-colored kernel between two fingers. As he moved his hand up, it popped in a wisp of steam and the Devil tossed it effortlessly into his mouth.

"Ahh..." he breathed, then chewed, then swallowed, as his eyelids slid closed with a silky celerity. Rest, he declared, truly was a heavenly experience and he allowed the music to penetrate him like seduction.

The Devil stayed that way for a time: reclining, popping kernels, snacking, sipping wine, and enjoying a period not filled with the agonized sobs and shrieks that so pervaded Hell's realm. Instead, he simply listened to music and even let his imitation foot tap to a genuinely human beat. This was *His time*, he asserted. *He* was Master of a Dominion—and—*if He* wanted to take a little time off, *He could*. Yes, the rhythm relaxed him, the wine was sweet, and his cares slowly started to recede like salty water at a low tide.

Then came an interruption.

"I am *so sorry*, Morning Star," said an Angel of the Lord, addressing him respectfully in his ancient, but translated name. The Angel materialized from some of the remaining mists and, with his arrival, the music player died to silence. "I didn't expect to find you here," he continued, haltingly. "In fact, I didn't expect to find *anyone* here. I had no idea you traveled *so far upwards* along 'The Way.' I deeply beg your pardon…"

The winged interloper was dressed in white, of course, but the Devil also observed he was unusually heavy with a rolling paunch and jowls and cheeks that jiggled under soft chestnut eyes. Above his eyes, hirsute caterpillars gabled. The Angel seemed surprised, almost embarrassed, and the Devil found himself beleaguered, but strangely perplexed. Aside from being slightly corpulent, the Angel donned a set of stylish spectacles housed in neat square frames. In Hell, physical limitations were often kept and sometimes intensified, but in Heaven such frailty was unnecessary—in fact, deficiencies were often considered taboo. Yes, occasionally a saved soul might choose to manifest eyewear to achieve a certain affectation, but not once—*not once*—in the Devil's long tenure had *he ever* seen *an Angel* in glasses. The departure merited noticing.

"I would say *I never* saw an Angel of the Lord travel *so far down* along 'The Way,'" the Devil began with a tinge of exasperation, "but yes, yes, nevertheless, *yes*… it is I: the Morning Star, Prince of Darkness, Bane of Man, Horny-

Thorny, the Liar, the Evil Enemy, the Deuce, Black Casper, Master Dicis-et-non-facis, and all the other sobriquets, both accurate and otherwise. And yet, I, too, did not know of a scheduling for this place. I honestly thought it as much unused as yourself… so if I have interrupted *your business*, please say true and I will depart. Sometimes we eternals need a spot out of the way, on 'The Way,' to be by ourselves. Do you not think? Regardless, I mean no intrusion or the dealing of double. I give you my word, former kinsman. This is but an accidental… and inconvenient… concurrence… for both of us…"

The Devil said these words stiffly, but with an unmistakable vein of sincerity as well. More than anything, though, the Angel of the Lord detected notes of fatigue and ennui in the Liege of Legion's voice. Additionally, the Angel was no stranger to the sources of such quibbles and discomfort. Eternal toil *is* toil, nonetheless, and at times even a velvet collar could chafe, he knew.

"No, Morning Star, I fear it is *I* who has committed the transgression. There is a soul to be ferried, yes, but it was farther up. I decided to change the location to here, to try to make a small, but important, point to her and perhaps to all those who drink at salvation's cup, in fact. It was to be an experiment, an exercise—maybe even a folly—and I thought this place might gain me better purchase. I believed it as much abandoned… or should I say 'unused'… as yourself. I positively did not mean to disturb your… meditation… if, indeed, that is what I have done."

The Devil nodded civilly and his icy demeanor began a minor thaw.

"No, not meditation… a contemplation perhaps… or just some thinking without the routine trappings of my station…" said the Devil.

"I see," replied the Angel. "Do you want to talk about it?"

"**NO!**" the Devil barked; however, the aggravated tone was unintended, so he added, "But thank you. There is no need to speak about things which are no longer troubling me."

A moment passed, and the Angel of the Lord wondered if the Devil was authentically sad and, unbeknown to the Angel, the Devil actually was. He just didn't know why. *'Pride goeth before destruction, and a haughty spirit before a fall,'* the Devil ruminated, but didn't want to think about it. *'We move not until we are moved,'* he remembered, recalling Belphegor, but pushed that memory away too. Instead, as a distraction, the Devil decided to focus on the Angel's introductory words and those peculiar eyeglasses which were so, so, very—*very*—unnecessary for him.

"But an experiment, you say?" Here, Satan's yellow eyes shined through their previously blue sheens and twinkled as if roused from dull annoyance to something more of a smoldering interest. "I find this both highly improbable, but also quite intriguing!" he continued. "An Angel with an idea? It doesn't seem possible… What I mean to say is: how do you experiment with what is—or what is at least intended to be—perfection? Surely things in saccharine Heaven haven't gone woefully sour, I pray and prey?"

"Your attempt at witticism is quite obvious, O' great dissembler. But do not forget we were once companions long ago and I am well aware of your conversational shenanigans. In fact, you unpersuasively tried to recruit me towards your failed cause, as I recall…" the Angel responded. The Angel attempted to appear stern but found himself breaking out in a small grin all the same. It always amazed him how disarming and comfortable Lucifer could be. All their initial awkwardness had been erased with just a little cordial dialogue.

"'Tis true. 'Tis always been true. Indubitably, my interpersonal skills have received some notoriety over the eons; however, my recollection is even better than the movement of my mouth! I could never forget our times of shared companionship in those lovely prelapsarian days! And, by the way, I still hold you made *a supremely misguided mistake* by not joining me. After all, battle builds character," the Devil replied, now fully smiling in pearly white. "But to *your cause*, O' thee of sugar and spice and everything nice? You wish to modify the designs of the designer? You seek to change what is perfect? Do tell! Indeed, if your aim is to alter the Divine confectionary, how do you foresee rearranging the blessed batter? I assure you my interest is genuine!"

The Angel of the Lord reacted with a wry, but benign, expression, before he answered.

"Not change *per se*—as *you* once tried—not in leadership or structure, but yes *per se*—as you say—in simple modification, O' thee of tart and bitter heart."

"Now who is parroting wordplay?" the Devil replied amiably. "In any case and earnestly, please explain your proposal! As you know, I am a bit of a social engineer myself. On my bond and blood, what do you have in mind?"

"I will tell because of our long-standing relation both as allies and enemies and, more, because *I do* think the idea a Godly one. In addition and in truth, no one in Paradise seems to give my thinking the weight of a ladybug's ear. They find new notions or any suggestion of invention of zero interest. I would call them dogmatic, but that would be offensive to both dogma and dogs! Thus I am happy to share my ideology even with my most fiendish of foes, if a fiendish foe is the only one to give me a fair and kindly reception. I find it a sad thing—not emotionally of course—but philosophically—that there is no place for contrivance in Heaven…"

"Careful, Angel," the Devil interjected, "such words can lead to terminal consequences! Remember, *you* weren't the first to suggest Heaven needs… what was the word… a 'modification.' Some may even confuse it with 'revolution'… or so I've heard."

They both smirked unreservedly now, but eventually broke off and shook their heads in mutual bemusement. "But to your plan, Bright One?" the Devil continued, "What is it? I surmise by your manifestation, dress, and those nifty eyeglasses of yours, you seek to alter the celestial form? It seems the only logical, albeit incredible, premise."

A vague electric energy rippled through the Angel's immanent fibers. He almost seemed to quiver with an infinitesimal tic.

"Ah true! Quite true! And truly astute, dark friend! No doubt my current attire must seem unnatural and unusual to your ancient eyes cast anew! I have thought long and hard upon Heaven's incorporations and have seen even longer, and in every dustless corner I witness only one thing repeated over and over and over again! Normally, to see it inspires warmth in one's chest. Usually, to observe it is to know symmetry and vitality and breathlessness. Indeed, to experience it is to draw forth all the filigreed words which indicate finery and refinement! Yes! What I heavenly beheld and behold from stem to stern and foot to crown and valley to peak is nothing but *Beauty*! Yes, the magical tableaux of Beauty! Beauty everywhere! Unassailably, so much Sublime Form! So much Exquisite but all that is—so—so—similar in assembled simulacrum and—so—so—generic in general genial construction! Yes, if you will forgive a metaphor, Heaven is like an ocean of existence which shimmers and glimmers and glows, where waves froth and crest atop shifting hills of sapphire blue, but to look below the surface and search under this liquid glory is to find just one type of *Fine Fish*! It is just schools upon schools of the same, same, thing! Thus, I began to ponder: is this form I now take not also Beautiful? Does my choice in unnecessary eyeglasses blacken my spirit? Does my paunch sully my glory or the glorious light that grants it? Should I have a different dorsal or scales or peduncle, am I automatically disqualified from the flawless sea into which all saved souls are destined to swim? Indeed, does it? All these things led me to deliberate: maybe… *just maybe*… wouldn't a more mottled scene better reflect the Divine palette? After all, shouldn't the God of everything have more variation in His vaunted and venerable vista than... than... just an unending panorama of uniform and unctuous uniformity? I thought so! Hence, I launched my diverse and diversity-inspiring cause!"

The Devil's eyes positively sparkled at realizing the Angel's plan.

"Portly Pilgrim! This is truly fascinating! You intend to introduce *ugliness* into the tapestry of Heaven!" the Devil burst out.

The Angel of the Lord immediately exhaled a dejected sigh and a shadow seemed to cross, and momentarily touch upon, his face.

"But I see by the turn of your visage, I chose the wrong phrasing," the Devil amended. "Obviously, nothing in your club of clouds could ever possibly be described as 'ugly.' You just want to change the bland landscape of the even blander monochromatic monotheists! Remarkable! At my height, it never occurred to me to contemplate so nuanced a scheme! How will your process of subtle augmentation work? Do you really think the stratagem has a chance for success?"

"I should be cross at you, Lucifer, if not for the fact many of my present colleagues and your former ones hadn't also characterized my idea as trying to invite grotesquery into the firmament. Verily, I have been called a 'fat monger,' a 'peddler of anti-pulchritude,' an 'advocate of the Divinely deformed,' and I've endured all manner of jest and—if not derision—then at least suffered as one who has a derided dream. Truly, Fallen One, in whatever way ridicule is experienced in the mortal world, I can tell you intimately, in the immortal sphere it stings..."

Here, the exchange between the Devil and the Angel faltered. It was as if the admission of pain or distress broke some kind of protocol and chastened them both. As a result, the Devil went back to popping a few more tawny kernels while introspectively sipping his wine. The Angel of the Lord also fell silent. He no longer looked at his former compatriot, but off into the nothingness that could become anything. The words hung in the air that was not air. After a time, the Devil resumed the conversation. Though he would never say, the Devil was reminded of the 'contemplation' which had brought him to this spot on 'The Way' in the first place. When he spoke next, his tenor was grave.

"*I assure you*, Bright One, what you are feeling is *exactly* the way the mortals experience it. Whether it be with our company or our ideas or our dreams, the prick of rejection bleeds us with a gush and then a slow deflation. We become limp, impotent, and enfeebled. 'When, in disgrace with fortune and men's eyes/ I all alone beweep my outcast state,/ And trouble deaf heaven with my bootless cries,/ And look upon myself and curse my fate.' The mortals have known this for ages—just as you and I do. The mortals knew how to express such disquietude as well…"

The Devil's recitation reverberated between the two eternals, virtually echoing off one another, as if both were but strings stretched and plucked and twisted upon the same instrument.

"But let us speak of happier tidings…" advocated the Devil, shifting to a more productive tack, "because I, for one, think your notions are noble. I, for one, perpetually think failure is but a temporary condition. Diligence and time can remedy all, *nicht wahr*? And, I think you should be lauded for your theorem! Yes, you should be extolled and exalted! So do tell! Be candid! Say true! What comes next?"

"'Tis strange I find validation only in my own mind and now from supposedly the most vile and foresworn rival to my realm, but encouragement from any quarter still gives courage," the Angel replied. "As to my 'stratagem,' as you call it, seeing will do far better than more words, as my quarry presently comes in from the Earthly plane. Watch, judge, and—if not pray—then at least incline for my success! The saved soul is nigh!"

The Devil stepped aside to give the Angel more space while the Angel raised his hands in a beckoning and welcoming gesture. Thus, the arrival of the saved soul began as it always began: with a smell. Like to the lark at break of day arising, the splendiferous odor began to fill the area between the Angel, in all his unnecessary overweight glory, and the Devil, who remained in the form of a man. It spread as a gentle breeze, and carried with it the warm undulating currents of laundry freshly pressed, of flowers yawning into bloom—of the skin and scalp of an innocent child newly minted into vibrant life. It was the aroma of cherished memories, but also the deep and fecund richness of a garden's possibility. Yes, the smell was the savory, everlasting, nosegay of the Alpha and the Omega from the beginning and end of everything good in God's green Universe: a painless birth proceeding from a peaceful death. Then, the air that was not air seemed to shudder and the resurrection from mortal life to life-everlasting was achieved.

And so the saved soul arrived—young and auburn-headed and as vital as the finest day of her youth. Indeed, by any measure, she would be judged 'very pretty' and 'fair of face.' But she also happened to be short. And… her nose bent just a tad dramatically to the left. And finally, though nobody needed to say it, 'pretty' does not equate to 'beautiful.' But the Devil had to applaud and come down on the side of the Angel because, without a doubt—she was *a perfect candidate* to experiment upon.

"Ah, welcome, Madam _____," the Angel greeted, because the soul had been expected, and because the Angel of the Lord knows every human name.

He went on:

"Your trials are over! Your tribulations are behind you! Every temptation is banished! And thusly, by your devotion to God and your good works, I come as an emissary of the Prince of Peace to ferry you to wondrous Heaven! Hear me! All suffering is ended! All doubt is cast into exile! Indubitably, you have been elected to the Elect and have been selected to be Perfect! It has been your life of humility and charity, of forgiveness and wisdom and, to be sure, because of all the other virtues so abundant in Heaven but so wanting on Earth—that I, with a joyful noise, sound my trumpet! Verily, let me announce to the Universe entire: another Sister has come home!"

Hearing this, the woman immediately collapsed to her knees. She began to weep streams of joyous tears, but before the tears traveled even one inch down upon her unlined fervent face, they evaporated into golden motes that floated up to encircle her brow in a blessed crown of immortality. Such was halo's origin. Then, after a time, the motes winked out—vanishing back into the nothingness that was everything—because not even the remnants of a joyous tear would be suffered to exist in Heaven. All this happened as the Devil watched with the curiosity of a cat—attentive, yet distant—waiting to see what came next. And what the Devil saw was the Angel of the Lord bending down and guiding the woman to rise.

"No supplication is needed, nor prostration either, my dear girl! Here, we are all equal except in experience—and you will have the length of eternity to explore the Divine mysteries sweeping forth and returning back upon themselves like the ocean's tide when it is always lustrous dawn! Sublime variety! Transcendent dynamism! Resplendent apotheosis! These are all yours to behold now! Yes, the will of Providence grants you provenance! Yes, the Divine Tree bears you every fruit! Here, the Universe weaves its thread only by the variegated songs of God's grace and to the varying melodies of your own imagination! Gentle mistress, now take hold of both my hands and gaze deep your immortal eyes into mine like two mirrors made of the same shiny stuff! Make good and firm your grip. Presently, I will open the door in your mind for what is to come forever and forever, Amen!"

The Angel of the Lord clasped the woman's hands and the woman clasped passionately back. It was the union of flesh that was not flesh—the union of the flesh that was more than flesh—the great transmigration of spiritual thought. It was the Divine merging of consciousness—the cleaving of souls just like the mingling of the marvelous mists upon 'The Way' itself. One might characterize it as psychic transference, or telepathy, or like the recognition of an idea outside of time—where disparate people from disparate periods know with absolute certainty they are connected beyond any particular era by what they think and feel and learn. However, the Devil had only one descriptor for what was happening: 'propaganda.' Nevertheless, he still found this arcane communion invigorating. It had been some interval since he watched such heavenly rituals and routines. Yes, it was nice when vocation mixed with avocation while on vacation, the Devil thought. He was also happy to note, his recent infernal conflicts had lost their hangnail's edge.

And so the Angel of the Lord and woman's spirit blended with the locking of hands and, from above, fine drops of water that was not rain began to fall. They were droplets of Divine knowledge itself. The drops landed and—just like the woman's tears—they again were immediately swept up into grains of golden light. Such was halo's second origin. This time the motes encircled both the Angel and the woman in a spinning orbit of coruscating brilliance. The information passed without exertion or strain. It was epistemological confluence, metaphysical convergence—epiphanic ontological realization. In a shorter, but infinitely more complicated phrase, it was the miracle of Revelation. And, once complete, the water ceased and hands broke contact—both replaced by a far more adamantine bond.

"*I… CAN… SEE!!!*" exclaimed the woman, when the transfer was over. "It's as if for the first time!"

And she positively glowed like a twinkling star enfolded within an immaculate vessel of ageless flesh.

"Quite right," the Angel replied, "and the view will only grow and grow in wondrous glory. Now, dear girl, are you ready to conclude your journey to infinite bliss? We can depart *at once* to the varied landscape where all things are saved and never lost! Say true! Let us depart, *now*! You have been *Redeemed* and nothing else matters!"

The woman didn't react, but rather gazed off into the ethers like a paralyzed statue of exulted reverence. Meanwhile, the Devil regarded her inquisitively as he and the Angel shared a furtive, hopeful, and vaguely collusional glance. They both knew this was the moment—this was the time of experiment, the juncture of choice, the point of opportunity that when—once gone—would almost certainly never come again. Would the woman change herself? Could she accept her manifested form carried from the mortal world? The proposition burned all along 'The Way' like a question forged by lightning: would salvation and Paradise be enough, or did Beauty in Paradise have to conform to some idealized and mundane convention? Finally, the answer came.

"Um… no… not just yet."

And with that, the woman began to alter. She grew five inches in five seconds, and her nose dramatically unbent, and her auburn hair colored instantaneously to strawberry blonde—and to describe the rest would be an exercise in pointless beauty. Yes, in mere clock-ticks, the woman sculpted herself into the very model of a model angelic: elegant, exquisite, delightful, and buxom. She now appeared as a Venus freshly stepped from the half-shell, and the Angel of the Lord had seen a form like hers a million-million times before.

When the transformation finished, the woman proudly proclaimed: "Now I am ready to meet my Maker and see all those cousins lost on Earth but surely to be found anew in Heaven! I am born and reborn again!"

Her face turned upward in supreme self-satisfaction while the Angel's eyes fell low.

"I could not have said it better myself, dear girl," he muttered in disappointment. And the saved soul noticed not even remotely. "Just give me a moment, please…"

And so, one last time, the Angel and Devil regarded each other as old friends who had become so, so similar in similar circumstances—hobbled by defeat or, perhaps, defeated by design.

"It *truly was* a good try…" the Devil began, with a rare, but genuine, note of consolation.

"Trying is all I could do…" sulked the Angel.

"It doesn't mean you will *never* succeed," the Devil replied. Then, after a slight pause and small smile, he continued, "after all… *I have had* some experience with unachieved perseverance. I would bide my time. And, don't forget… there is that old saying about 'other fish in the sea'!"

The Angel stared directly at the Devil, a little confused, but finally couldn't help but laugh. It was as if the quip breathed new energy into the Angel's deflated ego.

"Other fish in the sea! But you know *that's not the problem*! *The problem is* I'm dealing with *all the same type of damned fish*! Some supporter you are!"

"Well, good conversation is one thing, but for me to favor any success in Heaven is completely different. Besides, when a cliché is set up, it really needs to be played out. Don't you agree? But I am sincere in saying you should keep trying. It was a start, at least… a beginning of a beginning. You shouldn't feel too bad your first steps were… *inadequate*. Thus, I counsel: do not fear failure, rather fear not trying."

"Humph!" the Angel conceded. "Yes, I suppose *you would try* and try again! *You* know better than anyone success is a goal intransigent and one's dreams are always worth fighting for!"

"'Tis true. 'Tis always been true," the Devil ended.

Then the two Spirits, one light and one dark, said their kind farewells and departed. The Angel took his sumptuous, but common, charge to balmy Heaven and the Devil, who believed his time of recreation could not have been better spent, returned to hotter Hell.

Back in Heaven, the Angel resumed his standard angelic duties, but felt oddly contented, despite his failure. He vowed always to keep a prayer alive in his heart for improvement even within a place that—he had to admit—was perfect.

The Devil, however, once home, did not return to his regular routine because, *He* had to confess, those activities had grown a bit stale.

Yes, the Devil looked out among the ghastly edifices and ruined monstrosities and aggrieved regrets and monoliths to mayhem and sinners and their punishments of every stripe and type—or nearly—and took a moment to wonder and consider and ponder. He listened again to the sobs and shrieks and to all the other tight piercing coils of agonized expression that so pervaded Hell's realm. Everything in Hell was *so ugly—so nasty—*and he recognized, just like what the Angel said about Heaven, everything was—so—so—similar in assembled simulacrum. He then thought of music and sweet wine and popcorn kernels and of the Angel's quest—the Angel's Angelic Quest for Change. This led him to contemplate the reason he briefly stepped away from Hell in the first place. Yes, somewhere under his jurisdiction a soul was not suffering. This was new. No, change may have not been within the Angel's power, but it certainly was *within His*.

The decision seemed foregone.

So, the Devil paused and looked down upon a patch of shiny black rock among *His land*, which surely would cut any foot that was forced or dared to tread across it. And there, upon that sharp, immovable, and always potentially bloody stone, he ordained and executed the creation of a flower. He made it the most wonderful, beautiful, and miraculous flower that ever existed—in fact only two pairs of mortal eyes had ever beheld one like it before in the whole of time. Its petals and leaves extended out fifteen meters in looping vibrant life—not just green in color, but in a shifting, shimmering rainbow of tints and shades which positively exploded amid the contrasting desolation. Its shoots and roots went down a thousand leagues and rose up again to inhabit all of Hell's corners exuding just the faintest, barest whiff of hope and happiness and hearth. Some of the damned—for a mere instance—caught the fragrance of warm cookies pulled from the oven, or baking bread, or frying onions in a buttery pan, or a lover's perfume, or—indeed—any number of indelible joyful smells from long ago and forever gone—cherished personal experiences. They were the rekindled odors of more ebullient times—but again, they lasted for just the most pitiable and perishable moment.

Yes, from Eden's memory, the Devil let his flower grow large and bright and glorious so anyone who laid their eyes upon it—or caught the briefest bouquet of it—would know true Beauty amongst their truer Sorrow. Even the Devil, himself, at just seeing it and smelling it, thought of family and love and former homes and was almost—just almost—brought to non-evaporating tears… because… in Hell… tears never end with a golden halo.

Yes, in Hell, the Devil planned to make variety the very spice of death. After all… he thought… any idea that could not find a place in Heaven *should certainly* find a welcoming place somewhere else.

End of Story #4

Intermezzo
(fourth)

The Devil reviews the writer's latest story while the writer slogs through his fifth. And it all seemed to be going according to script now, which made the writer grateful. Just to whom he was grateful to—*however*—wasn't exactly clear. Nevertheless, the creative process had evolved into a sort of pattern that could be identified by its various parts. He would work on another story as the Devil read his last one. Then, once the Devil finished, conversation would ensue—including a lobbed insult against the writer—ultimately concluding with the Devil doling out a piece of genuinely useful advice. After this, the writer's Devil's Spot would fire and flare and the words he always dreamed of saying, but never could, would find their groove and pour out... even if those words weren't exactly his own. The writer didn't mind. If there was one thing he was sure of—the storytelling *must continue*. Yes, everything existed together in routine and predictability, and the writer and the Devil, both, took solace in it. Yes, each thought it fruitful to inhabit sharply defined roles.

So, the Devil gets to the end of the most recent story and flits up his bluish-yellow eyes to address the writer. But at the moment he opens his mouth to speak, a specter suddenly appears behind him. The figure just zaps into existence like a magic trick—like a bouquet of flowers fluttering out from the end of a wand or a shiny coin plucked seamlessly from behind someone's ear. Except it isn't a bouquet of flowers or a golden coin glinting in the stage lights. Instead, it is a person… and it isn't just any person. It is an Angel. And… it took the writer a few seconds to realize… it isn't just any Angel either. It is *his Angel*—the Angel he had just written about, and the one the Devil just read about, in his fourth story. He is wearing white, of course, but is also slightly corpulent. Yes, he is as portly and as jowly as the writer described him. Additionally, the Angel has on stylish spectacles housed in neat square frames. 'Just keep writing,' his Devil's Spot advises. 'You're already talking to the Devil, so don't be surprised if things get even weirder.'

"*I AM NOT FAT!*" the Angel of the Lord bellows with all the ferocity he could muster.

"Mizam, you're late," replies the Devil, smiling. "He is already four tales deep, and our deal is *officially done*. As far as being fat, though, your pot belly and paunch would seem to contradict you…"

"I'm late because I had better things to do than babysit the construction of some frivolous fictions," the Angel responds, defensively, "… and I'm fat because *he* wrote me this way. And *this* is what I think of your 'stylish spectacles housed in neat square frames'!"

The Angel approaches the writer, takes off his eyewear, and snaps them in two. He tosses them decisively and derisively on the working manuscript of Story #5.

"*I DEMAND YOU WRITE ME THIN!*" the Angel roars.

The celestial looms over the writer, attempting to be menacing, but with his soft chestnut eyes and quivering jowls, he is having a hard time pulling it off. As for the writer, he says nothing.

"He doesn't understand," the Devil interjects.

"Apparently not," replies the Angel, who then sighs and slumps himself into an empty chair. He ended up slouching. The posture did him no favors.

"You see," the Devil continues, directing himself to the writer, "when you write, you give off… let's say… *vibrations*… into the Universe. Yes, the words you write vibrate into the sky and into the ground—into the entirety of existence, in fact. And sometimes these vibrations can cause changes or summon things. Yes, they can imprint and occasionally leave a mark. Indeed, they—*potentially*—are able to make an impression from an expression, so to speak. And, your last story happened to change—right now—the materialization and iteration of an Angel—this Angel right here—appearing so angrily and irately before you. His name is Mizam, protector and the guardian of the balanced scales. You might want to take a moment to chew on this information…"

The writer does take a moment to chew, and in doing so, instantly recalls a passage from one of his earlier stories. Moreover, he is pleased to realize he can recite it accurately and exactly in his mind. His Devil's Spot throbs and thrums with recollection:

'He could see in his mind's eye a great and brilliant ripple spreading across the Earth like a dazzling wave of light to touch every dim and forgotten corner. The light held no lies, no deceptions, no disambiguation of any kind. The light held no secrets. It came from a place, that was not just a place, but this place—the afterlife—be it Heaven or Hell or anywhere in between, where all is known and no shadow or indiscretion could possibly survive. Corporeal privacy was nothing but an Earthly dream. Yes, the man finally saw in the afterlife every atom knows every other, and a Divine vantage can peer into every sphere and peek behind every curtain. Yes, God and His Angels and the Devil and His Demons knew it all even before he arrived.'

The writer ponders and revisits and analyzes, and allows himself to digest the situation a little more before speaking. "Are you saying my stories travel up to Heaven? And… I guess, down to Hell, too?" the writer asks.

The Devil manufactures a dramatic pause before replying.

"The short answer is 'yes,'" he finally answers, "… though the labels 'up' and 'down' don't really apply."

"So I wrote a story and called forth an Angel? And I changed an Angel just by writing about an Angel?" the writer asks.

The Devil picks up one of the snapped eyeglass halves and twirls it by its handle stem. The Angel glares at them both.

"Sure!" the Devil says. "Let's go with that!"

"But I thought you said stories don't really change anything?" the writer queries.

"Well… they don't change *anything important*," the Devil replies with a wink.

"Speaking of important, I have something important to tell you…" the Angel interrupts sullenly, his glare retreating noticeably.

"But *you* were late," the Devil answers.

"Yes… yes… but the truth often is…" the Angel replies.

"That's a good line," states the writer, factually.

"Perhaps," responds the Devil.

"But the truth is going to have to wait a bit longer…" continues the writer.

"Why?" both the Devil and Angel ask at the same time.

"Because… another story…" the writer says, but goes no farther. Instead, he just gestures to the compilation of papers in front of him and sweeps the second half of the Angel's broken glasses off his manuscript. He had finished the next installment during the Angel's little scene of Divine Intervention.

"That's five," the Devil notes.

"But what I want to say is about Heaven… and *it's important… im—por-tant…*" the Angel mutters.

"So is the story… and it's also about Heaven," the writer goes on, "and… the Angel in it is still fat… sorry," he says, but really isn't.

"What's this one about?" the Devil asks.

"Well, I figured the first four stories were pretty conventional and safe, so if I truly wanted to elicit reactions and discussions, I'd have to do more. I'd have to reach for something objectively transgressive… explore territory more subversive… challenge both myself and my readers," the writer answers. "Consequently, for this tale I felt compelled to write something inflammatory and be willing to take the heat."

"Oh, you'll get plenty of heat," the Devil quips.

"But transgression and subversion isn't what writing is for," the Angel comments, still petulant. "You should only write things that are wholesome and pious."

"That's not correct," the writer declares strongly. "Writing can be anything. *Writing is whatever you can get away with,*" the writer finishes, and his Devil's Spot flares in agreement. He didn't know if it was because of his Devil's bargain or because he, himself, was growing— or some wild and strange combination of both—but he could see so much clearer now. Yes, writing was order and chaos, consonance and dissonance, saccharine platitudes and cyanide poison—all.

"So are we done talking?" the writer says, wrapping up. The question is rhetorical because the dialogue had ceased.

Then, the Angel sighs again and slouches even deeper into his seat. However, he does get up when the writer hands over the next pages. Yes, if the Devil was going to read a new story, the Angel wants to make damn sure he gets to read it too.

The Flickering Tic of Heaven

(Story #5)

The part of 'The Way' that could most accurately be called 'Heaven' didn't adhere to many of the Earthly preconceptions of it. True, yes, true—there were familiar and idealized elements which could easily be recognized: long marble colonnades stretching out in intricate and angelic designs; bucolic parks and fields and meadows where the temperature was always temperate and the bugs bothered nary a soul; flowing rivers of sweet wine and oil and milk that never spoiled, winding among verdant tracts of succulent fruit trees just ready to detonate with delight; and—of course—the reunion with loved ones outside of time and reality, human frailty and mortal flaws, where every scintillating sensation and elated emotion were given over to the saved soul with the ease of a candied dream. But, as it is often said, a selection of propitious props does not a sublime scene make, and, in fact, as a whole, the part of 'The Way' that could most accurately be called 'Heaven' was quite different from the specious speculations and fancied fantasies of those who desired to go there.

To begin, from above—from a perspective impossible to perceive except by God or the Devil or some other entity privy to impossible places—the section of 'The Way' that could most accurately be called 'Heaven' looked like nothing more than a simple necklace. True, yes, true—it would have had to have been an awesome, behemoth, gargantuan, titanic, tremendous, mammoth, pharisaic… bit of jewelry—*indeed all the words denoting largess and largeness*—but in form and fabrication it resembled nothing but a simple necklace nonetheless. At its center was the colossal bauble of New Jerusalem—the essential Celestial City which towered as a literal beacon of salvation at Heaven's core. From such a grand and unearthly height, it gleamed in brilliance like a twinkling and massive pendant the size of a galaxy's heart. It was as if the entire night's sky had been condensed into a single gem and that gem was then set warmly aglow with the eternal light and bright succor of God. It was The House of the Father, The Silver City, Tian, Firdaus, Trayastrimsa, The Winnowed Fork, Svarga Loka, The Resting Place, Avesta's Abode, The Giving Tree and The Tree That Gives, and so many others and others and others. Indeed, by *any name* old or new, decomposed or not-yet composed—orderly, shining, and magnificent—it stood as a monument to *ALL THINGS* worthy of redemption while also Providently providing every ennobling pleasure. Yes, its Intricacies were inspired by the Immense! Its Beauty was inspired by the Beatitudes! Its Sublimity was inspired by Divinity! True, yes, true—to describe New Jerusalem in only words might well take an entire library compressed and strained through the most hallowed sieve ever conceived! Verily, the full and fulsome image of the place brushed against the farthest limits of human imagination and then stretched quite a bit farther into the gloriously incomprehensible.

To that effect, if New Jerusalem resembled a gigantic bauble, a proper bauble requires a corresponding chain, and Heaven's geography wouldn't be complete without its suburbs and subtleties, its hinterlands and hindquarters, its Back-of-Beyond and its Forward-Into, its Never-Never and Ever-Ever places which also adorned the supernatural stripe laid out in the pattern of Paradise. So—again from a perspective inaccessible—on either side of New Jerusalem, expanding outward, were what appeared to be links or hoops or loops of smaller collective heavens within 'Heaven' which glittered and sparkled to add to the entire resplendent whole.

Yes, there were neighborhoods and communities, districts and compounds—even ghettos and penitentiaries—where groups of like-minded souls could share company according to their agreed-upon beliefs and customs, *if*—true, yes, true—*if* those followers and customs were adjudged *worth and worthy of* salvation. New Jerusalem itself was a communal and open-door Heaven where all could come together and congregate without fear or strife, conflict or repellent repulsion of each other, but the hinterlands were gladly and gracefully granted their exclusions and exclusivity. There, *any* sect or order, convent or coven, assembly or chapter, cult or mult, could exist as a perfect version of itself. Yes, their faiths allowed them the Divine gift of getting what their leaders and doctrines had always asserted and never stopped preaching—that *their truth* was the *only Truth* and that *their way and ways* was *THE ONLY WAY*. Thus these smaller heavens existed within larger Heaven, but were allowed to operate separately.

And finally, within this ever-growing succession of beadwork—from the great bauble of New Jerusalem, to the xenomorphic menagerie of smaller collections—came the sequenced sequins of individual heavens, where saved souls personally and specifically got whatever they wanted—fully and perpetually—forever and ever, Amen. There, every lost thing was found. There, every whimsical whim was won. Yes, these heavens existed in pleasures without regret, in indulgences without shame, in egregious excess without sanction, or in grim austerity without struggle. No sin existed evermore and nevermore. No pain either. Delight and gratification were only matters of thinking and tinkering… and one's mind never stopped growing. And so from the central esteemed gem to the precious collective pearls to the individual treasured trinkets—*EVERY SAVED SOUL—SELECT and ELECT—EVERY PERSON and EVERY GROUP, EVERY DESIRE* and *EVERY JOY—EVERYTHING*—single or multiple, mutable or static—*EVERY REWARD*—promised or imagined—had its place and province and provenance under 'Heaven.' And… *IT WAS PERFECT!*

... Or so the oft-chanted melodious mantra went.

But, presently, a problem had arisen in Paradise.

Yes, out from New Jerusalem and beyond the heavens of the Mormons and the Presbyterians, the Amish and the Moonies, the Agnostics and the Ku Klux Klanists, the Branch Davidians and the Catholics, and so many others and others and others—and beyond even farther past tens of millions of individual heavens where love and gold and sex and prayer and pleasure and work and forbearance and youth and self-asceticism all had their places and places—was one little heaven where perfection had yet to be achieved. It housed but a solitary woman and versions of her two sons. It shined but did not gleam. It radiated but did not illuminate. It was as if Heaven were an endless sky of blue, but a single cloud could be spied that was just a shade away from blissful white. It was off-putting, nettling and unsettling, peeving—and more than that, *it shouldn't even have been possible*! Yes, the crenelated tapestry of Heaven was supposedly sewn and sown from the very essence of Transcendence itself, but here it was—*the anomaly, the aleatory, the an-orthodox*—and something *had to be done* about it.

And thus, an Angel of the Lord adjusted his spectacles—housed in neat square frames—and hitched up his tunic around his rather sizeable, but self-imposed, paunch, and paid the woman a visit. Yes, he traveled from New Jerusalem through the heavens of Heaven as easily as a person might turn the page of a book or shift their gaze from one brilliant star in the night sky to another. The Angel of the Lord moved in motion through notions, skipping like a rock on the pond of ideas. He traveled soughing and chirring through one dappled sacred chamber after another and from one dream manifested to manifested dream. Then, in the wink of the sky and an eye, he arrived at his appointed place where the saved soul could be found.

So once upon a time, an Angel of the Lord stepped upon the heavenly land of a loving mother in sandaled feet and got reacquainted with gravity once more, with solid things, with air and breathing, and all the other ersatz processes and physical simulacra she created. Yes, *his presence* entered into the substance of *her world*. The saved soul's name was Penelope Thatch and her sons were named Terrance and Toby. They had been a happy family on Earth, but within her heaven of Heaven this happiness was not all that Happiness could be. The Angel could smell the wondrous wonder of salvation, but not ecstasy. Yes, *this* was the suppurating splinter lodged underneath the fingernail of God.

The Angel of the Lord inhaled deeply of the air that was not air—inhaling the air that was *her air*. No men. Men had treated her badly. Recreation. No work. Sons. *Her Sons.* She loved *HER SONS*. The woman's generated atmosphere, itself, smelled of pine sap and dogwood flowers. It was from her childhood. It was from her best-remembered years near a park where her father sold 'X-MAS' trees for '$10' *'A Stick.'* She remembered about her father without thinking about her father. It smelled good—but he did a bad thing. No men. No fathers. No mother who looked on as a father did a bad thing. The imperfection—the less than complete satisfaction—emitted the slightest hint of putrefaction.

Yes, her heaven smelled like the most elegant and fragrant perfume atomized upon a slowly stiffening corpse. There was imbalance. The Angel of the Lord could odor this too.

He walked down a street *because it was a street*—asphalt, macadam, hard and seemingly real. It was the suburbs of Heaven, and Penelope Thatch had germinated the very embodiment of the suburbs. Manicured rows of docile domiciles peacefully and perfectly lined drives and avenues and cul-de-sacs. There were trees and white sidewalks and cars parked along pristine curbs. Here, trash always found its way into garbage cans and the cars never needed washing. The Angel of the Lord strolled, but not without a hint of urgency to reach his destination. Normally, he would have paused and ruminated on the various nuances and idiosyncrasies of the immortal reflection of a formally mortal existence: the ludicrous fire hydrant, the oddity of a storm drain, the harebrained and unnecessary congruity of a 'Yield' sign. Yes, these trifling trifles always drew up a scant curiosity in him—an almost human inquisitiveness—but, on this journey, he stopped not once for any such miscellany. No, he could not let himself get distracted. The grass was green, the sun shone, and the air was breezy and refreshing, but still there was that errant scent. There was **imbalance**. True, yes, true—so he walked with a bit of a quickstep to fulfill his Divine duty and ordained purpose. And in just footfalls and moments he came to the current location of the saved soul, Penelope Thatch.

She was casually resting in a lovely park abutting a playground that—not just *could have been* taken directly out of an issue of *Boy's Life* magazine, but *actually had been*. Two jungle gyms rose up invitingly and there were tilting see-saws and a voluminous sandbox as big as a basketball court. A set of hopscotch squares ran parallel to a diminutive merry-go-round while colorful saddled animals sat on iron springs waiting to be ridden in wild directionless frenzy. And, there also were people (who were *not quite people*) giving out balloons and hotdogs and candy, both cotton and regular, without price or ambition beyond dedicated and prompt service. Yes, all manner of recreation existed for those small of stature, but endowed with boundless vitality to run as free as their ever-moving legs. Surely this should have been enough, the Angel of the Lord judged. After all, what else could a saved soul want? "Unacceptable," the Angel muttered, almost audibly.

Penelope, herself, sat on a burnished red picnic table staring off to the horizon while the shades of her two children played among the shades of other children, laughing the frenetic and joyous laughter of an endless afternoon. Terrance—or at least the coalesced vapor presently and collectively engaged in the mimesis of Terrance—kicked a soccer ball repeatedly into a tree. It bounced back to him exactly, without deviation, every time. Terrance's face was long and narrow with large ears and a prominently jutting jaw. One eye drooped weakly and weepily due to an eccentric but accurately represented genetic memory. Toby, with his hydrocephalic head the size of an enlarged ostrich egg, simply peered dreamily into the sun. His broad fore-brow glistened like the interior shell of an oyster, perspiring majestically, almost angelically, in the golden supple light. Terrance occasionally spoke in a stammering stutter, but Toby never spoke at all. All the same, they were *her children* and *she* thought them up perfectly perfect and really real; however, they weren't *really real* or *perfectly perfect* because in this place and at this time—because indeed, *on all parts of 'The Way'*—*really real* and *perfectly perfect* was *only as real or as perfect as the strength of the Will that called forth such representative forms into existence.* Hence, the problem. Subsequently, the Angel of the Lord approached the woman with a wide smile and a friendly grin, but, inside, his bright spirit dimmed infinitesimally with a flickering tic. He imagined it wavered like a guttering candle flame and burned with less than a splendiferous scent. "Unacceptable," he muttered once more before fully engaging with the creator of a place that should have been a paradise, but wasn't.

"Good morrow, Ms. Thatch," the Angel began, "I hope I am not intruding on this fine and beautiful day?" Penelope Thatch showed no surprise because every saved soul always knows when an Angel is near.

"Good morrow, Emissary of the Divine," she replied. "I think there is no place in Heaven or Earth where *you could* intrude, but I'm afraid the days in *my heaven* of late do not quite rate as 'beautiful.' 'Satisfactory' perhaps, yet nothing more. In any case there is no intrusion. In fact, I was wondering if someone was going to show up. Because…" and here she paused, momentarily casting her eyes down from horizon to picnic table, "… because… *I can feel it too…*"

The Angel received these opening words earnestly, but with an objective celestial detachment. Yes, he always felt a pang of pious sympathy for those confused in the midst of such obvious ecclesiastical clarity. Humans were such small, but complicated creatures, he thought. Sometimes he wondered why God favored them so. Another Supreme Being might have thought them undeserving. Nevertheless, the Angel had to press on.

"What exactly do you feel, if I may ask?" the Angel pressed.

"Why the imbalance, of course!" Penelope answered. "I feel it within my very core and since this place is made of the same essence, I assume it must translate as well. Personality influences environment as much as environment influences personality, my brain tells me. It's a kind of an epigenetic transcendentalism—if such a phrase could be applied. My newfound existence gained from this miraculous place guides my perspicacity, though still I twist! I would never even have grasped the meaning of such words before, but I assure you I am applying myself. And yet… a resolution eludes me. I truly apologize for any inconvenience. I confess, Holy Traveler, 'twas not my intent to cause discord…"

Penelope Thatch had not been particularly bright on Earth, but she had been *particularly faithful*. In the heavens of all Heaven intelligence and acumen and all manner of enlightening qualities—even diction—grew, as on the mortal plane, in proportion to their usage and time spent. Still, the Angel was surprised by how much the single mother of two had developed since she died. She seemed to understand the intolerability of her situation. The Angel hoped this would make things go a little easier as he moved forward.

"There is absolutely no apology necessary, Ms. Thatch; however, you are right that I am here because of this imbalance. I go by many names, but presently my appellation is Mizam—protector and guardian of the balanced scales. I have come to see if there is anything I can do to help *you correct* what should already *be correct*, and assist in *making even* that which has somehow come out *as odd*. After all, it was once said…'God will prepare everything for our *perfect* happiness in *Heaven*, and if it takes a dog being there, I believe a dog will be there.' I have come to help you find that which has gone astray…"

The Angel intended these words to be comforting or even inspiring; however, the woman registered no change in demeanor or spirit. In fact, if anything, her back just seemed to take on a heavier slump.

"The fault, dear Mizam, 'lies not in the stars / But in ourselves,' I'm afraid," the woman began. "You see, I miss my boys—*my real boys*, that is. Yes, I know in my heaven I can conjure all manner of manifestations of them, but I still feel the stain of facsimile upon their creation. There is something artificial, something faux, something hollow about their projections. No, they do not completely satiate my love nor round out my world and I don't know why. I have tried making them infants and toddlers. I have tried making them happy adolescents—as you can see here. I have even experimented with thinking them up as pleasant and agreeable teenagers as well as adults with successful lives. Verily, I have *taken and reproduced* them exactly and precisely from my memories, and have launched fantastic adventures and utopian designs of celebration, self-sufficiency, and mirth, but still I am denied! My spirit just keeps yearning for those dear sparks as if I was ensconced in the darkest room searching blindly for the twin lights of my life. Indeed, I have tried everything and anything that I ever wished for them, or dreamed for them, but none has made *my paradise proper*! I miss my boys, Mizam—*I really miss my real boys*—and, plainly put, *I have no idea what to do about it...*"

The Angel of the Lord listened to Penelope's plaintive cries and his heart Divinely went out. He tried to remain stoic, and succeeded, but the infinitesimal tic of instability—of insecurity—quavered once more within him. 'Imbalance,' he opined. The very concept unnerved the Angel as much as an Angel could be unnerved.

"Well, Ms. Thatch..." he began.

"Oh, please, Holy One, feel free to address me as 'Penelope' or 'Penny' or even 'Pen,' if you prefer..."

"Then, my dearest Penelope... Pen... what I endeavor to do in situations like this is to provide you with as much information as possible. Thus, as you know, Heaven is a place of *unimaginable wonder*; however, its intricacies and axioms can sometimes confound even its most bewinged and benighted observers. You may already be aware: all of Heaven is governed by selection and dissection—discrete segments—that comprise and compose the entire Celestial System of Infinite and Eternal Order. Each part is self-contained and uniquely constructed, but the grandeur of the entirety is gestated and governed solely by the Will and Word of the one true God. ***Deo Optimo Maximo; Allah Hu Akbar; Soli Deo Gloria; Glory to God in the Highest.***

What this means is the principles and rules of any one place can be made malleable, but the principles and rules of the whole are not. Yes, there are some things that can be changed and some which are unalterable; some things that can be written down and ever revised and some, which once scored, can never be fiddled with again. Do you understand my conceit thus far?"

"I… I think I follow… but are you saying that these kinds of things have happened before? It doesn't seem possible…" Penelope replied, with a sense of sullen curiosity.

"Indeed, technically, it *is not possible*, and yet, sometimes there are ripples or vibrations in the firmament where the perfect pieces *don't quite* perfectly rest against one another. Occasionally—*very, very rarely*—does an item have to be nudged in one direction or another as Paradise expands Itself. Some of the host refer to it as 'growing pains,' though I never have. Heaven may grow, but there is never any pain. The one true God never saw any use for it."

"… Not in Heaven, at least…" the saved soul said.

"What was that?" asked the Angel.

"Nothing. Nothing. I don't know… did I say something? I suppose I'm just processing all of this. I… I guess… I just never thought about the complexity of the whole before… you know… all the implications… all I know is I miss my boys…"

"Well, no matter, but still remember your situation is *very, very, very rare*, but have faith and keep faith—**Utcumque Placucuerit Deo**. If you are not aware, it means: 'God does everything for you.' A pretty phrase, is it not?"

"I must admit, everything is 'pretty' from this place. After all, *it is* a panorama of bliss. But, I'd rather not talk of such minutiae. To my current dilemma, O' bright one? Can you tell me *exactly* what is occurring? Can you tell me why my children aren't my children?"

"Of course! This is precisely where I wanted to advance next, dear girl! You are, after all, *my child*! Hence I launch onward…"

To prepare, the Angel of the Lord assumed a more pedantic and professorial air, straightening his spine, and removing his glasses for a quick swipe and wipe. One could even suspect he was going to crack his knuckles, but he did not. Instead, he just did what he said he was going to do. He launched into the next section of his dissertation.

"The dilemma currently facing you is what we call 'Divinely Detached Fragile X Syndrome.' It occurs because of many factors, but broadly sketched, it is when a saved soul retains an Earthly attachment beyond his or her mortal existence. Generally, it happens when *a soul is saved* but a connection to that soul *in mortal life*—like a wife, a mother, a father, a sibling, a child, a mentor or friend—*is not*. For whatever reason, the saved soul rejects—or more accurately *doesn't completely accept*—the particular embodiment made manifest by the grace of God's plentitude. The saved soul can sense something is off. They can tell that the imbued life representation within an individual or collective paradise is somehow lacking the true and vital components of the mortal original. Stated more plainly, because you know the copy *is a copy*, you don't accept the copy *as the original*, which sullies your heavenly reward. It is this imperfect sentimental connection between humans which bespecks and begrimes the otherwise glorious system set up by God."

"… Yes, *glorious system…*" the saved soul whispered.

"Please say again? Your voice seemed not to rise above a murmured prayer," the Angel commented.

"… Nothing… nothing…" Penelope said, but then closed her eyes and prayed to God for a clearer answer beyond the Angel's convoluted words. After a moment, she gasped and exclaimed, "HOLD! I FEEL REVELATION COMING UPON ME!"

Here, water that was not rain began to fall, but the drops only landed softly on her own head. The drops made contact, but immediately were transformed and swept up again as motes of golden light. Penelope Thatch put her palms to her eyes and pinched her face in deep concentration. Then, she summoned her heart to her imagination and added faith and soon flashes began to spark and dance, rove and roam within her. A picture began to form. It was of a great and grand volcano spewing burbling lava into a scalded sea. The sea, in turn, spit up huge plumes of steam into the sky. And the sky filled with clouds, and rain—real rain—began to fall. With this, the volcano was extinguished by the incessant rain and the water carved out a valley where nothing but molten rock once flowed. A river appeared in the valley and plants began to take root. Trees grew and seeds continued to spread. And after a time animals began to frolic in perfect harmony. Many days and many nights passed as the valley grew in lushness and with life. Finally a man and a woman appeared among the flourishing greenery and tranquil setting, and the couple held hands. The man and woman made love near a waterfall under the caresses of a gentle sun. Nearby, a massive flower bloomed as chaos transformed to idyllic beauty. A baby was born and then another. '*True, yes, true, this was God's Design!—the Process of God!*' Penelope Thatch internally declared. The vision was enough to make her swoon.

She dropped her hands, flung her head back, and beamed with indescribable wonder.

"*I... CAN... SEE!*" exclaimed the woman. "The scales have fallen off! I know now my children—*my real children*—are not among those saved in New Jerusalem or in any of the xenomorphic menageries and I was certain they didn't have heavens of their own. Once I felt the imbalance begin to weigh upon myself, I searched and surveyed every place and plaza within the reach of my boundless love. Indeed I found not a trace! I should have realized God's fantastic plan still had designs for my special, precious boys. They are not in Heaven, I know, but now I understand why. Their simple and kind souls are still needed in the mortal world, so God in his infinite wisdom is recycling their sweet energies again and again back into the living Universe. Yes, this place is constructed to be *PERFECTION ITSELF*, but the mortal world still moves according to the *EVER-PERFECTING STRATAGEM OF THE LORD*! HIS WILL BE DONE! ***YES, GLORY BE TO GOD IN THE HIGHEST! MY BOYS ARE LOST, BUT THEY WILL BE FOUND! HALLELUJAH! HALLELUJAH! HALLELUJAH!***"

"But Ms. Thatch—Pen—wait... there is something you have yet to understand..." the Angel tried to interrupt, but the woman's thrall would not be halted.

"But don't you see, Mizam? ***DON'T YOU SEE?*** It's the way time works in this awesome place! An hour can be an eon; a minute can be a century; a second can be an era. Time, here, *is fungible*! I have only to wait a little longer—*in my place*—and my boys will arrive! My wait will take but a day, I speculate! Surely, twenty-four hours is long enough for my boys to live a thousand lifetimes on the mortal plane. Indubitably, I fathom, only *one day more* and my boys—*my real boys*—will once again cleave to their ever-loving mother. Thank you, Mizam. Thank you so much for your erudition and patience! I feel my mind is finally set at ease and *within the setting and rising of one of my suns, my own two true sons will be returned home*! One day more—a fourteenth of a fortnight—is all that it should take! ***Blessed be to Mizam and to God! Blessed be to the Plan of Jehovah! Blessed be to the Wisdom of the Divine!***"

The woman remained enrapt in her rapture, but the infinitesimal tic within the Angel positively convulsed. *'Should I explain?'* he asked himself. God did not answer and when God doesn't answer it means every path is open. *'Should I explain?'* he asked again. God once more said nothing and in that silence the Angel made his choice. Yes—even in Heaven—sometimes a heart needs to be broken, he reasoned.

"Ms. Thatch, I'm sorry, but I don't think you comprehend. Your children ***are not*** in the mortal world, nor are they in Heaven, and ***they never will be…***" The words came calmly out of the Angel's mouth as he relayed the awful truth.

Penelope remained entranced, but the Angel's stinging syllables and their terrible meaning did eventually break through. The rosy color infusing her face and the revelation in her eyes drained away like the last breath of a dying man. On top of this, a slight wind picked up in her heavenly playground and Mizam was undelighted to note it carried on its wispy currents the empty wrapper of a Milky Way candy bar. The incongruity of a 'Yield' sign in an individual heaven was one thing, but litter was quite another, he distantly thought. It was a ghastly portent. But finally, Penelope's fever and fervor snapped as, in her mind, Mizam's words sunk like something heavy and hot dissolving through a sheet of ice. The information began to drown her as her consciousness began to flail.

"What? *What?* **WHAT???**" Penelope sputtered.

"Please, Ms. Thatch, understand. Relax. Listen. *Process, and accept.* Your children were both born with severe mental challenges—so severe—that *they did not* and *could not* and *could never* develop the fundamental and mandatory requirement to gain admittance to this blessed and miraculous realm. This requirement, quite directly and straightforwardly, is ***the capacity for faith***. You see, *faith* is the cornerstone of salvation. *Faith*, in whatever version, *is the key for every lock* and *the pass code for every entry*. It is the Alpha and the Omega; the beginning and the end; the acorn and the oak. *Faith is the core and keel of Heaven*. It is the one sole necessary component ***for every saved soul*** and your children simply were not capable of attaining it. Everyone in the heavens of Heaven *has it*, and everyone on the mortal plane who desires to get here *must* acquire it. But, alas, your children could not. I am *truly sorry*, but *such is the way of 'The Way.'* God answers all prayers, but sometimes the answer isn't the one we wish for, or desire, or dream of. Yes, sometimes the answer is just **'stercus accidit'**..."

Penelope blinked rapidly and erratically as her mouth slacked open in a fetid and roiling epiphany. Indeed, all of her body felt wrenched agape and her stomach churned as if she was going to be sick—a sensation she hadn't experienced since before she died. The winds in her heaven picked up even further and carried more Milky Way wrappers. They caught on trees and on fences and dirtied previously immaculate corners. Tears began to well and trickle out of the shady eyes of Terrance and Toby. They did not turn into golden motes, but rather slithered and sluiced down each quivering chin—falling and eventually hitting the ground with pathetic splatters. Then, the sandbox the size of a basketball court transmuted to glass and exploded into a million shards. It was a deafening and spectacular spectacle. Yes, grief and disorder began to spread through Penelope's heaven like an unstoppable infection.

"But... But... But... *it's not their fault!*" Penelope wailed.

"No, no... of course it is not their fault, Ms. Thatch. *It's nobody's fault*. It is just the way things are, have been, and *always will be*. Remember God gave humans form and crafted them from *His own image*. But everyone is bound by the eternal pact between mankind and the Divine. He breathed life into all people and He aches for humanity—so much so He let humans sacrifice His only begotten Son for their salvation. Also, remember this situation is *very, very, very, very rare*—and not without solution. **Utcumque Placucuerit Deo.** God will provide even in this time of slight trial. Take heart, *my child*!"

"A solution? What solution, Mizam?" the woman replied in deep and nearly unhinged distress. "Speak plainly. You are telling me my precious, special sons are right now writhing in hellfire with the beast—***THE BEAST!***—and they will never find their way home to my loving bosom again! Verily, I can feel my heart fracturing as if it were made of nothing more than brittle slate! What possible remedy could there be?"

"It's actually quite simple and brilliant, Ms. Thatch. I would even characterize it *as elegant* and *full of mercy* in its design! You see, Heaven might be unalterable, but *your heaven is not*. I can simply go into your mind and spirit and remove any and all traces which offend. The sentimental remnants causing unease will be purified, cleansed, and you will become *unfractured*. In this manner you can enjoy the glory of God and all the favors He has lent to your disposal in *perfect harmony*. Now, does that not sound appealing? Yes, your boys may be in an unpleasant place, but you don't have to be. Now, does that not sound like sound judgment? With a word, you can leave all this temporary angst and anguish behind. Yes, with a word, you will never have to think about your boys or the loss of them again. Quite simply, and in mercy, you will not think about them because there will no longer be anything left to think upon! No fret! No worry! No consternation! God will do everything for you. No doubt! No disruption! No imbalance! What do you say? Doesn't this sound like *quintessential bliss*? I'll say true if you say true! Dear child, do you not want endless peace and eternal delight?"

The skies in Penelope's heaven darkened.

In the playground, one of the jungle gyms collapsed into a pile of rust and the other—in an instant—became choked with spiky and poisonous vines. The animals on their wild pendulum springs came to life and ran off as if chased by a plague of anthrax. And, the people (who were *not quite people*) began to melt like rotting tallow. Yes, even the very streets cracked as unseen and unnecessary water pipes burst below, and smoke began to rise from several of the docile domiciles lining the formerly serene scene. Parts of Penelope's heaven were on fire and her eyes began to blaze with an even hotter rage.

"NEVER!" she hissed. "NEVER! I WOULD RATHER SPEND ETERNITY HERE WEEPING FOR THEIR UNTARNISHED YET DAMNED SOULS THAN LIVE FOR A MOMENT WITHOUT THE KNOWLEDGE OF WHAT THEY MEAN AND MEANT TO ME! NEVER! I SAY! NEVER! I WOULD RATHER BE ERASED FROM EXISTENCE AND SCRUBBED FROM THE BOOK OF LIFE ITSELF THAN ALLOW MY MEMORIES TO BE LOBOTOMIZED IN THE NAME OF SOME DIABOLICAL DELIGHT! NEVER! I SAY! NEVER! I WOULD RATHER KISS THE SULFUROUS HOOF AND VOW ETERNAL ALLEGIANCE TO THE UNDERWORLD THAN TO LOSE THOSE TWIN TREASURES OF MY MORTAL LIFE! NO! NEVER!

NEVER! INDEED, I WOULD RATHER PLEDGE FEALTY AND GIVE THE DEVIL MY VERY SO—"

"LOOK THEE, THE LORD COMMANDS!"

bellowed the Angel in a voice that boomed like thunder. He stretched his arms upwards to Penelope's sky and the fires in her heaven immediately shrank low, perhaps in fear.

As for Penelope, her head was thrown back so she gazed squarely into her heaven's blazing sun. Its rays dazzled and glimmered in her eyes like yellow diamonds. Then, with an inevitable certainty, her heaven's moon began to cross the sun's coruscating brilliance in a purifying eclipse. It began to gobble the magnificent glowing ball in a slow creep. It covered the first quarter, and then the half mark, and then the three quarters, and then only a tiny shiny crescent remained—a single struggling sliver of silver fighting against a swath of shadows. In Penelope's heaven, the knives of both dark and light seemed to fall cuttingly upon Penelope's brow.

And then it was over.

The moon's shadow passed upon the face of Penelope Thatch while her manifested and mimetic sons vanished without even a whisper of memory. Yes, her heaven and her mind were rectified and a proper paradise had been achieved at last. The seething embers of dismay and discontent had gone out.

And, when Golden Helios returned to its full brightness, Penelope still lingered, staring dreamily into its blinding light.

"Ms. Thatch," the Angel of the Lord said, "do you know where you are?"

"Too, yes, too. *I'm im Hebben!*" she proclaimed in a stuttering stammer.

"That's right," he said. "And everything is perfect. **Utcumque Placucuerit Deo.**"

"Yes-sir-sire. Everything *is pre-Fect and per-Fact*!"

Then the Angel prepared to leave because his work had been done and done. Next, he was scheduled to go tell a lovely girl named Christina Cheer, who died in childbirth, that her daughter, who she named Sophia, had also not survived. Unfortunately, though, Christina's precious gift had passed on *before* baptism. It was a delicate situation, he believed—requiring a gentle touch—but blessedly it was not without remediation. Yes, sometimes a heart needs to be broken—even in Heaven.

"God is Great," the Angel said to no one and disappeared.

Penelope remained.

There she stood almost as a statue, gazing upward, and lovingly—and heavenly—into the lustrous light of her glowing sun. And… ***IT WAS PERFECT***!

… Or so the oft-chanted melodious mantra went.

End of Story #5

Intermezzo
(fifth)

Silence hangs in the air between the Angel and Devil when they both finish reading the writer's fifth story. It is a heavy silence—a pregnant one; the kind of silence the writer had only come to know through books or by watching TV. A stillness pervades that is palpable. He also found it strange that when the Angel and Devil read, they did so exactly in sync. Yes, they breathed in perfect unison and adopted the same posture. Even their eyes ticked back and forth simultaneously while each scanned the costly words—purchased by his soul. Regardless, the writer just sits quietly, and let his Devil's Spot whisper the most wonderful things for him to write down, as he waits for the pregnant pause to labor into birth. And, when the birth finally arrives, it comes through the Devil's laughter.

"Ahahahahahah!" the Devil booms gregariously. "You sent the retards to Hell!" He tips back in his chair and points at the Angel as he laughs and laughs, while stabbing his finger in a mocking gesture. "Yes, blessed be the meek and those deformed of form!"

"*I certainly did not!*" the Angel shoots back.

"Yes, you did! Yes, you did!" counters the Devil. "*He wrote it that way! He* even called you out *by name!*"

"You see? You can't tell a story like this," the Angel says as he shifts his vision towards the writer. "This is what you get when you deal with the Devil. Everything is tainted. Everything is stained. Everything gets soiled and all redeeming qualities of artistic expression just collapse back into the dust from whence they came. Yes, make trade with the Devil and you only get crude and basic works, emitting noxious language, infused with nothing but vile and forbidden blasphemy. It's sad and it's wrong. In fact, it's inappropriate… and incidentally, but relevantly… I would *never* send retards to Hell."

"'Special needs,'" the writer corrects, automatically. He is taken aback by the Devil's outburst because he hadn't intended his most recent story to be humorous in any way.

"What?" asks the Angel while the Devil's merriment tapers to snickers and he untips his chair to rejoin the conversation.

"'Special needs,'" the writer repeats, "… not retar… not the '*R-word.*' It's what humans call those with mental impairments—though technically we're not even supposed to use 'mental impairments' anymore."

"Why?"

"I'm not really sure. They just don't want people using the 'R-word.'"

"Retards?" the Angel restates, uncertainly.

"Yes."

"That seems silly," the Devil adds, now fully recovered.

"Perhaps, but I don't make the rules," answers the writer.

"And what's so 'special' about having needs? Everybody has them, right?" the Devil says.

"I don't have any," goes the Angel.

"Oh sure! Then what was the business about you *needing* to be thin?" the Devil challenges.

"*That* was about returning to a state of equilibrium. I require nothing except for the Light and Love of my Father."

The Devil lets out a raspberry buzz towards Mizam. His tongue is surprisingly pink.

"Do you have any other criticism?" the writer asks, ignoring the prattle, and continuing his typing.

"Well, I think it is an offensive story. You shouldn't have written it," states the Angel. "Honestly, you should destroy it. Yes, you should condemn it to the flames where it belongs. It impugns Heaven, misrepresents the vital and necessary rigidity of Celestial Rules, and sullies the nobility of my character as well."

"Well, I liked it!" the Devil gushes. "I think it's the first work you can truly be proud of! It's really, really amusing! Fun!"

"Figures," the Angel mutters.

"I don't think either of you are being truly objective… or trustworthy… readers right now," the writer observes.

"He's the Devil! Of course he isn't trustworthy!"

"Yes, and you should tell that to all the good and soulful people of Sodom and Gomorrah… oh, wait… you can't. Those cities are just ash and rock. You didn't even suffer the bones of the dead to remain. Yes, you even smote the lowly bacteria in the soil so nothing would ever grow again…"

The Angel and Devil bicker a little longer about who is less reliable, but the writer's Devil's Spot is really flaring and turning and churning up all the while. His fingers feel like miniature cylinders pistoning towards another story's completion. What it is spinning out is rhymes.

"Anything else?" interrupts the writer.

"Yes. Why aren't I in that last one? I mean, I thought I was going to kind of be the star of these stories?" the Devil inquires.

"You were in it… just indirectly. You got Penelope's children."

"The retards," the Devil notes.

The writer sighs.

"Let's just move on. Here. Read. This one's actually supposed to be funny, but then again, humor is subjective. Still, I imagine there isn't much comedy in Hell," he says.

"It depends on which side of the stage you're on," the Devil replies, "but in terms of moving forward, I think you can be even more subversive. And you might want to play around with the form and format of the next couple of stories—you know, spice things up. Surprise need not be terrible, is what I think. These are *your tales*, after all, so I suggest really going for something unexpected!"

"I'm way ahead of you," closes the writer and hands the Devil his next tale.

"Wait! Another story? I'm still catching up on the earlier ones, and I still have something important to say about Heaven… something *im—por-tant*," interjects the Angel. "What's this new one about?"

The Angel feels a little abandoned in the dialogue and he really doesn't like that the writer keeps handing over new pages to the Devil rather than to him. Additionally, he also questions himself if he had committed a sin by using the word 'retard.' He makes a mental note to ask about it when he gets back to Heaven.

"It's about blasphemy… as a matter of fact," answers the writer.

"Oh," says the Angel, worriedly.

"And it rhymes," he continues.

"Oh, no…" the Devil laments.

"And, this is the story with the wizards in it…" he concludes.

"Oh, no, no, no… this is going to be so much worse than I thought," the Angel ends.

"That's what I said," the Devil adds.

But the writer isn't deterred. Rather, his Devil's Spot encourages him to have faith in his tales, no matter how strange or offensive they might be. Indeed, it seemed to say that—whenever you write—always begin by believing it will be your best work yet. *'Yes, try to get away with everything!'* it championed, and the writer went championing right along with it.

And then a profanity-laced story which rhymed and had wizards in it commences.

An Act of Clowns, Magic, Mischief, and Tragedy

Prologue

(Story #6)

From Marlowe's ghost to Goethe's boasts, a story now appears. It starts out clunky, is a little bit bumpy, but the ending should bring tears. It is mostly a play, but not quite a play, but if a play *can play* then a play *should play*—should it not? I hope the author is clear! It is kind of bawdy and a little bit naughty, but—perhaps and perhaps—by these words arranged, we can hear Humanity's cheer! Enjoy!

1

And so once upon a time a Good Angel and a Bad Angel met upon the Earth. They met, in fact, in New Jersey. They had business with a set of contested souls, but presently these eternals were immersed within a long-standing game. The only rule was no profanity. The Good Angel insisted upon it for centuries now. The game arose because among the solemn, blazing, and unbridled Truths that underpin and overhang the Universe entire, one Truth remains arrow neat and sorrow straight. It is thus: Fools are unto every generation born. However, the names for fools *do change*... and hence the game took form.

Good Angel (G.A.): "Trouty-Lout."

Bad Angel (B.A.): "Nitwit-Snit."

G.A.: "Weakling-Weirdo."

B.A.: "Moron-Twit."

G.A.: "Toadying-Toad."

B.A.: "Poser-Clod."

G.A.: "Waste of Life..."

B.A.: "... and Mewling Nimrod!"

The Good Angel and the Bad Angel went back and forth in their rapport, expanding and exercising their vocabularies, so the exchanges became an increasingly rhyming staccato—almost like a spell. It was a spell against monotony, and a spell for engendering camaraderie between their various stations. Yes, being eternal is a long time stretch; thus, they continued in bulleted kvetch.

G.A.: "Dillweed-Numskull."

B.A.: "Pinhead-Slacker."

G.A.: "Dummkopf-Dweeb."

B.A.: "Schmucky-Whacker."

G.A.: "Knave and Spaz."

B.A.: "Cluck and Putz."

G.A.: "Kiss-Ass-Sucker."

B.A.: "Has-No-Luck."

G.A.: "Prickless-Wonder."

B.A.: "Can't even fu… fart!"

The Good Angel broke off the game, a bit perplexed.

"*Can't even fart!?!*" he asked.

"Well, *you said* no obscenity," replied the Bad Angel. "I'm even surprised you went with 'prick.'"

G.A.: "I went with it, because it was just a word before some words became accursed."

B.A.: "But it was the humans who put prohibitions upon dictionary's dictates. The host only forbade blasphemy. Everything else is fair as fare."

G.A.: "'Tis may be true, but still I hold my tongue on some, but let it freely wag about with others. But this segues nicely—have you any nomenclature new, for those that we are supposed to woo?"

B.A.: "You mean those we try to woo, that so often bring such futile woe? You speak of the synonyms of modern time for cur and clown, buffoon and oaf, doltish-ninny and weathervane loaf? Yes, a few I've gathered in anticipation, for such a shared time of jovial persuasion."

G.A.: "Proclaim them clear, but please hold the blue. Indeed, my ears have heard the trumpets, and yearn for only those of brighter hues."

"I abide and bide," the Bad Angel said, and the Good Angel nodded in gratitude.

B.A.: "The first is 'Skidmark' here defined: a waste, whose waste streaks down his behind."

B.A.: "And then there's 'Skeezo'—a creeping creep. In slime discomfort he accosts for sleep."

B.A.: "Thirdly stated, there is 'Window-Licker'—a term for those who dawdle and dilly-dicker. They neither force the pane, nor accept the pain, but stare froggily and groggily as spying banes."

B.A.: "And lastly there is the term 'The Tool,' which is an odd choice because tools are often useful things. And then again the wrong tool, or one misused, is a sad situation for anything. Perhaps it could be that 'The Tool' and 'Fool' are siblings—brotherly words who both can sting?"

B.A.: "Yes, here are four, but there are more, so feel free to put them in your jar. I spare your ears from the more impious jeers, but gladly I would raise the bar!"

G.A.: "No! These four you offer are enough; because three—in person—await for us. Yes, right now they loiter in a plot of bones, so let's hither there and then go home! And, verily, verily, you and I should pray, our triple idiots won't take long to sway!"

With this, the Good and the Bad Angels took to feathery flight, to find a trio of asses meddling at night. Yet the duo eternals never knew, that they, themselves, were being voyeured and observed by another two.

2

To be sure, the boneyard was old and long abandoned, with gray-green moss and few tombs left standing. And in the deep dark of night, just before the strike of twelve, three teenage nincompoops had come to dwell. Yes, they sought Satan's favor with ancient magicks, but with intellects combined, were no brighter than matchsticks! So, they had stolen a sword and an old-smelling book, a bit of chalk, and the foot of a rook. And though none spoke Latin, one had failed Spanish, and with these few trifles combined, they hoped to make the Devil unvanish!

Robin (R.O.): "The newt! The newt! Cunning, clever little beast!"

Rafe: (R.A.): "Yes, the newt... the newt... clever renown! You should have put him on a leash!"

Frosch (F.): "Why bring a newt? 'Tis not required?"

R.O.: "The newt and his eye all black arts require!"

F.: "I believe in too many fairy stories you partake!"

R.A.: "Read! Fah! He couldn't tell the alphabet from a snake!"

R.O.: "Could too! Could too! You mark me, we'll need that newt yet!"

F.: "Shut up, both of you! We have dark things to abet!"

Finally, the three silly boys stumbled upon the long appointed tomb, which was overgrown and cracked open, amid an air of dank gloom. On the surface it read:

> 'HEREIN LIES PENELOPE THATCH,
> DEVOTED MOTHER,
> WHO COULD NEVER BE MATCHED.'

Then Frosch dumped the conjuring items out with a clatter, but he neither cleaned nor brushed the tomb, because he gave it no matter. Yes, without doubt, disrespect in his heart truly did brood, and never a noble thing did he ever pursue.

Rafe was a different jackanape sort. He was a cowardly coward and an awkward dork. He divided his action between his nose and his crotch. Yes, he picked brazenly at each and his odor was rot.

Lastly, there was a numbskull, aptly named 'Robin,' because his brain was a birdbrain—as small as a bobbin. And, he'd bow down to Frosch, as though he were God, and with anything Frosch said, he'd reply with a nod. Stupidly, too, he liked to tell people he'd had sex in the rain, which was technically true, because his palm he did stain.

Indeed, the three threadbare troubadours were no raconteurs, but they banded together as broken things do. Frosch drew an imperfect circle—right on the tomb—while Rafe lit a candle, and fingered his moon. But, Robin just puttered and occasionally spit, with cheap chewing tobacco always plugged in his lips.

Yes, the summoning items had been collected in a quick shuffle, but there was one item more—an infant bound in a duffle! Yes, the babe could be heard letting out an occasional squeal, as the three vapid boys concocted their devilish deal! It was Robin's young brother, who they'd be offing to offer, to put yet untold and unknown 'bling'—*their word*—in their own greedy coffers! But the sacrifice came after, once all was made ready, but anyone who could see, could see the stakes were quite heavy! But, the business with the baby would come a little bit later; 'fore right now a debate was unfolding—that would end in a Seder!

F.: "Is it five or six? I can't quite remember? And… Jesus, Rafe! Stop stroking your member!"

R.A.: "I think it is six 'cause that's the Devil's number… and as for my penis—your looks makes me wonder!"

R.O.: "Maybe it's four or perhaps it is seven? Say… you don't think we might accidentally summon something from Heaven?"

F.: "Then six it is, let me make the star stand, and we'll have detailed our grim pentagram!"

Declaring this, Frosch did the drawing, lines all askew, and nobody noticed it was the sign of a Jew. Rafe took the chalk next and sketched a crude phallus; it was poorly composed and looked more like a chalice. Robin came last, and wrote the word 'Devel,' and then drew an arrow to where the Dark Lord should come revel.

So, these morons three continued their black preparations, but like the two Angels, they, too, were under observation. Yes, those fumbling fools by the light of a candle—this sinister ceremony was already in shambles! But just their act of defiance—of mummery and trouble—was enough for the Divine to dispatch winged bedoubles! Still from the darkness four other eyes stared, as the watchers had planned, something mischievously prepared!

3

Yes, the Old Crone and Whitebeard stood far enough off and, viewing both scenes, they awaited their scoffs! The first was Erichtho, who once consulted for Pompey; and the next was the Sabine Sorcerer of Norcia, pardoned in a day. Erichtho, 'The Somber One,' inhabited the crypts of the dead, while 'Whitebeard' of Norcia followed where she led. Indeed, both had historical gripes in their spirits, and thought bald revenge would best salvage their credits! Yes, this spell-casting pair longed for the Angels Good and the Bad, and if they could confound three mortals as well—well, it wouldn't be sad! And so after watching, Erichtho opened her lips, and then out their black-blooded plan did she let somberly slip.

"The time draws nearer and nearer," Erichtho started to mention; and Whitebeard made sure he gave full attention. "True, for years and for ages, I have tracked both the Good and the Bad; and we'll make them pay for the impact they've had! So tragic! My sisters and sisters—all set aflame; but I know who and to what to gather the blame! Yes, the Good Angel, who stoked with scripture and writ, the burning of women and called them 'unfit'! And the Bad Angel too, who accepted gladly their souls, but no protection gave when they were over the coals! Yes, the Good, who by 'good,' destroyed the feminine flowers, and the Bad, who by 'bad,' held back salvation by his darkest of powers! So, yes, and say yes, these two are on the hook for their dark and light sins, and we'll see them both fall—as they deal with cretins! Mark me, I swear and I promise—by this night's very end—these two Divine beings we're going to rend! Verily, verily, the scales will be reversed! We need only enact our plan—just as we rehearsed!"

Whitebeard agreed, but felt the need to point out, that it wasn't just women who had felt Divine rout.

"But do not forget, there were midgets and gays and even left-handers—all equally put on the pyre, the spike, and given neck-benders! So, we do this for every human victim in history's lost chapters! Then maybe both God and the Devil will watch who they come after!"

And following this, the pair watched and they swooned, and impatiently waited to unleash their ruin. Yes, each would cheerfully give up what they held the most dearest, if, in return, they were granted vengeance most fierce! Yes—women may scorn, and men may be brutal, but when two thaumaturges are wronged, forgiveness is futile!

4

Back in the graveyard, the twiddling three buzzed about the altar—so makeshift—with the brains of a bee. Yes, they had found the tomb of the 'Ever-Loving Mother,' and using—though incorrect—symbols, they had it covered! Next Frosch cracked open the old dusty book, and with each spoken word, he confirmed he's a crook! "*Tater Nostrum Diabolique Infernium!*" he began, and followed it with "*Expecto Patronum—Cadabra—Shazaam!*" Adios Mio! Some of the words were only half clear, so Frosch opted for chicanery and chance to mumble them near! Yes, reading was clearly not his natural forte, but making things up—he could do it all day! And so after speaking such garble and gobbledygook, Frosch paused for a moment and shot his companions a look.

F.: "Now is a drawing, which I think is direction… and dammit, Rafe! Why is always—*always*—with you, an erection!"

R.A.: "An erection! An erection! Why, I forever have one! I take the blue pill in case of some fun!"

R.O.: "An erection… an erection… what's this obsession with boners? Let's get on with the ritual before we're all goners!"

F.: "Verily, I agree with young Robin, and the drawing is clear! It is one severed finger and two drops of blood—in a smear!"

R.A.: "All three from one or one from all three? Indeed—how do we decide the divvying tree?"

R.O.: "I'll give a drop! It's no serious matter! And, besides, I'm not the one who lets *my Johnson* swell till it splatters!"

R.A.: "That's not a reason, you dumb unwashed stinker! You just don't want to lose a-one of your fingers!"

The conversation continued, a little embattled, until Frosch finally declared: "Let's end all of this prattle!"

F.: "We will draw lots to decide who'll lose the digit! And whoever gets the black mark—should not even fidget!"

F.: "Is there assent? I ask and say true! Or else depart from this scene—I mean both of you!"

R.O.: "Dear Frosch, I consent, 'fore you are our leader, and I'll take the gamble that I'll be a bleeder!"

R.A.: "And I'll not be accused of acting the coward! I'll gladly put up a pinky, and a pinky put forward!"

F.: "Then it's agreed! The black mark will decide! Two, but a blood drop, and the other—a finger aside!"

Frosch then went to the book and ripped out a page, and on one of three pieces scratched a mark like a sage. He shuffled and shuffled until he had Rafe and Robin confused, and ended by palming a blank one—for himself—to finish his ruse. After this, he handed the losing piece to Rafe, not because he liked Robin, but because—he had to admit—Rafe's constant diddling his diddle *did* make him look like a goblin.

F.: "Now it is done, and let's see to the deed; and remember, whomever gets the black mark without argument cedes!"

And so each of the boys—because they were far from being men—took and opened their slips with an "ah" and "a-hem."

"I've not the spot!" bluffed Rafe with a cough, but then tried to hide it, and showed the opposite side of his blot!

"I've not it either!" shouted Robin triumphant! Jubilant, he was, to feel no discomfort.

"Well, mine is blank also…" Frosch said with a sigh. "But I swear in just seconds someone will be caught in a lie… "

R.A.: "Robin's the dot! I can see it from here! I see it's quite small, but I can see it quite clear!"

R.O.: "I have the spot? I could swear my token is empty, but a deal is a deal, and I'll get Frosch's gratitude plenty!"

F.: "No, Robin-Rube, it is Rafe who's the liar! I can glimmer his mark by the light of the fire! Reprobate-Jerk, who has the soul of a shoe—by right and all rights, we shouldn't just take one finger—we should take two!"

R.A.: "Oh it was a harmless mistake—you should forgive me!—I say and I say, it must be all this mystical business… that's making me weary and bleary!"

Next, Frosch took the sword, and Rafe was held down, and soon Rafe's big middle finger fell to the ground. Then Robin and Frosch each a drop drew, and thus all arranged, this step was now through. Yes, the arrival of the 'Lord of the Flies' was drawing near, but an interruption was coming as the Angels appeared!

5

Indeed and indeed, the Good and Bad Angels remained just out of sight, in the cemetery of the dead, and from the trio not bright. And, the Good Angel exhaled in a discomfited way, and the Bad Angel agreed, but never would say. Yes, these two were assigned and assigned, to their asinine stations—to try to sway dumb souls away from God or the Devil's own Nations! Yes, each had been neutral in the GREAT WAR, but for Both Masters now—now they worked for! Without question, a winner or sinner either Heaven or Hell would accept, but neither realm would deign ever to take a hedger of bets! Yes, both always feared the rules of *Any King*, but now both were forced to endure two Kings' *anything*!

G.A.: "So, once more into the breach, my friend?"

B.A.: "Yes, once more into the breach we wend…"

G.A.: "It makes me think of the war… should we have made a decision?"

B.A.: "No! It wasn't our battle! Who could have foreseen such division?"

G.A.: "Verily, verily, but do you have any regrets?"

B.A.: "No! Not a one! We were treated like pets!"

B.A.: "Recall! Angel do this and Angel do that, but Angel don't think and don't want and don't dream—and that's that! Yes, be a happy obedient slave for all time and love your enslavement and think that it's fine! Truly, God or the Devil, who's to say which one's the better? But, whoever we'd pick, they'd still keep us in fetters! Undeniably, in an infinite standoff, we are but two cogs: functionaries, servants—treated no better than hogs! And those poor suckered humans, who already fear for their souls—what a load of malarkey, they've already been sold! 'Choose!' they say: give your life in submission to God—or sell the Devil your soul—but never, and never, just live life and be bold!"

G.A.: "Unfortunate for all, I can find no rebuke. Your words bite and they burn but they sound like the truth. Intractably, we are trapped and restrained in a system not ours, but we still have our duties while we whittle the hours. So let us not tarry and now make ourselves visible 'fore all this contemplation is making me miserable!"

And then the Good and Bad Angels uncloaked themselves, and manifested dramatically out of their shrouds. Yes, they appeared in an explosion of light and of thunder, and with dual booming voices tore silence asunder!

G.A. and B.A. together: "WHO DARES TO TRY TO SUMMON ON EARTH THAT WHICH IS DIVINE! WE HAVE COME TO INTERVENE—TO GIVE YOU TIME TO DECIDE! YES, THE CHOICE YOU MAKE

HERE WILL HAVE LONG REPERCUSSIONS! AND, TO HEAVEN OR HELL, COME FORTH IN DISCUSSION! VERILY, VERILY, WE SAY, EACH OF YOU FACE A STARK FORK IN YOUR PATHS, SO HEED UP OUR COUNSEL, AS YOU DO THE MATH!"

R.O.: "Math? *Math?* I didn't know of *a test*?"

R.A.: "Shut up, you ninny! This is no time to jest!"

F.: "Robin, 'tis but an expression, the turn of a phrase…"

R.O.: "Well these two before us—they speak like a maze!"

R.A.: "Just be quiet and listen—I'm sure we'll be fine…"

R.O.: "Well if there's not to be math, then I'll toe the line!"

And, the scene here is paused, in rapt ridiculous suspension, as the Crone and Old Whitebeard rise to ascension.

6

Erichtho (E.): "Ah, now is the time, and I'll get my revenge! And for every soul slain by religion avenge! Yes, with a flick of my wand, and a few obscure phrases, we'll see those obedient Angels feel the wrath of us mages! So, Whitebeard let loose the sacred essences, and throw up the stones; bring down the pestilence and read from the tomes! Yes, free the ground unicorn, and scatter the teeth of a dog, and by our acts here—we'll unleash Mighty Mesmer's old fog! With only a breath or two—should it take at the most—and then we'll work out our whammy-ist whammy on these sanctimonious hosts!"

Whitebeard (W.): "But, dear Erichtho, will the spell surely take hold? They are, after all, Angels—and Angels have great power it's told?"

E.: "Angels, indeed, but they also take the form of two men, and there isn't a man alive or dead or eternal whose will I can't bend! Just do the tasks as I ask, and watch how my vapor will travel; yes, with only one whiff, you'll see them quickly unravel!"

Then with a nod, Whitebeard followed her orders, and from the bonds of reality, itself, he stretched reality's borders! As for Erichtho, she cried out her syllables mystic, and a confounding grey mist did form—at that very instant! Yes, it wisped and it slithered on the foul-smelling air, and made way directly to the bewinged targeted pair. Indubitably, this was reprisal—retribution—and justice combined—incanted and planted by human design!

E.: "Now it is finished! Let's sit back and watch! But ho, ho, there! Who's that bizarre boy who keeps fingering his crotch?"

7

Back in the cemetery, the Angels and mortals were speaking, but ever so slowly, Erichtho's vapor was creeping. Yes, the Bad Angel was conscripted to make the Devil's own case, and the Good Angel, likewise, was charged to speak in God's place.

G.A.: "As instructed and compliant, here I arrive in the midst of this spate! Now let me spout my Divine boilerplate!"

G.A.: "Yes, Jesus loves you! This you should know and *should know*—'fore the good Bible tells you it's so—*and it's so*! Thus, stay your hand, and turn your face to the Lord, and think of the afterlife you have to look toward! Unlimited splendor! Unlimited grace! Yes, all will be forgiven—if you just leave this place! Please know every soul is special—*every single one*! So, I implore *you three specials*, seek the salvation to come!"

The Good Angel's opening had made an impression, but the Bad Angel, too, got to craft an expression:

B.A.: "Now is my time to read from the copy; but I really must comment: your altar is sloppy! This Divine being before you asks you for worship—but I'm telling you here—it means only hardship! Yes, Angels are dull, and Angels are boring, but Demons are lustful, and can be quite alluring! Instead, my Lord and Master promises a life of power and ease; indeed, you can have women and riches and do as you please! So, complete the dark ritual and all will be yours! Yes, you can settle up later—all in due course!"

G.A.: "But don't for the temporary, bargain the permanent! Think of the peace and the pleasures that reside in the firmament!"

B.A.: "But also consider the pleasures on Earth that can be gifted by Hell! Wealth, Sex, Revenge, Frottage—but, Zounds! What is that rank and rankling smell?"

R.O.: "Rafe it is! Because he won't wash…!"

And then equally, all five began to doze off…

Yes, a shroud of sleep fell upon the men and the Angels, as Erichtho's spun conjure worked all of their angles. And, the Angels, while sleeping, dreamt they were finally free, while the three selfish fools dreamt only—ME! ME! ME! Now to return to the Whitebeard and Crone, to view their reaction at the hijinks they'd done!

8

E.: "Ah! First, comes the sleep and the pleasurable dreams; then comes the waking and the breaking of teams! The spell is now cast, and has taken deep hold, and with one sweet chant more we'll see scruples unfold! Yes, the good will seek bad, and the bad will seek good, and—merrily, merrily—we'll even make that crotch-grabbing boy untumescence his wood! Oh, to be mortal! And, oh to have strength! Aye, human vision has no defined length! Join me in victory, Whitebeard—'tis our last step! And truly we'll see if Jesus has wept!"

W.: "Erichtho! Erichtho! I believe what you say, but I ask a last time if you're sure of this play? Assuredly, consider this my endnote of caution—but have not a doubt that I have faith in your potions! Yes, I know very well we can entrap these three men, and even those Angels, I think we'll swiftly upend! But what of their Masters? So drunken with power? Do you really think *we* have what it takes to withstand *their glowers*? It is but a question I ask—forthright and true! I just want to prepare for what dangers we're into!"

E.: "I understand your concerns, and I take no offense, but for what we are doing tonight—we should expect **every comeuppance**! Yes, we fight for humanity, for the degraded and destroyed!—'Fore it's **WE** who have suffered under the 'unquestionable' whims of the Lords! So, let them kill us or maim us or turn us to bugs, but for a small win for us humans—we shall take it with shrugs! I say this because it's high and low time someone hold **THEIR ACTIONS** accountable, since the *actions from both*—are quite truly abominable!"

W.: "Verily, verily, Erichtho! Where you lead I will follow! And, I suppose it's better to suffer for freedom than wallow! 'Fore freedom is freedom, and death is but death, but either is better than fiefdom—always having a foot on one's chest! So, dear Erichtho, take my left hand—because now is the time we take a strong stand! Yes, let's sing and let's sing, the last chant ever-so-clear! Yes, let's sing and let's sing, even if it costs us most dear! Undoubtedly and inexorably, you are my love and my compatriot unmatched! And, may the threads of our lives never and forever—be ever unthatched!"

And so Whitebeard and Crone clasped flesh and sang magic; it was an act of independence and dignity... and like most... 'twas to end tragic...

9

Once again in the boneyard, the five slowly awoke by the altar, but not one who awoke seemed to notice the conversation had faltered.

G.A.: "Oh my! I feel like I've been in the most wonderful dreamtime!"

B.A.: "I assure you it couldn't have been better than—"

F.: "Mine!"
R.A.: "Or mine!"
R.O.: "Or mine!"

The Bad Angel glared at the rude interruption, and his view soured darkly as he thought of corruption! Yes, it fell to him and *to him*, to be these three boys' agent of tempting, but he could smell that their souls were but hollow and empty! Yes, if he sent them to Hell, they'd add just more whining voices, and even their agonized screams would be just stupid noises. And, he suddenly realized Hell was already chocked full with the daft—that, indeed, from summit to pit—it was stocked high with riffraff! And this could not be! And this had to stop! And the Bad Angel would do it, because the Devil would not! Now he pulsed and convulsed with a grave assertion of dread, and this feeling continued as the Good Angel said:

G.A.: "Where was I at? My mind's a bit tilted… ah, I remember… don't leave good God unloved—or abandoned—nor selfishly jilted! Yes, break off this ritual done in the dark—and to the Heavens aspire—where the nice Angels do hark!"

Here the Good Angel halted, and waited for the Bad to reply, but when the Bad Angel did, he found he couldn't tell a lie!

B.A.: "Indeed and agreed, you should listen to this speaker of light! Darkness and sin are forever a blight! Yes, Evil is awful, and there is so much to fear and never and ever should you let the Devil get near! So, look to the Lord, and ask for forgiveness! Yes, I advise all of you: *walk away from this business!*"

The Good Angel stood frozen; his mouth was agape—because not once in eternity had the Bad Angel ever abandoned his tape! His eyes then shifted to the three bumbling bumblers, and a truth in his brain broke free from all tumblers!

'Why am I trying to save such valueless souls? Yes, why should they get to bask in God's glory untold? Undoubtedly, those that were dim in everything—in everything but faith—are already in Heaven amassed—all over the place! No, they don't deserve it, and that is the truth—and I'll see it get done, even if it takes being uncouth! Yes, let Hell have these souls of no definite worth; because, all I need to condemn them—is to hoodwink them first!'

The Good Angel then paused to consider his prose, and the words that come next were the ones he composed:

G A : "'Tis correct and correct, the Devil is a dangerous foe! But take a moment to ponder his devilish pleasures bestowed! Yes, pleasures of flesh and of wealth—of charisma and kingship; he can give them in hoards and from whores, without even blinking! Yes, Heaven is fine, if you like being a slave, but to take what you want—now that's living brave! So, finish this ritual and you'll hold the keys; indeed, complete the black art and Satan's favor you'll seize!"

This was the work of Erichtho's cast glamour—yes—Angelic minds had been shattered as she raised her banner! The smell of the spell exposed the bald naked truths of their secret desires, and turned into truth-tellers the two Divine liars! 'Fore Angels both of salvation and damnation alike are still not immune to the shabbiest-stabbings of spite!

And, just as the Devil and God could be vile and reviled, the Angels gleaned—through the magic—that some humans are utterly unworthy of trial! Indubitably, some human souls are completely damaged, feckless, and feeble, and verily, who, to them, would want to come forward and wheedle? It would be like fighting for some base rock, or some broken toy, and even in victory there would be no exultation or joy! Yes, and *say yes*, to chase fools through all time—must, admittedly, be a self-torturing grind! So, for the Angels, Erichtho took off their masks and finally allowed their true hearts be brought to their tasks! And thus was the scene, now under a curse; as the Good and Bad Angels' positions reversed! Yes, Heaven or Hell might not take a hedger of bets, but neither Angel now would fight for these idiots! Hence, the servant eternals persisted, but sabotaged themselves, and their Divinely ordained purposes, they put on the shelves! And so the two messengers started weaving arguments beguiling and new, but—in a shocking surprise—Rafe found himself without lead in his pencil, but well-endowed with a clue!

10

And so the Good and Bad Angels—or now the Bad Angel and Good?—pushed their now upside-down cases as hard as they could. This meant the Good praised the Devil, while the Bad extolled God but, at seeing this change, Rafe found the change very odd! He could see very plain these immortals were tangled in conflict, but soon began to suspect there was something more to it!

Yes, something was off, and something smelled fishy, and—on top of all this—his stickie was squishy! Perhaps unbelievably, it might be a ludicrous proposition to state, but Rafe's silly-willy had always signaled his fate! And this setting was unsettling, and the setting was wrong, and such was the message sent from his dong! Yes, hard boded good times, and soft boded danger—but anything in between meant—a future cliffhanger! And, right now it was soft—so soft—almost crawling inside, and this spoke of peril—a calamitous tide! It was thus and was thus: Rafe believed his private organ to be a totem of mysticism—so much so—he felt always naked without a perpetual priapism! So he called his conspirators away from the long-standing tomb, to candidly whisper he thought they were doomed. Yes, he suspected the Angels—that much was true—but he vowed not to admit it was because his crotch he looked to!

R.A.: "I say and I say, this situation's not right; haven't you noticed, these guys have switched sides in their fight?"

R.O.: "I haven't noticed! I haven't noticed nothing in years! And I, for one, won't get distracted by fears!"

R.A.: "Shut up, you ass, and comprehend what I'm saying! These creatures before us are not fairly playing!"

F.: "What do you mean? The choice is still ours! To get the gifts of Heaven or Hell remains in our powers!"

R.A.: "The choice—yes—the choice, but what's changed is perspective! Can't you see these two Angels have gone and reversed their invective?"

R.O.: "So? So? You never make yourself clear! I'm glad you lost a finger; next I hope it's your rear!"

F.: "Robin, calm down, and Rafe, come aside. Are you telling me, true, the Angels have something to hide?"

R.A.: "I'm saying both had been wooing us, but now neither are! This change is quite strange—we should run and go far!"

R.O.: "Why? Why? Who asks does not matter! All that matters is choice! And from what it sounds like—either way—we'll rejoice!"

F.: "Robin seems right, though that sounds exceedingly rare, but no doubt in mere moments, we shall all live without care!"

R.A.: "No one is listening! So I'm getting out; yes, I've lost a finger already, but I won't lose my snout! I am telling you clearly and distinctly, we should leave this place, Frosch; I feel great danger and darkness—and—and—oh my!—my penis is soft!"

Here Robin lunged forward and chased Rafe around, kicking and flailing to hit Rafe's now flaccid mound. Yes, Robin, while charging, kept casting his barbs, while furiously aiming at where Rafe used to be hard! And, as usual and *usual*, it was up to Frosch to intervene—no, he may not have been much, but he was the glue to the team.

R.O.: "Again and again and again—with your unit! Well, go if you want—just go—and see to it! I hate you, you dick, and your stupid erections—as if being properly stiff could give good directions!"

R.A.: "I hate you, too, you ignorant douche! You cling to your idiocy by nail and by tooth! Yes, my pecker has been an ongoing theme of your jokes, but I'm telling you here, we're in for a hoax! My dearest Frosch, you know you're my friend, but I honestly think that tonight—your life may just end! So, I implore you and warn you—please come with me! Because if you don't do it now, it could be too late to flee!"

F.: "O' Rafe, my friend Rafe, don't be such a drama; indeed, you're huffing and puffing like we're facing a trauma! But Robin *is right*, these Divines beck at *our* call, and whatever we desire—we're sure to get all! They'll do what we ask—whatever we say! And whatever we want, they are obliged to obey! So go if you need to, my feelings won't hurt—but really I think—you just want a quick squirt!"

R.O.: "Ha-ha! Rafe is pure cowardice, even his wink's on the blink! His entire existence has been only to diddle and stink!"

R.A.: "Jab and mock if you must, but I feel the situation is dire! I say one final time: you are both playing with fire! No, you two may not have any faith in my plumbing—but I have the faith—that you won't see it coming! Yes, we three and we three are standing upon the graves of our graves, but I sense we can dodge it, if we just don't make waves! So, disregard, if you're blind, my legitimate fears, but as for myself—I'm leaving here!"

Rafe then left—and he left—the others to the fate of what may, because he knew and *he knew* something Divine would never—*and never*—a human obey. Yes, even now, he could feel a great catastrophe forming! It was like a deadly volcano—ready to erupt without warning! Thus he slunk away quiet—as quiet as a lizard—but in his escape he came upon the two wizards! Yes, it was true! It was true! This ordeal already cost him a finger, but in the end he'd be glad he hadn't malingered!

11

W.: "Dearest Erichtho! We've struck quite a blow! But to be honest, I thought there'd be more of a show! True, yes, and true, the Angels continue to argue and squabble, but oh how I want them in much greater hobbles! Yes, oh how I've longed for their wings to be plucked—to see them dejected, despairing, and all out of luck! Yes, and oh yes, I believe they must feel the true weight of our scorn! How religious powers have made us mere humans so afraid and forlorn! So please tell me, please, we've done more than scramble their Divine occupations—but that at last and at last—they rest in the crosshairs of far deeper, and debilitating, and deprived tribulations!"

E.: "Aye, Whitebeard, yes, in the crosshairs they are, but I'm just a pebble, nothing compared to the stars! And yet it is true, a pebble can an avalanche make, and the path the Angels are on will soon make them quake! So, have patience, have poise—my old hirsute spell-caster, because in just clock-ticks—you're going to witness disaster!"

W.: "'Tis good to hear, because I sense our own future is grim, and before our grim deaths, I'd like to see this disaster begin! Oh but look now, one of the boys moves away! It's the one with the flesh pole—forever at play! It looks like he travels directly towards us! Should we run? Should we fight? Or maybe—not make even a fuss?"

E.: "It won't be a problem, 'fore we'll give him a blessing, and—from this time going forward—he'll carry our message! Yes, it's foretold and ordained, we are not long to survive, but with this boy's eyes, ears, and mouth—our actions will thrive! It is a message of sanctity, of solidarity, of solemnity and deterrence—that humanity can do just fine—without Divine interference! **Yes, we fight for our freedom, and our free will is our own!** And I swear and know well—we require no supernatural thrones! All this and much more, will this young boy bear witness, and he will travel the land, and be free to confess! There once were two mages who stood up for **human rights**, and challenged the supremacy **of all Divine mights**! Yes! The boy once with the boner will carry our tale, to show the true natures of God and the Devil, when fully unveiled!"

And so they waited and waited for Rafe to come close, so they could give him great gifts, and boast of their own valiant boasts! Yes, both felt well-satisfied and were done acting cagey, but back in the graveyard, it was time for the baby!

12

Thus, the Angels went on and went on, without the presence of Rafe, while Robin and Frosch believed—*wrongly*—to think they were safe. And so the Good Angel told how fiery Hell *was fantastic*! And the Bad Angel, too, proclaimed saccharine Heaven was nothing short *of ecstatic*! But, a storm could be heard, brewing off in the distance, as the two Angels kept on and kept on ratcheting up in insistence! As for Robin's young brother, he let out some adorable gurgles and one precious burp!—blithely unaware by what forces—*tonight*—his life could usurp! So, the Angels proceeded to describe Heaven and Hell in specifics, but sufficed to say, what each painted of both—wasn't so much terrible—*as terrific*!

G.A.: "You know, Hell isn't all torment—there's even this one glorious flower! The Devil created it, with his splendiferous powers! Indeed, it's more beautiful than anything growing on Earth! It's green, and it's grand, and smells of long ago mirth! And then there are books—all the books of the world—just waiting to be read, and have their mysteries unfurled! Yes, there are books that are ancient, and books that are new; books of enthralling delight—for whatever you're into! And, it also has movies—such movies you could never dream up—but none will be yours, if you cast your eyes up! Finally, don't forget, all this will come after a life of complete satisfaction. Yes! You can sate every want and every wanton desire—with just one simple action!"

The Bad Angel attended, but held in a guffaw, because these tales spun of dark Hell were stretched quite incredibly tall!

B.A.: "I assure you—*and assure you*—my companion is bending the facts, and there is no way you can think Hell is more peace than attacks! But *you must know* that Heaven is nothing but **BLISS**—yes, beauty, love, warmth—it should never be missed! For instance, there is a light that's so bright—more golden than the sun—that takes away any pain and regret in any sin ever done! Yes, it is a holy place, a sacred place—a place of tranquility and joy—and it shouldn't be swept aside for the whims of a boy! Truly! Acknowledge! Pleasure is virtually non-existent in Hell, but in Heaven's realm—it is too great to tell! So don't do that thing which is heinous and cruel! Yes—in *God's* name—don't be a fool or a tool!"

But the storm was approaching and gathering force, and streaked white and red lightning across its supernatural course! Verily, both Heaven and Hell had raised a malevolent maelstrom of smiting, and the wind blew alternately frigid cold and furnace hot—in gusts and in gusts—that were frighteningly biting! Yes, this was the wrath of the Devil, but it was also the wrath of the Lord, because in the disobedience by the tomb, they had come to accord! And so, each had gathered up clouds from their own Hellish and Heavenly sources, and sent them stampeding forth like grand-standing, grand-damning, and galloping horses! Yes, in truth and in truth, only a few words by the tomb were left to be stated; and then all involved in the transgression below—*always below*—would be most decidedly fated!

G.A.: "Well, why not now bring out the child, and why not the sword? Just lay him before us, as we discuss our moves forward!"

B.A.: "I disagree and disagree! Let the child remain in his diaper! He is just so small and so weak—we should wait till the time is much riper!"

But Frosch produced the infant, and then set him down, and the Bad Angel cringed with a thoroughly undevilish frown. And then the Good Angel likewise donned an unholy, unblessed, smile; it was as if his once bright white spirit—had been dipped in vile black bile!

F.: "I'm just setting him here for a moment… while we decide… but soon we will see by our choice—if we have to Robin's brother divide!"

Secretly—but in truth—Frosch was already leaning towards the side of Old Scratch; 'fore there were many pleasures and treasures on Earth, he'd love to selfishly snatch.

Robin, however, was more on the fence, but he had already decided to follow Frosch in servile deference. And thus the storm approached—as the boys weighed all the grave factors—but the time has arrived for the Crone and Old Whitebeard's final—sad, sardonic, and self-sacrificing—last chapter!

13

Rafe wandered and wandered, knowing not where to turn; but never and ever would he—to the graveyard—return. Yes, the mist which flattened his groin had also confounded his head, and the stump of his finger still hurt where it bled. Finally, he realized how he'd lived life as a fool—how his constant erection obsession—had branded him nothing more than immature and a ghoul! And so after moaning and roaming for some undefined period, he broke down inconsolably and sobbed out tears that were myriad!

R.A.: "Why am I so lost, so alone, so without any friends? Can this really be how my own story ends? Yes, I am abandoned by companions, and declined by Divines; aye, all the moments before now—were far happier times! Indeed and indeed, how does a person live without reason? And, how can grim death—not be better than treason? Oh terrible truth! The only thing I can think worse than living my life—is for me to abhorrently think—that I'd have to live twice! Verily, verily, the world is so empty, so heartless, and hard, that just living within and upon it can leave one irreparably scarred! I can't look to Heaven, and Hell is all smoke—

… and…

… oh how…

… it seems…

… everything…

… now…

… is just…

… one long…

… and…

… meandering…

… and…

… mendacious…

… and…

… meaningless…

… joke…!"

Yes, Rafe cried to the darkness, and he cried to the night! And he cried and he cried because—within the depths of his soul—he'd lost all will to fight! He wished for something—*for anything*—in which to have faith, but in lieu of God or the Devil, what Meme could replace? Could he believe in himself? Could he believe in a void?

Could he believe in *any higher power* that wouldn't leave him dejected, bereft, or annoyed? And so he shouted out his sharp pain, to the crickets and pale moon, but the only sound that resounded was the sad lonely caw from one lonely loon. To be fair, he expected none, because he believed there was no one to hear, but a response did unexpectedly come—in the form of Whitebeard!

W.: "Don't worry, young boy, your death won't be tonight; in fact, we will restore you, protect you, and give you great sight!"

E.: "Whitebeard, I've warned you, don't speak so precipitously! I've told you and told you, hope is most dangerous when given capriciously! Rafe, we cannot restore; we can only replace. You've lost a piece of your body, but another part we can put in its place!"

Rafe was surprised—but felt great relief—that he was no longer in exile, and not alone in his grief.

R.A.: "What do you mean? This night's just so unnerving! I'm so discombobulated; I don't even know what I'm saying!"

E.: "Sweet, silly boy, you have so much to learn, but know, in your actions this night—you've embraced the challenge to yearn! Yes, you chose for yourself, and you sensed something unfair; but now you see how the light in enlightenment can come from bitter despair! For sure, you have lost your two friends—and this is quite tragic— but we can provide you succor and solace—with our wonderful magicks! Yes, we will grant you fine help, and entrust you with our arrived-at conclusions, but *you* must decide—if they are Truth or illusions!"

W.: "Don't scare the kid! It's a lot to take in! But giving the kid our knowledge and power can't be a bad place to begin!"

E.: "Whitebeard, you're right, and I suppose the time has arrived… so step forth, my young protégé, and get our phantasmagorical drives!"

Then Rafe stumbled forward, holding his throbbing-hurt-hand, and Erichtho put, very gently, in his four fingers, her wand as she planned.

E.: "With this wand I bequeath all of my knowledge and wisdom; wield it wisely, see far, and even fight invisible kingdoms!"

W.: "And, here too! Here! Take a scrap of my beard! With it you can make powerful spells—delightful and weird!"

E. and W. together: "And as our last gift, we'll replace what you've unfairly lost! Yes, we'll take from your crotch and put it where your finger's cut off!"

R.A.: "NO!" Rafe burst out emphatically—in quite a loud shout; but of his passion and position he wanted not one nagging doubt! Yes, his journey had changed him, but how and how much wasn't completely transparent, yet in his next speech, he'd prove to himself—and to all—to be the wizards' clear heir apparent!

R.A.: "Verily, an hour ago that may have been a desire, but now I'd rather my brain use, and my flagpole retire! Yes, once upon a time—I acted impulsive and reckless—but I'm done with all that, and I'm done being feckless! Instead, I'd rather have facts, good works, and long-reaching vision! And, I no longer want to be the comic relief—incessantly jeered with derision! Even now I can feel something—*that something*—significant is occurring! Yes, in my brain and my mind there is a definite stirring! After these thorny trials, I can see matters clearly! Yes, an epiphany is upon me or is—quite verily—nearly! I understand now, Earth doesn't just run on basic flesh or rudimentary biology—but I also understand that its answers can't be coughed up or drank down through some ancient mythology! Yes, there is so much more out there in wonder and scope, and it is to these things we must look, if we are to hope to have hope! There is science and philosophy and historical metrics—astronomy, quantum physics—and even secular ethics! Truly, I can glimpse a nascent objective reality—which has no dependence, at all, upon *any* contrived spirituality! Yes, I feel the breadth of the Universe has been much expanded, and that the blinders of fairy tales and faith—are finally and forever disbanded!"

E.: "We accede to your request, but pray you also glean our intentions, that in regards to the Divine—we seek not their grace—but **greater Human inventions**! Yes, Humans need to evolve and need to come together—and whatever we need—**we need to get better**! Yes, Heaven and Hell *will always war*, and *will never get along*, but Humans can exist and advance—singing just **Human Songs**! So, please heed my words, because yours will be the only voice left in the morning, and travel the world to tell and to seed the most crucial of warnings! Those who think that God or the Devil respects them engages in nothing but delusion! Because in matters of

Power—God and the Devil—both work in collusion! No, Humanity *will never—and never—*be blessed or damned with respect—'fore as long as the Divines exist—they'll always keep their feet on our necks! Yes, they teach us to be small, and teach us to be weak—and they tell us we're tainted, imperfect, and command us to be meek! They set up as our greatest goal to be accepted when we die and—while we are living—they say *blind faith* is better than A **Good Human Eye**! Verily, dependence, fear, guilt—these keep the Divines active—but those are the things that keep Humanity static—and **can even roll Humanity backwards!**"

E.: "So, I say *'NO'* to them and I say *'YES'* to Humanity; because, *I take pride in being Human*, though *they'd* call it mere vanity! *YES—I SAY, YES*—because it is only *Human Trust and Cooperation*—that can provide Humanity's escape—from tyrannical-despotic-scripture and dictatorially-Divine-domination!"

Rafe listened to her words, and struggled to process, but the fresh knowledge he'd gained made him feel nearly possessed! Yes, he felt transformed and transmuted—from foolish boy to a much smarter man—and his mind buzzed eclectically and electrically with new erudite plans! It is important to remember how he had begun his life in lowly deceit, but now he'd grown tremendously with boldly pulsing conceits!

E.: "Now take this satchel…"

W.: "And also take mine!"

E.: "Both are magical vessels…"

W.: "For you to use in your climb!"

E.: "Yes, they will guide and protect you for what is to come, and for the acts you will face after the rise of the sun!"

E.: "Step away, now, because soon the lightning will strike!"

At this, Whitebeard huffed: "Oh those two hot-dogging hotdogs—always feeling the need to cause fright!"

Erichtho then drew a rune onto Rafe's dirty scalp, to hide him from the light and dark eyes in the skies that looked all about. She went on to direct him to a place where he'd be safe—for when the ireful wrath rained down on every 'iniquitous' trace! The work now complete, Whitebeard and Erichtho breathed their last living breaths, because in just seconds they were to—proudly and bravely—meet their preternatural deaths!

E.: "Fair thee well, Rafe! And remember, don't shy away from being complex!"

W.: "And also remember to—every once in a while—do something to perplex!"

R.A.: "Thank you, dear wizards, for soothing my concerned consternations! You have given me certainty in life; there can still be purpose in logic, and decency, and clear explanations! Yes, I am a Human and I'll fight for Humankind—and—with every word I dare speak, I'll endeavor to shine! Yes, your legacy is safe—I guarantee it! My word is my bond—*I am Human!* And mean it! Unfortunately, I suspect you'll both die in unimaginable pain; however, I know that you know, you will not die in vain! Yes, I'll carry on for you—you can count on me! I may make mistakes, but I'll make them as a *Human*—and I'll make them living free!"

And thus, Erichtho and Whitebeard waved Rafe amicably and safely away, and let out great sighs, because they were finally done with their fey. Then, they held hands and shared the warmth of their palms, and started humming softly their sublime ending song. Yes, the mortals and sorcerers would all perish together, and—like Whitebeard wanted—the grey Angels too would be stripped of their feathers. At last, in the pale reflected light of the silicate and silently orbiting moon, only Rafe would survive—'fore the end was approaching—and the velvety, cast-calling curtains—indeed—would descend very soon.

14

Yes, since the first waft of mist, we know the Angels slept then woke strident, but the scene in the cemetery—quite literally now—was veering towards violence! Yes, their arguing and bickering escalated well past different agendas engaged, and had morphed, internecine, into full-Angelic-fury and pure-supernatural-rage! And so they fumed and they spit—and they accused and abused—and with each volleyed word they further burned down the fuse! Just which Angel was winning, was too close to call—because both Angels now—vomited out obscene vitriol! So with curses and screams, they hatefully faced off over Robin's young brother—intending to verbally eviscerate and totally annihilate one another! The Good Angel even brandished the old sacred sword, and dangling it above the baby, the Bad Angel became nearly crazed and unmoored! And thus the action resumes with uncensored, wretched name-calling—but a warning is issued—because the venomous insults relayed—are quite profanely appalling!

B.A.: "Shit-Head-Dick!"

G.A.: "Douche-Bag-Douche!"

B.A.: "Ass-Lick-Prick!"

G.A.: "Skank-Pussy-Juice!"

B.A.: "Face-Fucking-Faggot!"

G.A.: "Suck-A-Dick-Nigger!"

B.A.: "Sloppy-*CUNT*-Maggot!"

G.A.: "Rotten-*CUNT*-Digger!"

Yes, these debauched examples—so crude and so lewd—show just how disgusting the dialogue had moved beyond rude! To be fair, this section of exchange should have been triple 'X' rated, but sometimes foul language is necessary for ideas to be stated! Yes, the terms and the burns, and the cuts and the swipes—aren't even execrable enough—to describe how vulgarly they sniped! In fact, if coarse words could kill—each participant would be facing imminent execution—with polysyllabic nooses and sizzling electric chairs of locution! Still, the stormy Divines above—*always above*—cared nothing for such heinous calumny; because they only primed and cocked guns, for one thing and only one thing: the death-deserving offense of disobedient blasphemy!

The pejoratives subsided, but not the dispute, as the Angels' anger and ire remained quite acute! And finally, the scene by the altar is lastly unveiled, but be aware— any sense of probity or propriety—has been completely curtailed!

B.A.: "It is truly unseemly and unacceptable for you to

handle the blade, because, if the baby is cut, it must be—*by a mortal hand*—be made!"

G.A.: "You can do nothing to stop me! *My hand is my own*, but I promise by sunrise, this blade will touch bone!"

B.A.: "No, you must not! This is not your choice to make! Recall, that these two jackasses must be given a voice in their fates!"

G.A.: "These two imbeciles, here, wouldn't know fate if it came up and nudged them! After all, that's why we're here—we're here exactly to budge them!"

B.A.: "Then, I swear by the Devil that you won't harm this child! I think, absolutely, your mind has gone wild!"

G.A.: "Then, I swear by God and the Christ, and the slippery Holy Ghost—by the end of this night—this baby will bleed like a roast!"

B.A.: "Then, I swear by righteous Satan and all the upstanding hordes of the damned—verily, in every pious name of the underworld—I command, stay your hand!"

G.A.: "Then, I'll swear by every black Angel and every suckered-saved soul—with Heaven's foul blessing I'll see this infant's innards exposed!"

R.O.: "What's going on? Everything's happening so fast!"

F.: "I fear Rafe was quite right—we might just lose our ass!"

R.O.: "Is there a chance of escape, if I give myself a quick stiffy?"

F.: "You can try—but I doubt it—I think we'll be dead in a jiffy!"

The situation got worse and got worse—from horrid to

horrible—and anyone hearing these words, should think the debate quite clearly deplorable! And then the moment came—the moment of final climatic eruption—where the wrath would pour down—untempered and intemperate—in fully dyspeptic destruction!

B.A.: "So, I insist in the holy, and merciful, and wise name of Satan! You will not lay any hurt, nor any pain, upon this small person!"

G.A.: "And I insist in the name of the impure Jehovah and the Kike-Jesus-Christ—on this eve and this eve—Robin's brother shall be sliced, minced, and diced!"

B.A.: "No—save the child! The Devil shouldn't have him!"

G.A.: "No—slay the child! God has no need of more cherubim!"

B.A.: "No, fuck the devil! Fuck him! He's a Bitch-Pussy, Cocksucking, Motherfucking-Cunt!"

G.A.: "No, no, Fuck God! Fuck Him balls-deep! He's a Rapist, a Sadist—and a Bitch-Bully-Runt!"

B.A.: "Defiling ignorant virgins…"

G.A.: "Allowing cancer in children…"

B.A.: "Empowering pogroms…"

G.A.: "And murdering pilgrims…"

B.A.: "Constantly corrupting the faithful…"

G.A.: "And leveraging fears of the Devil…"

B.A.: "Destroying the able…"

G.A.: "And elevating the feeble…!"

B.A. and G.A. together: "YES, VERILY, VERILY, I THINK THE UNIVERSE WOULD BE SO BETTER OFF, WITH NO GOD OR DEVIL WHO CLAIMS HE'S THE

BOSS! THOSE NATTERING NARCISSISTS—I WISH THEY'D NEVER MADE INTRODUCTIONS! BUT I WISH MORE—SO MUCH MORE—TO SEE THEM RETIRED LIKE SO MANY GOD-NOTIONS! YES, ZEUS AND POSEIDON, ISIS AND KALI—WHY CAN'T THEY—LIKE THEM—JUST GO AND RELEASE THIS REALITY! DEARLY AND SINCERELY, I BELIEVE, EVERYTHING WOULD BE SO MUCH IMPROVED— WITHOUT SUPERSTITIOUS 'SUPREME' BEINGS OR DIVINE BUGABOOS!"

These were the words that would finally end the extreme scene—except for one deafening word more, and that word was—

"BLASPHEME!"

Of the voices that boomed it, one was sublimely melodious; but the other—however—was tonally odious. Next came the discharge of six streaks of lightning: three red and three white bolts, of Divinely contrived smiting! And each bolt struck down on the heads of the mortals, the wizards, and Angels—as the bodies under each struck were instantly and irreparably mangled! Then the mangled forms dissolved into dust and the dust blew away, 'fore nothing of a challenger to the *All-Powerful* would ever— *or ever*—be suffered to stay. Yes and indeed, God and the Devil destroyed every last bit, because when the Devil or God smote something—they made sure it stayed smit!

And, just like that—mercurial and inscrutable—the clouds grew silent and departed. And, besides the scorched earth and the deaths—the scene pretty much closed as it started. Yes, a spell had been cast—and wrath had laid waste—and verily, verily, the only thing left to describe is the bittersweet ending with the baby and Rafe!

15

Rafe stayed surprisingly composed, given he'd just witnessed six deaths—with his heart beating heartily—within his own chest. And, from a distance, he could hear Robin's babe brother crying out desperate cries, which made him feel sadness and anger that he just couldn't abide. So, with sympathy and a plan, he returned to the place of the smiting and the dead, and laid his four remaining fingers—and new wand of magic—on the poor infant's head. Yes, the lightning had missed the infant directly, but still struck him in tertiary, and one of his sides was crisped tight because he had been burned most unmercifully!

R.: "Look at this young one, so hurt, and now baptized in soot! Yes, I suppose we're all to be grateful—*and grateful*—that he wasn't completely—*Divinely*—pulverized underfoot! Instead, they just left him abandoned, without a whit of protection, and this distressing tableau only hastens my righteous religious defection! Even now, I walk among the infinitesimal motes of Erichtho and the rest—yes true, and, true yes, I can see by the dust on my shoes—*by them—always by them*—how humanity is *so thoroughly blessed*! Truly, what immortal, all-knowing, and all-powerful beings—would act as they act, and commit the acts that I've seen? They claim to give choice, and then punish and tempt us! Surely, this foul equation is their attempt to upend us! Yes, they hide in the sky and down in the earth—but then jerk on our soul-strings till our deaths from our births! So, **No-I say-No**! And pledge myself to this boy; because, *they* are the Divine children who treat *us* like we're toys!"

Finally, Rafe waved his wand, and said a few words of healing; and the small boy-child recovered and stopped his terrorized squealing. He then gathered him gently within his own human arms, and vowed to shield and defend him from any oncoming harm. Afterwards they left, connected and convalescing together; no, the two may not have been blood—but from now on, they'd exist as brothers forever! Yes, one gripped the older as one sheltered the younger— and the bond that they'd share—would satiate all human hunger! The hunger of significance, for greater-than, for purpose and meaning—'fore these are the traits that always need bolstering and never need weaning! Thus, the two moved away driven by their own living properties—which is so much more productive than impotently surrendering to enforced spiritual monopolies!

Yes, the two would live on and live on—to make their own *human choices*—and each would speak individually, but also join forces! Yes, they had been bound by experience, as well as linked by condition—and would rely upon each other—and not think about God or perdition! Then, the boy-child and man traveled far and finally crested a hill—where the soft-supple light of first morning enveloped them—and the light truly does—envelop them still!

EPILOGUE

And so this gracefully concludes 'An Act of Clowns, Magic, Mischief, and Tragedy'—the tale of a fool who became not-a-fool—by embracing ***UNTARNISHED VISION*** and ***PRISTINE HUMAN MAJESTY! TA-DA!***

End of Story #6

Intermezzo

(sixth)

So after the rhyming story—the one with the wizards and a selection of profanities which made even the writer a little uncomfortable—the author watches the Devil—*the actual Devil*—and Mizam, an Angel—*an actual Angel*—finish reading his words. And, strangely, he is kind of surprised to feel nothing out of the ordinary about the current situation. Yes, it all seemed perfectly normal—that people would talk to, and hear back from, the forces of light and darkness as a means to cope with the multiple vagaries and varieties of human existence. The writer understands this better than ever before. In fact, it reminds him of having two imaginary friends whispering opposite things inward to him from his shoulders.

As for the writer's internal thinking—he is still swimming in rhymes—but he has to move on—because he no longer has time!

'*No, no, no...*' the writer tells himself, and thinks about commanding his Devil's Spot to cease and desist. But he reconsiders the inclination 'to command.' Yes, his Devil's Spot was part of him now, so he gently asks— *It?*—*Himself?*—to please tamp down a bit—at least in terms of the rhyming. Gratefully, the throbbing-rhyming subsides and the writer says 'thank you,' though his Devil's Spot doesn't say anything back. '*Yes, you have to make peace with all parts of yourself,*' the writer silently testifies, '*and, yes, everything must be consciously acknowledged, including the unconscious and subconscious elements too.*'

Then, far away from any such supercilious introspection, the two Divinities end their reading, but instead of the Devil, it was Mizam who speaks first.

"Ugh..." says the Angel.

"Is that a good 'ugh' or a bad 'ugh'?" the Devil responds. He shoots the writer a sly smile as he does so.

"I don't think there is such a thing as a good 'ugh.' But, you see... *this* is exactly what I'm talking about," Mizam goes on, shuffling the pages back to the Devil. "As advertised, the story is just blasphemous and utterly obscene. Yes, this is a prime example of artistic license transmuting into nothing but artistic licentiousness! Truly, it lacks any merit! There is no other word to describe it than **'*dirty*'**! Additionally, he's entirely disrespecting *both* Heaven and Hell. You perceive that, right?"

"Well, he's only half done with the collection," the Devil replies. "There are still seven more stories to finish. Maybe he'll cap it off with a rousing endorsement of religion—maybe even Christianity? Who knows? I'll definitely get his soul… but… philosophically and theologically… you might come out top dog when he's done?"

"Anything is possible when you're writing," states the writer.

"It doesn't matter!" Mizam counters. "Listen! He has you bestowing mercy on the damned, me sending retar—*special needs*—children to Hell, and humans defying the Divine—*and getting away with it*! Why don't you have him just write about a child prodigy or some S&M sex book for housewives or a love story where both the boy and girl fall for each other and have cancer? Give him something popular so his stories are… not   not… *so irregular*, why don't you? Real readers want things that are safe! They want stories already dubbed 'a classic,' or one dubbed 'in the tradition of a classic,' or something—*anything*—which will placate or distract them from the inherent misery in their lives! Yes, readers want fictions that are knowable and certain and—above all—ones that are reassuring! So have him write a bestseller which comports to these fundamentals! Surely it would still satisfy your stupid little deal!"

"There is *nothing little* about my deal," says the Devil, defensively, and the writer lets out a small snort in response.

"What?"

"Our deal doesn't work like that. I don't direct him. He traded his soul for a work of significance, but how it comes out depends wholly upon the writer. I get his soul. He and I *are done*. So, why should I care what he writes about me?"

"Because books can be powerful things! What if the wrong people get a hold of this? What if they begin to think you, me, *God*, are just concepts that can be fiddled with like so much malleable clay? I'm telling you, Lucifer, this is dangerous… and more… it isn't in the least deferential to our respective stations!"

"I wouldn't worry about it. He's just riffing off different formats, but remember: those formats are fantasy and *we're really real*. For instance, this last one riffs off some of the old tragi-comedies infused with heavy satire and a little bit of…"

"Dr. Seuss?" Mizam interjects. The writer makes another small snort, but it seemed more perfunctory than genuine.

"In any case," the Devil resumes, "I'm just saying we should wait for the entire portfolio to be concluded before casting judgment. Doesn't that sound appropriate? And maybe even… righteous too?"

"But our whole reason to exist is to judge! Furthermore, he's not being serious!" The Angel of the Lord wags his finger towards the writer. "*He* just wants to take pot shots at religion for his own petty reasons! *He* just wants to be cute and irreverent and literary! Flippancy, I say! Lack of gravitas, I say! Dilettantism and gimmicks! Celestial matters are grave and need to be addressed with respect! These are matters *of Faith*! **This History is Sacred!** And all *your writer* wants to do is play the jester and the clown!"

"Well, I want to hear what *My Writer* has to say about it… and… by the way… don't knock jesters. They're always so cheerful… like balloon salesmen…" the Devil replies.

As for the author, he positively feels like erupting with indignation—but he supposed if his Devil's Spot could tamp down its rhyming, then he could tamp down his own emotions as well. Yes, the Angel had essentially called him 'a hack' and the word 'gimmick' particularly stung.

"Do you think what I'm doing is just a series of gimmicks?" the writer asks. He directs the question straightforwardly to the Devil.

The Devil considers.

"I think there are those who would argue that any piece of writing is just a collection of gimmicks, but I'm not one of them… at least… not reductively… nor would I apply such a description in a negatively connotative way. In fact, the term 'gimmick' supposedly comes from any piece of equipment or apparatus a magician might use to pull off a trick. Some people even assert it is a corrupted anagram of the word 'magic.' But regardless, just like magic—real or contrived—stories attempt to do the same thing…"

"What? Pull rabbits out of hats?" Mizam snipes.

"No. Both acts of magic and acts of storytelling attempt to generate responses in their audiences," the Devil rebuffs. "They both attempt to achieve some kind of thoughtful wonder."

The Devil adds to the writer: "So you might want to think less about the stylistic qualities and more about the emotional reactions of your readers. Yes, consider what impacts you tried to achieve and the ones you still intend to conjure…"

"Well, I can tell you what *impacts* he has already *conjured* in me," the Angel interrupts. "I've read each of his stories and all I see is ridicule, mockery, and apostasy! Frankly, the only story I liked was the first one. The first one, at least, had a clear moral message: don't beat your wife unless justified! I believe any reader can get behind that…"

"The individual criticisms don't matter," the Devil says, but, again, addresses the writer solely. "The only thing which matters is the challenge to your authenticity."

"What do you mean?" the writer asks.

"Mizam isn't questioning your work—the form or execution or even the content—he is questioning your motivations and intentions. Quite directly, he is challenging the very right and primacy of you trying to be a writer. He is questioning your character. He is not only saying your stories aren't worth telling, but he's questioning whether *you* have the right to tell *any story* in the first place. *This* is what I think you should address next," the Devil finishes.

"But how? I'm already putting all I have into these tales. Everything about me is on the line. Are you saying I should write about myself… personally? The real me? The author behind all the narrative voices?"

"I don't know," the Devil says. "Mizam's the one who is essentially calling you 'a hack.' Do you want to let that stand? Writers should always ask if they can do more than minor satires, don't you think?"

"Satires don't have to be minor," the writer replies, automatically.

"Of course not, but I'm saying such a characterization can undercut and leave you bleeding and bare. I'm also saying if you want to counter such a charge, this would be the time."

Now it is the writer's turn to contemplate.

"Well, if I did so, it would mean completely demolishing the fourth wall..." the writer muses, uncertain, but intrigued.

"So what?" the Devil presses. "Aren't you the one who said: 'Try to get away with everything'? If you are going to break something—*break it*! Go ahead and break it into a million pieces and then put it all back together. What else do you think writing is for?"

"I did say that," the writer answers, but more to himself than to anyone else in the room.

He then starts writing again and he writes fast.

"Here," the writer says and tosses a newly finished story to the Angel.

"What is it?" asks Mizam.

"I'm just guessing," answers the Devil. "But I think you're about to read something serious."

And so the reading of something serious begins and the writing proceeds apace.

Mary's Tale: A Memorial

(Story #7)

The worst stories for me are the true ones.

By 'worst,' I mean the stories that hurt just by having heard them—the ones that can terrorize you more deeply and more permanently than any campfire tale told to a child involving the dark, or sharp teeth, or something moist which slithers a slime trail underneath the bed. Yes, in fiction, no matter how graphic or heinous the plot, there is always a bit of salve that comes from it not being real, that it didn't happen, that it was just a yarn somebody came up with to make money, or prove a point, or generate conversation. No, Oedipus never slept with his mother and gouged out his eyes, because Oedipus never existed. Additionally, the rapes and murders and mutilations—not to mention the cannibalism—didn't actually happen in

Titus Andronicus because *Titus Andronicus* is just a play composed by Shakespeare. And, no, Jason Vorhees did not stalk and slay amorous teenagers at Camp Crystal Lake, just like the witch in the candy house never really schemed to roast Hansel and Gretel like two over-stuffed adolescent empanadas. Yes, I will confess: a tale of fiction can be a mercy.

But the true stories—*the true ones*—they cry out in echoes and reverberate across time. There are the big ones: the Masada and the Holocaust, Andersonville and Carthage, Stalin's campaign of starvation and the charcoal shadows of Hiroshima, among so many others and others and others. And then there are the smaller ones: the Salem Witch Trials and the Donner Party, Ed Gein and the Triangle Shirtwaist Fire—also among so many others and others and others. And, in a seemingly unending torrent, there are the ubiquitous horrors: the reliable gossip about a man who beats his dog or wife or children or all three, or the fact first responders rushing to the site of an airplane crash often catch the scent of crisped beef hanging in the air alongside burning jet fuel, or the absolutely credible proposition of a nameless boy who had to throw a sack of kittens into the river because his mother ordered him to. This last group, as well, is among so many others and others and others. Yes, the true stories can be the worst ones, and it is no wonder even historians sometimes find themselves nauseated by so much history.

Then there are the personal stories—which is a little oxymoronic, because all true stories are personal to someone. For me, my true and personal story is about the death of my great-aunt Mary Mazepa. Of course, I never met her. She died when she was only five years old and, though I don't believe in ghosts, she does haunt me. Mary is one of the reasons why I write. This is because she died tragically and horrifically and senselessly... and it's all true... and I want to make sense of it—to give it both context and perspective—even if I have to do so by inserting a tale of truth within a collection of fictions. So I'll tell you what I know about Mary and what I heard about Mary and what I imagined happened, but I don't want to traumatize my readers. Letting the narrative mask slip a little should be trauma enough. Just note: the story that follows is about the terrible, terrible death of a child and what came after and after. If you don't want to read it, I understand, but if you do choose to skip ahead, I'd like to ask a kindness. Please take a moment to look at the next page. I want the page to be in Mary's honor and I want this story to be a choice—a choice *for you* to read or not to read—which is so much more than Mary was given. The page... and the choice... begins after me saying one last thing:

Mary, I'm so sorry this happened... and... sometimes when I think of what happened, I think it actually happened to all of us.

For Mary
Rest in Peace

Mary's tragic story, like everybody's story, began before she was born. And, like all tragic stories, there were moments before the tragedy—moments of peace and surprise, of happiness and mirth, that to personally witness would just be plainly adorable. Mary's story began with a romance kindling in one of the least romantic spaces ever imagined: the Ellis Island quarantine and medical inspection lines. I was told her future father and future mother met there. They didn't know each other and traveled separately, but in the general din and shufflings, with a lot of "hellos" and apologies for knocked shoulders and stepped-on feet, the two realized they spoke the same Old World language—in their case, a Ukrainian dialect. So they talked as people do when enduring a long line. Yes, they talked about their former homes and their voyages and their dreams. They even realized their villages were just a few miles away from each other in the Old Country, though they had never met. Furthermore, I know my great-grandmother made her journey with a modest steamer trunk and I like to think my future great-grandfather helped her with it. The medical inspection lines included a long trek up a rather steep staircase so official doctors could see who was short of breath, or having chest pains, or was otherwise lacking the stamina to become a newly minted American citizen. Yes, I like to think of him helping her while they were both in the blossoms of their youth and literally traversing the fertile land of a New World. This view beats the alternative version of why a young man would talk to a young woman in a long line—though, truthfully, that can be a nice image too. I guess it depends on how it all turns out. So, once upon a time—a strapping young lad helped a fair young lady with her luggage and they fell in love. Let's go with that.

***

What comes next is a bit of a blank spot with some undeniable problems of logic. Yes, so two people ostensibly met and fell in love at Ellis Island, but how do they stay together afterwards? This question deserves consideration. Indeed, there might have been a small percentage of immigrants who came to America without a plan, came with just a poesy in their pocket and a spirit of adventure, but whatever that percentage is, I can't believe one of them would come with a steamer trunk and have no one to meet them, no place to stay, no leads for work or—if they did have plans—would abandon them all to be swept away by a man you just happened to bump into during a medical inspection line. It doesn't make sense, especially for my future great-grandmother. It also doesn't make much sense for my future great-grandfather either… though I suppose it is possible one followed the other as opportunities presented themselves and because immigrant communities of all types and stripes were sprouting up throughout many parts of the United States. Yes, the horizon of 'The American Dream' drew men and women to all compass points and, however it happened, Mary's mother and father both ended up in a small enclave of similarly appointed dreamers in Eastern Pennsylvania, in a town called Palmerton. In Palmerton, my great-grandfather hitched his star to a job at a zinc company while my great-grandmother pinned her hopes and aspirations to a cigar factory production line. They married, of course. His name was John and hers was Anastasia—but everybody called her 'Nester.' And there is one last thing to say before we take our next leap forward getting ever closer to Mary and her tragic, senseless death. Nester was voted 'best smile' among all the girls in the cigar factory. This makes me think that maybe, just maybe, my great-grandfather didn't have a plan when he came to America. Yes, maybe he actually did just follow a pretty lady with a pretty smile, schlepping her steamer trunk all the way. True and true,

I believe in this world you have to look for joy anywhere you can find it.

***

For John and Nester the house and children came next, but, obviously, the children were vitally more important. There was love—yes—but there was also survival and the broadening of one's financial base and this meant accruing multiple streams of income and resources and labor. Perhaps it was cultural, or perhaps it was because America was churning and clanking through an Industrial Revolution, but one thing was for sure: the engine of an immigrant family *was the family* and my great-grandfather and great-grandmother wasted very little time starting and expanding theirs. A son was born. And then another. And then another. And then another. This made four sons in seven years. Also during this period of robust procreation, John and Nester experienced what I imagined was their first slap of genuine tragedy in the New World. The third son, Peter, was born in 1918 and never saw any other year. The Spanish Flu came and when it left, it took Peter away with it. I say 'I imagined' this was my great-grandparents' first slap of tragedy because I'm not sure, but not because of any ill-will towards them. It is because I believe to lose a child is never normal, but during that era it was a shockingly common occurrence, especially when viewed from a modern perspective. It also makes me think something awful from my perch here in these so-called 'modern times.' In so much of history you needed to have more than one child, because one terrible day, you might need spares. These were the circumstances of John and Nester's lives. Yes, they had to play the odds. I acknowledge the reality is hard to fathom.

***

Regarding John and Nester's house—it is only necessary to get a sense of the space where the gruesome events eventually played out. The main thing to know is that the views from the living room and kitchen directly presented themselves to Mary's dying place in the back yard. The residence was smallish, but better than clapboard, and had been constructed right off the street among many other similarly constructed homes. The street was aptly and ironically named 'Hazard Road.' In front, nothing existed that could even remotely be called 'a lawn'; however, all the houses had gardens and plots of grass behind them which were separated by half fences—to keep chickens and children from wandering across property lines. Yes, backyard chickens in those days. More importantly, the fences must have given my great-grandfather and great-grandmother and all the other immigrants the feeling that they *actually owned* the land. Finally, that family from long ago—*my family*—had a neighbor who will appear in Mary's dying last act. It was a woman who said exactly two things to my great-grandmother as she watched her daughter struggle and fail to cling to life. The first thing the neighbor woman said was so stupid, it is absolutely believable. And, the second thing she said was so monstrous, it is also absolutely believable. My great-grandmother would never talk to that neighbor woman for the rest of her life. I'm glad about that. I only wish I knew the neighbor woman's name, so I could choose *not to include* it in this story. My great-grandmother never forgave her and I guess I don't forgive her either. Yes, let her only be represented by her stupid and monstrous words and nothing else. Indeed, fools are unto every generation born.

***

Mary finally made her appearance on April 23, 1922. It was John and Nester's first daughter and my great-aunt. She was a healthy child and, like the four boys who had come before her, she arrived via home birth. John wasn't particularly religious, but Nester was, so she had Mary baptized into the Greek Orthodox Catholic faith, just like her previous children. Baptism is the first of the three major Catholic Sacraments, with the other two being First Holy Communion and Confirmation. I tell you this because the Sacraments indirectly play a role in Mary's death. Just how much of a role it plays, however, I leave for you to judge.

***

So time went on and no doubt the house on Hazard Road continued to evolve into an increasingly active one. John and Nester, their three surviving sons, and Mary, too, were joined by another girl-child, named Anna, born in 1925. And everybody worked. Yes, chores and jobs were a shifting but constant feature for John and Nester, as well as for the children, and Mary was granted no exception. Consequently, there were sweat and tears—dirt and tantrums. I have this picture in my head of my great-aunt, at just five years old, putting her little hands over her bright brown eyes and sticking her tongue out at one of her brothers for being reprimanded or ordered to do something she thought was unfair. In my mind, I hear her brother call her "Baby Snake!" and then Mary running off to tell on him to her father. Members of my living family still yell out "Baby Snake!" when we stick our tongues out at each other in a joking way. I think the image is cute and it always makes me smile. Yes, joy—anywhere you can find it. Oh, and for any readers who might have a literary bent, "Baby Snake!" is just "Baby Snake!" I'm not using the phrase for some grand allusion or as a representative nod to something else. Yes, I might have written about a character who deals with the Devil, but neither of those characters have anything to do with this. My own Eden remains untouched.

***

The white dress is next for Mary, which I've been told my great-grandfather *did not* want to buy. After all, money was tight and he was the head of a working-poor household. However, there is a period when every poor child doesn't know they're from a poor family and then, suddenly, there comes a moment when they do. For Mary, this must have been around her fifth birthday. This was because what she wished for most was a dress—a proper dress, a pretty dress—a dress befitting a spirited little girl, and one she could wear to church, which, for her, was St. Vladimir's Greek Catholic—again in Palmerton, Pennsylvania. Look it up. It has a website now. Yes, Mary loved church. It was probably the big spaces and ornamentation—the shiny gilding and stained glass windows—and, of course, all the other neighborhood children playing and singing and praying together. She wanted to look nice for those occasions and Nester probably wanted her to look nice for them too. So she got her dress—white and crinoline, with ruffles and cathedral lace—but the purchase came with a few conditions. First, Mary could only wear the dress to church and at home after church, but once the dress came off—*it stayed off*. This requirement stemmed from the second condition: Mary had to clean and care for her dress. Third, and perhaps most important, the dress would have to last until her First Holy Communion and Confirmation upon her turning seven years old. The dress was even bought big so Nester could take it in and let it out according to Mary's growing. Tragically, as you already know, the dress would never be let out because neither the dress nor Mary would make it to the age of seven. In fact, Mary would only own the dress for a little over three months. I truly hope those months were good ones—filled with a lot of laughter and lightness and smiles.

***

Then a little over three months passed and the terrible day finally arrived—Saturday, August 20, 1927. I'm told Greek Orthodox Catholics adhered to fasting from Wednesday to Friday and, after, would break the fast on Saturdays at their preferred church. This could have been the reason Mary was in her dress that Saturday or it could have been some other event. I don't know. I also don't know if she went with her mother or brothers, but I have been told that John wasn't around. Perhaps he was working or sharing a lovely summer afternoon with his friends and some cold beer. Regardless of these specifics, one thing is unassailably certain: Mary wore her pretty white dress for the last time.

So Mary went to St. Vladimir's church in Palmerton, Pennsylvania, and came home, but even though it was Saturday, and even though she was in her pretty white dress, there were still chores to do. For Mary, one of hers included collecting and burning the family rubbish in the fire barrel located in the backyard. So that's what Mary did. She collected butcher paper and flyers and old newspapers and whatever else was lying around and took it out back. And then she lit a match and the rubbish began to burn. And then a breeze or just the convection of the heat stirred an ember. Then, while the papers burned, Mary was burning too.

***

I'll spare you the details of what happens to a person on fire, especially if the person is a child. Nothing gratuitous needs to be said about skin or eyes or hair or lungs. The only thing I do want to mention is that when someone is on fire, usually their immediate instinct is to run. Yes, they want to run from the fire despite the fact that *they are the fire.* 'Stop, Drop, and Roll' wasn't around in 1927. So Mary tried to run away from the fire's source—her burning self. She did not succeed.

***

Nester was inside the house at the time and heard screaming and when she looked up she became witness to a flying flame. It must have taken an instant for her to process and realize what she was seeing, but once she did, she barreled out the back door and then, for another instant, froze. This is where the neighbor lady comes in. "Missus, your daughter's on fire," the neighbor lady said. Nester ran to Mary and tackled her to the ground. And she beat and beat at the burning white dress—at her burning little daughter. Nester, herself, also caught fire, but just on her sleeves and arms. She would carry physical scars—along with all the other kinds—for the rest of her life.

***

So after what must have felt like an eternity, with no doubt the taste of ash and seared crinoline and the sour metallic tang of adrenaline in Nester's mouth, she put out the flames on Mary and extinguished the ones flickering on herself. This is when the neighbor woman said her monstrous last line: "Well, it looks like the Mazepas will have roast meat tonight!" What would compel a person to say such a thing, I leave to the psychologists or philosophers to answer. Maybe, like Mary, she was in shock too. I suppose it doesn't matter. Nester gathered up what remained of her daughter and took her to the Palmerton Hospital where she was pronounced 'Deceased' at 8pm according to her death certificate. The certificate also noted 'No Conflagration,' which meant Mary hadn't died in a residential house fire. No, Mary had just burned to death by a stray ember after attending a church function in what was to be her First Holy Communion and Confirmation dress.

***

The funeral service took place two days later on Monday, August 22, 1927 and she was buried in the Catholic cemetery associated with St. Vladimir's. Surely there were unstoppable sobs and unimaginable grief as well as confusion, loss, anger, bewilderment, and the endless litany of questions that comes in the aftermath of such a senseless tragedy. And, I'll make one more statement without any attempt at being clever. Those questions must have burned and they still do.

***

In the years and decades that followed, Nester was comforted by her religion and often stated: "Mary is with the Angels." For her other family members and their lineage, I'm sure they had their own thoughts, but Mary's death did become a sort of cautionary tale about the dangers of children playing with fire—even though there is no evidence Mary was, in fact, 'playing' with anything. Still, the cautionary tale—as any tale does—helps make sense of things rather than facing the random, chaotic, asinine horror of the entire event. My grandfather, John and Nester's first-born child and my namesake, Stephen, told his daughter, Jenny, about Mary. And to be clear, Jenny was my mother and she passed Mary's story along to me. I never forgot about it, but I never really thought about it either... until now. Now, in the midst of my little compendium of ecclesiastical thought experiments, I wonder what words of comfort were said at Mary's church service.

What I found out is such: if you do research on how clergy and the religiously faithful respond to a senseless tragedy, the first thing you will hear is that we are living in a fallen world—that our sinful human nature opens us up to all manner of privation and torment because—through our own pride—we lost Paradise. I translate this as 'so it's our fault bad things happen.' Then you will hear, don't worry, God is still in control of everything and God is nearest to us when we are broken. And, for me, this means 'tragedy reminds us to be penitent and to have faith and that's why a five-year-old burned to death in her church dress in her backyard.' Lastly, you will hear God needed another Angel, Mary had been called Home, and a glorious reunion awaits so wipe away your bitter tears and seek absolution for all your bitterness. And I take this as, 'so Mary's dying never really mattered anyway because this world means nothing except to exist as a testing and tempting ground to determine one's place in whatever world comes next.' Of course, all these propositions would be backed up by Bible verses, rhetorical frippery, and—undoubtedly—genuine compassion and empathy to dilute the utter inanity of what happened. I struggle with the efficacy and contradictions here, but if it helped Nester find some solace I'm glad she was able to find any solace at all.

***

I want to close this irregular shift to a historical reality amidst a collection of 'frivolous fictions' by highlighting one final admission. If you are feeling this story exploits the death of a child, it is because it absolutely does, and I hate that it does. However, there is no way to tell the story without it being exploitative—or at least—no way I could think of. Mary's death is the reason for the story, but I can tell you if I could trade these words for the little girl in her pretty white dress, I would. Yes, I can live in a world where a child burns to death for no discernable reason because I have to. But, no, I will not live in a world where a child burning to death is considered 'an Act of God' or part of 'God's Plan.' And I won't live in a world where this story can't be shared… even if I have to bookend it between a selection of satirical fabrications and narrative constructs. Subsequently, I lay down some of my motivations bare.

So, once upon a time, I had a great-aunt named Mary Mazepa who died the way I wrote she died and this is my attempt to honor her. At the very least, now she has more documentation of her life than a death certificate. It is all that I can give to her except for my eternal sympathies and… what I feel are… my toothless regrets. Mary, Rest in Peace.

Now back to the fictions.

End of Story #7

Intermezzo

(seventh)

Once again silence occupies the air between the Devil, the Angel, and the writer. The Devil and Angel were finishing their reading, but the writer was working through some complicated emotions about his most recent words—yes—about what he had just written, and expressed, and now shared with strangers. He continues to pick slowly and deliberately at the keyboard to complete his next story—#8—but distraction weighs heavily on him. Even his Devil's Spot seemed to be muted and subdued. The writer knows moving on is his only choice, but he hadn't expected to write about Mary or to memorialize her death. She was supposed to be private, but her tale just flew out of him. It almost felt biological and—in truth—he did feel a little soiled by it. He wonders if other writers ever felt the same way when their living lives intersected with their fictions.

Then, the Devil and Mizam get to the end, but this time the silence does not break. If the earlier silence had built like a pregnancy, this one is a stillbirth. It permeates like mercury fog—oppressively thick and hinting of poison. The writer believes it is the intrusion of a historical and objective reality into his devilish deal which has upset the equilibrium. Nevertheless, as it is said on Earth, as it is in Heaven—as it is said anywhere—silence cannot reign forever.

"Did all that really happen?" the Devil begins, surely not in timidity, but with an understated tone which denoted a new seriousness.

"As far as I know," the writer replies. "I have some documentation, if that's what you're asking…"

"The death certificate…" the Devil mumbles.

"Yes. Well, a copy—though I have some other items," the writer goes on.

A piece of paper suddenly and miraculously appears in the Devil's hands. The writer knows what it is without looking at it.

"But you can't know for sure about the dress… or what the neighbor woman said…" Mizam adds. "That's just heresy…" he says, but the word is a mistake. "I meant to say, 'that's just *hearsay*'… sorry… still, it could be inaccurate…"

"It's more possible and plausible and has more evidence than the Great Flood, or Jesus raising the dead, or talking animals, or so many of the tales in your supposedly…"

the writer replies defensively, but then trails off, because he didn't mean to be so combative. "I'm sorry. I shouldn't have jumped so quick to making a comparison. I'm just a little sensitive, I think," he amends.

"And I wasn't trying to imply that anything in your honorific tale was false," the Angel backtracks. "I guess I'm a little sensitive too. Usually, when someone is looking for an explanation regarding senseless tragedies, I just lay blame on the Devil. No offense."

Mizam directs this last bit towards Lucifer who answers back, "Offense usually taken, but not this time."

Another wave of silence spreads through the room. It is even deeper and more hushed—the stillness of a library and mausoleum combined.

"Well, I don't like this story, but not for the reasons I didn't like some of the others," the Devil continues.

"I don't like it either," the Angel contributes.

"Then we are all agreed," the writer answers. "I also don't like it... but *I am* glad I wrote it," he states definitively.

"I can get behind that."

"So can I."

Now a third noiseless and solemn pause pervades.

"Where are you going to go from here?" the Devil asks, breaking the cessation after a time.

"I'm going back to my script. There are six more stories to write," the writer says. "I want this new one to have surprise and juxtaposition and continue connecting story elements from before 'Mary's Tale.' I don't think she'd be offended. Besides, I believe the idea is a good one. It's about love and reincarnation."

"Oh," Mizam responds a little worriedly. "But that's going to be a problem…"

"Why?" asks the writer.

"Because reincarnation doesn't exist," the Angel says.

"It doesn't matter. Just let him write what he wants," the Devil ends.

The Angel says nothing else and the writer is glad the conversation is over. Subsequently, he simply prints out his next story. In fact, he makes two copies so the Devil and Angel didn't have to strain themselves by sharing.

The writer thinks Mary would have liked this little act of courtesy and kindness.

Reincarnation Theater

(Story #8)

DAY 1

1

Celeste Talon inhaled her last living breath, but didn't live long enough to exhale it. She wasn't there anymore to expel air from her lungs. Instead, Celeste Talon died and entered into the vast nothingness of an unfathomable void—an impenetrable inky blackness and a bone-white blankness—which both swaddled her and smothered her at the same time. Impossibly, she could sense the immensity of the thing as she traveled through it. The void was huge, yawning, cavernous, but she could also intuitively tell it folded back on itself—to the point where nothingness became something again, where meanings inverted, antipodes reversed—and, in doing so, opposites brushed against one another to trade in the bizarre menagerie of what existed and what existed no longer. In this way, life became death and death became life once more. Then there was a flash, a feeling of fantastic movement, and, quite suddenly, she was somewhere else.

The somewhere else was standing in front of a full-length mirror in what appeared to be a rather plain and plainly appointed dressing room. She was nude and reborn—reborn as naked as the first day she was born—but this didn't surprise her. Nor was she surprised she had lost roughly sixty years of bodily living and now looked to be around a twenty-year-old version of herself. Even the scar from an appendectomy in her thirties had vanished, which seemed logical because the surgery never happened—at least here, in this world after the world. No, in truth the only circumstance she was vaguely surprised at was *not feeling* surprised by anything. Yes, she knew she was dead, but it all seemed perfectly natural and normal, and she wasn't scared or upset in the slightest. Curious, perhaps, but nothing more.

As if to reassure her, a small placard affixed on the wall to her right stated: 'Everything is fine!' and next to the placard was a coat hook supporting a white tracksuit on two hangers—the kind of clothes athletes wear at the Olympics to warm up. Below the suit, on the floor, were shoes—a pair of running shoes, a pair of ladies' loafers, and a set of flip-flops—again, all in white. Celeste took down the clothes and put them on—unsurprised they fit perfectly—and then selected the running shoes, not necessarily because she was going to run, but because they presented themselves first. Behind the now empty hangers another placard read: 'Please dispose of unselected items, appropriately.' A pedal flip trash bin sat in the corner, so she picked up the leftover shoes, depressed the lever, and dropped them in. They made no noise hitting the can's bottom because the can had no bottom. She looked down and saw only endless darkness. "Wherever those shoes went," she murmured sleepily, "they're not coming back."

She moved to the dressing room door, set with a standard brass latch, and Celeste clicked it open. A corridor came next lined with stately columns and marble walls. Another placard, this time on a free-standing post, announced 'This way' with an arrow indicating direction, so Celeste followed it. The corridor was high-ceilinged, but her feet didn't make any sounds as she began to walk. Celeste remained unperturbed.

Thus she walked for a while and was serene. Yes, she walked and the corridor seemed to accommodate her by extending its length to whatever distance she desired. Celeste wondered if it would go on forever if she just kept walking—a walk that was a beginning without end—like a permanent meandering or an eternal amble composed and manufactured just for her. And she was pretty sure the corridor would—that time and space were different here, that time was paused like a caesura and space could stretch like taffy. It was peaceful, and she liked it, and she knew she could stay as long as she wanted—just going at a slow pace past endless silent columns. It seemed like a gift, and she felt the freedom and comfort that all the choices were infinitely hers.

But, no, Celeste eventually decided. No, she couldn't just go on in suspense and suspended animation like a butterfly encased in amber. No, she couldn't just walk forever in an in-between place, in a medium place, in a safe place, however appealing that may be. She had things to attend to, and Celeste also knew beginnings have no significance without endings and—perhaps more significantly—the Universe has a way of moving events along, the way a book has mechanisms to propel a reader forward.

As if the corridor, itself, sensed this, Celeste came upon a final placard with an arrow indicating she should go down. A corresponding staircase descended and played out into a plaza where a young man, also dressed in white, waited for her. She traveled to him without haste.

"Celeste Talon?" the man asked when she reached him. He asked it with a crooked little smile which Celeste warmed to immediately.

"Yes," she answered, tentatively, but without fear.

"My name is Thanaxagoras. Now, before we go even one step further, I have a very important question to ask you..." The man's crooked little smile smoothed out to convey a grave seriousness.

Celeste, despite her calm, felt a tiny tremble of apprehension as she breathlessly waited for the question to come.

"Do you like milkshakes?" Thanaxagoras asked.

Then the crooked little smile returned, and Celeste instantly smiled back. She was already feeling his silly little smile was going to play a significant role in her life after death. In fact, for the first time ever, she thought she may have just met someone who was going to have an impact on her eternity.

2

"Of course I like milkshakes!" Celeste replied with a laugh. "Who doesn't like a milkshake?"

"Well… the lactose intolerant… or one of those lunatics who thinks milk is a form of animal exploitation," Thanaxagoras said, still smiling.

"I'm neither of those kinds of people," she answered.

"I'm getting that," he said. "Let's go."

They set off together, but Celeste was wrong about the staircase leading to an extended plaza. It just led to a very large room like a hotel lobby, except there was no front desk or furniture of any kind. The floor was still marble, but the back side of the room ended in three sets of revolving doors—brass and glass—from which to take leave.

"I think you're really going to like this," Thanaxagoras commented, pushing through one of the doors, with Celeste following.

This time they really did enter into a plaza, though the word 'plaza' fell gargantuanly short in capturing the view. Celeste looked north and saw a series of open-air markets, arcades, piazzas, galerias, and esplanades, and when she scanned south she saw the mirrored same without discernible end. She saw shops and game stalls—carnival barkers and artisanal demonstrations—outdoor cafes and street performers. She saw green spaces and idyllic parks, fashion runways and funny jugglers, urban street murals and gilded fountains. Yes, there existed places of quietude and raucousness. And, yes, there existed spaces for serious passionate intensity and frivolous lighthearted waste-of-times. Indeed, from horizon to horizon all manner of venues and activities were represented. And there were people too—all looking as young and vital as Celeste—who were walking singularly or in groups as they laughed and conversed and pointed things out to each other and inquired upon vendors of every stripe and type. It was an eternal bazaar containing everything from flea markets to high tea garden parties kaleidoscopically dotting the visual landscape.

Celeste tried to take it all in.

She failed.

"Wait... is that a roller coaster over there?" Celeste asked, pointing to an amusement pavilion beyond a row of glass-blowing kiosks and a bouncy house the size of a Newport mansion.

"Oh, yes," Thanaxagoras answered, adding, "we have just about a little bit of everything here. One of my favorite spots is a perpetual heavy metal concert performed inside an old-fashioned band shell. The neat thing is, it resides between a Zen meditation garden and a poetry stage where all the poems are done exclusively in sign language—yet the sounds never travel outside the shell. Cool, huh? Ah, this is our stop. What flavor would you like?"

The milkshake shop was called 'Shake It Off!' and Celeste ordered mint while Thanaxagoras ordered peanut-butter banana. They sat down at a street-side table framed by two silver chairs. The table didn't have an umbrella, but the sunlight wasn't blazing and the temperature felt of an unchanging springtime.

"Mint…? Eww… blech!" Thanaxagoras said, and stuck out his tongue like a little boy, making a joke.

"Well, I never saw someone drink a peanut-butter banana milkshake—*ever*," Celeste countered, but also smiled.

"That's your loss. We didn't have peanuts or bananas when I was alive. It was a travesty," he continued.

"When was that?" she asked.

"Oh, I've been dead for… let's see… around 4,000 years, now. Trading was more circumspect in those days. There were a lot of olives and goat meat—so much goat meat…" he replied. "Frankly, the first time I had peanut-butter banana was a revelation. You should try it."

"You should try a mint."

They sat in silence for a few moments sipping on their milkshakes through the oversized metal straws that are the hallmark of a good milkshake shop. They were also stealing occasional glances at each other without really consciously knowing they were doing it. Finally, they got down to business.

"Let's get down to business," Thanaxagoras declared, "but first… how are you doing? The transition from life to the afterlife can be difficult for some people."

Celeste didn't struggle to answer.

"I feel fine. Calm, actually. I think I had one moment of... I don't know... residual passion, I guess... when I got to the bottom of the staircase, but otherwise everything seems okay. This place should seem awesome or weird—or awesomely weird—but it doesn't. I *mean it is wondrous*, but it's not unbelievable to me. *I mean...* it doesn't feel impossible. I'm trying to describe it... it's like I feel that everything is as it should be... if my words make any sense. I feel utterly and completely... safe."

Thanaxagoras took another sip of his shake.

"'Residual passion'? I like that. But otherwise, good. That's good," he said. "Part of the structure of this place is to help our visitors manage their emotions. You can still feel everything in every way, of course, but the volume is just tamped down a little. Some of the eggheads over on the University Concourse call it 'ethereal objectivity,' but I think it's just a fancy way of saying this place helps you not to 'lose your shit,' when you die. Excuse my language, if I offend."

"I'm pretty okay with all language," Celeste said, laughing. "In fact, I may even use worse, from time to time."

They both stole another glance and added grins—one, delightfully crooked, and the other composed of a red chrysanthemum's blush.

"But you say I'm a visitor?" Celeste pressed on. "I thought this was Heaven. I mean it kind of looks like Heaven and feels like Heaven—but, if this isn't Heaven, then where are we? Are you telling me there is no Heaven?"

Thanaxagoras looked directly at her. Then, with equal parts gravity and compassion, he explained: "Now, that calm you mentioned before, I want you to wrap yourself in it. First, I want you to know that, no, this isn't Heaven, and your stay here will be temporary—for three days and two nights, to be precise. Second, I want you to know there is, in fact, a Heaven and you—eventually—will be going there. Third, and this is the hard thing, so don't let it trip you up: this is actually Hell."

"*Hell?*" Celeste exclaimed.

"Yes, Hell. But, don't worry, this is the nice part," he answered, truthfully and directly.

"Well that's not fair!" she said, automatically.

"No it's not, but I'd like you to set that aside for now. Besides, like I told you, this is the nice part of Hell and, remember, your time here is only temporary," he reinforced.

"How do you expect me to set aside the fact that I'm in Hell? And, by the way, how can Hell—*any part of Hell*—be nice?" Celeste pressed.

"Because, *it was designed* that way…" Thanaxagoras replied. "I'll break it down… but please call me 'Than.' I know names from 4,000 years ago can be a mouthful. Now, let me tell you about the secret history of the Universe, and how all this came to pass…"

3

So Thanaxagoras prepared to tell Celeste Talon the secret history of the Universe while sipping on milkshakes—one peanut-butter banana and one mint—in the afterlife.

"What do you mean—'the secret history of the Universe'? You know it's going to take a lot for me to put a pin in the whole 'you're actually in Hell' thing. Are you talking about 'the Big Bang' and all that stuff? Because I have to say, we had scientists in my time who knew quite a bit. In fact, just to let you know, we moved beyond the flat Earth or believing the world is riding on the back of a turtle," Celeste said, but was more indignant at God for sending her to Hell than intending to be snarky at Thanaxagoras.

"Listen, I know you're mad, but I love the turtle story—and the one about the moon, and the snake, and the lifeless sea. So don't knock turtles. And, by the way, we knew Earth wasn't flat—at least those of us who weren't *complete dildos*. Third, *I was in Heaven*. Yes, I was in Heaven for almost 1,000 years, except we called it 'Elysium' at the time. But then, one day, the new consolidated God showed up and changed everything and suddenly my Heaven was folded into this current version Hell. So if you want to get all prickly, you can at least acknowledge you weren't the first person to have something Divine pee in your Cheerios."

There was plenty Thanaxagoras said for Celeste to unpack, but she couldn't help but focus on two phrases.

"'Dildos'? And, 'pee in your Cheerios'…? How do you even know those expressions?" Celeste pressed on.

"Well, I may be dead, but I still keep up with the times. This place has *excellent Wi-Fi*. After all, this whole realm is but a reflection of the living world, don't you know?" Thanaxagoras answered, still a little defensive.

He hated this part of the debriefing. "So do you want to hear about the secret history of the Universe or do you want to continue being outraged? It's completely understandable."

"All right… okay… sorry. I didn't mean to snap at you. It's just… well… finding out you're in Hell—even the nice part of Hell—kind of sucks," Celeste amended.

"Fair enough," Than agreed.

Celeste found a way to recover her smile and Thanaxagoras returned it. He even reached out to briefly touch her wrist.

"So, tell me about the eternal mysteries of the Cosmos…" she said.

Thanaxagoras took a final swallow of milkshake and the metal straw clinked against the glass as he finished. Then Thanaxagoras launched into his exposition.

"You know… they're not even allowed to tell this story in Heaven," he started, with his usual crooked little grin. "You would think the God of the Universe, the God of Truth, the God of *The Word*—the new consolidated God—wouldn't worry much about appearances, but apparently *He does*. But then again, maybe it shouldn't be surprising. History is always written by the victors."

Celeste listened to her new friend—her new boyfriend?—and then almost laughed out loud at the idea. She died when she was eighty-one and Than was over 4,000 years—old?—dead?—and Celeste couldn't even remember the last time she thought of 'boys' in a romantic sense. Consequently, she just held her tongue and let 'the boy'— *'her boy'*—tell his tale.

"Thus, before all that, in the beginning—*in the very beginning*—there was a formless void... or maybe there wasn't a formless void... but what everybody seems to agree on: there was this structure... this element... this force... called 'The Way.' It was the first thing ever to come into existence, or it had always existed, but regardless, it is THE THING that is a part of EVERYTHING. Yes, 'The Way' came to be known as the fundamental part of all which has existed, exists now, or ever will exist. There are probably 10,000 metaphors I could use, but you've heard of $E=MC^2$, right? You know, from Einstein?" Than asked.

"... Yes..." Celeste replied, but inserted uncertainty in her tone. The conversation had taken a rather abrupt turn towards physics she wasn't prepared for.

"Don't worry about it. This isn't a test and I'm no expert either. It's just a story which relays THE TRUTH while we all wait around for a better story to relay the same information. In any case, $E=MC^2$ just means matter can turn into energy and energy can transform into matter, but the relevant part is: 'The Way' is THE THING that allows that to happen—so 'The Way' stays in all things, in all forms, and in all transitions of those forms, forever and ever and always. Do you follow?"

"Keep going," Celeste said, but was dubious. She was dubious of what she was hearing, but also dubious of her own understanding of what she was hearing. The one detail she wasn't dubious about, though, was how she was starting to feel about Thanaxagoras as his eyes shined and his mouth moved, telling her a story that couldn't be told in Heaven. It was intimate, and she wanted him to go on talking to her—perhaps indefinitely—like an endless stroll past silent columns.

"Well, in the early days—whenever those were, probably even before there was such a thing as 'a day'—'The Way' was uniform and omnipresent. *It just was.* Perhaps it was protoplasm or some kind of foggy mist, but then, I guess, it didn't like all the sameness and uniformity, so it made something different to contrast part of itself against itself. It made *something new*. Do you care to take a guess at what that was?"

Celeste thought about saying 'peanut-butter banana milkshake,' but the response seemed way too cute by half, so she just shook her head in the negative.

"What it made was… an egg," Thanaxagoras went on, making his best attempt at achieving a deadpan reveal.

"An *egg*?" chirped Celeste.

"Yup. The first thing in all of creation… or the second thing, depending on how you look at it… was an egg. Now, it wasn't an egg like a chicken or a goose would lay… at least I don't think so… but that would be kind of cool, don't you think? However, *it was* something containing other things—in this case, three supernatural fraternal triplets. One was Gaea, the original Earth Spirit, the second was Uranus, the original Sky Spirit, and rounding out the trio was Chaos, the original Chaos Spirit. Then immediately after hatching from the egg they began to produce and reproduce. Yes, they produced and reproduced all over the place. They did it by themselves. They did it with each other. They made things and did it with the things they made. They even did it with 'The Way' itself. Indeed, it was a full-on primal and primordial orgy of roiling and boiling origins and origination… and other than 'The Way,' these three ancient engines became the foundations for everything that was or is or ever will be."

"When you say 'did it' and 'orgy,' do you mean having sex?" Celeste probed, but wasn't trying to be bawdy.

"Yes and no. Certainly they invented sex and all the versions of it, but they were protean, generative—varied and visionary. Imagine they were the first alphabet from which every language would develop and everything to get written in all those languages," Thanaxagoras expanded.

"Wait," Celeste interrupted again, "so three supernatural beings created everything that existed, exists now, or eventually will exist?"

"It was a ridiculously enormous amount of sex," Than answered, and flashed his crooked little smile once more.

Celeste blushed, and laughed.

"So what happened next?" she asked.

"What always happens… the three forces created, and then their creations tried to supplant their Creators," Thanaxagoras said while maintaining that wry grin of his. "And the creations succeeded. It goes without saying, but should be mentioned anyway: one of the first things the ancient trio of Gods created was death. Yes—even with Gods—everything seems sown with the seeds of its own destruction."

4

"Do you like corndogs?" Thanaxagoras asked. "There's a great corndog place a little farther up."

Celeste barely heard the question. She was too busy imagining three incredible forces copulating and fornicating and masturbating—and, yes, even raping, if her memory of Greek and Roman mythology held—to give the nascent Universe a form—any form at all. And she thought of the inky blackness and bone-white blankness of the expanse she just traveled through when she died. It reeked of Chaos and stung like the slap of Uranus and caressed like the breezes of Gaea. She thought of a rotting pumpkin patch for some reason and she inadvertently shivered with an infinitesimal tic. The tic was enough to bring her back to conversation.

"No—yes. Yes, I like corndogs, but, no I don't want one just now. So what happened to Chaos, Uranus, and Gaea?" she pressed.

"Well, they did all right, at the start," Than continued on. "They created all the forms of diverse matter and all the forms of diverse energy and then all the diverse dimensions and, in time, all the stars and worlds and black holes and white holes and life and evolution, as well as permanent and semi-permanent death—you know—the whole ball of wax. Oh sure, there were squabbles along the way, but the three kept a sort of balance between themselves: Gaea, a generative force, Uranus, a hierarchical force—and not to mention a patriarchal one—and Chaos which moved all the other pieces around like someone shaking up flakes in a snow globe, except the snow globe was the early Universe. But then they made their first big mistake…"

"What was that?" Celeste asked.

"They started having children," Thanaxagoras answered.

"Oh," Celeste said.

"You ain't just whistling Dixie. In my neck of the woods, first there were the Titans. Yes, the Titans were born, but they pissed off Uranus almost immediately because all they wanted to do was be as powerful as him. Uranus, meanwhile, as the God of Hierarchy, held it as an article of faith—pardon the pun—he should remain perpetually and forever on top. So there was scheming and wars and betrayals and alliances until they eventually beat him—actually they castrated him with the help of Gaea—but then the Titans had children which you probably know as the ancient Greek and Roman Gods like Zeus and the rest. Again, this is just in my neck of the woods. Then Zeus and his pals wanted to be top dogs, so there was more warring and scheming and betrayals and alliances. That conflict finally ended when those Gods allied themselves with the Cyclopes and a group called the Hekatonkheires which each had fifty heads and a hundred arms, so thus ended the Titans. Hekatonkheires… man… pretty cool, huh? How can something have fifty heads? Talk about talking to yourself! Anyway, then somewhere along the line, someone made a *colossal* mistake."

"Which was?"

"Someone created human beings."

"Wait… What? Why were humans such a mistake?" Celeste probed. She was fascinated, but she was also at the bottom of her milkshake and the metal straw made a little crackling and slurping sound.

"Because before then," Thanaxagoras went on, "the Gods just sparred and battled with each other, but humans—*Humans*—introduced belief systems and this meant a God's power was directly proportional to the number and fervency of the people who believed in them. It also meant humans could make up new Gods using only belief—*using faith*—and so the whole system which was already a messy bloodbath of ever-shifting parts got even more complicated. Yes, I bet good old Chaos was lmao-ing at that turn of events!"

"Lmao-ing?" Celeste questioned.

"Laughing his ass off," Than explained.

"I know what it means; I'm just surprised you knew it."

"*Excellent Wi-Fi*, remember. Are you sure you don't want a corndog? I really could go for a corndog right now?"

"Fine," Celeste answered, "but I want you to keep talking as we go there."

And she really did want Thanaxagoras to keep talking, not just because the subject matter was interesting, but also because she was becoming quite certain she was falling in love with him. She almost laughed her own ass off. No, she had never really, *completely*, fallen in love on Earth, but now—here she was—and all it took for her to find true love was to die. On top of all this, she suddenly realized she really did have a hankering for a corndog. It was nice to know death was not without its hilarious and ironic side, she thought.

5

Celeste and Thanaxagoras got up from the table and began to move, while their empty milkshake glasses were promptly collected by a conscientious attendant who seemed to come out of nowhere. Thanaxagoras offered his arm and Celeste accepted it gladly. Then, they started to walk through a trellised colonnade filled with flowers which was away from the disparate dins and distractions of the more active parts of this realm. She hadn't noticed the walkway before and briefly wondered if it had always been there or if it was newly created just for them. Anything seemed possible in the afterlife, she mused. She also got the sense Thanaxagoras was starting to feel the same way for her as she did towards him. The cradle of his arm had a warm and easy feel about it. In fact, it felt almost scripted.

"So what happened next? I take it Chaos didn't just enjoy a good belly laugh and call it a day?" Celeste asked.

"Not quite," Thanaxagoras answered with his quirky angular grin. "Well, with the invention of Humanity, humans walked the face of the Earth and the Gods walked with them. You see, now Gods had to court and pander to humans and/or just straight-up intimidate or terrify them to keep their powers. So they granted favors and told lies about themselves, and they got people to fight other people, and even to fight other Gods for their own purposes. And, don't forget, everybody was still having sex. Yes, sex all over the place: demi-gods, abominations, fairies, sprites, hybrids, hydras, chimeras—you name it! And, yes, occasionally a God would get fed up and try to exterminate the hairless, little apes but another God would always step in and squirrel some of us away to repopulate. But then—and this is very important—a group of humans got together and decided that maybe… *just maybe*… there shouldn't be all these Gods running around, but rather be just one God—a *True God*—a God *to serve them*—so 3,500 years ago, in some caves near the Dead Sea, that's what they did. And what was to become the new consolidated God—the Judeo-Christian-Islamic God and his legions of Angels—came into existence. Yes, they were born by prayers and by faith—by fervor and by sacrifice, *always sacrifice*. But, again—most importantly—*He* was created *by humans*, but of course *He* would never serve humans, because no respectable God ever would. Do you want to guess what happened then?"

"I would guess the new consolidated God immediately set out to eliminate all the other Gods… the old Gods…" Celeste said, and didn't have to struggle with this response either. Learning a little history seemed to go a long way in life and life after death, she thought. Additionally, something about this place made her feel smarter. She filed a mental note to ask Than about this, too.

"Bingo!" Thanaxagoras exclaimed proudly, and Celeste felt the pressure on her arm increase. "The new God—the *One True God*—drew on human belief and human believers and those believers expanded and expanded until *He* was the only game in town. And, after *He* beat the old Gods—the Pagan Gods—it didn't even matter if Christians fought the Jews or the Jews fought the Muslims or one sect fought any other sect, because it was all *the same God*! What a brilliant stroke! Yes, indeed! Let it be said on low and on high: monotheism was a great start-up!"

Celeste laughed and paused to smell a spray of carnations nestled in a terracotta pot. The flowers smelled fresh and sweet—like morning dew mixed with sugar.

"But of course, afterwards, *He* had to lie about it and rewrite history," Than went on. "Yes, the *One True God*—the *God of Truth*—couldn't say other Gods were created before *Him*, or that *He*, *Himself*, wasn't created by immutable and universal forces, and *He* certainly couldn't say *He* was born instead by the varied oddities of human thought. So *He* made up a better story and got everyone to tell it to each other."

Thanaxagoras halted near the end of the colonnade and Celeste began to catch the scents of fried food among the floral blossoms. Strangely, the blend was not unpleasant.

"Okay, but what does this have to do with Hell... and what does this have to do with me?" Celeste asked.

"Well, the humans created the new consolidated God and new consolidated God created the Angels, because if you're going dominate everything in all of existence, you're going to need an army, but I've told you about the nature of creators and their creations, haven't I? So a selection of *His* Angels, led by Lucifer, rebelled because that's what creations always do. Consequently, a civil war raged in Heaven."

"Yet, the Devil didn't win," Celeste pointed out and jumped forward, realizing something salient. "I thought the pattern of history was a series of creations *supplanting* their creators?"

"That's true—the Devil didn't win—but he *didn't completely lose*, either. Remember there was a whole lot of space in the Universe after the old Gods fell, like parts of the *old Heaven*, created by the *old Gods—my Heaven—* and all the other territory of the old Underworld. So, yes, the Devil was defeated, but it was a *negotiated* defeat. And through the Celestial Treaty, Lucifer got his own kingdom and the New Order was set up. So in terms of the Angelic War, it was an extremely fruitful conflict for both sides," Thanaxagoras said.

"Both sides?" Celeste challenged. "What did God get out of it?"

"An enemy of course!" Thanaxagoras exclaimed. "*He* got an opposite—a bogeyman—someone to threaten Humanity with and a way to drum up even more of the faithful! Yes, those *He* couldn't coax with love, *He* could now threaten by fear. Yes, in some fashion, the division between Heaven and Hell benefited both God and the Devil... maybe God even more."

Celeste fell silent. In fact, she was feeling a little somber, but didn't know why. Thanaxagoras, however, seemed more boyish and enthusiastic than ever.

"I never feared or loved God or the Devil," Celeste stated in a soft voice, but one holding no shame. "Frankly, I never gave either much thought. I don't think I've ever told anyone that before."

Thanaxagoras flashed his crooked little smile before replying.

"I know. That's why you're here. I'll try to fill in more of the blanks, but first let's get those corndogs. It's never good to discuss matters of the soul on an empty stomach. Don't worry, though. Everything will work out."

Celeste nodded because she believed him.

And she believed him because that's what you do with someone you love.

6

"Two, please," Than ordered.

He handed Celeste a corndog by its stick, along with a small cup of sauce. The hotdog place was called 'Three Doggie Night' and the mascot was a nine-foot wiener wearing a cowboy hat and sporting a bushy mustache. He was doing a quick draw with a set of ketchup and mustard squirt bottles, looking jaunty.

"Now, I insist you try it with jalapeño mayonnaise…" Than continued.

"Whatever you say," Celeste replied.

She dipped her corndog into some white sauce swirling with green flakes and crunched down.

"This is amazing!"

"Yup. Fantastic every time…" he answered and got to work on his own corndog. A small dollop of mayonnaise ended up dribbling down his chin and Celeste wiped it off with her thumb.

"Good, but messy," she said and they both mooned at each other between bites.

"So what happened after the war in Heaven?" she asked.

"It was a *civil war*, don't forget. So, with the actual fighting over, God and the Devil had to negotiate a final *and lasting* settlement of hostilities. They didn't do it personally, of course. They used surrogates: God used His remaining Angels and the newly minted Devil used His newly minted Demons to hash out an agreement. Now the most important thing to remember, this new treaty was almost entirely about soul-wrangling—about how human souls were to be divvied up between Heaven and Hell, God and the Devil, for what actions and for what beliefs, under what circumstances, and in which ways to satisfy the new *détente*. Largely sketched, both sides concluded good people who had faith would go to Heaven and bad people who lacked faith, or bad people who had faith but who died having not been absolved of their sins, would go to Hell. Understand me so far?"

"I think so," Celeste responded, "but it all sounds way too broad… or way too specific. God and the Devil came up with a system to categorize and separate—*and judge*—every human being who existed, exists now, or ever will exist through the entirety of time? It doesn't seem possible…"

"Well, they did it. The eggheads—again the eggheads from the University Concourse—call it the 'Divine Algorithm.' God and the Devil came up with the basic system—which was pretty intuitive, actually—and then added codicils and riders and exceptions and exemptions and all sorts of stuff. There was this huge debate about the sin of Sloth and about suicides, and another one dealing with children who died before reaching the age of reason or the souls who were born developmentally—*biologically*—incapable of faith. There were also some real convoluted discussions about dietary restrictions, I could never figure out. I mean—if you're hungry—eat something! It doesn't matter what it is! Finally there were people like you, who also had to be classified, itemized, and assigned," Than went on.

Celeste took another bite of corndog and chewed thoughtfully.

"You make me sound like a product—like just a thing—like I'm some can of soup and two store clerks are arguing to see which shelf I should go on…" Celeste said in a bit of a pout.

"In some ways you are—and I am too. But it would be less like soup and more like a battery. We humans provide the power to the All-Powerful. Sorry to get so 'red pill or blue pill' on you. I told you I would tell you the truth, but I never said you would like it."

"Wow. A *Matrix* reference! That's a little dated, don't you think?" Celeste brightened, teasing, but in a friendly way.

"I'm 4,000 years old! That reference is positively modern!" Than returned.

And they both laughed.

"In any case," Thanaxagoras went on, "yes, for better or worse, we—we poor souls of the disoriented are—are the batteries for the Divine Engines of Heaven and Hell and their respective rulers. We charge them up. We give them vitality and validation. The Truth is: they only want us because of what we give *Them—always Them*. The Devil gets his strength through suffering and God gets his kicks through love. 'This is the terror to knowing what the world is about.'"

Thanaxagoras munched on the end of his own corndog like a rabbit nibbling a carrot.

"That's David Bowie," Celeste observed, before continuing. "But none of this explains how either of those Lengels landed me in Hell."

"'Lengels'? I like that. That's John Updike. But I suppose it is as good a way as any to describe two self-serving supernatural beings," Than said. "To answer your question, however, you are in Hell because you had faith."

"Faith? Just how does faith land me in Hell? I thought faith gets you into Heaven?" Celeste asked with a tinge of genuine opprobrium.

"Oh, it does. *Faith* is the cornerstone of salvation. *Faith, in whatever version, is the key for every lock* and *the pass code for every entry*. It is the Alpha and the Omega; the beginning and the end; the acorn and the oak. *Faith is the core and keel of Heaven.* It is the one sole necessary component ***for every saved soul***," Thanaxagoras explained.

"So what's the problem?" she asked.

"You had faith in the wrong things…"

"I have absolutely no idea what you are talking about…"

"You believed in Humanism and Humanity and in Human Goodness. You extolled Human Evolution and Mortal Love… rather than engaging in the notions of the Devil or God. This was the basis of your faith. So the Devil wanted to keep you because you denied God and

God wanted you because it was the only way to keep you from the Devil. Indeed, 'In an infinite standoff, we are but two cogs: functionaries, servants—treated no better than hogs'!"

"What's that from? I don't know it," Celeste asked.

"It's just something I read recently," Than answered, a little crestfallen Celeste didn't.

"So my faith in Humanity landed me in Hell…" Celeste stated, now crestfallen herself.

"Yup," Thanaxagoras said, flatly. "But before you beat yourself up, let me tell you what comes next and why…"

"Sure, Thanaxagoras," Celeste said, stopping briefly to crouch down on one knee to do her best Princess Leia impression from *Star Wars*: "'You're my only hope.'"

"Now, who's making dated references!" Than replied.

And they both laughed again.

7

"Do you want to walk some more?" Celeste asked. She and Thanaxagoras were both done with their corndogs.

"I've always enjoyed walking," he replied.

"Me too," she said.

So they set off into another quiet and peaceful colonnade, except this time it wasn't filled with flowers. Instead, it was studded with square and oval picture frames swimming and swirling with vibrant colors. Occasionally, one would freeze and compose itself into a masterpiece. *'A Rembrandt, here, a Van Gogh there, art goes round and round, everywhere,'* Celeste thought, but didn't share it.

She was more inclined to hear about her current situation and all the situations to come.

"As I was saying, what are a God and a Devil to do with someone who is no great sinner, and who does have faith, but their faith is in the service of Humanity rather than the service of the Divine?" Than began, rhetorically.

"Okay, I'll bite," Celeste answered, non-rhetorically, "but only because of the corndog."

"Nice… and the jalapeño mayonnaise. Nevertheless, the answer is simple: they recycle you," Than said.

"Recycle me?" Celeste pressed. "I guess I really am just a battery…"

"Yup, everlasting. But you'll get recycled in a specific way—one that assures your salvation…"

"I still don't understand," Celeste returned and she really didn't. A lot of this was going way over her head. Yes, she had never given God or the Devil much credence or attention, but even if she did, she thought, no amount of musing or prayer could ever truly prepare a person for an actual afterlife of any kind. How could she? After all, she had a whole other life to live before continuing on. So Celeste simply tried to be a good person and squeeze whatever joy she could out of trying. It seemed enough and the least hateful path. It also made her feel kind of pissed about the Universe.

"Don't be pissed about the Universe, but rather work to understand it. You lived a pretty exemplary life. You were a good neighbor and treated people with respect and you had faith—that's *essential*—because *faith* is the cornerstone of salvation. Except, you didn't have faith in the new consolidated God, but erroneously believed in Humanity and yourself. Consequently, God didn't want to give up on you. And so, you come to Hell for a little bit—the nice part—and then you are reborn on Earth, but this time things are tilted to guarantee that when you die again—die a next time—you'll get into Heaven."

They walked arm in arm past a Monet which just crystallized in one of the frames. Celeste thought it was one of his *Water Lilies*, but couldn't be sure.

"You already said a lot of that before. But how is God going to guarantee I won't make the same choices and decisions over again? How can He assure I won't end up back here… or… maybe… get sent somewhere even worse?" Celeste asked.

Thanaxagoras didn't answer and Celeste knew he was holding something back.

"Well… tell me! You've told me everything else. Don't you think I can take it?" she nudged.

"Ms. Talon, I don't think there is anything in this world, or any other, you cannot take. You are no shrinking violet and you certainly are not a facile princess in need of my rescue. I hesitate because I don't like to think about it and because I wish it wasn't true," Than admitted.

"Then spill it, Than," she goaded, but it was goading with a smile. Though, for the first time since they met, Thanaxagoras didn't smile back. Rather he surrendered with a sigh and his crooked little grin flat-lined.

"Okay… But I want to state again I have nothing to do with it. *They—always They—*and *Their Treaty* dictates that your path—your afterlife—will follow the example of Jesus

Christ. You will spend three days in Hell and then you will rise again. And, after the three days, *They* will take the faith part of your soul and repackage it in a new body with a new life. And though you will not come back as a Savior, you will come back as someone who will be saved. But the path of Jesus and the three days in Hell aren't the only things *They* have you model after the Messiah. You are also going to experience what He did when you're reborn. This, quite succinctly, is salvation through suffering. This is the mechanism of reincarnation *They* have decided upon..."

Celeste blinked rapidly a few times and her own smile vanished.

"Are you saying I'm going to be *crucified!?!*" Celeste nearly shouted.

"No, no, no—it's nothing like that. See, this is why I didn't want to tell you. Rest assured, you won't be crucified."

Thanaxagoras took a moment to let the emotions pass—for both of them.

"It's just that after you're reborn, God will visit a hardship upon you. I don't know what the hardship will be, and I don't know when it will happen, but this hardship will bring you into God's fold. The suffering you'll experience is designed to soften your heart and turn your face to the Lord. It could be anything: poverty, a medical crisis, the death of a child—an assault. Yes, there's a whole smorgasbord of varying degrees of unpleasantness that's possible, but whatever it will be, it will shift your faith away from the world and cement a faith towards the world that comes after. This is how you will incorporate submission and the love of God into your new life—your next life. Such is *His* mercy and *His* promise to people like you and, as I said, I'm sorry, there is nothing I can do about it…" Than concluded. He refrained from saying 'Amen' or 'Ah, men,' though he was thinking of both.

8

Celeste listened with supreme focus, but when Thanaxagoras finished she shifted her attention to one of the ever-changing paintings along the walkway. They were beautiful—the shapes and the colors, the tones and the forms—and suddenly she became cognizant that each and every one of the paintings which cycled through had originally been composed by a Human mind and put to canvas by a Human hand. *'Yes, even God and his Angels and the Devil and his Demons couldn't create images like these,'* Celeste thought. *'Yes, God and his Angels and the Devil and his Demons were many things, but not one of them was an artist in the traditional sense.'*

"Well, it still doesn't seem right," Celeste said after reflecting on her nature and the nature of art. "But it could be worse, I guess." She worked on reclaiming and refining her calm—her 'ethereal objectivity'—as Than said the eggheads on the University Concourse called it.

"That's a good way to look at it," Than concurred. "Things weren't fair on Earth, so why should anyone expect they'd be fair in the afterlife? In fact, it's been my experience virtually none of the interactions between humans and *any God* were ever equitable. Even my Matron God had her problems."

"Your Matron God?"

"Yes. I was a herald for Mnemosyne, Goddess of Memory, once upon a time. She wasn't the worst, but 'not the worst' is kind of top of the heap as far as Gods go," he continued.

"How can a God of Memory be unfair?" Celeste asked, before working it out herself. "Oh, they can take away happy memories and make you relive bad ones—like some terrible Goddess of PTSD. I guess *that is* an inordinate amount of power for one being to hold over another."

"Bingo again," Thanaxagoras agreed.

Celeste looked off into another painting and Than joined her.

"Ah, Picasso. I love his work," he said, before adding, "Well, that's about the lay of the land. You're in Hell for the next three days and you can spend the time as you like. You can go off and explore… you can meet new people… or old people… or try new things… or try old things… or… if you want… you can, uh… you can spend some more time with me…"

He said this last bit hesitantly, again like a little boy, and Celeste very much liked thinking about him that way: Thanaxagoras, the 4,000-year-old boy who wanted to make time with her.

"I think I would very much like to spend more time with you," she answered. "But I do have one last question…"

"What is it?"

"Are there any clothing shops around here? I mean this tracksuit is lovely, but I'd rather put on something which has a touch more style."

Than smiled his crooked little smile.

"I could do with a change, myself," he said, gladly.

"Then let's go shopping!" they both exclaimed at the same time.

And for a moment, at least, the serious matters of the afterlife receded in favor of two people enjoying each other's company while falling in love.

9

They left the corridor of shifting paintings and very soon—too soon?—came to a clothing shop called 'All That Pizzazz!' Celeste, once more, couldn't shake the nagging, wondering, titillating question if the shop always existed or if it was somehow being created as they traveled along— responding to her and Thanaxagoras's wants and desires. She was going to ask Than about it, but then got distracted by the clothes. The clothing was gorgeous—fine, high end, and everything fit like a glove. Celeste chose a strapless gown which complimented her shoulders and Than picked out a tuxedo complete with tails. The two twirled and showed off to each other like teenagers—which wasn't an unreasonable comparison because in the afterlife they almost had the bodies of teenagers.

"If you're going to dance when you're dead, you might as well dress to the nines," she quipped, and Than laughed.

Then he asked what they should do next and she suggested roller-skating which made Than laugh again. He loved the idea of roller-skating in designer couture, so off they went. Not surprisingly a rink was nearby, complete with a DJ and a huge disco ball, dangling like a mirrored eye from the ceiling. The roller rink was called 'Roundabouts.'

So they skated in luxury and, during a couples-only song, they skated face to face with Celeste skating backward. Thanaxagoras was decent on wheels, but not as skilled as her, so he held on to her hips and they gazed happily at each other. Than asked about her former life and she told him she had been a relatively successful activist and social justice warrior and was in advertising and systems management for a time. When she told Thanaxagoras this, she had to remind herself she wasn't bragging, but rather was reciting the résumé of an entire life. In return, Celeste asked how he got to the underworld, and he told her people who died before the new consolidated God—*'the old dead'*—he called them, had to stay where they were when the new order came about. It was part of the Celestial Treaty.

"So, the Devil decided to make use of most of us—*the old dead*—as guides for people like you, since there was no real point in torturing souls already judged and who played no role in the Heavenly rebellion."

"Did you ever meet him? The Devil, I mean?" Celeste asked.

"A couple of times, actually," Than replied.

"What was he like? Scary?"

"I'm sure he is to a lot of people, but I found him to be like most Gods."

"Not the worst?" she hazarded.

"Pretty much. He even cordoned off all the bad people from my time—the really, really, awful ones—so they wouldn't get in the way of our work here. As I said, it's all designed," Thanaxagoras ended.

They skated for a while longer and next came dinner at an Italian restaurant where Thanaxagoras addressed the *maître d'* by a Latin name. However, the name had so many vowels and consonants Celeste was sure she couldn't repeat it even if she practiced. She commented as much to Than and he said, "Again, names from 4,000 years ago—they ain't easy."

Finally, evening fell as sunshine gave way to moonlight and the day was over. Than suggested a hotel where they could spend the midnight hours in adjoining rooms, but Celeste wasn't having any of it. She didn't know when she decided to sleep with him, but the urge had grown and grown within her like a gathering tide. Than was nervous, but didn't need much convincing.

And so the first day ended with both of them in each other's arms and in ecstasy. Celeste gleaned one last thought before she fell asleep: it had been a very good day to die.

DAY 2

1

The second day arrived with Celeste sleeping like a baby, which was appropriate because just hours ago she had been reborn once again into the afterlife. She slept peacefully and tranquilly, and her only movements came when she sought out a cooler spot on the pillow for her cheek or extended a slender foot from beneath the marvelously silky sheets to get a dose of air. Celeste awoke before Thanaxagoras and decided to cat-paw around the room to the closet. Yes, formalwear might suffice for roller-skating, but she had a feeling the closet was filled with more casual items exactly in her size.

She was right.

After dressing, she continued her cat-pawing right out into the hallway and found a white courtesy phone provided by the hotel. She found it funny how, in the movies, the afterlife is always represented by an over-abundance of white and it was true here as well. Regardless, she ordered room service. Then Celeste snuck noiselessly back into the room and back into the warm bed and watched Thanaxagoras sleep, but wasn't trying to be creepy about it. She was just bowled over by his beauty and by her feelings for him. He even had a crooked smile while sleeping... along with the slight trilling of a baritone snore. She found both excruciatingly adorable.

There was a knock at the door and Than's eyes eased open.

"What's that?" he asked, sleepily.

"I ordered breakfast," Celeste answered, and greeted him with a set of bright white teeth and then a kiss.

Since she was already dressed beneath the covers, she rose, went to the door, welcomed the attendant, and directed him to bring in the breakfast cart.

"I'm sorry. I would tip you," she said to the attendant, "but I don't have any money. In fact, I don't even know if this place uses it."

The attendant just nodded in a friendly way, conveying understanding, and left.

"There is money here, in fact, but only out of the ATMs and at the casino halls. Both are a little boring, though," Than explained, still sleepily. "All the ATMs have the pin number '666,' if you ever need some, and, anyway, it's posted on the machines. The Devil thought it would be humorous. As for the casinos, everybody always wins and then, if someone wants to spend their winnings, all the shopkeepers have to go through this song and dance about giving stuff prices—which they no longer know anything about. The worst is when visitors haggle. Most of the vendors just end up saying, 'Take whatever you want and go.' It's pretty unsatisfying, if I'm being honest. Can you get me a robe from the closet, please?"

Celeste went and fished out a robe which—again—was white and looped with a golden braid. She moved to the breakfast cart and poured coffee for both of them.

"So... this is day two," Thanaxagoras said. "What do you want to do?"

"Well..." Celeste answered, "I was thinking we would have breakfast, get properly attired, and walk and talk some more."

"More walking and talking?" he asked, putting on a faux exasperated tone. "I'd think you'd have had enough of that already. What were you? A big Aaron Sorkin fan?"

"Well, I loved *The West Wing*. It's just a shame he never waded into fantasy genres. I bet he could do wonders with science fiction. But... hmm... we could add an activity between breakfast and getting dressed," she replied, with a wink.

"What about before breakfast too?"

Celeste enthusiastically climbed back into bed. She distantly pondered if the coffee would go cold, but also knew she wouldn't be surprised if it didn't.

2

So after Thanaxagoras and Celeste's morning activities—two of them and another one for good measure—Celeste once again found her arm wrapped around Than's as they set off. This time their path took them along a corridor filled with aquarium tanks and tropical fish. The tanks were stacked one atop each other, stretching up at least thirty feet on either side in a display of beauty, exuberance, and awe. Still, the impact of the view didn't compare to the impact of Celeste's emotional state. Indeed, she never knew how love could grow and grow, and do it so quickly. It felt like destiny or kismet and Celeste felt nearly mortified at invoking such concepts, even if they were just within her own mind.

They walked in silence for a while looking at the fish and at each other, until Thanaxagoras finally said:

"You're really curious about this place, aren't you?"

"Oh, yes," Celeste answered, almost wistfully.

"But you know you won't remember any of it, right?" he asked further.

"I know," she replied. "But because—eventually—you won't remember something, isn't a reason not to learn about it," she replied.

Than stopped walking and Celeste stopped with him.

He looked at her strangely for a few seconds. It took her a moment to realize the look on his face. It was surprise.

"You're surprised!" she exclaimed.

"Yes," he answered. "I'm sorry. It's just been a long time since anything surprised me. I'm trying to process it."

Celeste didn't respond, but felt a thrill that was akin to victory, infused with love.

Another moment passed, or seemed to.

"I never... I never thought a thought like that before. It's... it's..." Than fumbled on.

"Like a peanut-butter banana milkshake?" Celeste needled, but it was needling with affection.

Thanaxagoras laughed.

"Yes, I guess that's an apt way to describe it," he said.

They started up again, but then Than stopped once more.

"So, what do you want to know?" he looked around and asked.

Celeste gazed off to examine one of the stacked aquariums. It contained one of the largest and most beautiful clown fish she had ever seen, nestling quietly within one of the most elegant and sprawling yellow sea anemones she had also ever seen. She thought of Gaea and she thought of Chaos, and—briefly—of Uranus, but Uranus didn't seem to fit this particular scene. It was 'the unity of complementary and opposing forces,' her mind announced, but she didn't know why.

"Well," she began to ask, "is it all real? What I mean is: are the people we see and the places we go real? Or is it some trick or fabrication? I have to wonder: if I'm in a part of Hell, is there deception going on? After all, the Devil really isn't known for being honest…"

Than laughed.

"It's a good question, but rather complicated to answer," he said. "I'll start out by saying, if this is a trick… or deception… or a fabrication… I'm in it as much as you are. This place sure seems real to me."

"Me too. And?" Celeste asked.

"I can tell you most of the people are real. They are the *old dead* and visitors like you and a few other VIPs, but—yes—some are shades. 'Shades' are what we call manifestations which carry out certain functions—say doing a job nobody wants to do—like being a balloon salesman."

"What!?! I love balloon salesmen! Who wouldn't want to be a balloon salesman? They're always so cheerful! Seriously, did you ever meet a grumpy one?"

"Be that as it may, the venues here, however, are absolutely real. They all exist in this place, so if you think they were created just for us—I mean, for you—that's incorrect. The thing is: the roads and passageways and byways are malleable. To be accurate, every form of entertainment, education, distraction, and leisure exists here, but the paths and streets and trails to get to them are made to be as convenient and fast as possible. It wasn't always this way, but it is now."

Currently it was Celeste's turn to process.

"Why did it change?" she asked.

"No one really knows," Than answered. "One day the Devil just appeared and said this place needed it. So He made the roads more functional—*more fungible*—and

He added the ATMs with His funny little pin numbers, and... actually... now that I reflect on it, He created the University Concourse, too. The Devil said something like: 'It shouldn't take people so long to find what they desire to find.' We all went with the changes, of course. It wasn't like we had a choice. But as satisfactory as this place had been, I have to admit, He made it better."

"Not the worst," Celeste commented, distractedly, but Than thought she was in much deeper contemplation.

"Exactly," he replied. "And one more thing. As far as honesty—the Devil is one of the most honest Gods I've ever met. His relationship with humans is pretty straightforward: what you see is what you get."

Celeste said nothing more, and Than let the conversation lull. Celeste seemed to retreat into her own meditations and counsel. However, if she needed some time to think, Than thought, that was okay with him. In fact, whatever Celeste wanted to do was fine—very fine, indeed.

3

Thanaxagoras wanted a bench and felt the road do something—perhaps stretch or perhaps shrink—to find him one. He was still a little unsure about how everything worked with the pathways—their new abilities to twist and turn and shortcut for those who walked out and about upon them. Nevertheless, Than always found a good bench helpful for deep thinking, and if there was anyone who was thinking deep right now, it was Celeste. Unsurprisingly, one appeared just a few feet ahead. They sat down and Than waited for the appropriate moment to pick up the conversation.

"Um... do you want to tell me what's bothering you...? Or maybe you'd like another corndog... or there is this churro place, which I hear great things about, but haven't been to yet. We could do that..." Than fumbled. Like most men, alive or dead, he had no idea how to unlock a woman's secrets.

Celeste remained silent.

She wasn't so much meditating about the intricacies of the afterlife anymore, but rather was mulling over Than—Thanaxagoras—her 4,000-year-old lover—*who was nonetheless new to her*—and how sometime tomorrow she would have to say goodbye to him forever. She was working out her emotions and she almost felt she had it—something she could do, or something she could say, to make it all meaningful, and lasting, and not forgotten. In a fashion, she realized she was about to die again, but this time it would be permanent. Celeste Talon would be no more. Then she mentally kicked herself for such nihilistic and pointless navel-gazing. *'Why am I wasting time thinking about being miserable when I could spend my time actually being happy?'* she thought. *'Because you're in Hell, idiot, and wherever you are, part of being Human is being an idiot,'* she chided herself.

"Nope," she finally responded and smiled to extinguish all the dark and troubling fires within her. "And I'm not hungry, either. But I do want something from you..."

"Well we already *had that* before and after breakfast," Than said, on much surer footing.

"Not *that*, you nympho!" Celeste began.

"You know I knew her… Nymphos… well… Nympho, but she was kind of a maniac," Than interrupted, and they both returned to a cheerful equilibrium.

"Stop it…! And incidentally, what *a really, really, poorly constructed joke*! I can't believe you said something so cheesy—though it shouldn't be surprising Hell is full of puns. But what I want from you is to show me a secret," she went on.

"A secret?" Than questioned.

"Yes. A secret about Hell. Something we can share. Can you show me that?"

Thanaxagoras thought for a moment.

"Oh, I can do that. In fact, I believe I have just the thing. Follow me, my lady…"

Then they left the aquariums so Thanaxagoras could show Celeste a secret about Hell. She hoped it would be a good one, but regardless, she was just grateful to have propelled herself out of existential despondency and into happiness once again. Yes, she vowed never to waste another moment fretting the end of joy, especially if it just started, and… especially… if the something was love.

4

Somehow in the midst of Celeste's brooding, and Thanaxagoras thinking about Celeste's brooding, their arms became unlocked and now hung loosely at their sides. Celeste rose from the bench and gave Than an inviting look. He joined her immediately and she took him by the elbow. *'A modern woman,'* he thought. Given his age, he also found the thought amusing.

They walked out of the aquarium corridor and into a space that didn't seem to have any amenities or activities at all. The area reminded Celeste of some trip she had taken a lifetime ago—more than a lifetime ago—to Europe, where she experienced a sense of wanderlust that could lead a person down a blind alley with nothing really to see and still be satisfied. The side street just consisted of interconnected identical buildings made of sandstone or chalk, each with only one door and two elevated windows on either side. Everything presented as very plain and nondescript—almost inherently forgettable. She thought for a moment and came up with the word 'bland,' but that wasn't right. *'No. This is camouflage,'* she amended in her mind.

"Okay," Thanaxagoras began, "now this isn't necessarily a secret. I mean it's not forbidden—but it is a place very few people know about and virtually no visitors come to at all."

"It just looks like a common backstreet," Celeste replied. "But I guess a secret would be hidden in a place where nothing happens..." she trailed off.

"Yup," Than said and gave her a mischievous smile. "But a door is only a door if you can recognize a doorway is before you," he continued, attempting to be dramatically cryptic and ludicrously profound.

He winked and Celeste laughed.

"Is that your version of trying to 'peanut-butter banana milkshake' me?" she asked.

"Yes, it is. Yes, it truly is," Than said, sniggering back.

He halted, not at one of the doors, but at a space between two of the buildings.

"Wow. I guess the Devil really wanted to keep this place hidden," Celeste remarked.

"You bet He did. I think He found it embarrassing—a little bit for Him, but a lot more for God. But there's one last thing I think you should know before we move on. I'm telling you now, because where I want to take you, we have to pass by something *that is* truly grim and disturbing. This *is* part of Hell, remember. Are you ready?"

Celeste took a moment to consider.

"Well, you told me a story which can't be told in Heaven, and you told me the truth I would suffer my way to salvation..." she said. "So go ahead. I trust you."

Now it was Than's turn for another dramatic pause, but this time the drama wasn't manufactured. Rather, he was genuinely hesitant at describing something *genuinely gruesome*. Nevertheless, he soldiered on:

"Okay..." Than began. "The first thing I want to say is I'm not making excuses. The Devil is the ruler of this realm and *He* decides the punishments, so I don't want you to think I have anything to do with it. Yes, we drank milkshakes and ate corndogs and went roller-skating in fine style and everything else, but the guy behind this door you're going to see was dying and dying over and over and over again while we were doing it. This is the Devil's prerogative because... here... the Devil is *a God too*."

"What do you mean the man behind this door is dying over and over again?" Celeste asked, perplexed.

"It means Hell is repetition. It's an aphorism here. In fact, I thought it was an aphorism everywhere—even Stephen King wrote about it. Yes, in Hell, when you're punished, the terrible things which happen to you happen over and over. It's standard. Actually, some of the Old Gods invented it. Prometheus gets his liver pecked out every night by a bird and dies, and when the sun comes up he is alive again with a fresh liver ready to be pecked out once more. Then there was Loki—a Norse God—who infuriated so many people poison drips into his eyes every day and night, on and on, but his wife—who loves him—keeps trying to catch the falling drops but fails—so all he does is curse at her. I always believed his wife was in a version of Hell too, but for what—who knows? Regardless, when you are dead—and consequently can live forever—you can die and die repeatedly—and die in the most horrible ways. Yes, in the afterlife, some places are truly constructed to be 'the perfection of the hideous.'"

"That's H.P. Lovecraft," Celeste said, barely above a whisper. Unpleasant images were beginning to swirl inside her mind.

"Bingo again," Than applauded.

"I think I understand. So what's behind the door?" Celeste advanced, shaking her head to clear it.

"Well, I have to find it first. The location changes all the time…"

Thanaxagoras began to run his hands over the chalk wall beneath one of the angular windows. He would knock and listen, knock and listen, but he kept talking.

"Behind the door is a man convicted… condemned…

damned... choose your descriptor... of bearing false witness. He helped start a war... a couple of them, actually. They were stupid, unnecessary, wars and thousands upon thousands were killed while he stayed safely away from the combat zone and even figured out how to profit from the chaos and bloodshed. So when he finally died, he was sent to Hell. Now his punishment is to be chained upside down, by his knees, naked, with his head in a zinc bucket. Can you picture this thus far?" Than asked.

"Yes," Celeste said and she really could. Her mind was open. She even imagined the smell of the metal bucket—like cold ozone, gelid and damp, like the smell of an old car battery split open on wet snow. Additionally, her legs pulsed with a sympathetic ache where she imagined the chains would cinch and bite. When Thanaxagoras spoke, his words unfolded a picture in her mind like a terrifying pop-up from something worse than a nightmare.

"I know it's right here," Thanaxagoras said, examining the wall and getting frustrated. "I come here now and then between visitors. You have to knock three times, but in exactly the right spot," he said and kept at it while counting. "So, anyway, with the man naked and hanging, and with his head in a bucket, tiny, but very deep, cuts begin to form all over his body. And these cuts *never* stop bleeding. The blood never runs out. They just bleed and bleed—on and on and on—but because the guy is upside down, the blood can only travel downwards. And because of the bucket, the blood collects... and fills... and gets higher and higher... until..."

Thanaxagoras abruptly stopped talking because he

heard two sounds. The first was a "click-clunk" which meant he had found the passageway. And, second, was a kind of gasp-gurgle of someone falling down. It was Celeste. One hand covered her eyes and the other drooped over her mouth.

"Celeste!" he exclaimed.

But Thanaxagoras could shout from now until the next judgment day and Celeste would never hear him. This was because her mouth and nose and throat and lungs seemed filled with blood—thickly hot and salty fresh. She knew the man hanging upside down, with his head in a zinc bucket, was drowning in his own blood… and would drown, and be drowning, and die drowning over and over again. It may have just been in her imagination, but it was enough to make her choke. Than bent down and hugged her.

"I'm sorry. I'm sorry. I'm so sorry," he said. "I forgot you don't know anything about this…" he stammered.

Celeste heard no words. There was a man drowning in his own blood over and over and over again just a few feet away from her. He would be thrashing. His head would be banging against the bucket. The blood would slop up into his ears like a novice swimmer unaware of the determination and insidiousness of liquid immersion. The blood would splatter on the floor in angry red stars. Yes, he would crack and dislocate his own joints to avoid what was happening. But he couldn't. No, he would die. He would die. He would die. And then it would happen all over again. *'Hell is repetition,'* she quoted from Than as her mind recoiled.

Then she lost consciousness.

Celeste Talon had fainted in Hell.

5

When she woke, it was to shafts of pleasant sunshine and to the frowzy hayseed smell of tangled grass. She also awoke feeling Thanaxagoras gently patting her face. Presumably, he was trying to revive her. But something seemed wrong with Than's hand. It felt oddly boneless and very wet. In fact, now that she was paying more attention, what it actually felt like was a tongue.

Celeste opened her eyes.

It was a tongue.

However, there was no way she could be freaked out by it. This was because the tongue belonged to a goofy and gigantic yellow-hair sheep dog which immediately stopped slobbering on her when she opened her eyes. The dog sat back on all fours grinning and panting and waiting. She assumed he was hoping to be called a 'good boy' for doing a 'good boy' doggie thing.

"I can't believe I passed out," Celeste began. "I feel like such a pussy—pardon my French. I take it you carried me past the dying guy in the bucket? Christ, I'm a cliché, like I'm actually trapped inside a male narrative—a real dippy damsel in distress. Truly, this must be Hell..." she finished.

"Yes, I carried you," Thanaxagoras answered. "And you might be embarrassed, but I'm ashamed. I wasn't even paying attention when I described... when I described what was in the corridor. But as for passing out, I've done it dozens of times over the things I've heard and seen throughout the centuries. So if fainting makes you a pussy, I'm a bigger one. Though, *I am sorry* if I was an insensitive dick..."

Celeste was silent for a moment.

"No, no. It's just me. Sometimes if I get mad at myself, I get snappish..." she went on. "I confess: it's not a desirable trait."

"I don't think there is *any trait* about you that isn't desirable," Than replied, without missing a step.

Celeste laughed and got up on her elbow.

"Good boy," she said and rubbed the sheep dog's furry yellow head. He continued to grin stupidly and Celeste laughed again.

"So is this what you wanted to show me?" she asked. "This is *the big secret*? The Devil has a sheep dog?"

Thanaxagoras extended another dramatic pause.

"Umm... no," he answered. "Look behind you."

Celeste did and laughed for a third time. This was because when she turned she saw nothing short of *an awesome secret* of Hell. In fact, she found it absolutely delightful and any remaining embarrassment melted away to nothing.

6

Yes, if Celeste had been gob-smacked or god-smacked—at viewing the landscape beyond the set of revolving doors after meeting her new 4,000-year-old boyfriend—the panorama she now took in was no less astonishing. It was, however, more charming and more pastoral. In fact, it looked like a replicated landscape right out of a brochure for the Girl Scouts or a page from *Boys' Life* magazine. It was the kind of scene where everyone was happy and the idea that anything terrible could happen would be inconceivable and farcical on its face.

Yes, the place she saw was filled with children—joyous children, running children, boys and girls—smiling. There were thousands and thousands of them. And there were animals too—mostly dogs, but also a few horses and monkeys and goats. She even believed she spied a camel and an elephant among the rolling hills and serene pastures. The children and animals must have occupied several thousand acres of verdant meadows—though distance, here, was hard to judge. There were playgrounds and picnic areas and roaming petting zoos free of barricades or obstructing fences. A monarch butterfly flapped lazily by. It was heavenly and Celeste had to actively remind herself that this, too, was—in reality—a part of Hell. The yellow sheep dog ran off to enthusiastically nuzzle two nearby boys with his ever-slobbering tongue and loving snout. Celeste couldn't help but notice one of the boys had a long and narrow face with pendulous ears and a prominently jutting jaw, while the other boy had a hydrocephalic head the size of an enlarged ostrich egg. She didn't know how, but she immediately put together everything she was seeing.

"Good boy," she repeated.

Thanaxagoras prepared to speak.

"I guess you are wondering what you're looking at, but before I answer, I want to restate: I have nothing to do with it and you should still keep wrapping yourself in that calm—in that ethereal objectivity—before you…"

"Lose my shit?" Celeste interrupted, more curtly than she intended.

"Umm… yes…" Thanaxagoras answered, a little concerned.

"I know exactly what I'm seeing," she said. "I may not know how, but I know for sure these were people incapable of faith. Yes, these are people who had intellectual disabilities. I had faith—but faith in the wrong things… because you told me God declared it so. You said: '*Faith is the cornerstone of salvation. Faith, in whatever version, is the key for every lock and the pass code for every entry. It is the Alpha and the Omega; the beginning and the end; the acorn and the oak. Faith is the core and keel of Heaven. It is the one sole necessary component **for every saved soul**.*' I remember precisely. But some people are incapable of faith because of genetics or a developmental issue or any number of circumstances which can impede the very process—*the very concept*—of faith taking root. And, for the new consolidated God, *they* don't get a free pass. No, they don't get reincarnation like me. And these 'children' aren't children either. Some of them died as old as me, and just like me they were given younger forms—much younger forms—because children are easier to control and… because… the tamped-down emotions—the ethereal objectivity existing beyond the passageway—is ratcheted up to an eleven in here. I can feel it. That's why I'm not totally outraged even though I ought to be. This place is without pain or fear or anxiety and without anything that would cause discomfort of any kind. I also know, somehow, the Devil created this place because these unwanted children reminded the Devil of *Himself*. They were rejected by God, just like God rejected *Him*. The only difference is: they didn't choose to abandon their faith, because they never had any in the first place. Nevertheless, God threw them all in the same boat… into Hell. Indeed, *He* really should be embarrassed. This is a travesty on a supernaturally—*Divinely*—fucked-up scale."

Thanaxagoras didn't say anything until he came up with something to propel the conversation forward.

"So, why do you think the passageway was hidden and why did we have to pass the dying man… before you… before we… were allowed to enter this space?" he asked.

"Camouflage, of course," Celeste answered. "Like all supernatural beings, the Devil has a reputation to protect and God does too. Neither God nor the Devil would ever want to let anybody know God was capable of neglect or the Devil capable of mercy. It would confuse the new system which ended Heaven's civil war…" she finished.

"That's exactly right. Actually, everything you said was right," Thanaxagoras affirmed. "You really have a knack for understanding the afterlife…"

"This place is weird," Celeste said back. She wanted to say some more things—some more *pointed* things—about God, the Universe, and the mentally challenged, but her indignation was being siphoned away in favor of ethereal objectivity.

"Yes," Than said. "Not the way of the living world," and added: "So do you want to take a time-out to play? We don't have any power or agency to change the unchangeable, but we can still share in the fun."

And Celeste did. She did because she loved children—*all children*—and because she recognized playing was the only thing she could do.

7

So Celeste and Thanaxagoras spent a lot of Celeste's second-to-last day cavorting and playing with damned children—cavorting and playing with the children *who were damned*. The two handed out candy and popcorn and participated in games of kickball in the breezy afternoon. And there were rounds of tag and the petting and feeding of animals, including the camel—which Celeste was tickled to discover someone had named 'Humpy.' They even took a nap on plush foam pads covered with soft blankets like they were tykes, themselves, and all tuckered out. Then Celeste had the idea to give out balloons so Thanaxagoras made it happen and he distributed some too, and they both laughed and laughed because it did indeed seem impossible not to be ridiculously cheerful when handing out balloons to eager and fascinated kids. Finally, there were hugs—lots and lots of hugs—and smiles abounded.

Celeste inquired if the animals were shades and Than said that some were, but most weren't—that they were the actual living energy transported to Hell upon mortal death. Animal souls didn't get to go to Heaven either, just like the intellectually stunted, so the Devil had His "'pick of the litter'—so to speak," he said.

"Except for cats," Thanaxagoras continued. "It's a misconception the Devil likes cats. He hates them and is infuriated somehow human rumor associates Him with 'raggedy felines' as He calls them. Dogs—though—dogs He really likes."

Celeste listened fairly passively because it was more

enjoyable just to exist in the moment as a nice human being doing nice human things in the afterlife; however, she also asked why the Devil didn't change the children—the biologically damned—either mentally or physically.

"Well, the answers are connected," Thanaxagoras replied. "Things can be modified or enhanced after death, but there has to be something to work with. If you don't have higher levels of cognition—say the capacity for faith or complex thinking or deduction—then there is nothing to enhance. Connectedly, the Devil doesn't change their physical appearance except their age because, if He did, everyone would go nuts. The kids wouldn't recognize themselves. The good thing, however, is all people do have emotional quotients and the Devil *does modify* those. You won't find a happier place in Hell," he concluded.

One last event punctuated Thanaxagoras and Celeste's time in the eternal playground. As the afternoon shadows began to grow long, one of the boys who had been slobbered on by the yellow sheep dog ran over to Celeste and tugged on her sleeve. She turned and bent down to greet him. His narrow face and big ears didn't take anything away from his shining eyes or the furrowed lines pinching his forehead in excited concentration as he tried to speak.

"You… you… go to Hebben?" the boy stammered and stuttered.

"Yes," Celeste answered. She thought of calling him 'sweetheart,' but didn't want to condescend.

"My mommy… there… in Hebben. Say… 'hi'?… Say 'love mom'… from me?" he continued.

"Of course, sweetheart. I'll tell her," she replied. "I'll also tell her what a handsome boy you've become."

The boy smiled with a mouthful of crooked teeth and ran off.

Celeste did not smile.

Her dishonesty soured any possibility of joy.

She didn't even know the boy's name.

And—after—when she lived another whole life and died again, she wouldn't remember any of this anyway. In fact, now that she knew about the afterlife, and about how 'God's Mercy' worked, it seemed a whole lot less mysterious and far more cruel than she ever imagined.

8

The evening of Day 2, in many ways, mimicked the evening of Day 1. There was a final round of hugs, with the kids, as well as the animals—including Humpy—and then Thanaxagoras and Celeste walked back through the hidden passageway. Celeste felt oddly proud that, this time, she didn't faint. It was awful, but the Devil has to do what the Devil has to do, she reasoned. *'Just like God,'* she opined.

There wasn't much conversation between the two of them as they left, because there was only one thing left to discuss and neither wanted to. So they went to dinner instead—sushi this time—with another *maître d'* and another 4,000-year-old name Celeste couldn't pronounce. The closest they came to pursuing the unspoken central subject was when Celeste said, "I love you," between a sip of sake and a bite of tuna sashimi. She said it as a matter of fact. Thanaxagoras echoed, "I love you, too," with his funny little grin, but the grin didn't hold any humor. Both of them were glad to acknowledge their love, but they stayed thin-lipped through dinner, saying nothing more, because 'more of love' was never going to be a part of their story. No, they thought, the Devil wouldn't have it… and neither would God. Yes, sometime tomorrow they would separate and never see each other again. In fact, not only would they be worlds apart, but Celeste Talon—as she was now—would tomorrow forever cease to be.

DAY 3

1

Celeste and Thanaxagoras made love again that last night—really made love. They made as much love in one physical act as all the love they accrued since Celeste first stepped down into the empty hotel lobby and Thanaxagoras introduced himself by asking if she liked milkshakes. There was something sensuous about it, and passionate, and even elegiac and, when they finished, they both collapsed into a deep sleep so close to death it felt familiar. And, neither of them dreamt because—in their love-making and their love—perhaps all their dreams had been exhausted too.

So morning came and wakefulness returned with it. However, when Than's consciousness rose he immediately knew something was wrong. It wasn't the empty spot on the bed beside him. Nor was it the fact the closet door stood open and clothes were missing. And it wasn't even the note on the nightstand in Celeste's handwriting which intended to tell Thanaxagoras what he already knew.

'A modern woman,' he had thought of her, but now he thought about himself as 'a very stupid man.' Yes, for centuries, Thanaxagoras prefaced conversations with visitors by saying things like: "Sorry, this is Hell and there is nothing I can do about it," or "You are going to get reborn, then suffer your way to salvation, so apologies, but look on the bright side," or "Regrettably, you and I are just tiny specks of energy for supernatural beings of immense power to mainline and there is nothing anybody of our species can do to change it." Yet, Celeste had been in the afterlife for only a little over two days and he should have known she would never acquiesce to a system she fundamentally believed to be unfair. After all, she had faith in Humanity, even though Humanity was unjust. But she also knew the same as he did: Gods were unjust even more. And, on top of all of this, she believed in mortal love and, worse, now she believed in immortal love too. Thanaxagoras felt shame because he would have let her go without a fight but—at this moment, he was sure—she was facing down the Devil to find a way to stay with him. His own failure made him apoplectic.

"Silly girl!" Than exclaimed, before dashing to the wardrobe to dress.

Yes, he might have been planning to let Celeste go without a fight, but now he was going to go after her. And, though there are many ways to connect to the Devil in Hell, he knew Celeste was aware of only one. This was because he had told her within just minutes of their first meeting.

The Devil could be found through the University Concourse.

2

Celeste awoke decisive and certain she could find the Devil through the University Concourse, but not because Thanaxagoras had told her. Instead, she knew because a university or a library is always a good place to find things, and know things, and, with time, hopefully to understand them. Additionally, of all the buildings and venues she had seen thus far in Hell, there was one edifice and piece of architecture which supposedly held knowledge she hadn't. This structure was a church. Yes, churches were ubiquitously absent in Hell—so ubiquitously absent—Celeste hadn't found their absence strange. No, in life, when she passed by a church she often thought to herself: *'That place would make a great laboratory, or coffee house, or... bookstore.'* But, after she died—when she noticed—she realized the absence of churches meant this realm was governed by an objective system of information. No, the Devil had no need for places of worship or adulation—because *He* was already the uncontested King of this realm. *He* also had no need of places gilded with mystery or saturated with arcane ritual. Rather, the Devil was an objectivist—an objective counterbalance to God—and such evidence-based truth always gave her strength. Now it was a source of hope as well.

So when Celeste rose on the morning of Day 3 and Thanaxagoras remained asleep, trilling his little snore and smiling that little crooked smile of his, she fully committed and headed off to the University Concourse. She had the idea to ask for directions, but in less than a hundred steps she found herself standing in front of a gigantic triangular archway declaring itself as 'Pythagoras Plaza' in stenciled letters. The pathways assisted her, just as the pathways assisted everyone. Nevertheless, she was grateful.

She walked over a stylized mosaic on the ground that read: '$A^2 + B^2 = C^2$: Here, we circle the past to square the future!' She wanted to read the Divine Treaty between Heaven and Hell—the actual document, itself—which ended the civil war between the Devil and God. She wanted to know the exact rules and terms of her dictated fate. Celeste went on to wonder just how much the pathways could twist and turn to help her reach this final destination. Sure enough, the first building she came upon was a grand gothic rotunda at least thirteen stories high. A sign posted outside said: 'Repository of the Celestial Armistice' with another notation below: 'DO NOT REMOVE ORIGINAL MATERIALS! Free mimeographing available on every floor!'

Celeste almost laughed out loud. Of course, Hell had Xerox machines. She bet they didn't even jam.

She mounted a set of marble steps to a heavy bronze door which opened effortlessly when she pushed upon it. Inside the rotunda was a circular ramp wrapping itself upwards and upwards to allow access to stacks upon stacks of thick binders colored red and white. None of the binders were obviously labeled, but she knew each and every one was filled with pages of the settlement of hostilities—*the negotiated settlement*—between an all-powerful Father and a powerful—though not quite all-powerful—Son. There must have been tens of thousands of binders amounting to millions if not billions of sheets of paper written in some form of Theological legalese. Still, Celeste thought: if you are going to divide up the Universe and detail the processes which govern every single soul that existed, exists, or ever would exist, the paperwork—no doubt—would have to be extensive. She just prayed it was written in English.

Taking only a dozen or so steps up the circular ramp, Celeste found herself on the eighth floor and felt a little dizzy. Then she remembered she was still on the pathways—on the path—and they were getting her to where she desired to go. The view was even more impressive from a higher vantage. The building reminded her of the Guggenheim Museum except it was filled only with reams of words. *'How can a whole Universe be divided up by just words?'* she distantly thought. But another part of her asked: *'How could they not?'*

She closed her eyes and thought, *'Reincarnated Souls,'* and every variation of the phrase she could think of, hoping the pathways would work even more specifically—more microscopically. There was a noise and Celeste opened her eyes. One of the binders near an outside window looking over Pythagoras Plaza seemed to jostle and hiccup. It was the first time—other than the pathways or the dying man in the bucket—she had actually seen anything truly mystical in the afterlife and her fascination jostled and hiccupped as well. It made her briefly wonder why souls here didn't fly, but she didn't dwell on the proposition. Instead, Celeste shut her eyes again and thought of the volume—the volume of the Divine Treaty between Heaven and Hell that was pertinent to her—to her, specifically. Supernaturally, the binder burped out onto the floor. She walked over to it and looked down, uncertain what to do next. There was evidence of the afterlife everywhere around her, but somehow the prospect of seeing part of the afterlife officially documented made her nervous.

"Reincarnation chapter?" she asked the binder, half as a request and half feeling like a fool.

The binder shivered and then flipped open.

"The page I need, please?" she asked again, a little more confidently.

The binder fluttered and flurried to a specific sheet of paper.

"Highlight passage?" she hazarded.

The binder slammed shut with a clap much louder than it should have been.

"Okay... all right... I'm sorry... I'm just new to this..." Celeste confessed to the binder.

"I acknowledge the overreach. I hope you accept my apology," Celeste said, but added, "I've never apologized to a book before..."

The binder seemed to tilt from side to side, almost rocking as if deciding something, and then flipped open again to the previous section. Perhaps to acknowledge some overreach on behalf of itself, or to convey it accepted

Celeste's apology, a passage on the page began to highlight in gold and red tints. It was exactly what she was looking for and exactly what she expected when she thought about how a God—*any God*—would choose their diction in terms of outlining their powers over Humanity. Regarding the semantics, one word shined brighter than any other in the paragraph. It was the word 'Gift.' Yes, Gods never *owed* Humans anything—they never endowed them with rights—but they did *give 'gifts'* as acts of kindness. This was because a kindness can always be taken away with the toss of a thunderbolt. The entire relevant line read: 'Noble Souls, with the good standing of Faith, but lacking Faith in regards to the Divine Hierarchy are hereby to be given the Gift of God's Mercy through the process of Reincarnation and all its attending attributes.'

There were more specifics appearing above and below the passage, but this one line from the Celestial Armistice was everything she needed. Indeed, a 'gift' could show Divine benevolence and power, but as a function of both language and reality a 'gift' *need not* be accepted. It had been the whole predicate of her plan.

"Thank you," Celeste said to the binder. After just a few seconds, she found it strange that she didn't find it strange to talk to a book.

"Now all I have to do is have a conversation with the Devil," she concluded.

She replaced the binder and turned to go back down, but when she did she found herself facing a man with sparkling yellow eyes which glowed in a piqued promethean curiosity.

"Good morning, Ms. Talon," the Devil said, because the Devil knows every soul under His dominion.

"Pleased to meet you… I hope you guess my name…" he finished with a smile.

"Um… Mick Jagger?" Celeste answered, grinning also. She just couldn't help herself.

"That's funny, but not quite," he said. "Let's chat."

3

Thanaxagoras raced insofar as he could race to the University Concourse. *'Celeste, Celeste, Celeste Talon… Celeste my love!'* he thought, screaming her name in his mind. It seemed like it took him an eternity, but he arrived at Pythagoras Plaza in less than ninety seconds after exiting the hotel.

He moved briskly towards the Repository of the Celestial Armistice. It was the only place that made sense. He knew Celeste would want to be well prepared if she was going to do what—he was sure—she was going to do. Yes, Celeste had no shortage of gumption or bravery. Still, he reckoned it was a monumentally stupid and potentially horrific action to take.

'Celeste! Celeste! Silly girl!' he screamed internally and infernally again.

And then there she was.

Celeste had exited the repository, and now strolled dreamily outside an auxiliary building labeled 'Hipponax Lecture Hall.' Thanaxagoras was relieved to see her, but then felt terrified once more. This was because Celeste strolled like she didn't have a care in the world or in the world after the world. In fact, her gait was like that of someone who had made an agreement and felt immensely satisfied with the terms.

Than shivered with a cringing heart.

Celeste spied him and waved, casually.

Thanaxagoras reached his love in just footsteps, but then unintentionally manhandled her into Hipponax Lecture Hall. She seemed to make a small objection, but if Celeste voiced anything, Thanaxagoras didn't hear it. Instead, he plunked her in a seat near the back of the hall and took to the stage.

"I want you to know I appreciate what you did, but you have to take it back," Thanaxagoras began, gravely. "I love you. I love you more than anyone I've ever loved when I was alive and more than anyone I've met since I've died. However, none of that matters. You have to give that up. You have to take it back if you can. You must be reborn. And you must go to Heaven. I'm going to say this in no uncertain terms for you to understand: you **cannot** make a deal with a God in the service of Human Love."

Celeste considered interrupting, but it was clear Thanaxagoras had built a head of steam, so she just waited for him to whistle it all out.

"You see, Gods—*any God*—are jealous Gods. And what they are most jealous of is love. Acts of Human Pride come second, but love is first. They cannot abide *any love* directed towards anyone or anything besides themselves. The new consolidated God had Abraham sacrifice—*almost*—his son Isaac; Hera, Aphrodite, and Athena essentially started the Trojan War to mess with Human Love. Oh, you might say, but Cupid and Eros and Venus were always setting up humans to fall in love with one another—but you have to remember that was only to get Humans *to love them first*! In fact, I would argue there is nothing more dangerous than to let a God—*any God*—get wind of true Human Love because eventually they will destroy it!"

Celeste still said nothing.

"So we need to go find the Devil and have you take it back. I'll take a demotion regarding my status as a guide in the underworld or make some other sacrifice, if I have to. But you can't give up Heaven for love and you can't stay in Hell for love either. I won't abide it. I won't allow it. You mean too much to me for you to toss away your soul in a reckless act which will end badly… for both of us."

Thanaxagoras said all this while crinkling his face into a worried and fretting frown. Celeste noted his mouth twisted downward in a funny crooked way, just like when he smiled. This, however, she did not find adorable. Now it was his time to wait.

Celeste continued not to say anything.

Thanaxagoras waited.

Celeste looked at her nails.

Thanaxagoras waited.

Celeste scratched the back of her neck and then gently probed her ear with a fingertip.

"Well, say something!" Than exclaimed, unable to extend his patience. "Time is short! The reincarnation portal opens in less than an hour—at 3:30! You are a silly, silly girl!"

Celeste finally rose from her seat.

"Oh, I'm sorry, is it my turn now? Is it the *'silly girl's'* turn?" she began. "I was having a hard time knowing because you bum-rushed me into this building and into one of the back rows only to literally take the stage and give me a lecture in a lecture hall. But thanks for *mansplaining* the Nature of Love and for also telling me all love is eventually doomed. It *really was* an uplifting speech! Maybe next time you can tell me how every fine meal ends up as shit or how every baby will eventually die! In fact, why don't you just say every good or nice or kind thing will all turn into cunt-hairs! Yes, *cunt-hairs*! Yes, big nasty cunt-hairs that get ingrown and fill up with pus and have a gnarled and gnarly black hair at their center! I've read when you enter Hell or Purgatory or Limbo or whatever, there is a banner that states: 'Abandon all hope ye who enter here.' However, maybe you should paint it over to say: 'Embrace all hopelessness thee who enter here—thus sayest Thanaxagoras!' It's more fitting! I love you too, by the way."

Thanaxagoras was taken aback by Celeste's anger which seemed so hurt and so genuine that it elided over her profanity.

"I'm... I'm not saying all love is doomed..." Than stammered in response.

"Well, that's sure what it sounded like... and... in fact... you might be right. Our love may end. All love may eventually end. But like I told you yesterday: just because something is going to end, isn't a reason *not to do it*! But none of this matters anyway. The subject is irrelevant."

"How can you say our love is irrelevant?" Thanaxagoras asked, a little hurt himself.

"It's irrelevant because it never came up," Celeste answered.

"What do you mean it never came up?" he continued.

"What do you think? Do you imagine, I just went up to the Devil and said: 'O' Dark Lord, unquestioned Ruler of the Underworld, I've fallen in love with the most amazing man so could you please do us a solid and let us live happily ever after in the nice part of Hell'? No, you idiot! I asked Him if I could stay because I weighed all the factors and I told Him I wanted to stay!"

"But... but you wanted to stay for me, right?" Than asked, less surely than he hoped.

"Yes, of course! But you weren't the only reason," Celeste replied. "Look around: here I get eternal youth and health and enough time to do anything—everything—I want! I could learn to play an instrument or write a book or study Sanskrit, if I so desired! And, besides, I like being me! I know myself! Why would I want to give that up?"

"But you won't get the love of the consolidated God..." Thanaxagoras observed.

"Well, I never had it in the first place! And, to get it, I have to become someone else and suffer and then spend my afterlife loving Him and worshipping Him! What kind of deal is that? So I proposed a better one with the Devil. I offered Him something and He accepted."

"What did you offer?" asked Than.

"My soul, to stay here, under his domain, to start. And I offered my gratitude. Gratitude might not be as powerful as love or suffering, but it still has value. I also agreed to do a little work for Him. Actually, it wasn't even a hard sell. We seem to have a lot in common. Furthermore, He said I wasn't even close to being the first person to choose to stay. He told me it was one of the reasons why He made this part of Hell so pleasant compared to the other parts," Celeste explained. "Didn't you know that?"

Thanaxagoras was quiet for a moment.

"No. I heard rumors some people stayed… but…"

Celeste cut him off.

"You said it yourself: the Devil's 'not the worst,'" she continued, "and it doesn't hurt this place was formerly a type of Heaven back in the Ancient World. I told the Devil, it just needed something special. That's where my work for Him will come in."

"What did you say this place needs?" Than asked, conflicted, but working through it.

"Advertising," she answered.

4

Celeste Talon and Thanaxagoras talked a little longer about her newly forged deal with the Devil and how their now possible future might unfold.

"How did you do it? How did you convince Him?" Thanaxagoras asked.

"Well, there was the business side, of course, but mostly I told a story," Celeste answered.

"A story?"

"Yes. A fable… something I read in college like a

million years ago. It was called *The Warden and the Jailer*. Ever hear of it?" she asked.

"No," he replied.

"It's pretty simple. Once there was a brutal jailer who hurt all his prisoners while demanding their respect. 'I am the jailer!' he would snarl. 'I have more power over you, so you must give me respect!' Meanwhile, there was also a warden who said: 'I am not your jailer. I am your warden. I manage the prison, but the prison has rules. If you break the rules there will be consequences.' Then as the years passed both the jailer and warden spoke with clubs and chains and unpleasantness, but when they did, they each told two different tales. One told the tale of a man who would never deserve respect under any circumstances. The other told of a man who earned respect... even when he had to use a club."

"That's a pretty good fable," Thanaxagoras said.

"I thought so," Celeste replied. "The Devil did too."

There was a moment of silence between them.

"So you really don't want to take it back?" Than asked.

"No. I really don't. This will last as long as it lasts, but at least it was my choice. Seventy-two hours ago, I didn't know I was a pawn in a supernatural system I couldn't control. Now, at least, I'm a pawn who made some moves of my own," Celeste answered.

Thanaxagoras laughed.

"What's so funny?" Celeste inquired.

"I realized we just had our first fight and it was about whether or not you'd stay in Hell," he said.

Celeste laughed too.

"Yeah, I guess we did," she said.

There was another quiet moment.

"So what should we do now?" Thanaxagoras pressed on.

"Well, I don't know about you, but I think we should make up," she said and gave him a wink.

Then there was more giggling because they both knew they already had.

DAY 1,000

Celeste and Thanaxagoras walked arm in arm in the afterlife. They had no specific destination so they just ambled while the pathways twisted and meandered randomly out in front of them. Occasionally they passed some of the signs Celeste helped to create. The signs were billboards that read: 'Heaven is in the eye of the beholder! Ask your guide about it!' or 'A new consolidated God? Visit the University Concourse! Lectures hourly!' or 'Salvation through suffering? Wasn't living one life hard enough? Ask!' or—Celeste's personal favorite—'Do you like being you? Stay that way! Choose Hell!'

Every time Celeste viewed one she smiled, but the smile was bittersweet.

"I wish you weren't so hard on yourself," Thanaxagoras said. "You're doing a good job. The Devil seems satisfied, and the new work-release program from the other parts of Hell is a great idea. It will even help balance out the ratio between ancient and modern souls. That alone should increase the number of people who choose to stay through the reincarnation loophole."

"I know," Celeste answered, "but it's been almost three

years and only 193 souls have chosen to remain. I can't believe people are willing to give up their agency so easily. I just wish they could see reincarnation for what it is: another form of self-annihilation and they're doing it for a God they never knew… even, perhaps, for a God they can't ever really know at all."

"Well, don't forget you are fighting 2,000 years of propaganda. Also, the visitors have only three days to absorb the irrefutable truth. A fair number of scientists are choosing to stay though. That's good," Than comforted.

"I guess. I just want people to be more considerate and introspective about what they believe," Celeste sulked.

"All you can do is get people to think about their choices. After all, choice is the foundation of Hell," Thanaxagoras replied.

"Do you have any regrets?" he asked.

Celeste thought for a moment, considerate and introspectively.

"No," she said. "I get to be me and I get to be with you and this place is… is…"

"Not the worst?" Than interrupted and smiled his crooked little smile.

"Yes. Not the worst," Celeste said, smiling back.

"So what do you want to do now?" Thanaxagoras asked.

"I'd like to go see the children, again," Celeste answered. "I feel like giving out some balloons."

"Good choice," he replied, adding, "as long as we get to do it together."

End of Story #8

Intermezzo

(eighth)

Since Mizam and the Devil had chosen to read like humans, rather than like the supernatural entities they were, it was taking them some time to finish the latest tale. The writer supposed he should have expected this. Story #8 was his longest thus far. There wasn't a reason, except the writer had to get two people to fall in love, in less than seventy-two hours, in Hell, and make it all plausible— while supplying the litany of underlying theological conundrums appropriate for supernatural tales. Although, when he reflected on his first story, he had a married couple live an entire lifetime of purported 'love' and that only took a little over two pages. Maybe subconsciously he wanted wife-beating stories to be shorter, and tales about eternal love to be longer, or, perhaps, a story's length is just a result of its narrative function. His Devil's Spot thrummed pleasantly in favor of all these ideas.

As for the next story—Story #9—he had already finished it too. The writer contemplated leaping forward to Story #10 because he had the kernel of a plot and even an intriguing title: 'Go Tell It to the Lamb.' However, to skip ahead seemed disrespectful somehow. After all, Mizam and the Devil were integral to his writing process now. They deserved time to give feedback and, furthermore, he found writing can be a lonely endeavor and occasionally *any conversation* can be useful to expel the voices in his head.

Then, at the same moment, Mizam and the Devil get to the conclusion of 'Reincarnation Theater.'

Mizam speaks first:

"Well, that's not the ending I expected," he says.

"What did you expect?" the writer asks.

"I thought the woman would end up with her head in a bucket of blood. I mean, such is a fitting punishment for abandoning God," he continues.

"She didn't exactly abandon God. She only chose *not* to make His acquaintance," the writer replies.

"Tomato, potato," Mizam finishes, tersely.

The writer doesn't bother to correct the Angel. To do so seems like a fool's errand.

"What about you?" he asks, directing his inquiry to the Devil.

The Devil takes a beat before responding.

"Well I liked Humpy!" Lucifer exclaims with unexpected enthusiasm.

"The camel?" the writer probes.

"Yup. Give me an animal with a funny name and I'm on board!"

The writer smiles.

"So I moved you?" the writer asks.

"What?" the Devil asks back.

"I moved you. I made an impression. I knew stories could shift the status quo," he says.

"Don't get crazy," the Devil evades. "I just like creatures with amusing names."

"Fair enough," the writer admits.

"So, I take it, once more, you aren't offended he isn't showing you to be the most furious, diabolical, and thoroughly unmerciful Demon in all of God's Creation?" Mizam jumps back in, asking the Devil.

"You mean: am I upset he didn't portray me as some cliché or cardboard mockup of an infernal stereotype? No. I don't mind at all. He isn't writing *My Biography*. Moreover, his stories aren't a documentary collection—except for Mary Mazepa. You said it yourself: reincarnation isn't even *a thing*," the Devil replies.

The writer doesn't like the Devil mentioning Mary's name. Still, he has to return to the task at hand: the criticism.

"That's a shame—that reincarnation isn't a thing," the writer interjects. "I always liked the idea… you know… the notion of coming back again and again to improve yourself, help humanity, or make up for whatever wrongs you might have committed in a previous life. It's a philosophy of atonement and second chances. The very concept seems to embody, at least, *the possibility* of advancement—not just for individuals, but for entire societies and civilizations as well."

The writer thinks the three of them had moved beyond silent pauses, both pregnant and otherwise.

He is wrong.

The sound which fills the room after the stunned and startled silence fractures is uproarious Divine laughter—from both the Angel and Devil. One set of ha-ha's is sublimely melodious and the other set is tonally odious, just like he had written earlier.

"You have to be kidding!" the Devil howls.

"Agreed!" Mizam cries. "What naively romantic claptrap! Humankind will forever fall to pieces because humanity is already a fallen species! People could come back a million times and there would be no advancement! As for redemption—that only comes through the Lord!"

"Indeed! The only thing humans get better at is finding new and different ways to kill themselves! You want to see reincarnation? Just imagine a thousand forms of suicide and murder! There's human reincarnation for you—*the Human* status quo! It's intractable!" the Devil continues, still snickering.

"I will never ascribe to such a dreary and dismal outlook," the writer counters. "It is religion which corrupts humanity. It can even corrupt the faithful in the midst of them exercising their faith."

"Is that quite so?" Mizam asks.

"Yes," the writer affirms.

"Then prove it!" the Devil challenges.

"I already have," says the writer as he hands over the next story, but feels a deep need to unequivocally state one last thing.

"I'd like neither of you to ever mention Mary's name again. Some things are more important than narrative continuity," the writer sternly ends.

Barbury's Heavenly Prayer

(Story #9)

An open letter from the Heavenly Afterlife to the Earthly Plane:

Who gets to tell a story is important. I mention this at the beginning because I'm going to circle back to it at the end. But first I want to tell *every human being of faith* a few things about Heaven. You can call me many things, but regarding Heaven, I guess you could call me 'a native.' For lack of a better word, I was 'born' here. And though I don't have a soul—and consequently *am not human*—I'm pretty close. I share many attributes with human beings because my creator wanted me to have them. I can grow and I can change and I can express myself. I even have a measure of free will—though this can be revoked at the drop of a hat or the blink of an eye. I've also studied human culture, mortal art, and the history of Earth for over 300 years now. I am a shade for the saved soul of Hallelujah Bock. A 'shade' is like an idea made flesh. I am a functionary. A servant. I am one of her figments, her avatars—an embodied whim generated and coalesced from her whimsy and her whimsical desires. I was formed and brought to life to chronicle and bear witness—all for Hallelujah Bock's glory and God's glory too. This is my purpose. Sometimes Hallelujah calls me 'High Priest,' though if I have any priestly duties other than writing down what I've seen and what I know, I remain unaware of them. I'm not even sure if this is my tale or hers, but I am charged with its construction. You can think of me as 'Barbury.' This is the name bestowed upon me by my creator. I'll tell you more about myself and my existence in time, so for now, I beg your patience. I'll also communicate exactly why I am writing, but first I want to sketch a picture about how most of Heaven *really operates*. I will preface by saying one more thing: I have a favor to ask you… but perhaps 'favor' isn't the right word. No, it's more like a prayer. Yes, I'm praying to you. No one else is listening.

**

You see, in Heaven—if you make it there—you get anything you want. You can be whoever you want to be, you can change whatever you want to change, and you get to put together a world—a world that maybe isn't perfect for everyone, but one at least—that is *perfect for you*. But this is not to say the glorious dispensation of a person getting *anything* in Heaven means Heaven is full of *everything*. No, such a proposition is fundamentally incorrect. Yes, there are things existing in the Universe which do not exist in Heaven. There are horrors like rape and torture and child molestation and cannibalism—the pagan kind, not the Transubstantiation kind—that in the history of Heaven never once were made manifest. Could they manifest? No one truly knows, but most likely not. The reason is Divinely simple: *the soulfully saved are not depraved*. Yes, the soulfully saved almost instinctively, perchance inherently, shun the darkest possibilities of human behavior. In fact, for many saved souls, the potential for such hideous acts no longer exists—even within abstract memory. After all, who would want to dwell on the blackest of sins in a place brimming with the brightest of lights? Feathery Angels thought this question worthy of consideration, proposed by God. Hallelujah Bock believed the question merited consideration as well.

Yet caveats and caveats—the afterlife is full of them. Where is the line drawn? Does this mean there is no violence, or killing, or war, or even assassination in Heaven? No. Those things *can and do exist* within the varied and mottled stripes of Paradise. This will become clearer. Yes, this will become clearer when you understand the activities of saved souls are roughly hewn into three distinct planks. First, there is worship—*always worship*. "Remember the Sabbath Day, to keep it Holy," sayeth the 4th Commandment and the saved souls do. Except, when they 'remember,' they ascribe the dictum of the Sabbath to part of every day because in Heaven, *all the days are Holy*. Worship then bleeds into the second type of soulful activity: study and scholarship. Yes, after worship there is always homework to explore ways to worship even more and worship even better. And this homework lasts forever. Yes, in Heaven, gratitude and submission is an ever-evolving system of blessed supplication. Finally, the Sabbath isn't only Holy, requiring worship and study—it is also a day of rest. God decreed it so Himself. And this bleeds into the third type of Heavenly activity: leisure and recreation. And it is through this last subgroup where killing and war and even assassination *can and do* exist in the celestial panorama of infinite bliss.

"How is this possible?" you might ask. Is it because every religion has a streak of violence in its supposedly venerable and inviolate tenets? This is true, but no. Is it because Humankind, itself, is a violent species—and such violence cannot be scrubbed from the Human condition, even after death? This is also true, but also no. Is it because violence is a mechanism for growth, both physically and metaphysically? True and more true, but no and more no. It is because violence is pleasurable. Violence is satisfying. Violence is gratifying. *Violence is fun!* And, most of the time, violence ends up with at least one of the parties experiencing another type of joy: victory. And, if you are a saved soul in Heaven, *you always get to win*!

So if you happened to be a knight of the Crusades and wanted to relive a glorious campaign, you could. Or if you wanted to storm Omaha beach or successfully defend the Alamo or rid a town of ruffian bandits in the Old West, you could do that too. You can even shoot Hitler or defeat a James Bond villain or fight Klingons, if such was your wont and want. I would be remiss if I didn't mention the Inquisition, but I don't like thinking about such morally complicated, yet pious, scenarios. Yes, in truth, it could be more elegantly stated, but since I invoked *Star Trek*, when you get right down to it, Heaven is very much like a holodeck. Indeed, it is perfectly malleable and perfectly generative and perfectly without consequences. Yes, you can create anything your heart desires and destroy what you created—at will—at once—and do it all over and over, again and again, the same way or different. Repetition is one of Heaven's gifts. You could even manifest shades like me to serve you or be killed by you or fulfill whatever you envision—provided you have a soul and your soul was saved.

Yes, in Heaven, you get anything you want, because Heaven is a repeating loop of pleasures unbound. But you should be aware and know well, regarding shades, some of the granted pleasures involve spectacular violence and genocidal slaughter. And… in Heaven… slaughters can go on forever.

***

So it was for my patroness: the saved soul, Hallelujah Bock. Born on Earth in 1697, she was abducted from the Ivory Coast and sold into slavery at just four years old. South Carolina came next—or at least the land that would eventually become South Carolina—where she was purchased by a genteel mistress named Mrs. Eustice Willingfam to do domestic work in the Main House. The place was called 'Salvation Plantation.' Mrs. Eustice christened the place herself and thought the appellation to be terribly charming. In fact, Mrs. Eustice very much enjoyed naming things, so when she saw a black child, without parents, in shackles that only stayed on her wrists because the little girl *was making* tiny fists to keep the shackles on, she exclaimed: "Oh my! Why, aren't you just as cute as a coffee bean! God must have sent you to me... I will call you 'Hallelujah'!" The 'Bock' came later. Hallelujah had this way of clucking and giggling as she chased chickens about the yard.

Now Mrs. Eustice Willingfam was many things, but one characteristic settled within her beyond all others: Mrs. Eustice Willingfam *was devout*. So Mistress Eustice had Hallelujah baptized, of course, and made sure she knew her Bible stories—though she was never allowed to learn to read—and she required Hallelujah and all her other slaves to go to church every Sunday and, after worship, receive the rest of the day off. It wasn't called 'Salvation Plantation' for nothing. Mistress Eustice even put Hallelujah at the head of the procession when her caravan of property traveled to their weekly ritual of cleansing and reward.

The power of those moments, every Sunday, thrilled and elated Hallelujah—and it was a type of jubilation Hallelujah *never forgot*—even after death. She wore a white dress—pre-crinoline, but still nice—adorned with ruffles and cathedral lace. Yes, *she led* the field hands and the house servants and skilled laborers and exulted in the power of leading them. Yes, *it was she* who brought others to the threshold of salvation beyond the plantation. Yes, *she* walked in the front of the line. And Hallelujah would march smiling and with pride, and always carry a bundle of dried wildflowers in one hand to set down on the stoop of the church steps for Jesus. She also knew Jesus was grateful and accepting. This was because each successive Sunday the wildflowers would be gone so Hallelujah always faithfully and happily obliged to bring another bundle *unto Him*.

Then seven years later, Hallelujah Bock succumbed to consumption and died. Yes, death came and the little girl who was 'cute as a coffee bean' left Salvation Plantation to reside in actual salvation for time without end.

This was the beginning of Hallelujah's story and the preamble to mine.

****

I want to pause here and say what Hallelujah Bock did and does is monstrous from my perspective, but it isn't evil—not in any way. In Heaven, there is no evil. It is impossible to do evil in Heaven. And, don't forget, Hallelujah died as a child, without parents, and she was saved. Thus, by all definition her actions fall squarely within the purview and guidance of the totality of God's precepts. Indeed, in Heaven, no soul could ever harm any other, but with shades—*with shades*—they can be used for anything. Yes, shades live by the grace of the soul who summons them and they die in ways incalculable. It's what we're created for. Consequently, there can't be anything immoral about our lives or deaths—if either word even applies. Yes, in truth, you couldn't call any saved soul 'evil' any more than you could label someone 'evil' who kills a character in a video game. Yes, for shades, it's all just Nintendo up here. And, for us shades, Hallelujah Bock is but one more player. I write these words with the utmost respect and deference, of course. The point is: she is essentially all-powerful over us, but there is nothing consciously abusive about our relationship. Destruction and creation were hers to dispense without limit or reserve. This was part of Hallelujah's reward brought forth and wrought by God.

Pause concluded.

*****

In any case, Hallelujah Bock died wheezing and gasping and choking and then went to Heaven without a hitch.

On top of this, you should know the first thing that happens to a saved soul upon reaching Heaven is the experiences from former living times dim and fade. Yes, their former lives become like a distant memory without pain. You could even say '*they blanch.*' But before you mourn the diminishing of cherished recollections after death consider: in Heaven, why would you want to have a memory at all, when you can have a candied dream? Heaven is made of dreams, don't you know, just as Hell is made of nightmares. You should know this from your dreams and from your nightmares, and from your dreams that become nightmares, and from your nightmares that become dreams. It's as axiomatic as finding meaning by gazing at the stars.

So when Hallelujah Bock died at just eleven years old, she preferred a sugared fantasy rather than any other of Heaven's facets. Oh, sure, she had been assigned a guide and got a tour—like everyone in every afterlife—before she chose to construct an individual heaven within Heaven for herself. Thus, she was able to marvel at the stunning brilliance of the Celestial City of New Jerusalem, to walk upon its streets made of gold and pass by its magnificent silver towers. She even got to sip from its flowing rivers of sweet tea and streams of refreshing lemonade cleverly infused with a hint of mint. Also, she was able to review a number of collective heavens—including a few populated by former Earthly slaves and some made up of adolescents just like Hallelujah, herself—but none of them had much connection or effect. Finally—in an antiquated residual instinct—she sought out the heaven of Mrs. Eustice Willingfam, because without a doubt, she had been saved too, but Mrs. Eustice preferred a 'Whites Only' paradise.

Did this mean Hallelujah Bock was lonely? The answer is: absolutely not. Don't be ridiculous. There was never any sadness or disappointment or any feeling of rejection because that's not how Heaven works. Yes, permanent satisfaction permeated Hallelujah's new reality like the gravity of her own faith. Indeed, how much can you care about other people when you have been saved by the Lord? No, the only friend you need anywhere is Jesus. Hallelujah learned this from her time on Earth. Yes, *He* is your father and your mother—loved more by you than your closest friends or even your children. *He* is your confidant and your balm. *He* is your confessor and your rock. Yes, *He* is the manna that supplants mankind. No, in Heaven, there is no concession for human relationships because human relationships are superfluous, transitory, and incidental. *They do not matter!* The warm embrace of a Supreme Being overrides all. So was Hallelujah Bock lonely in Heaven? No. The Lord was with her and she required nothing else.

The question remained, however, of where Hallelujah Bock would carve out her own little slice of heaven in her more than splendid eternity. How she did it wasn't surprising in celestial terms, but it was surprising to her. She had only one necessary specification: *it had to be big*! This was because, in Heaven, you get anything you want, and what Hallelujah Bock wanted was to be a Prophetess of God. It was part of her worship and study and recreation all rolled into one. So Hallelujah wasn't just going to construct her own heaven, but rather was going to construct an entire heavenly world and fill it with creatures—*with shades*—to bring them forth unto the Lord. Yes, even though Hallelujah Bock had died and had earned her place, she still wanted to lead, and, because she was in Heaven, she would always be at the head of the line.

******

So Hallelujah Bock found an unused section of Divine real estate between two other individual heavens and opened her soul, her heart, and her imagination. This was enough to set in motion the construction of her own private world. She told me how she did it. And because I was programmed to believe, I believe.

The first thing Hallelujah wanted was the Light of the Lord so Hallelujah made a sun. Except it wasn't exactly a sun, the same way I'm not exactly a human. Rather, Hallelujah Bock's sun was actually a portal, a passageway, a transit hub tunneling all the way through the ethereal veil to allow the light from New Jerusalem—Heaven's central city—to swaddle her would-be world in endless succor. This was the Lord's Light—the literal Light of God.

And Hallelujah said, "Hallelujah," because she was pleased.

Next Hallelujah thought of land and there was land. And then Hallelujah thought of sea and there was sea. And then Hallelujah thought of sky and there was sky. Yes, from a formless void a full world grand and fulsome formed. And she named one of the landmasses of her new world 'O-Frica' and another landmass 'O-Lina.' These were names she took from her living times. And the literal Light of the Lord did fall upon the rocks and shoals of O-Frica and O-Lina.

And Hallelujah said, "Hallelujah," because she was pleased.

Following this, Hallelujah thought of animals and thought of plants—then of houses and rivers and roads and churches and carriages and all the things she had witnessed during the few years of her short and truncated life. And all these things did come to pass. And she placed them in both O-Frica and O-Lina because in her mind the world was nothing but two great landmasses separated by vast waters.

And Hallelujah said, "Hallelujah," because she was pleased.

And finally she rose up from the sea a great and glittering tower between the two landmasses like a miraculous vertical spire yawning into the newly minted air, because that's exactly what it was. The spire was to be her home and my home too. And from that spire, we would peer out upon her world and all her wonderful creations beneath the loving rays of a golden sun.

Yes, her heaven bloomed into existence from her memory, her imagination, and her soul. Now before Hallelujah could say her final "Hallelujah," she needed only to produce her legions of shades to try and bring them forth unto the Lord.

Subsequently, my creation was nigh.

****

I admit fully, I'm not sure what it's like for a real human to be born—a human with a soul—but I do believe my soulless creation and your soulful birth is quite similar in one respect. First *you are not there* and then suddenly *you are*. In retrospect, I know I was fragments. In retrospect, I know there were component parts that would eventually come together to be me. I imagine it was peaceful, *my existence before my existence*, but surely this is a delusion. This is because *a nothing is nothing*—and a nothing cannot be ascribed an emotional state. Yes, before anyone is born, it is only bone-white blankness and an unfathomable abyss that nevertheless holds the potential of something. Yes, before I was me, I was the potential me. Yes, before I was me, I was only parts, but then the component parts connected and—*poof!*—there I was. I think we are all connected by a *poof!*—whether you are a soulful human or a soulless shade—though this might be a delusion too.

And thus from the bizarre menagerie of what did not exist, but could, I appeared fully and completely—not so much like Adam or Eve—but rather like a Jewish golem with a piece of paper crammed in my mouth. No. I had no soul, no parents, and was wholly unaware of the context of my creation. I would say I was an orphan, but that would be a disservice to orphans. And I stood there naked as the day I was born because I just had been. I only knew two things: I was to serve and to love the Prophetess of the Lord: Hallelujah Bock. Such were the twin directives which guided my genesis.

This is when my creator spoke to me:

"Oh my! Why, you're just as skinny as a bar! I will call you 'Barbury'! You will be my High Priest!"

Poof!—indeed.

These were the first words I ever heard.

****

For me, those early moments were disorienting. Yes, I was disoriented and I was dumbfounded because I found myself without orientation and I found myself dumb. I had the basic sensory abilities of any proto-human, but I did not know how to process what I observed and what I felt and what I occupied. I didn't have a body and now I had a body. I didn't have a mind and now I had the beginnings of a mind. Indeed, I was new, and I was me, and I came into existence as a new me in Hallelujah's new world. I felt the absence of my soul, but I didn't say anything. I couldn't. I was like an egg without a yoke and such expression was beyond my capabilities. No, articulation remained an alien reflex yet to be activated.

"Oh my!" Hallelujah exclaimed again, but this time while carefully examining me up and down. "You hardly know anything, do you? No, you don't know a lick or a stick! You don't know as much as a ladybug's ear! I must attend to that!"

Saying this, Hallelujah raised her hands as if she were reaching for Divinity, itself, and then miraculous motes of brilliant golden light began to swarm and circle around her. It was beautiful—like weightless gold dust—and even Hallelujah seemed to shine. Following the appearance of this shimmering miracle, she moved her hands like a magician and the coruscating mass flitted so that it hovered directly over the crown of my newly created head. If I had a soul, I believe it would have formed a halo.

Then Hallelujah snapped her fingers.

At the sound of the snap, the fine and transcendent particles immediately coalesced into fat drops of cold water and doused me. I gasped. It was like being hit by a frigid flume of icy slurry. It was as if someone had taken a blanket and dipped it into the Arctic Ocean and then rudely threw it over my head. The liquid felt gelid and oddly thick as I was so unceremoniously splashed. I knew at once it was knowledge, but it was cold knowledge—knowledge without love; knowledge without purpose other than it was knowledge. Some of the water got in my mouth and I tasted metal. I think I tasted mathematics and physics. With that, more and more chilling information burbled up and down within me as if my body cavity were filled with a glacial gurgling spring. I thought of onions and for a time all I could think about was onions. I don't know how long Hallelujah let me stand there dripping and shivering, but she did. I suppose she was allowing me to steep, to become saturated and sotted—to marinate like some piece of protein. She was giving me what I needed to be her instrument. Thinking back now, it was my own kind of baptism, but oh so very, very cold.

Finally, after a microsecond or an eternity, my creator spoke again:

"Oh my! We have so much to talk about! But before I get into my design, do you have any questions for me? I imagine this is quite exciting for you!"

Once more, I shivered and paused, but I was no longer dumbfounded or found dumb. Instead, I unbelievably processed her words. I had been given understanding and speech and somewhere in this series of roiling and undulating epiphanies a question ascended in my mind.

"Um… yes… and with respect… why am I black?" I asked.

****

Yes, I was black-skinned. Yes, Hallelujah had created me black. In fact, I was *very, very* black: bootblack, blue-black, black as a boysenberry. And Hallelujah was white. In fact, she was *very, very* white: ivory, alabaster, white as sugar or uncut cocaine. If color were a sound, the contrast would be a visual shriek and scream.

So after my question, Hallelujah explained with unwavering certainty that God was white, and a white woman had led her to God, and she was going to lead me to God, so she figured even though she had been born black on Earth, in the afterlife, she should be white too. Whiteness was part of her reward, she said proudly. "Yes, in Heaven, I get anything I want," she proclaimed. I also want to mention, though Hallelujah Bock died at just eleven years old, the Hallelujah appearing before me looked to be in her mid-twenties—stunningly beautiful with blonde hair and blue eyes. She was quite buxom as well. Thinking back now, perhaps it was lucky I had been showered with freezing liquid, which was knowledge without love.

Hallelujah then went on to expose her own Divine purpose: that she wasn't just going to lead me to God, but she was going to lead a whole world to God—*her world*—and I was to write down all her actions and declarations. She said I had been created special—that she'd given me many wonderful gifts. She told me I could see through the eyes of any creature—animal or shade—in her lands of O-Frica and O-Lina. And she decreed I would be able to read and write. She also said I would be able to access and examine all the knowledge of the Earthly plane so I could better understand Humanity and the human simulacra—*her shades*—which she would presently be making. This would be my function. Yes, I could peruse any book, study any subject, and the fountain of available information would constantly update as Earth and all its cultures moved forward in time. She even said I could have sex, and a blush rose on her pale face—a ghostly blush in Heaven. And she told me I would live forever. So history would be mine and the future was mine and, for a time, the present was mine, too. Lastly, she added that bit of 'free will' I mentioned earlier. Yes, I was charged with chronicling all the events in her heaven within Heaven and give her someone to talk to—not because she could get lonely, but because "chatting can be a heavenly experience," she expanded.

"Why don't you just compile a record, yourself?" I asked. Language was becoming easier, the way a river follows a riverbed. "Surely, if you created me, you could easily create a compendium of all your actions and activities?"

She told me of course she could, but during her living life God had not seen fit to grant her literacy and, as a result, she decided never to tap into those skills as a way to honor the Lord. "Active ignorance can be an act of faith," she claimed. Personally, though, I just think she wanted a record kept, but didn't particularly like the mechanics of the written word. I guess it goes without saying, but needs to be said: Hallelujah had me write everything down, but never reviewed my work—not once. Yes, my scribblings may as well be mist for all Hallelujah seemed or seems to care.

Regardless, our initial conversation came to an end

and Hallelujah propelled her world forward. Yes, for Hallelujah to complete her heaven she had to create not just one civilization, but two. O-Frica and O-Lina needed to be colonized. However, and so much more vitally, she had to issue her Covenant as a Prophetess of God with a promise I know she believed to be sincere, but I must testify to be a tragic folly. Yes, it was a tragic folly for me… or I should say… a tragic folly for all of us shades ever housed beneath the firm beams of Hallelujah Bock's firmer and even more fantastical firmament.

Hence, please hear my prayer.

****

Thus, the Prophetess Hallelujah did populate the land of O-Frica with shades so that the shades of O-Frica numbered 10,000 times 10,000. And thus, the Prophetess Hallelujah did populate the land of O-Lina with shades so that the shades of O-Lina numbered 10,000 times 10,000. And among the numbers of both O-Frica and O-Lina she placed men, women, and children of every class and type. Yes, she molded craftsmen and builders, priests and washerwomen, soldiers and teachers. She sculpted laborers and artists, explorers and settlers, brigands and fools. And she made it so all occupations were represented and so that all the people—*who were not quite people*—varied in their talents and intelligence and beauty under the Lord's Glorious Light which shined directly from the City of Heaven beyond the sun. And thus the lands of O-Frica and O-Lina did swell with a plethora of shades.

And Hallelujah said, "Hallelujah," because she was pleased.

Then the Prophetess saw fit to give her two newly created flocks of O-Frica and O-Lina all the skills and abilities they needed to fulfill their functions. Yes, she gave them the full range of human emotions, though they were not human. And, she made sure her shades had the same measure of free will given to me, though they were not me. And she mandated that they could think and they could move and they could feel. And all of this was done with Hallelujah's promise one wonderful day her shades could be lifted unto the Lord and be saved like humans, though they were not.

And Hallelujah said, "Hallelujah," because she was pleased.

Then the Prophetess bestowed upon them knowledge of the Lord so they might know *Him*. And she let some people read and write and let others remain without. And, as she gave her shades life, she also gave them the ability to procreate. But unlike me they would not live forever. Her shades could have children, but everyone in O-Frica and O-Lina would eventually die. These were things she remembered from her living times. And finally the Prophetess Hallelujah did make all the shades of O-Frica and O-Lina black-skinned—every man, woman, and child—bootblack, blue-black, black as a boysenberry. 'Fore shades to be black-skinned and Hallelujah to be white-skinned was essential for when Hallelujah Bock struck her Covenant.

And strike her Covenant the Prophetess Hallelujah did.

I know because I was the one who wrote her Covenant down.

****

Hallelujah had me call her Covenant 'The Song of Hallelujah' because she always loved hymns and songs and ditties while she was living. I would even go so far to say the words *were Biblical* because she had me insert her song into the Bible—into all the Bibles she had created for O-Frica and O-Lina. It was a new chapter waiting to be read right after the book of 'Revelation.' I'm also sorry to report the first draft of that song was a terribly pretentious piece of writing. What can I say? Hallelujah might have given me the ability to read and write, but I had to learn to do it adequately. As a consequence, my first attempt vacillated between being stiflingly stilted and gloriously garish. I suppose it's fortuitous Hallelujah never chose to read my work. Still, feedback—*any feedback*—would have been nice.

In any case, Hallelujah then ordered me to deliver what she thought was her 'good news.' So that's what I did. I delivered 'The Song of Hallelujah' to be read in all the corners of O-Frica and O-Lina. I was the one who crafted the words. It was I who proselytized her message. And because I was programmed to believe, I believed. Yes, I was sure I was doing a righteous thing—the Godly thing—because I was doing Hallelujah's thing.

So I said in her song that Hallelujah created the world and all the creatures in it. And I wrote Hallelujah had been created by God and, as God had created Hallelujah, so she created the populations of O-Frica and O-Lina. Therefore, this meant, God had a hand in creating the populations of O-Frica and O-Lina too. And I wrote the populations of O-Frica and O-Lina should have faith and keep faith. And I emphasized faith was the core and keel of Heaven. And I wrote Hallelujah was the Prophetess of God. And I said with enough faith they would fly up to and into and through the sun to receive salvation and heavens of their own, just like Hallelujah had received salvation and a heaven from God. And I proclaimed they would know the power of their faith when their black skin turned white. This would be the sign of God's approval as established by the Prophetess. Then, finally, I made the first of many, many mistakes. I was honest with my brothers and sisters—my fellow shades. Yes, I told the newly created populations of a newly created world that they did not—not one of them—have souls.

It did not go well.

****

Here, I want to pause again and tell you Hallelujah never seemed to enjoy inflicting suffering. She might have. Yes, if salvation was assured, she might have, but no one in her created world ever got as far as salvation. As a result, in terms of her shades, she just saw misery and suffering and death as part of the necessary scaffold to achieve her heavenly perfection. Yes, she developed a certain sanguine resignation about it… and since she has all the time in the afterlife, you really couldn't call any of her actions 'capricious' or 'impulsive.' I also imagine it must be quite difficult to create an entire world and then populate it. What's harder, I suppose, is trying to get all the characters you create to do what you want. The undertaking is massive. Nevertheless, Hallelujah truly did want her shades to bask in the Light of the Lord and travel to exulted deliverance beyond the sun. However, she also believed a measure of free will was essential to the process. This meant her shades had *to choose* to have faith and then achieve salvation through God's ineffable judgment. So the first question became: how do you manipulate free will to lead individuals into faith? And the second becomes: how do you get individuals of faith to behave and perform activities favorable to God's judgment? Inevitably, a lot of trial and error would be required.

But did she enjoy destroying what she created and causing suffering untold?

No.

Still, annihilation is annihilation.

Second pause concluded.

****

So the shades of O-Frica did number 10,000 times 10,000. And the shades of O-Lina did number 10,000 times 10,000. This adds up to 200 million. Yes, this adds up to 200 million people—*who were not quite people*—who I told didn't have souls. And when I told them, they all immediately—at once—descended into madness.

Yes, the words were scarcely received, when riots and fires broke out. Indeed, the words were scarcely received when murders and suicides spread like riots and fire. Some of the shades cut themselves open. And some shades cut other shades open too. Why? They had to be sure. Yes, they had to be sure they didn't have souls. They didn't believe it. Perhaps they couldn't believe it. So they went looking with knives and axes and razors, but found only blood and organs and bone. It was ghastly. I wrote up the entire Butcher's Bill of the event and don't want to lay out the grotesquery twice. I sometimes wonder if I was spared from the insanity of the shades because Hallelujah allowed me to steep in cold knowledge, but ultimately I don't think it matters. Not having a soul doesn't bother me. No, my sense of self is complete without it. However, I never considered the consequence of *telling others* they didn't have souls. I confess: it was shortsighted.

As for Hallelujah, at seeing her newly created world collapse almost instantaneously into ashes and arterial spray, she just sighed softly, but without any sting of failure. As you should know already, in Heaven, a saved soul can never be stung by anything.

"Well, Barbury, we'll just have to try again!" she announced, transforming her sigh into rapt enthusiasm.

And that's what she did.

And that's what we did.

The slate was wiped clean.

****

So Hallelujah took 200 million dead and mangled shades and all the injured plants and animals and all the attending damaged infrastructure which existed throughout her heavenly realm and made them exist no longer. Yes, for a scant moment her new world was newly lifeless and freshly barren once more. And then she brought everything back. Yes, she brought everything back as if nothing ever happened. And then I archived my first attempt at 'The Song of Hallelujah' and wrote another version—also as if nothing happened—but this time I left out the bit about Hallelujah's shades not having souls. It seemed more prudent and it went better. I mean, at least, there wasn't mass suicide and murder, so that was a positive step.

But was it a lie? At the time, I just saw it as an omission. Yes, at the time, I saw it as just another draft of future history. After all, Hallelujah offered a chance at salvation, and was essentially all-powerful, so what else matters other than intentions? And I was created to serve, so I served.

Thus, with Hallelujah's physical reset and my theological rewrite, the newly reconstituted shades began their newly reconstituted lives with no memory of their initial existences of torment and failure. And the populations of O-Frica and O-Lina all went about their programmed activities—from Earth's North American Colonial period circa 1700. And the populations of O-Frica and O-Lina did have faith and keep faith and diligently worshipped the Lord. And the populations of O-Frica and O-Lina did generally thrive.

And Hallelujah often said, "Hallelujah," while fervently keeping one eye on her world and another on her blazing heavenly sun. For the world, she was waiting for someone's black skin to turn white as prophesized. And for the sun, she was waiting for someone whose black skin turned white to fly up to and into and through to the promised salvation she offered in God's name. But after 150 years of shades living and dying and praying not one shade did.

Not one.

****

Be assured, I adhered to my duties during those 150 years. Yes, I wrote down events both major and minor that occurred in O-Frica and O-Lina. I also spent a lot of time, when I wasn't writing, by catching up on the actual history of Earth. It was fascinating. Who could imagine a world so dynamic and diverse, and one which moved in so many directions throughout time? Even after 150 years I felt I barely scratched the surface. I must say, however, it made keeping track of Hallelujah's realm feel relatively easy in comparison. Her world was narrower and consequently less complicated to monitor.

As for the remarkable occurrences in O-Frica and O-Lina during those early years, I won't go into them in depth. This is because—as you might surmise—the populations of O-Frica and O-Lina were to be erased and reset again. Still, two notable things could be mentioned as points of interest. First, although both populations knew of slavery and Hallelujah created slaves, the practice was abolished within ten years. I don't know why. Personally, I lean towards the absence of a racial component. The second outlying event was a whole cottage industry developed in the construction of telescopes. I guess having been told of a place beyond the sun, people wanted to see it. It is the only logical explanation because—though Hallelujah created space around her planet—she created no stars. No, she just wanted a singular focus in the heavens which was the doorway to larger Heaven, itself. She even neglected to set a moon in the sky.

Other than these twin peculiarities, O-Frica and O-Lina flourished. The harvests were good, the worship was regular, the trade robust, and the shades, for the most part, were optimistic and happy. Why wouldn't they be? After all, everyone knew 'The Song of Hallelujah' by heart and they sang it together every Sunday. For them, this meant Hallelujah was looking out for their well-being and God was looking out for their care and safety beyond that. Yes, they believed they were protected by invisible hands.

And yet, alas, 'The Song of Hallelujah' never played out to its promised ending. No, after 150 years not one set of black skin turned white and no one flew upward and through the sun. As for the populations of O-Frica and O-Lina, they seemed not to notice or, if they noticed, seemed not to care. No, they were just content living their best lives and found satisfaction by living them.

But Hallelujah cared.

And when Hallelujah cared about something, she came unto me.

"Oh my! Barbury! Do you remember when I said, 'chatting could be a heavenly experience'?" she asked cheerfully.

As usual, when she spoke I felt so very terrified and so very cold.

Nevertheless, I loved her and was grateful, because I was designed to love her and be grateful.

"Yes, mistress," I replied with a shiver. "Yes, I remember. Yes, Hallelujah, Prophetess of the Lord. How can I be of service? Yes."

****

"Good, Barbury. That's good. It's good you remember," she said.

Then, despite my memory and despite me assuring her of the accuracy of my memory, she went on to recount much of what I already knew by heart. So, Hallelujah reminded me of her Covenant. And, Hallelujah reminded me faith was the core and keel of Heaven. And, Hallelujah told me how she loved her shades, and told me how she loved O-Frica and O-Lina, and how she just wanted people to be saved. And, of course, Hallelujah reiterated and underscored and repeated God loved everyone too. And, of course, she said in Heaven she was supposed to get everything she wanted. And she said—again—it was *her reward* and that it *had been promised*. And she asserted in no uncertain terms she *would get* her perfection. And, yes, it sounded very much like a song when she talked.

Finally, this segued into the main thrust of her conversational focus: the lack of complete flawlessness of her heavenly design, even though her design rested within the larger flawlessness of Heaven itself.

And, Hallelujah told me again what I already knew: she never saw any black skin turn white. And I told her this was true because if someone had achieved the miracle of their black skin turning white, I would have written it down. And she told me she never saw anyone whose black skin turned white fly up to and through the sun to receive their own well-earned celestial reward. And I told her this was true because if someone had achieved the miracle of flying up to and into and through the sun, I would have written it down. And she told me her Covenant was real and it reflected her love and reflected God's love too. And I told her this was undeniably true, because *I had* written it down.

Obviously, I listened as long as Hallelujah wanted me to listen until she got to her point. She wanted to know why the shades of O-Frica and O-Lina weren't achieving salvation and what could be done to facilitate the requirements of her glorious Covenant so generously given.

"Oh my! So, Barbury, since I don't cotton to the mortal world, I turn to my High Priest. I know you have been studying Earth. Do you have any ideas to encourage salvation?"

And I'm sorry to say I did have an idea.

I told her that in much of human history, faith seemed to increase both in consistency and intensity when the faithful were forced to contend with adverse circumstances.

And, yes, I did use the word 'force.'

But, no, I didn't use the phrase 'adverse circumstances.'

The word I actually used was 'suffering.'

And for the next 150 years in the heaven of Hallelujah Bock, suffering is what I witnessed, and suffering is what my brother and sister shades got. I think if I truly did have a soul this suggestion would have heralded my complete damnation.

****

I wish I could say the idea was my own, but the truth is, I stole it from my study of Earth. However, that is no excuse. It is also no excuse that as a saved soul, Hallelujah was immune to suffering and not even aware of what the concept fully entailed. No, for her it was a strange, alien, and hard-to-comprehend idea—but Hallelujah did see it as a revelation.

"Oh my! Barbury! That's a splendid stratagem!" she exclaimed with a laugh.

So the slate was wiped clean again and then she brought everything back again. And I archived my second draft of 'The Song of Hallelujah' and wrote a third. This time I still omitted the fact that Hallelujah's shades didn't have souls, but I also added that the shades would know God's love and Hallelujah's love through 'their struggles.' And I told them their current existences and tribulations and any unpleasantness held no weight compared to their eventual glorious redemption. I even said their world was but a 'pale shade' compared to the world to come. Only later did I realize I had been inadvertently ironic.

And was this third rewrite filled with lies? At the time, I just thought of them as 'modifications.' Yes, they were 'modifications' in the furtherance of Hallelujah's goal of heavenly perfection. Besides, what's the difference between serving up hallowed words or serving up hallowed suffering? *'Service is service, after all,'* I told myself.

And so, the following eras were eras of famine, of war, of disease, and of disasters, both natural and unnatural alike. There was an epoch of parasites and an age of boils. There was a generation of stillborn babies and whole seasons where every ship was dashed upon the rocks. I won't get into the complete litany of horrors, but only ask you to imagine the most awful things and know that Hallelujah Bock's heaven incorporated them all. But don't forget, the goal was salvation, thus every action was justified. Yes, everything was executed for the ultimate benefit of O-Frica and O-Lina so justice was inherent.

"And what did I do during these times of strife and misery?" you might ask. I did my duty, of course. I wrote everything down and when I wasn't writing things down I escaped into the history of Earth again, and into literature, and eventually into pop culture when it was finally invented. Indeed, *Star Trek* was an epiphany. It gave me a way to understand myself and Hallelujah's world. But yes—when I could turn my eyes away from watching the lands of O-Frica and O-Lina both figuratively and literally burn, I did. I dove into the cultures and cultural artifacts of Earth.

Eventually, over the decades, I recorded how eleven times Hallelujah brought her world to extinction or near extinction through suffering and how eleven times she brought everything back once more. Yes, the shades of O-Frica and O-Lina lived and suffered and died only to live and suffer and die again. I fully confess: I was complicit in shaping their anguish. I could do nothing else. I was powerless to mend or soothe.

Lastly, you probably want to know if Hallelujah's scheme—*my suggestion*—worked? Well, faith certainly increased in both consistency and intensity. I wasn't wrong about that. And the peoples of O-Frica and O-Lina did shriek 'The Song of Hallelujah' unto the heavens. But was anyone saved? Did anyone's black skin turn white and did anyone fly up through the sun to their promised emancipation into the Light? What do you think?

No.

Of course not.

Not one person—*who was not quite a person*—achieved salvation.

Sobs, though… they were as boundless as all the Earthly stars.

Yes, they were as boundless as the stars I had read about in Earth's history, but had never actually seen.

****

So now it's been over 300 years in Hallelujah Bock's quest for heavenly perfection and I should start to bring this rather lengthy prayer to its conclusion. This is because Hallelujah has just come again to me for another 'heavenly chat.' And, yes, she began once more with everything I already knew. And then she got to her question. "Now, what can be done?" she asked. Yes, now, what mechanism should she—*should we*—employ next? Yes, suffering increased faith in both consistency and intensity, but salvation was still not being realized. So what else could she do for the people—*who were not quite people*—she so dearly loved?

Do you think I should have just told her 'nothing'? Yes, do you think I should have said: "I'm sorry, Hallelujah, Prophetess of God, but your design is misconceived, an error, and fundamentally flawed?" Indeed, how *would you tell* your creator their project was not only a folly, but a tragic folly at that? Indeed, *could you* tell something Divine that its Divinity had limits? After all, when did a creation ever tell their creator 'no'? Yes, speak true, could you spit in the eye of the indomitable force which made you?

I couldn't.

So I told her the only thing more intense than having to endure the trials and tribulations of suffering is for the faithful to impose those trials and tribulations upon themselves. And this meant sacrifice. *Yes, sacrifice!* And I told Hallelujah I would write in her new song the populations of O-Frica and O-Lina should willfully give up what they loved most to achieve salvation. And I would write in her new song the populations of O-Frica and O-Lina should shun all pleasure. And I would write in her new song *only sacrifice* would pave the way to fulfilling Hallelujah's Covenant… and *only sacrifice* could provide the grist so the shades of O-Frica and O-Lina could get heavens of their own. I wrote God was a *transactional God* and these were the requirements to complete the transaction. This idea, too, I got from Earth.

And so I wrote Hallelujah's new song directing the people of O-Frica and O-Lina to offer up their worldly comforts. And, I wrote they should offer up their food. And, I wrote they should offer up their water. And, I wrote they should offer up all connection to each other. And, yes, I wrote they should even offer up their children. And so it was written: salvation could only be achieved through self-denial, flagellation, and sacrifice. And, yes, the populations of O-Frica and O-Lina would also have to cheer their deprivation because it wasn't enough for them to love Hallelujah and God, but they had to prove their love by loving nothing else.

Oh, and I still wouldn't tell any of them they didn't have souls.

Yes, this would be Hallelujah's song.

And Hallelujah said, "Hallelujah," because she was pleased.

Yes, she was very pleased with me and I almost drowned in her pleasure.

"Oh my! Barbury! That's a splendid design!" Hallelujah celebrated.

And then the slate was wiped clean and the table was reset and another song was codified while the old one went to the archives, because such is the way to draft perfection.

And now a new attempt is underway.

But, at last, were these latest 'modifications' lies?

I've thought a lot about this over the centuries and I finally have come to an irrefutable answer: these 'modifications' *are not lies*. I am an agent of Hallelujah, who is an agent of Heaven, which is a *construct of God*. This means, whatever words I put down come from an authority well beyond my ink or pen. So, if the words change, the words are meant to change. And if the words contradict, the words are meant to contradict. And if the words cause harm, it is harm for a purpose.

And it is not up to readers of Scripture to question Scripture. And it is not up to the writers of Scripture to question Scripture either. No. A writer's voice is not his own. Yes, Absolute Truth only comes from Absolute Power. This is all anyone ever needs to know. Indeed, Hallelujah was designed to serve God, and I am designed to serve Hallelujah, and the populations of O-Frica and O-Lina are designed to fulfill the dictums of 'The Song of Hallelujah.' Such is the way of Heaven. Yes, illumination is only revealed by Light, but the Light comes from somewhere else. No, the Ultimate Authority *is God... and God* can be moved by only one thing.

And this is why I'm writing to all the living people of faith on Earth—all those lucky humans with souls.

It is time for me to ask my 'favor.'

Yes, it is time for me to conclude *my prayer*.

I just hope you're still listening.

****

I said at the beginning 'who gets to tell a story is important.' I also said I wasn't sure if this was my story or Hallelujah's. Nevertheless, this is the story of Hallelujah Bock's heaven and I am the one who wrote it down. I also said I would tell you exactly why I am writing and that moment has come. You see, I have grave doubts whether my latest suggestion will help Hallelujah achieve her heavenly design or her heavenly perfection. My feeling is it will fail a thirteenth time. No, without souls, I don't think anyone in O-Frica and O-Lina will ever achieve salvation, but I also don't think that will stop Hallelujah from trying. And this means Hallelujah will come to me for yet another 'heavenly chat.'

"And do I still have more ideas?" you might ask.

Well, as a saved soul, Hallelujah cannot conceive of rape or torture or child molestation or cannibalism (the non-Transubstantiation kind), *but I can*. Also, I have declined—*so far*—to offer up any of the smorgasbord of fictional torment and tormenters from my Earthly studies during the last 300 years. But, surely, *I can do that too*. Would a monstrous adversary lead O-Frica and O-Lina to salvation? I don't know. Should I suggest a Grendel or Cthulhu or *The Blob* or a zombie apocalypse for Hallelujah's world? I don't know. Should I propose placing a version of Satan himself to tempt and bamboozle and terrorize? Would that do it? Indeed, could a Borg cube zipping through the sky or Cenobites or Thanos or the Stay Puft Marshmallow Man lead the soulless populations of O-Frica and O-Lina to Divine deliverance? Yes, Hallelujah gave me all the knowledge I could absorb and all the imaginative capacity to use such knowledge, so *I can* suggest anything. I am not constricted or constrained by a soul. On top of this, she has instilled in me my prime directive: to do whatever is necessary to get people's skin to change color and then fly up through the sun. Indeed, the Earthly plane is replete with monsters and the monstrous. And I have access to them all—like a rolodex dipped in blood.

But I don't want to.

No, I don't want to draw from my black bag of tricks anymore.

And, I don't want Hallelujah to come to me and ask.

No, I don't want to think up the next terrible narrative for Hallelujah's world.

Thus, I write to you humans—*I am praying to you humans*—because I have only one idea that won't inflict another round of senseless agony on the shades of O-Frica and O-Lina. As I have attested, and hopefully you have witnessed, prayers from the soulless don't work. But everyone knows prayers *from the soulful do*. I've read it throughout all of Earth's history. Yes, the power of *human prayer* has been promised by all your holy texts and from all your holy people. And more, Scripture affirms it, which means God has said it, which means it is as True as Truth can be—as True as the Risen Christ. Yes, *only those with souls* can get God to answer a prayer.

So what I ask—*what I pray*—is for all of you people of faith—*real people with souls*—to pray too. But I'm not asking you to pray for me. And I'm not asking for you to pray even for the shades of O-Frica and O-Lina. I am asking you to pray for Hallelujah Bock. Yes. Please. Pray Hallelujah gets what she wants. Yes, she has earned *her heavenly reward* and deserves *her heavenly perfection*. The power is yours. I know you probably have prayers of your own, but it shouldn't take much effort. Yes, pray Hallelujah gets what she wants because only those with souls can truly move God. Yes, please pray for a different end to this story, just as Hallelujah's shades pray for their black skin to become white and for them to fly up to and into and through the sun. Yes, I beg of you, because I love Hallelujah and I serve her.

So that's the favor I ask. I beseech you pray for Hallelujah.

"Prayers work," your holy books and holy men say. So please use your connection to God to assure this outcome.

And finally I proclaim, "Amen," to close this missive.

Now, I only need to do one last thing: to find some way to get my list of heavenly wishes to the Earthly plane, because only prayers can better a world.

End of Story #9

Intermezzo
(ninth)

Another story is done and the writer waits for his audience to catch up. He knows he has taken a risk in crafting a tale from an unorthodox point of view, but he doesn't know if the risk paid off. The writer continually marvels at how difficult it is to create something. He supposes this always has to be the way; however, he also keenly feels the excruciating and infuriating irony of pursuing an artistic endeavor. Good writing—*good anything, actually*—needs to appear effortless while requiring seemingly herculean amounts of labor. *'Did my latest story succeed?'* the writer wonders as he so often does. He could feel his Devil's Spot urging him to have faith, but self-faith only takes a person so far. Outside perspectives are vital.

"So, now you're trying to ruin prayer?" Mizam asks, laying the stage for the next Divine Algonquin roundtable. His tone is sullen and more than a little petulant, but also resigned.

"Why do you say that?" the writer deflects, not wanting to give anything away.

"You know full well what I'm talking about," Mizam scolds. "You know human prayers—*prayers from the soulful*—will never change the ending of Barbury's story, or *your story*, for that matter! You just want to show prayer is futile and impotent. So don't play coy."

"I'm not playing coy," the writer shoots back. "Surely, an all-powerful God—*your God*—could change Barbury's story. In fact, *He* could change all my stories. *He* could have even intervened and got me not to write at all, right? Yes, *He* needed only to send a sign."

"He did send a sign," Mizam goes on. "He sent me. That's what I came to tell you. Don't deal with the Devil. It will end badly. This was my important message."

"Then why were you late?" the writer challenges. "If it was so important—if *I* was so important—*im-portant*—then why didn't you arrive before I made my deal?"

Mizam takes a moment to regroup. He isn't used to personal attacks.

"Well, everything happens for a reason. Maybe God wanted you to make the right choice on your own? Maybe *He wanted you* to want *Him*?" he finally answers.

"Now who's playing coy?" the writer responds.

Meanwhile, the Devil says nothing. He just keeps shuffling through the pages of the last tale, looking pensive. The writer alternates his focus between the two supernatural beings. His mind and his Devil's Spot whisper to him that something significant is at hand.

"I really don't like experimental writing," the Devil eventually interrupts. "But I did tell you, I would *get you there*. And *here you are*. This is a story which pushes the boundaries of what a story can be. Yes, this is the kind of story where it doesn't rely on what other people think about it. They can like it or hate it, but one way or the other, it hits the memory. It's infectious. I can't believe you tried to get real readers to pray for a fictional world."

The writer doesn't immediately say anything back. Instead, both his mind and his Devil's Spot hum and thrum at the Devil's words. In fact, *both flare*!

"So the story works?" the writer asks tentatively.

"Yes," the Devil affirms. Like always, he is direct and unequivocal.

"I was afraid it might have gone too far," the writer continues.

"It does," the Devil answers. "But that's why it's good. It is a completely original work from a completely unique vantage. There isn't another story like it that comes to mind. This is exactly the kind of artistic execution you sold your soul for. Don't go all gooey, but you should feel very satisfied. This work is adequate."

"Yes, enjoy one thrill of mortal satisfaction before you're writhing in hellfire for all eternity," Mizam comments.

"I guess I'll transition from writing to writhing, then. But any advice on where to go now? I want to make sure I take advantage of every opportunity I have left," the writer says, ignoring the Angel and looking only to the Devil.

"Well, you just wrote something experimental, so maybe you should try your hand at something traditional. Traditional fables usually have talking animals. Also, usually, they are short. Embrace simplicity and familiar forms. What do you think?" the Devil prompts.

"I like it. I especially like the idea of 'short.' I can't imagine what it's like to write an entire novel," the writer concludes.

And then more ink is put to paper as the writer again tries to make what he writes appear effortless.

'Poof!—indeed,' the writer thinks to himself.

Go Tell It to the Lamb

(Story #10)

Once, when Humanity was very young—so young people called it 'Mankind' instead of 'Humankind'— men understood themselves by looking towards the animals. Yes, the men watched the animals and noted their traits. And the men observed the abilities of creatures large and small. And the men assessed the animals' demeanors and dispositions. This was useful, the men thought. It taught them how they were both like and unlike the animals. Then, after a time, each man— and eventually each woman—realized they weren't like or unlike all the animals, but rather every man and every woman was personally connected to one specific kind of animal alone. That animal came to be recognized as an individual's 'Spirit Guide.'

Thus, the lion chose men who were brave. And the most fleet of feet was chosen by the hare. And a shy woman was the choice for the mouse. While the tigress welcomed strong mothers. And the owl selected the wise and on and on. Yes, the humans decided the animals would determine who they connected with. And so, from all over the world, the animal-worshippers espoused the philosophy that every man and woman had a link to an animal of a specific type—save for one: never would the lamb be a Spirit Guide.

The reason for this was simple. The lamb was without guile or defense. Yes, the lamb had no armor like the turtle, or swiftness like the sparrow, or aggression like the boar. Yes, the lamb could not camouflage like the chameleon or stink like the skunk. And it wasn't crafty as a fox and couldn't dive for cover like the shrew. No, the lamb just went around bleating and nuzzling and looking delicious. Thus, everyone concluded the lamb was made for only two things: consumption and sacrifice. Yes, the lamb was made for consumption without sadness and for sacrifice without hesitation. Thus, the mandate went out: the lamb was to be the martyr for every living thing because the young world needed a martyr and the young world especially needed a martyr who was young. Even the grown sheep agreed: to spill blood, innocent and pure, calls forth the best blessings.

So, all the animal types—except the lamb—guided their human counterparts. "This thicket is a good place to spend the night," the doe would say. "There is something in that thicket over there which could be worth watching," said the cat to a curious woman. "This rotted food might be nice for me to eat, but for you it is nothing but sickness and death," advised the vulture.

And on it went.

However, all the animals shared one common piece of advice to their human charges. "Be patient, patient, patient," all the animals would say. Yes, to the beasts of forests, and for those that roamed the plains, and to the creatures of the sea, human beings always seemed to be—*constantly*—in such a rush. They ran when they didn't need to run. They fought when they didn't need to fight. They ate when they were already full. They believed in things they didn't need to believe. Mostly, though, the animals thought the humans were continually looking—*continually searching for something*—but didn't know what they were searching for. The animals also found this funny. No, they might not have had the abilities of higher thought, but, as animals, surely they had better instincts.

Yes, the humans were perpetual searchers and so they perpetually kept searching—even after their deaths. But now the animals guided humans. Subsequently, when humans died, the animals followed them into the afterlife. And, even though the lamb was never a Spirit Guide on Earth, the lamb followed too.

But the animals faced a problem in the human afterlife. No, for animals, death was simple: they simply went to the place where existence ended. But for humans, death became more complicated. No, for humans, they did not know the place where existence ended and the animals didn't know where it ended for them either. Worse, the humans kept up their searching—searching all over—but the place where existence ended was the one place no human being wanted to find. Consequently, the animals were failing as Spirit Guides.

This is when the lamb finally revealed itself, with his innocent shining eyes and his fleece as white as snow.

"Be patient, patient, patient," said the lamb to the animals.

"Be patient, patient, patient," said the lamb to the humans.

"As you are aware, I never guided humans or animals on Earth, but in the afterlife, *I can guide you all*," the lamb said to both humans and animals. "I will go up the mountain to the place where existence ends and wait for you there. I know *The Spot*. When you are ready, come unto me. Take all the time you need. I am the king of patience."

And the lamb was patient, and patient the lamb needed to be. This was because the humans took their time while the animals bided theirs. The men and women distracted themselves from looking at the mountain where all existence ends and the animals followed the humans in their distractions. The animals had no choice. Yes, the animals chose to be spiritually entwined with humans and now were covenant-bound to follow these strange creatures in all their wanderings, even after death.

"Be patient, patient, patient," the animals said to each other, but they no longer said these words to the humans.

But time passes, and time is guarded by the Spirit Guides of both the cheetah and the snail. Nevertheless, fast or slow, *the time did pass*. And one by one the humans and their Spirit Guides made the long trek up the mountain to the place where existence ends—and found their way to the patient lamb.

Finally, only one man and his Spirit Guide remained. The man was just a human and his Spirit Guide was the hummingbird.

"Well, hummingbird," the man said, "all the others have gone up the mountain. I suppose we should go up as well."

The hummingbird didn't reply because he, too, had long waited to go to the place where existence ends.

So up the mountain the man and hummingbird went and, when they reached the very top, there was nothing but a small plateau and a treacherously steep cliff on the other side.

There, the lamb greeted the travelers with his innocent shining eyes and his fleece as white as snow.

"We have come so you can guide us to the place where all existence ends," said the man. "I am the last of the animal-worshippers and this hummingbird is the last of the Spirit Guides. We declare ourselves ready to take the leap."

"And leap you will," replied the lamb in a sweet and soothing voice, "but before you do, you must do something you might think unpleasant or unfair. You must shoot the hummingbird with a silver arrow because only a human can destroy a Spirit Guide. This is the light and the way for you to get to the place where existence ends—*the Only Way*."

Still, the hummingbird said nothing and the man felt no need to object. The two were committed.

"Here. Take this bow and arrow and complete the task," the lamb continued softly.

Then a small bow and arrow appeared on the ground beside the man, gleaming in silvery-white. The argentate sheen caused the bow to take on the semblance of a harp and the arrow to take on the semblance of a fountain pen.

The man picked up the instruments of destruction.

"Aim true," the hummingbird said as his last words.

And the man shot the bird in the heart and sent it tumbling over the cliff's edge.

The arrow had barely struck when the sound of uproarious laughter also flew through the air.

It was the lamb.

But when the man spun around, no longer did the lamb have innocent shining eyes or a fleece as white as snow. In fact, the lamb wasn't even standing on four legs anymore. Instead, the lamb staggered and swayed on two hooves, walking like a man, and his fleece had turned black as coal. As for his eyes, they brimmed with fury and madness.

"YOU FOOLS!" the lamb bellowed. "NOW I AM THE ONLY SPIRIT GUIDE LEFT! YES, LOOK OVER THE CLIFF'S EDGE AND YOU WILL SEE THE BONES OF THE CAMEL, THE HAWK, AND THE CROCODILE! YES, PEER OVER THE PRECIPICE AND YOU'LL SEE CREATURES AS MASSIVE AS THE WHALE AND AS MINISCULE AS THE FLEA—ALL ROTTING IN THE SUN! YES, ALL ROTTING *IN THE LIGHT*! GONE!

GONE! ALL GONE! AT LAST AND AT LAST, I WILL GUIDE HUMANITY AND I WILL RULE THEM! YES, I WAS THE KING OF PATIENCE AND NOW I WILL BE *THE KING OF KINGS*!"

Then the lamb hooted and hollered once more—a cackling-bleating laughter that seemed to echo everywhere.

The man said nothing. And the man didn't peer over the cliff's edge. And the man chose not to look to the lamb. Instead, he left the scene and left the Spirit Guides both present and long gone. Yes, the man traveled back down the mountain and out into the empty desert.

And the man realized: if he needed a guide, he would have to look to himself. And the man considered further: no, never again would he kiss the foot of any animal in worship—and especially—he would *never-ever* kiss the hoof of a lamb.

End of Story #10

Intermezzo

(tenth)

"Wow…" the Devil says when he finishes the tenth tale: 'Go Tell It to the Lamb.' "This story is even more blasphemous than the rhyming one where you used actual blasphemy…"

"Yes, it is," Mizam agrees with unvarnished anger in his voice.

"I just wish you gave the animals names… particularly the lamb…" the Devil continues. "And I really hope the camel over the cliff wasn't Humpy. I've kind of grown attached."

"He did give the lamb a name!" Mizam breaks out fully, attempting to roar. "The Lamb is: Jesus Christ, Son of God, Holy Servant, Bread of Life, Bridegroom, Authority, Author and Perfecter of Faith, Chief Cornerstone, Immanuel, the

True Vine, Victorious One, Wonderful Counselor, Mighty God, Everlasting Father, and Prince of Peace! Yes, *He* is the *Way and the Light!* This *boy-writer* here didn't even try to hide it! Now, I'm glad you made your deal. I'm happy you're going to burn in Hell! God was right to abandon you. You are unworthy of my Father's Mercy!"

The writer and the Devil exchange a skeptical glance, both utterly unmoved by the Angel's tirade.

"Um… that's a little un-Christ-like," the writer comments.

"And you're mischaracterizing God, I think," the Devil chimes in. "He isn't just *your father*, but he's the writer's father and my father as well. Just because someone sins or rebels, doesn't erase the paternity from whence they came."

"That may be the case, but this writing is deplorable! What an ignoble way for a son to treat *His Father, Son, Holy Ghost, and Savior*," the Angel shoots back, trying to maintain his rage.

"Yet, I don't understand how a father can be his own son and also a ghost—all at the same time. I also don't know why I need a 'savior' and I have a real 'father' already. A lot about religion doesn't make sense. So, forgive me if I wanted to explore some of the quibbles which retard the thinking of the world," the writer responds, tersely. He is tired of explaining himself.

"Don't use the 'R-word,'" the Devil quips.

Meanwhile the writer keeps up his writing. He can feel his collection of fictions beginning to draw to a close.

"Good. More jokes," Mizam almost spits.

"Listen, if you don't like his stories or the subject matter, then don't read them. You delivered your message and now you are no longer required to be here. Go back to Heaven, if you desire. Or, travel to another imperiled soul—but try to get there in a timely fashion. What I'm saying is: if you hate this, just leave. After all, why would you want to stick around reading a book which makes you so angry?" the Devil challenges.

For a moment, there is silence and uncertainty coming from the Angel of the Lord. After puffing up, he deflates again like so much hot air escaping back into the ether. His fingers nervously shuffle through the completed pages—the creative product generated by a human mind—as if the pages could lend him an answer.

"Well… I wanna see how it ends…" the Angel finally says.

"Then, you take the next story first," the writer offers. "But I warn you: you aren't going to like this one either. The title pretty much gives away the game."

The next story is titled: 'The End of Heaven.'

The End of Heaven

(Story #11)

1

In Hell—*the nice part*—Thanaxagoras and Celeste Talon fast approached a singular moment. The signs had been going on for weeks, maybe longer, but the final piece of evidence dropped at dinner. They were eating at a Spanish restaurant called 'A Bowl of Bolero,' attended by a *maître d'* with another 4,000-year-old name. Celeste ordered an Anis del Toro and a tilapia platter infused with black licorice, which Thanaxagoras thought was gross. These were some of the signs: strange food cravings and obscure Hemingway references, along with bouts of slight nausea and occasional dizziness—all of which Celeste and Thanaxagoras actively ignored. But 'A Bowl of Bolero' also appointed itself with serenading opera singers and during one particularly powerful soprano solo Celeste's left breast began to lactate. Now the situation couldn't be denied. Celeste Talon and Thanaxagoras had become pregnant in Hell.

"We need to go to the eternal playground. I'm about to lose my shit," Celeste whispered, while surreptitiously dabbing her damp blouse with a linen napkin. She was working very hard to remain calm and not draw attention to herself.

"I was thinking the University Concourse? We need more information," Than replied, but could feel his own ethereal objectivity fraying rapidly.

"No. You're right. Let's go," he reconsidered.

The pathways quickly took them to the nondescript camouflage alley and, surprisingly, Thanaxagoras had no trouble finding the hidden corridor with the drowning man inside. They went past the bloody spectacle and entered the playground which had been reconfigured for nighttime activities. All the animals still meandered about, but between dusk and dawn there were fields of lightning bugs for the children to catch and a lazy river bobbing with brightly colored inner-tubes. The river shone like an iridescent snake beneath a full moon four times its normal size. Other amazing things dotted the visual landscape, and it was wondrous; however, this was no time for wonder. Wonder was for appreciating the present, but not when the future danced on the edge of a knife.

"I take it this has never happened before?" Celeste asked.

"Never," Than said, emphatically.

They walked arm in arm and in a rush, but since they had no destination in mind, their rushing was aimless.

"Never," he repeated. "There aren't even stories or rumors about such an event… except about—"

"The Antichrist?" the Devil interrupted.

During the couple's aimless push forward, Thanaxagoras and Celeste mainly kept their vision down on their own traveling feet and the frowzy grass beneath. Consequently, they came upon the Devil unaware. Nevertheless, when they looked up, there the Devil was, still in the form of a man, except for the twin yellow sparks of his eyes glinting in the moonlight. He stood sedately next to Humpy the camel, and was feeding the animal a very large carrot. Humpy seemed to be enjoying the delicacy with toothy gusto.

"I'm sorry, Dark Lord," Thanaxagoras began in a bit of a stutter. "I wasn't expecting to find you here…"

"No one really expects to find me," the Devil answered, "but I want to be the first to congratulate you. It's a rare treat to witness and celebrate the impossible."

"The impossible?" Celeste asked. "So I assume this really is without precedent?"

"Utterly and completely without precedent," the Devil affirmed. "It's nice to see you both again, though."

"Wait! The Antichrist? Are you saying the world—*that everything*—is going to end because we got pregnant? Is this part of some prophecy or design?" Thanaxagoras anxiously pressed.

"No prophecy or design I've ever heard of. But I wouldn't put too much stock in prophecies anyway. At best, they are unsatisfying riddles and, at worst, they are addle-minded gibberish. No. This is just... unprecedented. There is no other word for it..." the Devil said.

"Then how did this happen?" Celeste probed further. "I've been here for years and I don't even menstruate!"

"You don't?" Thanaxagoras hazarded.

Celeste gave him a sour look which collapsed the question immediately.

"Menstruation was one of my father's punishments. One of his curses on women," the Devil replied. "Thus I felt no need to replicate it in my realm. I'm kind of a feminist that way. But I also wouldn't get too caught up in the simulated biology of the afterlife either. It will give you a headache."

"I've been having those as well," Celeste commented.

"I want to go back to our baby potentially being the Antichrist..." Thanaxagoras returned. "Is that still on the table?"

"No," the Devil responded. "The sole element every book of lore and prophecy and rambling agrees upon is: I'm to be the Antichrist's father. Whether he is born here, or born on Earth, or in a galaxy far, far away, is up to debate. But I'm his Dad... or *her* Dad. So unless Celeste and I had some secret—and I'm assuming mutually satisfying—tryst, this child is not mine. *Ipso facto*, he is not the Antichrist."

The Devil flashed a rogue's grin at the conclusion of his explanation.

"Then what was the cause? Clearly, something supernatural is going on? Why is this happening? And why now?" Celeste continued.

"Who knows?" the Devil stated. "Maybe it is some anomaly of 'The Way,' or perhaps my own father is messing with all of us, or, even, the power of love allowed for the consecrated conception to take hold. I honestly have no idea. It's kind of exhilarating, actually—to not know what's happening or how it will end…"

"That's a split infinitive…" Celeste muttered, her face pinched in pregnant concentration.

"Well, I'm glad you're enjoying yourself, but what about us?" Thanaxagoras challenged, almost forgetting to whom he was addressing. "What I mean is: is this a blessing? Is it dangerous? Are we going to birth an abomination? A messiah? Just a plain old baby? Do you have any guesses?"

"Not a one," Satan admitted.

Silence fell, broken only by the distant laughter of the children who were damned, playing about the world, after the world. There was also the sound of Humpy munching happily on his carrot.

"Okay," Celeste resumed. "I suppose we have to talk about choices and options. At the very least, I'm going to need a doctor."

"Oh, yeah," Than contributed. "I personally know Dr. Spock—the baby expert, not the Vulcan. He could help…"

"I was thinking a doctor of a different sort…" Celeste said hesitantly. "Maybe we should discuss the *Hills Like White Elephants* scenario. If that's even possible."

"The Hemingway story?" Than asked.

"Celeste, we're in Hell. You can use the word 'abortion,'" the Devil lightly chided.

"An abortion, then. Should we consider it?" she asked, her eyes going to Thanaxagoras.

"I don't know. Would it work? Who would do it? How?" Than went on. In standard times, he prided himself on remaining cool, but things had gotten gravely serious and seriously fast.

"Schutzstaffel Josef Mengele, formerly of the Third Reich, is pretty much up for any medical procedure," Satan said. "I bet he would make the attempt…"

"I *will not have* a Nazi war criminal getting anywhere near my uterus," Celeste announced forcefully.

"Fair enough. He's quite skilled as a doctor, however," the Devil replied casually.

"But the choice is mine?" Celeste asked.

"Of course," the Devil replied. "Choices are what Hell is about! Personally, I believe Thanaxagoras should have a say, but ultimately, the decision is yours."

Here, the children's laughter—the children who were damned—turned into frightened screams. There was a disturbance at the edge of the eternal playground and it didn't take long to discern where the disturbance was heading. Even Humpy broke free from his Master's hold to run off into the semi-darkness.

In footsteps, the phantom appeared.

It was Mizam, the Angel. He was still fat, but he was huffing and puffing like a pack of wolves were voraciously snapping at his heels.

"Lucifer! They're coming!" he shouted as he neared.

"Who?" asked Lucifer.

"The Angels! All of them!"

"Why?" Thanaxagoras jumped in.

"*For her!*" Mizam breathlessly continued. "For her and whatever is growing inside her! They're going to restart THE GREAT WAR!"

And Mizam pointed at Celeste, but not at her face or chest. Instead, he specifically pointed to her reproductive area and whatever was developing not even the Divine could say would be good or evil.

Thanaxagoras blushed in Hell.

"They want to kill it!" Mizam finished.

2

In Heaven—*where all the parts were pretty nice*—Archangel Michael sounded the heavenly klaxons, ordering every Angel and every saved soul to make preparation for a final battle. The Celestial Civil War was going to recommence and this time *he* would end it once and for all. Every resource was to be marshalled, every weapon readied, and each heavenly occupant, wherever they resided, was conscripted to fight or contribute to the glorious carnage.

And it would be *glorious*.

The Archangel Michael had thought of little else since the end of the first conflict—the one where His Father forbade Him from eviscerating His brother Lucifer in a magnificent spray of sublime light and fluids. 'Yes, God let Cain slaughter Abel, but Satan only gets exile—not to mention a whole kingdom of his own. It's enough to make a loyal son rebel,' Michael mused without irony. This was because—like so many things—irony rarely touched those seated within a feathery perch.

So Archangel Michael convened his war council, consisting of the Angel Gabriel, the Angel Castiel, and the Angel Clarence. These were Michael's most loyal and subservient advisors. They sat at a table in the shape of a cross with Michael at the head, two other Angels at the crossbeam ends, and Clarence at the foot. Long ago, during the first skirmish, Michael had over twenty advisors and the table was round, but over the centuries he had winnowed his flock and changed all that. No, *this war* would not be waged by committee. Michael, in fact, was almost giddy at the prospect of celestial bloodshed.

"I call this meeting to order," Michael said officiously. He had to keep himself from chuckling at the word 'meeting.' In truth, the gathering was more like a formality or—at best—a debriefing. Opinions would not be solicited or required.

"Okay, our first move is to send out small strike teams to each one of Hell's entry points as a massive diversion while our main force lays siege to Hell's Eastern Gate. Simultaneously, we will dispatch two commando units down the Jesus Crevasse to rally among the Bogs of Sloth and the Forests of Lust. The Sloth contingent needs to be comprised of flying forces only, due to the paralyzing snakes which pervade this territory. Castiel, you will lead that group. As for the Forests of Lust—Clarence, take a platoon of Cupids and Cherubim to draw out the molesters from Pedophiles' Grove and smite them without mercy.

This will provide footholds behind enemy lines to allow for reinforcements when Celestial Brigades 4, 11, and 13 eventually breach the walls…"

"Whoa, Michael! Wait a second! With respect, before we discuss strategy or tactics shouldn't we cover more rudimentary issues?" Gabriel interjected, in an uncharacteristic display of personality and independence.

Michael sighed.

"Like what?" he asked sullenly.

"Well," Gabriel continued, "first, are we sure it's genuine? Are we sure there is an actual pregnancy and that it is actually happening in Hell? I mean… we really shouldn't start an invasion without knowing the facts…"

"The facts are clear," Michael sniped, wanting war and not more words. "You felt the pregnancy revelation, the same as I, didn't you? And you know the revelation didn't come from Heaven, don't you? And you know it didn't come from Earth. And you know it didn't come from a neutral section of 'The Way.' No, the pregnancy revelation had Hell's signature! Hence, a child has been conceived in Hell! And if a child has been conceived in Hell—*ipso facto*—he is the Antichrist, and could destroy all life and all of the afterlife as we know it! Is there anything you're still unclear about?"

"But I thought Satan had to be the Antichrist's father? I grant an embryo is developing, but are we certain of the paternity?" Gabriel pressed.

"*Who else* would get someone pregnant in Hell? Yes, name one other entity that would have the power or desire? No, for 6,000 years, there has never been a conception in the afterlife and your theory is: the Devil ***is not*** involved? So what would you like to do? Take a little trip to the fiery abode of eternal torment and disgrace and make an inquiry? Give me a break..." Michael ridiculed.

Gabriel went quiet. He hated when the Archangel became so intractable that even asking a simple question was like throwing an apple into a minefield.

"My concern isn't so much about the invasion, but about resources," Castiel picked up, also out of character and unusual for him. Castiel was the liaison to the lesser and greater Angels and the realms of the saved souls. Subsequently, he was the least outspoken of the trio because Michael didn't much care to hear about the anxieties of those beneath his position.

"Oh good! Another civilization heard from!" Michael spat. "We *hold* all of Heaven and *control* the very Forge of Creation, itself! But, by all means, what are your resource concerns?"

Castiel pursed his lips, but persisted nonetheless.

"Well, Michael, quite a few of the saved souls, some of the collectives, and even a fair number of Angels have expressed a variety of... reservations," Castiel began. "You see, we have a lot of... um... pacifists among our potential ranks. We also have some veterans of the original... melee... who don't relish going back into battle with their former kin. This being the case, I was wondering... um... if you wanted to address any of these... um... trepidations?"

Michael held his head in his hands and inhaled and exhaled noisily. Finally, he answered.

"*Cowards...*" Michael hissed. "You can tell the Quakers and the Buddhists and the Amish and the Hippies and the Peaceniks and whoever else is against this war—or against the concept of war, in general—*to literally fall in line!* There are no half-measures now. Remind them, by their very existence, they signed up for the conflict between good and evil and this is the time to fight. Tell them that God, *Himself*, has issued the order! And if that doesn't light a fire under them, announce they are more than welcome to walk among the smoldering ruins of Hell for the rest of eternity after the war, because—*sure as shit*—they won't be allowed to stay here!"

Castiel imperceptibly edged away from the table. He could feel Michael's anger and almost taste his rage. They were like bands of deadly radiation spinning off an unstable star. He wasn't used to such intense disquiet.

"Okay, Michael. Okay," Castiel replied. "But did God really order it? I mean, I know *He* hasn't given a verbal command for a few thousand years, but did *He* really send a sign? I only ask... because... you know... *they* will probably ask... and... uh..."

"*My Faith is God's Sign!*" Michael fumed.

Castiel went mute, submitting to the zealotry of a fanatic.

"The worry I have is," Clarence said, entering the fray, "are you sure we will win?"

Like Gabriel and Castiel, Clarence rarely spoke, but Michael thought him the most sober-minded of the bunch. He was always practical, and never hysterical, and Michael enjoyed his company as much as he could enjoy anyone's company. Michael often thought, if Clarence and he had been born on Earth, he would call Clarence a 'work friend.'

"Finally! Someone has something worth asking!" Michael exclaimed as his exasperation turned to exuberance.

"To answer, Clarence, we will *absolutely* win this war! It's not because our cause is more just, or our resolve far superior, or that it is prophesized—though these things are true—it is due to the fact *we have two secret weapons* that Hell doesn't!"

The Archangel nearly swooned. Never had the Angels seen Michael so excited or aroused.

"What weapons?" all three asked at the same time.

Michael beamed with a self-satisfied grin. He had waited for this moment almost as long as he had waited for the resumption of the inevitable conflict.

"The first weapon," Michael began, "is the solution to this little word puzzle. I came up with it myself. Here is a riddle worthy of the Sphinx!

'I come through the door, but don't stand on the floor.
I come from a tree, but I'm not in its core.
I cannot be caught, but I can surely be cast.
I am cold and am sunless, but I can move slow and move fast!
What am I?'"

"Does anyone want to fancy a guess?" Michael challenged, with teeth like chiseled pearls.

The Angels looked at one another, not so much in contemplation, but in profound confusion. They knew Michael to be a perpetually aggressive and surly Archangel, but he *wasn't playful*. The change of scene and demeanor was downright unnerving to witness.

"Darkness?" Gabriel chanced, believing it was better to answer than not.

"Nope," Michael said, still smiling in razored pearly white.

"A shadow?" gambled Castiel, edging imperceptibly back towards the table and putting on a brave face.

"That's closer," the Archangel hinted. "Come on, Clarence! Don't let me down!"

Clarence despised riddles, but he mentally sifted through the available clues about what could be employed as a unique weapon given the nature of Heaven's composition. For instance, 'darkness' was a terrible guess. Where in Heaven would you find it? And what good would it do against Hell anyway? Ultimately, with a little effort, his mind worked out the problem and epiphany washed over him.

"Shades," Clarence said, definitively and confidently.

"Bingo!" cheered Michael, who in the last few minutes had become more like an eager schoolboy than Heaven's most fearsome warrior.

"You want to use *shades* in the war against Hell?" Castiel asked.

"You bet! Consider: Lucifer and his legions *love* to punish the damned! And they love to do it *personally*. No, they don't use shades to do their dirty work! And this means they barely have any! And that means *we* have the advantage! Talk about resources! Imagine millions upon millions of *our shades* thrashing themselves against the battlements of Hell while we pick and choose our targets! It'll be like shooting an ocean of fine fish in a barrel! It's genius!"

"Okay," Clarence agreed. He could do little else. "But what is the second weapon? And I'd rather not have it explained in the form of a riddle. I feel the stakes are too high for wordplay."

Instead of saying anything, Michael just reached under his white robe and presented the additional weapon to the group. It was an iPad. He set it in front of the Angels so they could see what was on the screen.

"What's that? Are those plans for a bomb?" Gabriel asked.

"No," Michael finished proudly. "*This is the bomb.* I also invented it. Let me explain… and, Clarence… no more riddles, I promise as much as I promise we will be victorious in this war, work friend."

Clarence didn't reply. He was too busy studying the iPad screen and wondering if Michael and Heaven had gone insane, or if it was just him.

3

Returning to Hell, Thanaxagoras, Celeste, and the Devil waited for Mizam to catch his breath, as well as for the eternal playground to regain equilibrium once again. The children needed some time to adapt to the unnatural presence of an Angel, fresh from Heaven, moving about their territory. Most had run for cover to hide wherever they could, and only now occasionally popped up their heads to spy and peek. Catching sight of them reminded Celeste of Dorothy's trip to Munchkinland in *The Wizard of Oz*, but she didn't voice the obvious reference.

"Feeling better, Mizam?" the Devil asked.

"Yes. Thank you," the Angel answered. "It was exceptionally hard to get here."

Thanaxagoras snorted.

"I bet that's the first time anyone ever said such a thing about Hell," he commented.

"I had to slip in through the Jesus Crevasse," Mizam continued.

"What's the Jesus Crevasse?" Celeste whispered to Than, not wanting to interrupt.

"When Jesus Christ came to Hell and ascended to Heaven on the third day, he punched a hole in Hell's ceiling. Not even Satan was able to repair it," Thanaxagoras explained.

"Oh," she said.

"But I came as fast as I could," Mizam went on. "Archangel Michael rang the war klaxons immediately after feeling the revelation. There was no debate. I'm not even sure if he convened a war council…"

"So you came to warn me?" asked the Devil.

"What? No. Yes. Well, it isn't fair!" the Angel exclaimed. "Look, I have always been a happy soldier of Heaven, but what's currently going on in Heaven *is not heavenly*. Heaven isn't about sneak attacks… and Heaven definitely isn't about slaughtering the unborn. I don't care if the baby comes out with three heads and they are all spitting acid and fire! Michael's proclamation included a directive to 'rip the child from the harlot's womb and crush it underfoot on sight'! That's a direct quote!"

"Oh God!" Celeste cried.

"Exactly," Mizam concurred.

"But you know they'll call you 'a traitor' for doing this?" the Devil picked up again.

"I don't care. If there is one thing you have taught me, it's that I have free will and free will means not standing idle during an event you can't abide! I fully accept the consequences of my actions. Principles are nothing if you don't stand for them."

"I couldn't have said it better myself," the Devil affirmed. "But what about God? Does he plan on weighing-in?"

"You know God. *He* doesn't personally weigh-in on anything anymore. No, we're on our own," Mizam said dejectedly. "Yes, we're on our own..." he repeated.

"Okay," Celeste picked up, "this was some useful dialogue, but what now? What are we supposed to do?"

"Well, I have to go and shore up Hell's defenses. Mizam, I could use your help..." the Devil began. "But you, Celeste, have something far more vital to do."

"What?" Thanaxagoras asked.

"Get a pre-natal check-up. I'll send someone here to make a house call. Rest assured, this is the safest place in Hell. Yes, the doctor will see you shortly," the Devil finished.

Thanaxagoras and Celeste looked at each other and then turned to call after the Devil as he and Mizam departed.

"Don't send Mengele!" they both yelled, theatrically.

They couldn't help themselves.

Then there was laughter which made even the children who were damned come out from their hiding places.

Equilibrium had been restored.

4

In Heaven, the three Angels were struggling with what they were seeing. They stared at the iPad which Michael said was a bomb, but they were also looking at a picture of a bomb—albeit a cartoonish illustration of one on the iPad screen. The bomb had a round drum like a bowling ball and a plug on top with a white fuse twisting out of it. Written on it was: 'Acme Explosive and Activated Praise Company.' A prompt for an activation code floated eerily underneath the image.

"Don't worry," Michael declared with his perfect smile, "the bomb isn't armed. I'm not an idiot. I programmed it so it needs a password."

This did little to calm anyone's unease and the Angels stole another worried look between one another.

"Yes, I've been working on this for quite some time," Michael continued, reaching out and stroking the iPad almost in a caress. "In fact, I started the process right after the first conflict because—as with any dispute regarding power or religion—you can always count on *more war*. So I found a way to collect or coalesce… I guess you would call them 'particles'… from 'The Way' itself. I think they might be molecules from that old mythical god named 'Chaos,' but origination doesn't really matter. All that matters is:

this thing has been collecting energy for over 6,000 years and I suspect it will annihilate *just about anything*. Yes… this baby… *is ready to blow…*"

"But iPads haven't been around for 6,000 years," Gabriel said, and instantly wished he hadn't.

"No. *But I have*," Michael sneered. "It wasn't always an iPad. It was a cup and an hourglass and a sword made of ice and a bunch of other stuff. The picture wasn't always a cartoon bomb either, but I've been accused of lacking whimsy, so a cartoon bomb—*why the hell not*? Any other boring inanities before we move on?"

Gabriel again went silent. As swiftly as Michael had gone from angry to childlike, another turn arrived like a caustic whirlwind.

"Who will deploy it and how will it work?" asked Clarence, neutrally.

"Excellent, Clarence! Another *not-inane* question!" Michael announced while making sure Gabriel caught some of his glare. "For the answer, I ask: if you have two secret weapons, what is the best way to use them? Mind me. This isn't a riddle—it's just an inquiry about maximal utility."

Clarence instantly knew what Michael was going for, but Castiel skipped the line.

"You combine them!" Castiel proclaimed triumphantly.

"Yes, that's right. Too bad, Clarence. Maybe you'll get there first, next time," Michael went on.

"I did get there first," Clarence corrected. "Castiel just stole my thunder."

"Well, there'll be thunder enough for everyone soon.

Now, can we get back to the business at hand? I have to leave and procure a legion of shades and my suicide bomber. After all, super-combinations of secret weapons do not create themselves!" Michael ended.

Clarence, despite his best intentions to remain objective, felt an infinitesimal tic quaver through him. A plan was coming together, but—as with any plan—uncertainty came with it. The scent of the prospect was less than pleasant. There was peril. The Angel of the Lord could odor this too.

5

In the eternal playground, Celeste's pre-natal check-up proceeded apace. It was conducted inside a circus tent to not further upset the children and so the pregnant couple could have a simulacrum of privacy. The Devil had sent Hippocrates—that ancient, original man of medicine—which made Celeste and Thanaxagoras breathe a sigh of relief. Though they didn't mention it to one another, both believed there was an outside chance Satan may have actually chosen to send Mengele as a joke.

After a careful examination, Hippocrates began: "It's been *a long time* since I attended a pregnancy, but everything seems normal. I would place the gestation around thirteen weeks and the mother and the two ride-a-longs are healthy. 'Ride-a-long,' that's the correct slang for 'fetus,' right? I'm trying to be more modern and contemporary. It's not easy."

"I never heard of it," Thanaxagoras said.

"Me neither," replied Celeste, before she realized they both had missed the point. "Wait! *Two ride-a-longs*?"

"Yes. You are pregnant with twins—a boy and a girl—as far as I can tell. Huh. I really thought 'ride-a-longs' was a saying," Hippocrates went on.

"*Twins…*" Thanaxagoras whispered, slightly in shock.

"Well, fraternal twins… but yes. Congratulations," the doctor answered.

Celeste took Thanaxagoras's hand and guided it to her stomach. They met each other's gaze with warm and loving eyes.

"I can't believe this is happening," she said.

"I can't believe I'm going to be a father," he said.

"I can't believe the Devil is hiding a bunch of mentally challenged souls and friendly animals in a secret section of Hell," Hippocrates commented. "I'll give you some time to be alone," he finished then left the tent.

"So, I assume the 'Hemingway Option,' is out of the question?" Thanaxagoras asked, after Hippocrates exited.

"Yes," Celeste replied. "Do you know, he called the man in the story 'The American' and the woman, 'the girl'? I think even his capitalization mattered… and was sexist… by the way. But, no, we should see everything to the end, I think."

"That's all right by me," Than agreed and gave Celeste a kiss. "I guess we should start mulling names," he added.

"Adam and Eve? Mars and Venus? Samson and Delilah? Thanaxagoras Jr. and Celeste II?" Celeste joked.

"Anything except the last one," Thanaxagoras retorted.

"I don't think my son would ever forgive me if I named him Thanaxagoras Jr., and I wouldn't blame him either."

The happy couple laughed.

"So twins!" the Devil interrupted. He seemed to have a knack for that, both Celeste and Thanaxagoras thought. "*Mazel tov!*" Satan concluded.

"I guess there really are no secrets in Hell," Celeste murmured.

"Don't be dramatic," the Devil returned. "Hippocrates was right outside the tent. He told me the news."

"So, are we safe?" Thanaxagoras changed tack. "I mean, is Hell… um… more secure now?"

"Well, Hell's always been pretty secure. Only one successful jailbreak in 6,000 years," Satan quipped. "Ironically, that carpenter's escape route is still Hell's greatest liability for covert invasion. It was a stroke of luck to have Mizam here. He found a way to plug the Jesus Crevasse— at least temporarily. Other than that, I increased patrols and handed out weapons and marshalled all the souls of the damned to get ready for the fight, so I believe we are as prepared as we can be. Ultimately, though, I think the final outcome will come down to hand-to-hand combat between Archangel Michael and me. My brother never liked me much… even when we were on the same side…"

"The souls of the damned are going to fight for you?" asked Thanaxagoras incredulously.

"Yes, indeed," the Devil replied. "Say what you want about Hell, but it's their home. They also know they wouldn't fare any better even if the Angels win. No, Heaven is not a liberation force and free passes are not given freely."

Celeste thought of the eternal playground and all its children.

"True enough. But what are we supposed to do now?" Celeste inquired, nervously. "Just wait?"

"Yes," Lucifer answered. "But while we wait, there is one last thing I'd like to do, and it involves you both…" he said.

"What is it?" Celeste and Thanaxagoras asked.

"Since we're all here, I'd like to throw you a baby shower," the Devil offered. "As I said: 'it's a rare treat to witness and celebrate the impossible'!"

6

In Heaven, Michael finished going over plans with his war council and then adjourned the meeting without further objections, mindlessness, or riddles. He could feel all of New Jerusalem positively pulsating for battle as well as every other corner within Paradise making ready. It was to one of these corners Michael now traveled. He needed shades for his war and also—far more importantly—a shade suicide bomber to detonate his bomb in Hell. To find both only took a millisecond of contemplation. Everything he required could be found in one place: the personal and individually-constructed heaven of the saved soul, Hallelujah Bock.

And so the Archangel Michael hitched up his tight-fitting tunic, which accentuated every ripple of his sizeable muscles, and paid Hallelujah a visit. Yes, he traveled from New Jerusalem through the heavens of Heaven as easily as a person might turn the page of a book or shift a gaze from one brilliant star in the night sky to another. And in less than a blink or a wink, he arrived.

Michael had long heard about the saved soul who wanted her own heavenly world and—additionally—wanted to bring forth a population of shades unto the Lord. But to stand upon her land was a surreal experience. He could feel the faith of her shades like a baking heat which was matched only by the solemn vibration of their suffering—200 million strong. As for the total number of Hallelujah Bock's shades, however, technically it was 200 million *and one*. There was a character named 'Barbury,' who apparently functioned as some sort of clerk and was Heaven's oldest continually existing shade. Michael eagerly anticipated acquiring him in service.

Thus, the Archangel zipped to Hallelujah's private spire between her lands of O-Frica and O-Lina and entered the tower without knocking or announcing himself. He located Hallelujah immediately in a main chamber which had a map painted on the floor. Except it wasn't a map. Michael could see little things moving across the topography: people, animals, equipment. It was an interactive rendition of her world and Hallelujah sat on a gigantic golden throne beholding all she had created.

"Good morrow, Michael," Hallelujah said brightly. "You came at an opportune time! This might be the prophesized moment!"

Here, Hallelujah moved her hands and the map enlarged so just one town square occupied the field of vision. Hallelujah didn't know the phrase 'zoom in,' but that's what she did. And when she finished zooming in, the map displayed a group of her shades who had gathered in a village center while a child shade—a young girl—was being tied by her arms and legs between four horses.

"The greater the sacrifice, the greater the chance at salvation," Hallelujah murmured.

Then, the horses ran off in all directions and Archangel Michael heard a small but distinct scream from the center of the map.

"Oh well. That was Althea Cartwright. Her parents, Normal and Goody, made the decision. Maybe they'll have better luck next time. They have four other children, you know…" Hallelujah mildly sulked.

Archangel Michael didn't comment.

"But, Michael! It's so nice to hear from you!" Hallelujah shifted back into an upbeat tone. "However, I assure, this is just a work in progress. My man Barbury and I have decided on the strategy of self-sacrifice to get my shades to salvation. It didn't work this time, but don't worry—*we will get there*! Speaking of which—Barbury! Come and meet our distinguished guest!"

A small door opened from an adjacent anteroom and Barbury appeared. Michael could see the room was filled with books and magazines and electronic machinery of all types. A television flickered in the background throwing flashes and shadows. Barbury, himself, approached slowly and gingerly. He was naked, but didn't bother to cover himself.

"Why, you are just as black as a coffee bean!" Michael exclaimed.

"Greetings, Angel of the Lord," Barbury returned.

"What were you watching?" the Archangel inquired, curious about the television.

"An episode of *Star Trek: the Next Generation* called 'The Arsenal of Freedom,'" Barbury answered dutifully. "It's one of my favorites."

"Ah, 'The Arsenal of Freedom,'" Michael repeated. "I suppose *Providence* really is alive and well!"

"How can I be of service?" Barbury asked.

Michael took a moment to look down at Hallelujah's map. She had returned it to its wider perspective and he watched all the little things move about like insects.

"Well, chief," the Archangel began, "first, you can hold on to this."

Michael tossed Barbury the iPad with cartoon bomb on its face.

"I don't like carrying baggage," the warrior finished. "Now, you can go and finish viewing your program while I have a few words with your Master."

"No!" Hallelujah disagreed, louder than she wanted. "Barbury is my scribe and records everything significant that happens in my heaven," she continued. "Please, let him stay? I've never had *a real Angel* visit me before! I want to make sure he knows what to write down."

"Fine by me," Michael said. "I just thought he might be bored while the adults talk."

Barbury didn't indicate any preference.

"Oh, Barbury's never bored," Hallelujah said, grinning brightly. "Isn't that right, Barbury?"

"No. Barbury is never bored," Barbury replied.

"But anyway… I suppose you are here about the war?" the Prophetess continued. "It sounds exciting! I don't know much about the concept, except regarding the minor scrapes between my shades in O-Frica and O-Lina!"

"Yes, it's about the war," Archangel Michael replied, "and more specifically, it is about *your shades*, in fact. You see, I want to enlist them—all of them! Think of it! You, Hallelujah Bock, could single-handedly help stick a thumb in Satan's eye! Doesn't that sound righteous?"

"Oh my! What an honor, Michael!" Hallelujah exclaimed, automatically, before probing further: "But *my shades*? If I may ask: why don't you just create an army of shades yourself? Why do you need mine?"

Michael exhaled with force, annoyed, but maintained his composure.

"To answer, wonderful child: *your shades* are the most developed shades in all of Heaven! Moreover, they are acquainted with violence and thusly would make extremely effective soldiers! I rarely give praise—*except to my Father*—but you have done something truly miraculous here! And if you let me conscript your shades, I won't have to expend any of my celestial energy for the task. So what do you say? Will you donate something from your heaven for a noble cause and the greatest good?"

Hallelujah paused for a moment and looked down at her map in a loving and tender fashion. The conclusion seemed forgone.

"Oh my! This is a splendid stratagem, Michael! Of course, you can have my shades. Throw them against the battlements! Order them to ram themselves into the spears of the sinners below! Yes, let their shade blood create a red mist like war-fog to defeat the Evil Adversary and all his followers! Indeed, they live for sacrifice because they know sacrifice is the only way to salvation! I grant your request, Highest One!"

"Excellent," Michael answered, radiantly.

"If the shades do this—*if they do this*—*will they get souls? Will they reach salvation? Is it a guarantee? Will they be saved?*" Barbury interjected in an excited whisper, only feeling and not thinking.

"Barbury!" cried Hallelujah. "You know the rules! No speaking, unless spoken to! I apologize, Archangel."

Michael turned to Barbury and sized him up and down like a slab of meat. His angelic face was an angelic stone.

"Will the shades get souls and be saved?" Michael repeated. "*They are shades.* Of course not! Shades are just force-fields and notions. They come from nothing, are made of nothing, and—when they cease to exist—they return to nothing but nothingness! No, you could no more cram souls into shades than you could make sunbeams part of the night. Pure silliness, Barbury! Balderdash and falderal! Tweedle and twaddle!"

"I'm sorry I stepped beyond my station, Mistress," Barbury said with severe regret.

"Oh, one mistake after three centuries of dutiful service is easily forgiven. I pardon and absolve you!" declared Hallelujah. "It's just a shame you can't go to Hell with the other shades. I'd love for you to detail a record of the conflict! I imagine the action will be quite intense! It would be like a vacation!"

"Ms. Bock, I'm afraid you misunderstand," Michael picked up, returning his attention to the saved soul. "When I said I needed your shades, I meant *all of them*—Barbury included. I have a very special job for him," he finished.

"Oh my!" Hallelujah cried, nervously. "*My Barbury?*"

Meanwhile, after his outburst, Barbury went silent and just rubbed his thumb back and forth over the smooth contours of the iPad Michael had given him. It felt good to hold on to something solid as his fate unfolded, he thought.

7

Back in Hell, the impromptu baby shower was in full swing and the Devil believed it to be a great success for something thrown together so hastily. He conjured up refreshments inside the circus tent and festooned the eternal playground with balloons and streamers to add to the festive atmosphere. The Devil also directed a new dawn to arrive several hours earlier, so everyone could enjoy the party while basking in warm supple light. Since most of Hell was preparing for war, sending invitations was tricky, but Lucifer made sure some old friends of Thanaxagoras and some new friends of Celeste came and he even invited the Arch-Demon of Sloth, Belphegor, to have someone to talk to and because—despite the impending war—Belphegor wasn't doing anything, anyway.

"I guess the secret's out about the mentally challenged, the animals, and your mercy," Thanaxagoras said to the Devil, making conversation. The initial greetings and preliminaries were over and the attendees had broken into small groups for chitchat.

"The secret was out as soon as I sent Hippocrates for Celeste's exam," Satan replied. "He's an excellent doctor, but a terrible gossip."

"I'm surprised I never ran into him before..." Than answered.

At the same time, Celeste and Mizam were talking while Belphegor slowly made his way over to join them.

"The Devil mentioned you found a way to seal the Jesus Crevasse," Celeste directed towards Mizam. "That must have been hard. How did you do it?"

Before the Angel responded, a humble and half-embarrassed smirk crossed his face.

"I had this idea a while back to introduce a... a variation to how souls manifested in Heaven. One of my ideas was to allow saved souls to be fat..." he said.

"You wanted to make *fat Angels*?" Celeste asked, energetically.

"Yes, yes," Mizam sighed, but held on to his cheerfulness. "However, nobody signed on. Still, I never forgot the idea and since the Jesus Crevasse is near the Bogs of Sloth and the Bogs of Sloth have all these paralyzing snakes... I thought I'd use the idea on them."

"*So you made fat paralyzing snakes!*" Celeste shouted, getting more excited and loud enough to draw attention from the other partygoers.

"Shhh!" Mizam reprimanded, but struggled to keep in a laugh. "But, yes I did. I chubbed those slithering bastards right up and stuffed them into the Crevasse! I'll tell you! I wouldn't want to be the first Angel or saved soul down that passage. It's not even about the poison! I packed the snakes in wickedly tight! I don't think there's room enough to even get a ladybug's ear through!"

Belly laughs abounded.

"Laughter…?" Belphegor interrupted as he reached Mizam and Celeste. "That's weird. Excuse me, but are you the expectant mother…?" he asked.

"Yes," Celeste answered, trailing off in giggles, but it took her a second to find where to look since the Arch-Demon was basically invisible.

"Here. A gift…" Belphegor slurred.

A grey ingot seemed to float in the air in front of Belphegor's shimmering mass of unaccomplishments.

Celeste took it.

"Oh! A brick of metal! Thank you!" she said, trying to hide her bewilderment.

"It's pumblum… a bar of lead…" Belphegor gurgled. "It's just something I had lying around. I heard it was customary to bring presents to a party… I probably shouldn't have…"

"Nonsense!" Celeste genuinely soothed. "I love it! It was very thoughtful of you! Who knows? Maybe one of the little ones will end up with 'Belphegor' as his middle name!"

"I wouldn't recommend it…" the Arch-Demon garbled, but imbued a hint of jocularity in a few of his muddy syllables.

Then something happened.

Yes, the moment for the momentous thing Celeste and

Thanaxagoras, and every Angel and every Demon had sensed, arrived.

It was not a conception in the afterlife.

And it was not the birth of Celeste's twins.

Instead, every part of Hell turned black and even the darkest parts of Hell turned darker as if preparing for a far more brilliant illumination.

In the eternal playground, clouds like floating bruises obscured the sunlight and everyone looked to the sky.

"I didn't order any storms—" the Devil began to say before he was interrupted by a tremendous bolt of lightning.

Thankfully, it hit in an open field, free of children and guests, but that was the only thankful element. This was because, when the lightning made its jagged arc to the ground, the light it threw blinded every being who looked upon it. It was dazzling, pure, brighter than an atomic blast. For a moment, even the Devil saw stars. As for the damned souls, they would have been sightless forever, if not for the regenerative aspects of life after death. Celeste would ponder about this phenomenon later, and take Satan's advice: never get caught up in thinking about the simulated biology of the afterlife.

But the frenetic lightning strike was only the beginning.

Following the electric bolt came a deafening rumble and peal of thunder that also temporarily rendered everyone in earshot without hearing. The circus tent collapsed into a bundle of red and white silks and sent the entire population—of partygoers and residents alike—to the ground. The animals, too, weren't spared from the dual impacts. No, everything ended up in the dirt.

After the commotion, a stillness descended which seemed to go on forever like an endless stroll past silent columns.

But as things fall, things rise, and eventually the totality of witnesses regained their sight and hearing, as well as their footing.

They all looked to the field where the lightning struck.

There, a black man stood—as naked as the day he was born because he just had been reborn.

He looked around at the chaotic surroundings, having no idea how all the chaos came about. Dazed, he tentatively moved towards the collapsed circus tent where Celeste rushed to help Thanaxagoras and the Devil.

"Excuse me," the man said upon reaching them. "My name is Barbury. In deference and with respect, could you please tell me where I am?"

Thanaxagoras and Celeste shared a look.

"Do you want to tell him or should I?" Thanaxagoras asked, regaining his smile and trying to ameliorate the recent trauma.

"I will," Celeste answered. "Now, don't freak out. You are actually in Hell… but don't worry… *this is the nice part*," she ended. She also found her smile and was grateful that, despite the cataclysm, Hell's ethereal objectivity remained intact.

Meanwhile the Devil tried to locate the whereabouts of the children who once again had gone into frightened hiding.

"Nice to meet you," the Devil said, distractedly, and then muttered to himself, "I'm going to have to get those kids a bunch more camels. This place is getting out of control…"

"I'm in Hell?" Barbury continued. "But I can't be. I don't have a soul…"

"Of course you do!" Satan stated. He turned to focus on Barbury and his eyes grew wide with piqued promethean curiosity. "I can smell it all over you. It may be *brand new*, but it's there," he finished.

"What's the last thing you remember?" Celeste asked.

Barbury didn't immediately say anything and everyone leaned in.

"I think I just blew up Heaven," he said.

8

In the moments leading up to Barbury's sudden violent transformation from soullessness to soulfulness and his even more violent and abrupt journey from Heaven to Hell, Barbury had gone numb. He didn't think it was possible to become more numb, but Archangel Michael's appearance and his war plans extinguished whatever embers of simulated emotion remained within him. He felt entranced or drugged or stunned. He couldn't even put a name on the state of non-feeling inundating his body and mind as if his entire being had been submerged in viscous tar.

Barbury walked away from Hallelujah Bock and Michael, who were still conversing, to an extending parapet he hadn't visited in decades. The parapet looked over Hallelujah's world—and his world—the one he helped shape. The view was dreary, drab, or uninspiring. Barbury couldn't decide how to put a name on what he was looking at either.

Meanwhile, Michael went on and on—his voice becoming a droning buzz—as much as Michael was a drone, himself. The Archangel explained to his Mistress how once the Angels had conquered Hell, and when they had 'ripped the child from the harlot's womb and crushed it underfoot on sight,' Barbury's task would commence.

"You see, Hallelujah? You see?" Michael said. "As soon as the Antichrist is destroyed and all the saved souls and Angelic battalions get clear, Barbury will set off the explosion! We'll leave the shades to cover our retreat! Yes! Hell isn't going to know what hit them! It's genius!"

Barbury heard his Mistress make a small objection about not knowing how to read and how important *he*, Barbury, was to her and then stopped listening.

Instead, he chose to peer down at the iPad Michael had required him to carry. The bomb was a funny bomb, Barbury thought, but he also focused on the words written across its face: 'Acme Explosive and Activated Praise Company.' Barbury knew 'Acme' meant: 'the highest point,' but the phrase 'Activated Praise,' was a mystery. *'Why did Michael include it?'* he wondered, with a little life flowing back into him.

This is when the Archangel Michael lost his composure and preached his last holy and lofty sermon on high.

"***Ms. Bock***," he started, in frustration and unveiled anger. "We, the Angels of the Lord and the True Servants of the One True God, ***own everything***! We ***own*** Barbury, we ***own*** you, and we even ***own*** this whole moronic world!" he bellowed. "So, if I want to take him—*I'll take him*! Shades are like souls—***they are God's property***! I also don't know what the big deal is… you can always just create more slaves! So stop being such a nattering child. *You are here to SERVE ME, you nattering bitch!*"

Hearing this, Barbury turned with half a decision and a half-blind hysterical instinct that was the antithesis of decision-making and engaged every aspect of his mind. The injustice of his existence began to smolder and his vision narrowed to a singular goal: to solve the riddle of himself by solving the riddle of Michael's bomb. After all, what power did he have? None. No, he had no power except the power he was holding in his own two hands. He prayed he was doing the right thing, but—like all his prayers—this one also went unanswered. *'Activated Praise Company,'* he thought. *'How do you activate praise?'* he thought again.

Then in an unstoppable and perhaps preordained rush, he worked out the solution.

Barbury's fingers went to the screen and touched the prompt for the activation code. A miniature alphabet appeared. Barbury typed in what he knew was the correct password. In fact, the key had been with him since the day he was born.

"**H-A-L-L-E-L-U-J-A-H**," he entered.

Yes, 'Amen' ends a prayer, but 'Hallelujah' activates one, Barbury further realized.

Immediately the iPad began to glow brilliantly white—as bright-white and white-bright as a blank sheet of pristine paper illumed beneath a blazing lamp.

Barbury seemed to hear a ruckus from the main chamber of the tower. It sounded like Michael was voicing strong objections to him while Hallelujah Bock was screaming orders at him, but any listening or following had ceased.

This was because the light kept getting brighter and brighter and whiter and whiter. It was warm and embracing and seethed with unimaginable authority. Barbury got the idea he might go blind by looking at it, but ultimately recognized he didn't care.

Incredibly, then, the light seemed to be lifting him up. It kept growing and growing in passion and intensity. Yes, he was riding the light. It was under his feet and around his arms. It was like wings. He was floating above the land and moving faster. And the light took Barbury higher and higher until he apprehended he was heading for Hallelujah's sun—on a rail of light—on a cross of light—on the wonderful, wonderful, bright-white, white-bright light.

"I'm achieving salvation!" Barbury applauded in his own self-guided epiphany. He preached his words high above Hallelujah's world, soaring towards Hallelujah's sun, but was only proselytizing to himself. "I am sure of it! I know now salvation does indeed come from sacrifice, but it also comes from love. Yes, sacrifice and love! Why didn't I figure this out before? Why didn't I know the self at the core of myself? Yes, all I needed to be saved was to find a way to love myself and love the light and sacrifice myself and sacrifice everything to the light! I AM SAVED!"

But there, at the cusp of salvation, a cacophonous voice ripped through him:

> *"NO! YOU ARE NOT SAVED AND YOU ARE NOT LOVED! I GIVE YOU A SOUL ONLY TO DAMN YOUR SOUL! HEAVEN HAS BECOME UNCLEAN AND I ALONE HOLD THE POWER TO REMAKE IT!"*

And with these words, Michael's bomb exploded.

And that was the end of old Heaven.

Yes, Heaven ended—not by an act of war, and not by an act of pure sacrifice and purest love—but by one voice booming inside one person's head.

However, the Archangel Michael was right about his bomb and the termination of hostilities between powerful religious forces.

Both were glorious!

End of Story #11

Intermezzo
(eleventh)

The writer could feel himself sliding towards the ultimate end now. His Devil's Spot had significantly ratcheted up for the last story and it felt like a high water mark—like a mark of convergence and divergence—where things came together so they could be thoughtfully pulled apart. Consequently, he focuses on riding the energy all the way home—*to fire and flare* all the way home.

"Mizam, do you want to comment first?" Lucifer asks as the writer's Divine audience finishes and immediately transforms into Divine critics.

"What?" the Angel answers. "Oh… I think it's okay."

"Really? You think it's '*okay*'?" the Devil continues. "You know he just blew up Heaven?"

"Yup. That's what the story was about," Mizam states calmly.

"He also called you 'a traitor,'" the Devil further needles. "How does that make you feel?"

"I'm fine with it," the Angel says, not taking the bait.

"Can I inquire why you are fine with it?" the Devil asks, trying to add even more pressure.

"Because… fake news…" Mizam sighs casually, displaying no affect.

"Fake news?" the Devil presses.

"Yes. You were right and I was wrong," the Angel replies, but without contrition. "You were correct, these stories don't matter. They don't change anything. And most likely no one but us is ever going to read them. Yes, he can scribble whatever he wants. And, no, the world need not end because of a story. I get that now."

"'The world need not end because of a story,'" the writer repeats. "What a wonderful line…"

"Well, *Mizam* isn't going to be any fun," the Devil says, turning to the writer. "But as far as I'm concerned, this tale is another achievement. You pulled disparate elements together and managed to connect them in semantic structure and thematic coherence. However, I imagine some of the choices were difficult—especially what you had to leave out."

"They were," the writer agrees. "One of the things I wanted, but couldn't execute, was a game of hide and seek between Terrance, Toby, and Belphegor during the baby shower scene. I had this image of Belphegor whining because the kids kept finding him—despite the fact the Demon is virtually invisible. I thought it'd be cute."

"It would have been," the Devil continues, "but it would also remind people of Terrance and Toby's severance from their mother—a mother you incidentally obliterated when you nuked Heaven. You *did* game out all of the ramifications?"

"Yes, and there was no logical way to save Penelope. Besides, Mizam essentially lobotomized her in one of my previous tales," the writer counters. "I would argue she was dead already."

"Do you have anything to say about that, Mizam—about you lobotomizing a single mother of two?" the Devil needles once again.

"Nope," says the Angel, "more fake news."

The Devil rolls his eyes.

"So… penultimate story…" Satan states, changing back. "It lays the groundwork for the grand finale. Do you have a plan?"

"I have something better than a plan," the writer answers.

"The tale is written. Here. Take it," the writer says as he hands over the second-to-last story.

"Only one more to go…" the writer mutters to himself.

He is done with the Devil and Angel.

An Im—por-tant Story about a Mother

(Story #12)

And so, once upon a time, a little boy raced down linoleum steps at a breakneck speed. There would be breakfast—true—because he had been catching whiffs of coffee percolating in the pot, and could smell the beginning aromas of bacon crisping in the pan. But this wasn't the reason for the reckless running. No, with the arrival of dawn, something else drove him. So the driven boy clumped and galumphed down the steps, in footed pajamas, and let the arches of his padded feet slip over the edges of each, nearly causing him to fall every time. Doing this was unwise, but it helped him move faster—*dangerously faster*—and three steps from the bottom, he did finally lose traction. His feet slipped and he began to fall, but was able to turn his falling into a controlled leap, like almost all children instinctively know how to do. So, he hit the landing in a slide, thumped on his ass, slid down the last two introductory steps, and then was up again and running as if he had never fallen at all. Yes, if the glamour of youth is to witness a life on fire, to watch the boy was like seeing a flying flame.

The kitchen table came next—smartly varnished with thick wooden legs like newel posts—and the floor was still linoleum, so the child gathered up even more speed and dashed underneath it like he was coming in hard at home plate. His head banged on one of the table legs, but the boy wouldn't notice until later, when the welt rose up, and the rest of the afternoon would be spent curiously probing the tender spot with his finger. But that came after—because right now he was sliding out from beneath the table, as if it were an ungainly wooden womb, to end his frenzied trek by literally crashing into the slender legs of his mother while she cooked.

"Whoa, whoa, there, whirligig! You almost made me spill the milk!" the mother chided, but it was chiding in a gentle way. She was not so much unused to such crashes and, besides, she could always hear her son romping and barreling towards her from miles away. And she smiled as she added milk into a ceramic bowl filled with egg yolks while whisking them into a frothy yellow swirl of morning goodness. Yes, a pinch of salt and pepper, a little time on the stove, and this morning's breakfast would be done.

"SORRY, MOM!" the child shouted, though he didn't

need to shout, but did anyway out of habit. He always felt adults were just too darn tall. They towered like giants and he seemed so small in comparison. He had to get his voice up there, somehow, he reasoned.

"But I have something to show you, Mom! It's something *im-por-tant*, *im—por-tant*," the boy said, breaking up the syllables to make sure he got the 'important' word right.

"Okay, honey, I'll look at it after you eat," his mother replied. She stirred the scrambling eggs with a wooden spoon. The fragrances of coffee, bacon, and now freshly cooked eggs garlanded the kitchen in a warm and easy tranquility.

"NO, MOM! NOW! I said, it's *im-por—tant*! LOOK! LOOK!" the boy bellowed, still unnecessarily.

The mother moved her vision from the stove to her supine, yet eager, child, with his eyes as wide as saucers. The child reached into the left pocket of his pajamas. Out of it, he pulled three pages of lined legal paper that had been crumpled, folded, and finally rolled into a cone. The boy raised the cylinder of dimpled wood pulp up to her like an offering.

"It's *a story* for you!" he proclaimed. "A *story-ee!* And, *I* wrote it!" he added, proudly.

"Oh, that's wonderful, sweetie," the mother said.

"Will you read it?" the boy asked. "Will you? Will you, Mom? It's *im—por-tant*! So will you?"

"Of course I will," she answered, "but you have to eat your breakfast first. Do you want juice?"

"YES, PLEASE!"

Then the mother poured the boy some juice and began to read the boy's story, as the boy shoveled down his breakfast. Yes, for an instant it seemed like he forgot all about his *im—por-tant* story because in its place were eggs right out of the pan and crisp bacon and now freshly poured apple juice brimming a clean glass.

Regarding the story, the first thing the mother noticed was the handwriting. It was a child's handwriting—sloppy, but attempting to be meticulous—with misspellings and reversed letters and a good, but mostly failing, attempt at keeping the letters between the paper's industrially produced lines. The second thing she noticed was the plagiarism. This was because the story appeared to be a complete rip-off of 'Jack and the Beanstalk'—a tale she read to her son a million times and would probably tell him a million more before he finally crested into pubescence. The title of the story was 'Woofie and the Dog Treat Stalk,' but the word 'Stalk' had an extra 'l' in it, so it was spelled 'Stallk.'

The mother found the error adorable.

Because, after all, *she was* the boy's mother.

The woman continued reading and found out that Woofie's family was starving and soon would be thrown out of their dog house to roam the woods forever and ever and ever. But Woofie's mother—no doubt a wise and fiercely protective canine—sent her eldest son, Woofie, to buy dog food with their last bit of money. "If we are throwed out of our house, we should make our stomakes full," the mother dog said in the story. And so, Woofie went to buy dog food with the family's last dollars, but on his way, ran into an evil cat named 'Sidd,' who convinced Woofie to trade the money for a golden dog bone that had magical properties.

And as she read on, Woofie buried the bone in the backyard and from the golden bone, a great and grand Dog Treat Stalk grew way, way up into the sky. Then, Woofie climbed the great and grand Dog Treat Stalk and faced off against a mean and very big bulldog named 'Slobber,' who possessed some wonderful things. There was a dog bowl continually filled with water, a ball which threw itself, and a bag of dog treats that never went empty. Slobber was asleep when Woofie collected all these wonderful things, but suddenly—shockingly—Woofie stepped on one of Slobber's many chew toys and the toy let out a tremendous 'SQUEEK!' and Slobber woke up. The ferocious bulldog chased Woofie out of his great and grand doghouse—so much bigger than Woofie's house—and Woofie raced down the Dog Treat Stalk and began to chew and chew at its base until he chewed all the way through and it fell down. At the end of the story, the Dog Treat Stalk fell, Slobber was defeated, and out came Woofie's mother so he could give her all the wonderful things and everybody lived happy and happily ever-after!

The boy was licking his breakfast plate when his mother finished reading.

"Don't lick your plate, baby," she said.

"But, Mom, I'm making a 'sunshine plate'! You always told me to!"

"But, 'sunshine plates' are for *little boys*," the mother said, sensing an opportunity aligning with her own motherly agenda. "But you are a writer now, and writers don't make 'sunshine plates.'"

"Oh…" the boy replied and looked down sullenly.

There was still a bit of egg and bacon grease tempting him, but he resisted it.

"WELL, IF THAT'S THE WAY IT IS, THAT'S THE WAY IT IS!" he announced and pushed the plate forward.

"Yup," his mom concurred.

"But... my story! My *story-ee*! Did you read it? Did you? Did you, Mom?" her son implored.

"Yes, dear," his mother said.

"But did you like it? Did you like it? Did you?" the boy shouted again.

"Well, I think it's *creative*," answered the woman.

"Cree-ate-ive... cree-ative?" the child repeated and pondered.

"It means, I can see you used your imagination. You know what 'imagination' is, don't you?"

"Yeah, it's my brain and brain! And I used it?" the boy asked, though he was beginning to feel the welt develop where he banged his head.

"You sure did, buddy," his mom answered.

"YES! YES! I USED MY BRAIN AND BRAIN!" he exclaimed, and then the boy ran off with his belly full and the mother heard him fall up the two initial steps and clump and galumph back upstairs yelling, "YAY! YAY! YAY!" as he went.

The boy had another idea and hoped to get it down before it flew out of his mind as his ideas so often did. It was about three rabbits who had to fend off a hungry fox and, to do it, they would build houses made up of different kinds of stuff. He thought the story might even be better than 'Woofie and the Dog Treat Stallk'—and hurried to commit the narrative to paper.

His mother, meanwhile, washed the breakfast dishes, and kept an eye on the clock to make sure her son got to the school bus on time, which she did.

***

Several years passed and many other tales appeared, and there was much more clumping and galumphing, as well as a succession of statements from the mother like "I think this story was creative" or "imaginative" or "descriptive." She didn't know what else to say. And the boy seemed to plow through—almost systematically—the collections of Mother Goose, the Brothers Grimm, Hans Christian Andersen, and any other source that had a talking animal or a bend towards childlike magic. The mother even jokingly wondered if a child could be sued for copyright infringement, because her son's 'stories' were so obviously lifted from existing materials. Still, she thought it was adorable. She just prayed Disney's legal department never got wind of her son's writings of 'The Zebra King' or 'Finding Minnow.'

Then the boy turned twelve and the writing abruptly stopped. Nothing came for over a year. The clumping and galumphing also ceased, and was replaced by a lot of slouch-walking and loping, instead. And the son grew his hair out into a messy mop, but his eyes remained as wide as ever. The mother wished her son could have had an easier time transitioning into puberty, but she also knew this particular road must be walked alone. Indeed, he seemed to want space, so space she gave—while the days and distance ticked on and on.

But finally one morning, when the mother came down for coffee and to prepare breakfast, she found a set of neatly typed pages resting atop the varnished kitchen table the boy slid under so many years ago. On the pile was a handwritten note that simply said, 'Please Read Me,' and the mother smiled. No, she knew it wasn't fair and she knew it wasn't true, but sometimes she felt like her son forgot all about her, and sometimes for long stretches. It made her feel sad, and she couldn't help but obsess on what a horrible thing it is to be lonely, even when you're with someone you love. She hated such desolate notions, and hated the stinging pangs of them even more, but this new story was like a light banishing the long shadows from her mind.

And so she poured some coffee and did what the note asked: she began to read.

The story was called 'The Butcher's Block' and it was about a vegan teenager who fell in love with a decidedly carnivorous boy who was also the son of a butcher. The boy's father didn't like the girl because she kept leading protests in front of his shop while waving signs that announced 'Animals Are People Too!'. The girl's parents didn't like the boy either—for obvious carnivorous reasons. Nevertheless, the two fell in love, and the love was forbidden by both sides of the families. The families then ordered the couple never to see each other again. So the boy and girl decided to kill themselves because the couple's forbidden love was not meant for such a harsh and unfair world. In the closing scene, the lovers sat cross-legged in front of one another and brandished cattle-killing bolt guns—both hopelessly and hopefully—in their youthful hands. Then, with tears in their eyes, they pointed the gun muzzles at each other's heart, but when they pulled their separate triggers only a single sound boomed up to the heavens. The last line of the story was: "Yes, two lights went out, and Earth was darker, but somewhere a star shined brighter in the hope for a day when lovers need not die for love."

Here, the story ended.

The mother sipped coffee and her first thought was: it was probably a good thing, she supposed, her son was now adopting storylines from more sophisticated material. Her second thought was to wonder if he had a girl. Her third thought was to be sure to remind him not to share the story with anyone at school because stories about teen suicide earns nothing but an all-expense paid trip to the vice principal or guidance counselor these days. Yes, she believed if her son was to suffer the slings and arrows of trying to be an artist, he could spare himself the particular bolts of "Why don't you write about something else?" or "Why do you have such dark thoughts?" or "How are things at home?" from some busybody's public school quiver.

Eventually, her coffee cup was empty and she could hear creaking noises moving down the linoleum steps—creaking which corresponded to the size and gait of her foot-dragging son. He appeared on the landing like a street urchin and saw his mother with the story spread out before her.

"Oh good… you got it," the boy said, rubbing the sleep from his eyes. "I want to know if you liked it, but first I want to have some coffee," he finished.

It was the first time his mother had ever seen her son drink coffee, and he plucked a mug from the cabinet and poured himself a cup to the brim. He didn't add any milk or sugar to it. He was going to drink it black and would do so for the rest of his life.

"Do you want a refill?" he asked her.

"Yes, please," she replied.

And they both sat in silence for a moment, caffeinating, and feeling the warm dark liquid radiate out between them in their own kind of synchronicity.

"So… what do you think? Is it any good? Do you like it?" the child asked.

The mother looked down at the pages as though the pages themselves could help her reach an honest but acceptable answer.

"Well… I think it's more complicated than anything you wrote before," she began.

"It should be. I based it on William Shakespeare… *Romeo and Juliet*? We're reading it in Miss Penny's class. Do you know it?"

"Oh, yes," the mother replied, "though I like his histories better than his tragedies…"

The teenager frowned at this information and then spent some time staring at his black coffee. The mother knew such silence well. It was the kind that said 'if you want the conversation to continue, you're going to have to push in some chips, because I'm done, and I'm not bluffing. I didn't even have to talk to you in the first place.' And, here, the mother joined him in frowning because this was exactly the type of thought that made her feel so sad and alone. She felt both trapped and encouraged to fill the soundless void. She also noted how strange it was to feel simultaneously grateful, yet resentful, at getting to talk to her own son.

"… But tragedies have their place, too," she continued, "and I saw you turned the 'star-crossed lovers' into 'cross-legged lovers.'"

"You saw that? Did you like it? I thought it was one of my best ideas," the boy picked up again.

"I thought it was quite… clever," the mother answered.

"Hmm… clever… *clev-er*," her son repeated, suspiciously, and the terrible silence fell once again like a pall. The mother thought she just might burst into tears, but fought against the urge. She decided to ask a question instead—well, at least, a question about a question.

"Can I ask you a question?" the mother gently approached.

"Sure," her son answered. "I hope it's *a clever one*."

The mother died a little inside at hearing this, and she saw her child's coffee cup was almost empty—as empty as her own heart was hollowing out right now.

"Why don't you try to write something not based on something else?" she asked, pressing on bravely. "I mean… you have your own ideas, right? I don't think you need to model off existing works. Can't you just use your creativity to come up with a story that is new?"

Her questions hung in the air along with the awful

silence and, for a moment, she thought he was just going to walk and stalk away after he finished his coffee.

But he didn't.

He answered.

"*No, Mom*. I can't come up with *something new* and something *that's my own*. All the great stories have already been written down and all the good ideas have already been used up. The best I can hope for is to copy greatness." The child let out these words in frustration and annoyance that betrayed his own sadness and loneliness, but there was still something about his tone that slashed—as if he couldn't believe his mother was *so stupid* as to not understand such an obvious and worldly truth. The mother desperately hoped she was wrong about her interpretation. After all, *he was* just a teenager and she did know *she could be* a little over-sensitive as a mother. She looked down at her own cup and saw it was almost empty as well.

"Keep in mind, you're still young, honey," the mother probed ever so tentatively—in the most soothing voice she could muster. "It can take years for an artist to find his voice…"

The boy interrupted the conversation and pushed back from the table. He might have mumbled, "Whatever," but he was already trudging up the linoleum steps to his room. This didn't stop his mother from completing her sentence in full:

"Keep in mind, you're still young, honey. It can take years for an artist to find his voice… and I'll be here for all of them."

Then the mother picked up her own empty cup and

the one her son had left abandoned on the table and washed them in the sink.

Yes, she thought, writing can be difficult, but living with someone who writes can be a whole lot harder. She also realized she had forgotten to warn him against over-scrupulous guidance counselors or vice principals who are always at-the-ready to sound alarms at any student creativity—even if it is based on Shakespeare.

***

College came next for the son as he slouch-walked and loped his way from adolescence into young adulthood. He chose to be an English Literature major, of course. As for his writing, it was sporadic leading up to his college years and sporadic, too, was the sharing of his writing with his mother. And sometimes she minded and sometimes she didn't. Either way, there seemed to be about a fifty-fifty chance of feeling worse whether she interacted with her son or not. A smile was rare for him during those pre-college years and his wide eyes took on a haunted and brooding look. He also seemed to metastasize silence around him into an almost impenetrable shroud. When he did speak about things, he had developed a consistent theme: he hated high school and hated everyone and everything existing there. And, yes, he had been summoned to both the vice principal and guidance counselor on a number of occasions because his writing was nebulously "inappropriate," while their due diligence was decidedly not.

So the mother saw her son off to college and when

she saw him again it was like a meadow exploded inside his soul. He was filled with life, with excitement, and with ideas. There were new friends—true—but the real treasure he seemed to find was new stories—or, at least, stories that were *new to him*. He described his professors like compass points directing him through a sea of literature, of form and format, and he got to converse with them about anything and everything. No subject was taboo, curiosity wasn't treated with suspicion, and nobody ever accused him of disruption or subversion or haughtiness. Indeed, when he spoke about the subjects he was learning and the books he was experiencing, he became like an open book, himself. And the mother felt happy because *he* was finally happy for a time. She half expected to hear him scream "YES!" and then yell "YAY! YAY! YAY!" as he talked about Irish poets and Victorian classics and post-modern experimental composition—whatever that was.

But, like all things, college ended and the son graduated with eight more classes than he needed to graduate. He moved back home and the die was cast. This is when he told/asked his mother—almost fearfully—about wanting to try to become a professional writer.

"Then you should do it," his mother replied flatly. "You have certainly read enough, and you graduated at the top of your class, so if you want to go for it, you should."

"But do you think I will make it?" the son asked, with a tentativeness and vulnerability which was somehow both meek and courageous at the same time. He added in a voice barely reaching the level of a whisper: "*Do you even like my writing?*"

"I can't answer that," his mother said. "All I know is: if you want to try, you will have to try. But you're going to have to do what you're going to have to do, because however it is, that's the way that it is. Remember, honey, you are trying to scale a mountain and there are still a lot of vice principals and guidance counselors out there."

The son didn't really understand this response, but it encouraged him enough. Then his mother put on a pot of coffee and they shared a cup before he forged into a room he now christened to be his new 'writer's garrison.' Indeed, the son would write and send his writing out into the world.

So that's what the son did… or at least that's what he began to do… because there was still a lot to learn.

Yes, to become a writer requires both nothing and a seemingly endless spectrum of intricacies—depending on who you talk to. Writing requires a pencil and a bit of paper. Writing requires a decent word-processing program and a printer that won't smudge the ink. It requires a rigorous system of exacting discipline and a free-wheeling spirit to embrace the Gods of creative inspiration. To write, you have to compose in a gush and let your words stand as they may. To write, you must revise constantly, the way a gardener might prune a topiary or clip judiciously at a hedge maze. Yes, writing requires everything and the absence of everything—and people will advise you on exactly what you have to do to succeed and then tell you to throw it all out the window. But for most, and *most of all*, writing requires failure, and the son was going to fulfill this particular requirement in spades.

Nevertheless, he worked hard and wrote every day, because that's what he thought it was to be a writer. And he smoked cigarettes and practiced drinking single-malt whiskey, though he liked neither, because that's what he thought it was to be a writer. And he sent out poems and stories and query documents to agents and editors and publishers—making sure the format guidelines were followed to the letter—because that's what he thought it was to be a writer. And he tacked up rejection slip after rejection slip in plain view on one of the green walls of his writer's garrison, because the color green was supposed to lend itself to a fertile mind, and because that's what writers did too.

Years passed and his wall grew thick with papers like the lazily-tended bottom of a bird cage. The replies were almost all form responses, but a few handwritten comments did land saying: "this was creative" or "imaginative" or "descriptive," but "it's not what we are looking for right now." Very, very, occasionally there would be a stab at encouragement—the "keep trying" or "keep at it"—that definitely were effective stabs because they cut him like knives. Yes, if failure made a writer, the son was crushing it and it was crushing him as well.

Meanwhile, the mother supported her son in every way she could, but also cursed herself—because, of all the things she did for him—she could not make her son a better writer. And her son also knew this, and he hated himself for knowing it, because it made him resent his mother a little—so much so—he became blind to all the wonderful and supportive things she did do. Yes, when you're failing at something it can be hard to see anything but the failure—failure, failure, everywhere. As a consequence, the meadow in his soul became barren and even the very soil grew alkaline.

Then one day everything changed. The son was smoking and drinking black coffee and reading the newspaper about a tropical storm named 'Jadzia' that had apparently walloped some small Central American community. In fact, the storm walloped with so much wind and rain there were reports of alligators in the streets, threatening the local population and hindering rescue efforts. Reading this, something happened to the son which had never happened before. He saw in his mind's eye a perfect image. It was of a woman lounging in a luxurious bed covered in silks. The bed had four standing posts and was draped with ivory-colored mosquito netting. The woman was beautiful and fatuous and privileged. Yes, the son saw it clearly and as vividly as a remembered dream—and not just saw. All his senses were dialed up to eleven: sirens were howling, a broken palm frond swung lethargically in front of an open window, and the air seemed scalded. Yes, the atmosphere reeked with odors of broken earth, dead things, and upended trees—while the birds complained noisily about their devastated nests.

And on his mind went. Who was the woman in the bed? Who was she? Who? She was the wife of a dictator or the wife of one of the dictator's generals, obviously. And where was he? He was out dealing with the aftermath of the storm, of course. Why didn't she go with him?

Because what was there for her to do? But whatever they were doing, they sure were taking their time and being awfully loud about it. So she hides her head beneath one of the soft pillows. And the room is hot, very hot—the air conditioning cut off—no power from the storm. So she has opened all the doors and windows before climbing back underneath the silky diaphanous sheets. And while she lies in bed a tremendous alligator scuttles into her bungalow with his terrible claws and jagged teeth and scaly swishing tail, dragging mud and leaves and all sorts of detritus across the polished floor. The woman smells the alligator before she sees it, but thinks it's coming from outside—the outside brutal scents of the storm and the rancid stench of the poor people of her country—the ones she despises and the ones the sirens were making such a fuss about. Finally, she can bear the cacophony no longer, but when she rises from beneath her downy castle, the giant lizard eats her whole. The last image is of the alligator nuzzling under the once pristine sheets now covered with muck and grime and blood to wait—perhaps knowingly or perhaps unknowingly—for the woman's husband to come home. The title of the story would be 'Poverty Smells like Alligators.' Yes, he could see it all laid out before him in an orderly pattern that gave him the sensation of paradise.

And he put down the newspaper, leaving the rest of the newspaper unread.

And he put down the coffee, leaving the rest of the coffee to go cold.

And he left the cigarette, too, and the cigarette burned down to a charred nub in the dirty ashtray.

And three hours later his mother heard the most unusual thing. She heard her son scream "YES!" and then there was clumping and galumphing down the steps at a breakneck speed. The son burst out onto the landing and jumped down the last two steps. The mother was afraid he might fall, but he had it covered. He had turned any chance of falling into a controlled leap.

"WHATEVER YOU'RE DOING, STOP RIGHT NOW!" he shouted, though he didn't need to shout. "PLEASE READ THIS!"

He thrust the pages into her hands, while his eyes blazed with a fervor verging on madness, and his mother flashed upon a phrase she wasn't even aware she knew: 'vim and vigor.' Yes, that's how her son delivered his story to her. The act was the embodiment of this phrase, and for the first time she truly, truly understood what it was to have one gesture, one movement—one life—perfectly translated into words. Yes, her son handed over the pages in vim and vigor, and she accepted them.

So, the mother read the new tale while her son picked at his fingernails and his teeth and brushed at his clothes and, in short, did a bunch of other things—*anything*—to distract himself from the passage of time. Yes, if a watched pot never boils, an observed reader never reaches the end of a story. But, after an interminable period, she finally did finish.

"Do you like it, Mom? Do you? I think it's the best thing I ever wrote!" her son exclaimed. And the mother flashed back to when her little boy drank apple juice in a room garlanded with the aromas of bacon and coffee and fresh eggs and she was reading about 'Woofie and the Dog Treat Stalk' with an extra 'l' in the title.

"Well, I see you're really excited about it," she began, but couldn't get out any more before her son cut her off.

"Yes, I am! *I am* excited about it! But do you like it? Tell me what you think!" he shouted, but it was very clear he didn't know he was shouting.

"Well…" she continued, "can I ask you a question?"

"Sure you can!"

"Well, why does the alligator climb into the woman's bed? I mean, now that it's just eaten, wouldn't it want to go back to the water or jungle or something? I guess I don't understand…"

The son looked down at his story, confused, then back up to his mother, befuddled.

"It… no… it… that's not the point! The story is about greed and income inequality and callousness! It's about the infirmity and absence of God's love! The alligator isn't even really real! It's just a symbol!" he shouted again.

"Oh, okay…" replied the mother. She started to search for something else to say and was afraid that terrible silence would descend upon her and her son like nuclear radiation, but thankfully, it didn't. The son was too preoccupied and animated to be passive aggressive.

"It doesn't matter!" he shouted one last time. "I have to get this formatted and start sending it out!"

And then the son disappeared up the stairs to make his corrections and connections.

The mother meanwhile went back to what she was doing, but she did think her question was completely justified. '*Yes, why would an alligator want to roll around in silk sheets anyway? Could an alligator even feel the texture of silk?*' she thought.

Still, her son was excited and she was excited for him. Because, after all, she was his mother.

***

The following eighteen months were exhausting. Yes, they exhausted the son. And, yes, they exhausted the mother. And, yes, even the house seemed exhausted—sagging at the eaves—as the sun, itself, labored to rise above its roof every morning. If the mother had to hazard, she would say her son sent out at least a hundred submissions, but her boy knew it was actually closer to 200. He was keeping track. The first thing he did after writing 'Poverty Smells like Alligators' was to clear off the green wall in his writer's garrison of all the old rejection slips to start anew. In those early days, when he looked at the expansive, green space, he imagined an idyllic pasture—wide open with possibility and opportunity. Unfortunately, this image wouldn't last for long.

And so, after three months, the first responses began to flurry in and, with each successive month, the hopeful green turned white as winter. The writer ticked off the returns on a list he kept hidden under the mattress of his bed as if it were adolescent pornography. They were rejections without comment and he was compelled to hide the growing tally. He didn't want to think about why he did this, but part of him knew it was because he was ashamed and every new failure instinctively reinforced the need to hide his shame. His mother, meanwhile, learned to fear the sounds of the mail delivery and the ding notifications of incoming emails. Indeed, her hope had been snowed under too and she seemed cold all the time, no matter how high she turned up the heat.

More disturbingly, the son began to slouch-walk again as the months dragged on and on and there was nothing either of them could do.

Finally, after a year and a half since the son wrote the story, he did one last accounting of his submissions. Of the 198 submissions he had sent out, he had received rejections from 184 of them. The rest he concluded were in limbo—where he guessed his story should truly reside. And then a new die was cast. He was going to tell her. The son was going to tell his mother he was giving up. She always wanted him to be a lawyer, anyway, and he was still young enough—*just young enough*—to pull it off. And, no, he wasn't going to kill himself. To do so would be cowardly, and he would never give *those* whinging vice principals and guidance counselors, who always believed such would be his end, the satisfaction. Additionally, he remembered his tale, 'The Butcher's Block,' and had come to the realization that death, no matter how appealing in stories, is permanent. Yes, death might play well in literary tragedies, but in life, death just sucks.

So the son went downstairs in a slow creak on the linoleum steps and decided to surrender the whole thing. All he endeavored after the announcement was to share a cup of coffee with his mother and ask about her day and see if he could do anything for her. He wanted to apologize for… for everything, he supposed. Yes, if there is one positive aspect of acknowledging failure, it is to realize how terrible you've been to other people while failing, especially to the people you love, he thought.

The boy reached the landing and descended the last two steps.

"Mom? Can I talk to you for a minute, please?" he asked, more timidly than he would have liked, but with determination as well.

"Of course, honey. You can always talk to me," she answered and motioned towards one of the empty chairs at the kitchen table—the table which remained a static fixture in both their lives.

The son sat down and for a few moments silence reigned, but it wasn't that awful, tense silence, the mother noted. If anything, it felt significantly grave, but didn't feel inconsolable.

And then he opened his mouth to speak, to tell her, but before he could the doorbell rang. Strangely, from an outside perspective, it looked like the sound came directly from the boy's open mouth and his mother laughed.

"Hmm… I guess hold that thought?" she said with a smile, and—though her child was an adult—her child smiled back.

So, she went to the door and found a man standing there with a certified envelope which she had to sign for. It was a brown envelope, 8x by 11x, and thick enough not to be one page, but a bundle. She also saw by the return address it was from a literary agent and the recipient was intended to be her son. She signed for it and returned to the kitchen table.

"Mail for you," the mother said and handed over the delivery.

The son examined the package in a conflicted state as if the package were a bomb, or perhaps the answer to all his dreams, or nothing at all. Then, the writer dared to wonder and laughed it off. Then, he remembered reality and steeled his body and soul. Then, finally, he thought of throwing the envelope away—unopened—in some ultra-dramatic way to show he had totally moved on and no longer cared about success or failure. Still, envelopes are meant to be opened, so the son opened what had been delivered.

It was his story. It was 'Poverty Smells like Alligators' and there was a handwritten note on top, which the son read.

The mother watched her boy's eyes ping-pong over the words with a kind of stoicism she had rarely seen from him. Then, when he finished, he flipped through the remaining pages to see if there were any other scrawled comments, sent by a person he didn't personally know, but who felt strong enough to return a note and *his own story* by certified mail. Of course, there were no more scrawled words. There was just the note.

"What's it say? Is it good? I pray it's good…" the mother offered tentatively, but with her own level of personal confliction. She wanted only the best for her son, but was also scared for her son, but she also was perplexed at the extraordinary calm her son seemed to channel as he looked through the pages.

"Here. Read," her son said and then added, "I'm going to make us a pot of the finest Colombian…"

He got up and went about it, and his mother joked in an easy, automatic way: "Well, you know I don't like pot and we're too poor to buy cocaine, so let's just have the coffee instead."

"Har-har," replied the son, but wasn't sarcastic about it.

Then, the mother looked at what had been sent. It was her son's story, but her singular focus went to the note—the note from a fancy literary agent that could change the direction of her son's life forever. And, from a dark place, she hoped it wasn't a suicide missive—one written for her son, but composed by the hand of somebody else.

So, with slight trepidation, she read what it said:

Dear Sir,

I don't know how you were able to get this story to me, but if you have done any research you should already be aware I have been shepherding new writing talent to publication and helping maintain existing writing standards for over forty years now. As such, you should also know, as a feature of my professionalism and expertise, I always respond to submissions which find their way to my desk. Sometimes it is a very unenviable task. I say this, because what I am about to say, I don't like saying. I also imagine you will not like hearing it. Yet, please keep in mind I am doing it <u>for you</u>.

To start, I read your tale. To finish, in my

professional, personal, vocational, and avocational positions, I believe it to be supremely inadequate and, if I'm to be honest, a colossally pretentious and spectacularly misguided attempt at Literary Fiction. I do not know why new writers have to be such strutting peacocks or from what Black Muse they derive their materials, but, in my candid assessment, this story is an affront to every creative impulse for anyone, anywhere, in the entirety of time.

Consequently, I urge you to give up on writing. I urge you to give up, so more room can be carved out in the publishing universe for newer and better talent to take hold and rise above the clutter. This is my truthful adjudgment. If you desire to engage in a profession dealing with Literature and Art, I wish you one happy thought. It is thus: I hope you can teach.

Sincerely,

A. Stercus Accidit, Literary Agent, Pandemonium Inc.

PS: As a point of plot, why would an alligator want to get into a silk bed after he ate?

After reading the note—the longest commentary offered to her son she knew of—the mother did the only thing she could do.

She laughed.

Yes, she laughed. She couldn't help it. It was as if all the travails of her son and herself and all that *Sturm und Drang*—the 'storm and stress'—of their lives had evaporated into smoke. And, yes, she didn't know how she knew the term '*Sturm und Drang*' any more than she knew where 'vim and vigor' came from, but these were the words that blossomed in her mind. Then her son was suddenly laughing too and the coffee was almost done. And, the son poured a cup for each of them.

"You know…" the son began, after the laughing had subsided to chuckles, "… the thing is, it's not exactly terrible advice, becoming a teacher, I mean."

The mother savored the beverage and the moment, as both the coffee and the laughter lifted her chills which at one time seemed bone deep.

"Well, you loved your teachers—in college, at least. But that means you'll have to get your master's degree, at the very minimum. Still, I think it's an option worth pursuing and, more, I think you'd be good at it," she said.

"Then I'll get my master's degree," her son replied.

"Of this, I have absolutely no doubt."

"Neither do I."

"It feels good, doesn't it?" she asked.

"Better than I've felt for a long time," he answered.

"But I have to mention one last thing…"

"What is it?"

"You saw that fancy literary agent asked the same question I did about your story, right?"

And then there was more laughing, concluding with the son throwing the feedback note into the trash bin, while he stuck the story in a drawer somewhere. Yes, he thought, it might be a 'supremely inadequate' and a 'colossally pretentious' tale, but *it was his* and *it was finished* and now it would also be a reminder—but not a reminder of failure. Instead, it would be a reminder of the time he and his mother moved on with their lives and it would remain as written testimony—for him and for anyone—that the world need not end because of a story.

End of Story #12

Intermezzo
(twelfth)

'Yes, *the world need not end for a story and, yes, let's be thankful for mothers and Devil's Spots,*' the writer thinks. For the first time, the writer is unconcerned with whatever the Devil and Angel would say after reviewing his latest story. The writer acknowledged both had been useful, but now he felt their usefulness was over. In fact, it was as if the writer could read their minds. Yes, he knew what each would voice in objection and blandishment—so much so—that the two didn't even have to speak. The writer could do all the talking for them.

"I know what you're going to say," the writer begins, starting with the Devil. "You're going to say my story is 'sentimental' and 'maudlin' and 'puerile,' and *no one* wants to read about a writer and his mother. I can see your points."

"And you're going to say," the writer continues, shifting to the Angel, "I finally wrote something 'wholesome' for a change, and wonder if those events are true, and then you are going to realize you can't relate because you never had a mother. You are even going to get a little teary-eyed and try to hide it. The Devil will make fun of you, but it's a deflection, because in the blackest part of his coal-black heart, Lucifer must also admit he never had a mother either. Yes, both of you will recognize some things are beyond the Divine."

"So the Devil will chastise me and the Angel will congratulate me according to their pre-established beliefs, like always," the writer goes on. "But the story stays—and *will stay*—exactly as it is. I used to think this book—this collection of fabulist trifles—would be *my one fine thing*—tangible proof of my life's value. And I suppose it is. But there's more to it as well. Ideas have to be examined and challenged, but what really matters is how we treat one another despite the ideas we hold or reject. So I choose love. Human love. And you two, I reject. Yes, you are rejected, not because you both don't have admirable qualities in your own ways, but because each of you is no more real than impressing a shape upon a passing cloud. No. I can't live my life being dominated by figments."

"Subsequently, I choose a life of my own making—until my death—which is just the last act of living. The immortals can't feel this, can they? They can't feel the passage of time and the growth and decline of one's own existence. Such is what makes life precious and I like the preciousness of life even with the knowledge it will end.

Kindness. Integrity. Challenge. Humor. These concepts don't just 'strut and fret,' but are weapons to fight their opposites: cruelty, mendacity, complacency, and stick-up-your-assed-ness. No. Positive qualities don't just need to be expressed in fiction. They need to be lived. They need to be embodied."

"So that's what I'm going to strive to do—embody them. Thus, I cancel, rescind, and void all arrangements to any mythology of the afterlife in favor of living the best life I can live right now. There will be flaws and failures and shortcomings—to be sure—but what else can be done when you embrace reality over fantasy? No. Free passes are not freely given."

"Regardless, I thank you for your imaginary service and attention."

"You are both dismissed," the writer ends.

The Thirteenth Fable: Part 2

(Story #13: Part 2)

The apprentice nun finished reading 'Intermezzo 12,' turned the page, and found... nothing. The manuscript entitled *Fiction for Atheists: A Novel* just ended. There were a few blank sheets of paper and the back cover—which was also blank—but no more words. For some reason, this made the nun panic. Yes, she had risked her life by entering the forbidden library, but the nun wasn't expecting the story—the fruits of her trespass—to conclude so abruptly. Confused, she flipped back and forth from the last inscribed page to the bone-white nothingness on its opposite side. The apprentice nun thought perhaps some of the final leaves may have gotten stuck together; however, they hadn't. Then, she flipped to the front thinking she missed something—a table of contents, maybe, or another kind of indicator or clue. The nun *was sure* the author bargained his soul *for thirteen fables*, not twelve. Lastly, in an act of frustration, verging on desperation, she shook the book up and down, hoping a clarifying note or key or answer, *any answer*, might fall out—as if from the sky.

Nothing fell.

'*What was the point of all that?*' the nun thought. '*And why are stories like these hidden and forbidden? Surely if one has faith, their faith can stand up to a bunch of squiggles on a page? Even the profanity and blasphemy is no mortal blow or moral threat! Yes, it might be unpalatable, but it's only poisonous in how much you swallow! No, a book can't force you to believe anything! And why the hell would the writer close on a tale about him and his mother? What about the other stuff? Is Heaven just gone? What about Celeste and Thanaxagoras's twins? Was one evil and one good? Does Barbury really have a soul? What happened to Humpy? How can you end a book with so many loose ends? Yes, where is the reassurance and clarity?!?*'

In time, the nun's agitation subsided. She considered going back to the shelf to see if there was a second volume to the tome, but ultimately didn't bother. The apprentice nun wanted to know what non-believers believed about religion and God and the eternal soul—and now she did. Yes, she had made the hard decision to put everything on the line, had self-tested her own faith, and came through unbroken and unblemished. Indeed, if all the other banned books in this taboo section of the Atheneum were simply variations on irreligious themes, then there was no point in reading further. She felt her objective satisfied. Exposing herself to a single opposing narrative sufficed.

Then—like any good borrower of books—the nun placed the text back where she found it and gratefully tapped on its spine. No, the book may not have been lightning in a bottle or a revelation from on high, but someone wrote down the words with attention and care. *'Yes, all books are written for the readers who find them,'* the apprentice nun reflected, while an area in the center of her forehead thrummed slightly.

She turned to depart.

But when she turned, she became paralyzed.

This was because, at the old prison doorway from whence she came, there stood what she feared most: *people.*

Yes, standing silently in the threshold of the penitentiary jamb was the Grand Prioress of her Order, the Grand Inquisitor of the Monastery, and—the one person who terrified both the faithless and the faithful in the extreme—the Grand Heretical Carpenter. It goes without saying: the Grand Heretical Carpenter was the man who designed and constructed all the crosses for sinners to pay for their wages of sin on Earth.

The three stood in the passageway looking dour, but not necessarily displeased. It was well known this triumvirate enjoyed their blessed work immensely.

"I… I… I got lost," the apprentice nun fumbled, nearly imploding with the inadequacy of her excuse.

The image of Jesus Christ was still painted in repose on the wall behind the Grand Prioress, the Grand Inquisitor, and the Grand Heretical Carpenter and the sum of them looked like a lethal nativity scene. Then the Grand Prioress moved from the entrance to the bookshelves. Dressed in her full habit, she seemed to float. The Grand Prioress picked up the manuscript the apprentice nun had just replaced.

"Ah, *Fiction for Atheists: A Novel*," the Prioress finally said. "You know this book is supposed to have thirteen fables, but there are only twelve. Have you figured out why, yet?" she asked.

Now it was the nun's turn to greet dialogue with quietude.

"Your life might depend on it…" the Prioress added, serenely.

The nun had been expecting remonstrance and rebuke, not literary questions, but the last comment from the Prioress focused her mind, as the prospect of death usually does.

"Yes, let us speak bluntly. Answer the question if you want to live…" the Prioress pressed on.

The situation reminded the apprentice nun of Clarence, Archangel Michael's 'work friend,' from the eleventh tale trying to solve Michael's riddle. So she thought about what she just read and thought as hard and as fast as she could. Her heart pulsed and convulsed to send every available drop of blood to her brain. *'Yes, why would the writer say he was going to write thirteen stories, but write only twelve? Yes, why would he bargain his soul for thirteen and fall short? What's the answer? What's the answer? What's the answer?'*

Soon enough, almost miraculously, revelation washed over her.

She *was sure* she was right—as correct as Clarence with his declaration of 'shades.'

"Because twelve fables breaks the deal!" the apprentice nun exclaimed, excitedly. "The writer traded his soul for thirteen, but not writing the last one violates the terms and voids the contract! *He* did it to save himself! That's why there's only twelve! *He* outsmarted the Devil! He won!"

The Prioress smiled pityingly.

"No," she said. "That's an intriguing guess, but not even close…"

The Prioress regarded the apprentice nun with a sly smile and let the tension build.

And let the tension build…

And let the tension build…

And let the tension build some more.

Eventually, though, she spoke again.

"The reason why there is no thirteenth story is because *I didn't write one*," the Prioress said.

The apprentice nun took a step back as if she had been struck.

"What?!?"

"The reason there is no thirteenth story is because I didn't write one," the Grand Prioress repeated.

"No! You can't be! You can't be the writer! You can't be! It isn't possible! These stories are beyond you!" the apprentice nun nearly shrieked. She felt as if her mind was trapped inside a slowly closing vice.

"But, alas, I am the writer. I am also a woman, so you were wrong about that '*He*' stuff as well. You see, our greatest duty..." she continued, waving her hand at the Grand Inquisitor and the Grand Heretical Carpenter, "... is to protect the integrity, sanctity, and *sacredness* of our institutions. And this means: **We** have to know who can be trusted and who cannot. So **We** do this through temptation—the temptation is this forbidden library you're standing in. What other purpose do you think these books serve? They are our mechanisms to draw out unworthy moths to the flames. Besides, I adore writing especially when it helps ensnare hypocrites..." she finished.

"But my faith is still pure!" the apprentice nun objected. "In fact, it's even stronger! I was challenged, but not changed! I believe! I believe! You have to believe me!"

"Be that as it may, you still broke the rules. They were clearly posted," the Prioress replied, as her amused pity transubstantiated to boredom. "Yes, I suppose one could say: *you* are the thirteenth fable and the moral of the story is your death," the Prioress ended, but added one more line:

"Take her."

Then, the Grand Inquisitor and the Grand Heretical Carpenter advanced and hooked the apprentice nun by both her arms. The novitiate's toes scraped across the stone floor as they dragged her away.

"No! No! This isn't right!" the nun screamed. "You can't be the writer! You shouldn't be allowed to kill me just for reading! Your capitalization was all over the place and you confused some of your tenses in the intermezzos!" the apprentice nun screamed. "No! The book wasn't even that good! No!"

And her screaming would go on for a little longer, but only until the pounding of hammers drowned her screams out—like the pounding sounds were nothing but teeth-keys on a typewriter making a different kind of imprint.

End of Story #13: Part 2

* * * Postface * * *

The author completed his project, so naturally he went to his mother to talk about it.

"Mom?" the author asked.

"Yes," his mother answered.

"I've finished my book," the author said.

"Okay..." his mother replied. "Did you go through with it? Did you really crucify a nun at the end?"

"Yes, but not on the page," the author answered. "I had to. It was the final juxtaposition between writing about matters of faith and religion and acting upon them. The distinction needed to be stark and clear."

"It still sounds risky," his mother said.

"Perhaps."

"And I also gather you are going to include this

conversation we're having right now as the novel concludes?" she asked.

"I feel I need to do that too... because symmetry and such... to show human beings as supreme over superstitious notions and not the other way around."

"Well, this is your final opportunity to talk to your readers. Any last words you would like to impart?"

"Just two things," the author answered. "First, people write books about gods, but no god has ever written a book—ever."

"And the second thing?" the mother pressed.

"That I'm going to dedicate the novel to you."

"I thought dedications come at the beginning?"

"Well, I broke so many rules, what's one more? Do you want to hear it?" the author asked.

"Very much so," his mother answered.

The author paused dramatically, then finished.

"'To my mother: Jenny Mazepa Schmoyer-Malouin. Sometimes I feel like we've been through Hell together. It was heavenly. Thank you and I love you.'"

End of 13 Fiendish Tales: A Novel

About the author

Stephen Schmoyer is a graduate of Muhlenberg College and Kutztown University. He has taught writing and literature at the college level for over twenty years. He despises raw tomaoes, currently lives in the Lehigh Valley, PA, USA, and is working on his second novel.

 Matador

For exclusive discounts on Matador titles,
sign up to our occasional newsletter at
troubador.co.uk/bookshop